The Eagle and the Tiger

Tim Davis

ISBN: 978-0-9862758-2-1

Book design: Dean Fetzer www.gunboss.com

This is purely the work of fiction. I call it reality fiction, insomuch as this story could have quite possibly happened, but to my knowledge, it didn't. Any real life similarities to any of the characters in the book is purely coincidental. There was a battle at Dak To but the battle depicted here is purely fictional.

I would like to shout out a special thanks to all the people who helped on the book: Len Dorsky, editor in chief, Austin Muhs, without him the book wouldn't have been published, and to John (Cazzie) Karczmar, my man in Delaware, a friend I have known forever. Thanks guys, your help is much appreciated.

GLOSSARY

AO – area of operation

ARTICLE 15 – Infraction of Army rules resulting in both a fine and disciplinary action

ARVN'S – army Republic of Vietnam

BOOCOO – pidgen French used to mean many

CP – command post

DAISY CHAIN – string mines together so one detonator activates them all

DI-DI – Vietnamese for go or hurry

DINKY-DAU – Vietnamese for crazy

KLICK – kilometer

LAAGER – position

LIMA CHARLIE – slang for loud and clear

LP – listening post

NDP – night defensive position

NVA – North Vietnamese Army

PAVN – peoples Army of Vietnam

REMF – rear echelon mother fucker

RPG – rocket propelled grenade

SHORT – slang for time left to serve on one year Vietnam tour of duty

SITREP – situation report

SKATING – slang for slacking off or shirking a duty detail

STRACK – squared away soldier

TI-TI – Vietnamese for small

THE WORLD – G.I. slang for the United States

XIN LOI – pronounced Zin Loi – means sorry about that

CHAPTER 1

The Eagle Lands

Sitting on his helmet, the wind blowing in his face, Billy Fleming looked out of a helicopter as it began its downward descent.

"Man, down there is the third herd!" (Herd-nickname for 173rd Airborne Brigade),

A grinning, eighteen year old soldier named Peyton said, emphatically jabbing his index finger at the mountain outpost below them. "We're gonna' be with the baddest dudes over here! All the way, man!"

"Yeah, airborne, all the way," Fleming responded thinking of the tragic comedy that had overtaken his life. He wasn't even supposed to be here much less go "all the way." But tragedies and comedies aside, all his concerns whittled down to just one: he desperately wanted to live. He can't remember the feeling of wanting to live life as ever being so intense, so desirable. And this wanting, this desire, wasn't blatant self-indulgence. He was nineteen, in the flower of his youth; he was supposed to live life passionately, with desire. Yet here he was careening down a path that could easily end in death at such a tender age.

The helicopter continued descending downward toward its final destination: a makeshift camp located in the Central Highland's mountainous jungles, a stone's throw from the Laotian border. Foxholes and fighting hootches dotted the landscape. Fatigue shirts, tee shirts, and other clothing articles hung on clotheslines strewn along the compound. Fleming thought it looked more like a shantytown village from the other side of the tracks than a combat soldier's base.

The helicopter dropped down on a red clay landscape.

Fleming and five other replacements jumped off the chopper, shielding their faces from the red dust kicked up by the helicopter's whirling blades.

Haggard, thin soldiers, resembling refugees from a concentration camp, made their way toward Fleming and the other new arrivals. Most were shirtless with bandanas tied around their foreheads. Some wore peace sign necklaces or beads; others, obviously the more religious ones, had olive drab cloth rosaries hanging around their necks. The men were all a reddish color, seemingly a permanent stain from the red dust and clay that was everywhere.

"Well lookee' what we got here," an African American soldier shrieked, grinning from ear to ear. "Cherry ass motherfuckers."

"How many fuckin' days you got left?" another asked. "Three hundred and fifty what?"

They moved closer and Fleming almost lost his breath. His nostrils filled with the acrid, ammonia stench radiating from men who hadn't bathed in weeks. He suppressed gagging and had a momentary sensation of wanting to vomit.

One man stepped forward and studied them – pus-oozing sores ran up and down his arms. He leaned this scabby, pus filled appendage on another man's bare shoulder. This man's fatigue trousers were rotted out in the crotch. Some of his penis and scrotum hung out exposed. A strawberry red scabby pus-oozing rash ran up and down his thighs.

Fleming couldn't imagine himself ever being in this same condition.

"What do you think, Doyle?" The crotch exposed man asked. "I give them a week, maybe two."

"I dunno,' Fields," Doyle said, his brow furrowed as if giving the matter a lot of thought. "Three of them could last a week. The other three...maybe a month."

A skinny man made his way to the group. He wore glasses and was maybe five feet six inches tall. "Break it up and start taking this shit down. Leave nothing for the gooks."

The men immediately scattered and went about the task of tearing down their makeshift home.

The small bespectacled man intensely eyed the replacements. "My name is Levine. You will call me sergeant, until I tell you differently. Did all you assholes get that?" His accent was thick east coast.

"Yes, sergeant," everyone answered.

"Good. Ya' all got it. You're some smart motherfuckers. You're some lucky fuckers, too. We been in this stinking hole for forty days straight and today they're pulling us back to the rear."

"But, sarge," a man named White complained. "We just got here."

Levine thrust his face inches from White. "What the fuck did I just tell you?"

White's eyes widened. His face was a mask of fear and confusion.

"I ain't even putting up with a cherry dickhead whose gonna' get me and all my men killed because he can't listen to men who know more than him."

A moment of silence passed. White's face turned red with humiliation.

"What the fuck did I just tell you?" Levine demanded threateningly.

White's eyes darted, confused, trying to deduce what the fuck he was just told.

Levine jabbed a finger, hard, into White's chest. "I told you to call me sergeant, dickhead."

"Yes, sergeant."

"Yes, sergeant what?"

Another moment passed.

"Uh…yes, sergeant, sir.

Levine blasted him in the chest with an open palm.

White fell backward to the ground.

"Yes, sergeant. I won't ever make that mistake again," Levine corrected him.

"Yes, sergeant. I won't ever make that mistake again." White repeated.

One man at a time, Levine made intense eye contact with each soldier. "Make the same mistake twice in da' Nam and you get wasted. You fuckers will listen to everyone out here who says anything to you. You're the lowest scum on the totem pole – cherries. Cherries get themselves wasted. Now I really don't mind that. But when you get my good men wasted, we got a problem, a big motherfucking problem. You don't listen so help me fuckin God I got ways that will get you wasted in a week and I ain't afraid to use them. You fuckers got that?"

"Yes, sergeant," everyone answered in unison.

All of a sudden, Levine's eyes laser beamed on Fleming.

"You're a Spec. 4. How the fuck did you get to be a Spec. 4? You been in country before?"

"No, sergeant, this is my first tour."

"How long you been in the Army?"

"Ten months, sergeant."

"How the fuck did you get to be a Spec. 4?"

"Sergeant, it's a long story."

"I got fuckin' time."

"I got an advanced promotion out of A.I.T., (Advanced Individual Training)."

"They don't give advanced promotions to Spec. 4 out of Infantry A.I.T. Are you lying to me, dickhead?'

"No, sergeant, I ain't Infantry. I didn't go to Infantry A.I.T."

Levine peered at with a wide-eyed, open mouth expression of disbelief. Then he sneered. "Jesus Christ, I got a man in my unit who ain't Infantry. I need that like I need more gooks. What's your motherfucking story?"

"I ain't supposed to be here. I'm supposed to be in another unit. This is a mistake."

"I know it's a mistake, dickhead. That's pretty fucking obvious."

A moment passed.

"What I gotta' wait all fucking day?" Levine said. "Tell me about your mistake."

Telling this story would lead to describing all the tragic comedy since it would mean telling the whole story and Fleming knew the whole story was better left untold. "Sergeant, the Amy lost my orders and I got sent here. The clerk in Nha Trang said not to worry. It happens all the time. They'll find my orders eventually."

Levine smiled an evil glowing grin. "Well there it is. What if during the find my orders eventually time, you get zapped, which is a very real end fuckin' result out here? Are you supposed to not worry about that?"

"Well, no. I mean yeah, sergeant. I don't wanna' get...you know...zapped."

Levine studied him a moment, and then started chuckling. "JENKS," he called over his shoulder. "Get over here. You gotta' hear this new guy."

A thin, tall man sauntered toward them. He swaggered cockily, each step oozed with self-confidence. A dozen other men followed; eager to hear Jenks interrogate the new guy.

"This cherry says they lost his orders and he ain't supposed to be here. He said the REMF (Rear Echelon Mother Fucker) clerk told him not to worry."

"Is the REMF clerk sweating his balls off in the field, cherry?"

"Huh?"

"Will the Gooks be trying to kill the REMF clerk cause I can guaranfuckingtee' you they'll be trying to waste your ass?"

"Well I don't–"

"You're a John Wayne motherfucker is that it?

"Huh?" Fleming said, his confusion growing by the second. Jenks' rapid-fire delivery of questions was mind-boggling. "No, it ain't like that. There's really nothing to worry about. The clerk said it happens all the time. I'll be outta' here in no time."

"And you believe that?"

"Well, uh…yeah. He had no reason to lie,"

"Ain't that sweet. What we got here is a cherry who believes people. We got a name for cherries like you. We call you dumb motherfuckers who're gonna be dead in a week."

Everyone started laughing, even the other cherries; men who also had the credentials to become dumb motherfuckers who're gonna' be dead in a week.

Jenks held his hands in the air, signaling for quiet. Everyone stopped laughing. "Tell me about this unit you're supposed to be in. How come you ain't with them? What kind of unit is it?"

"It's top flight. I got a security clearance, top secret."

"This motherfucker's CID (Criminal Investigation Division)," another man said.

"He's dumb, but he ain't that dumb. If he's CID he wouldn't be telling us he has a clearance."

Jenks eyed Fleming for a long moment then the twinkle of enlightenment slowly entered his eyes. "I'm a dumb motherfucker who enlisted, there it is. This recruiter tried to get me to join a top-flight unit. I mean he said these guys were STRACK. I mean they had their shit together. The problem was I couldn't get in, didn't qualify. I smoked too much pot, drank too much beer. This cherry must be something else."

"Like I said it's top flight.'"

"Uh huh. Top flight. Is it called the A.S.A.? The Army Security Agency?"

It was just as Fleming had expected; he had known that telling the story was going to turn bad. "Yeah, that's the unit."

"Well there it is – they are top flight. They're so top flight ya know what the recruiter told me?"

Fleming knew but didn't want to know – didn't want Jenks to tell him. "What? What did he tell you?"

"They're so top flight, they ain't even in Nam. Did he tell you that?"

It was exactly what Fleming had known and had been told. "Uh, yeah."

"Then why you here? If they ain't here then how the fuck you get here, cherry?"

"That's a long story."

"I like long stories. We," he made a sweeping gesture with his arms indicating the men around him. "We all like long stories. Except for watching cherries die, there ain't much real entertainment around here, get my drift? Tell me your long story."

Fleming was seconds away from revealing all the tragic comedy, and that would lead him further down the path of more ridicule. "I joined a unit called the A.S.A. The A.S.A. ain't in Nam. But they really are. You see they change their name to Radio Research when they go to Nam."

"Why all the name changing?"

"Something called need to know. Everything works on a need to know basis."

"I need to know the answer to my question. How come you joined a unit that ain't in Vietnam and you're in Nam?"

"It's the need to know again. The best I can figure is civilians can't know the A.S.A. is in Vietnam cause in a way they ain't and, for some reason, civilians don't have the need to know they ain't here. Once you're in the Army you get the need to know that the A.S.A. goes to Nam, but when they go they change their name to Radio Research."

"Did anyone follow that?" a soldier asked, dumbfounded.

"Yeah, I did," Levine replied. "In Queens it's known as bullshit."

"It sounds like bullshit, but that's how secret organizations work, I guess." Fleming knew his argument was pathetically weak, but it was all he could think to say.

Jenks jabbed a finger in Fleming's chest. "It sounds like secret organizations work that way so secret organizations can lie to dumb fucks like you and get them to join. That's what it sounds like to me."

Everyone started laughing.

"You are about the dumbest motherfucking cherry I've met in a long motherfucking time," Levine said laughing along with everyone else.

"No, no, no," Jenks yelled above the laughter. "Cut the cherry some slack. He got screwed but we all got screwed. We're all here in da Nam, ain't we? Before we crown this cherry the dumbest motherfucker we've met in a long motherfuckin time, we gotta' make sure he's worthy of that title. "

"Jenks is right," Levine said soberly. "Shit's gotta be earned."

'How many of you fuckers enlisted?" Jenks asked. "And how many of you enlisted for three years because the recruiter fed you bullshit about how only draftees go to Vietnam?"

Both Jenks and Levine raised their hand along with more than half the gathered men, which by now is most of the platoon.

"Everyone with their hands up enlisted for three years and is sweating his ass off in da' Nam. The rest got drafted for two years and they're sweating their ass off in da' Nam. Face it, dickheads, all us three year swingin' dicks are dumber than the two year swingin' dicks. Now this A.S.A. shit is different. I know. They wanted me but, like I said, I wasn't up to their standards. This cherry was. Now, they told me they were so good the enlistment was different. How many years did you enlist for to get in this top flight unit, cherry?"

Fleming could feel his face literally drop. "I enlisted for four years."

"God, you is dumb," an African American soldier said.

Everyone had a comment ranging from an explosive motherfucker to laughter and everything in between.

"There it is. You're out here with us sorry fuckers cause some swinging-dick clerk made a mistake. And it all started cause some cheese dick recruiter promised you wouldn't be coming here. And because you believed him, you actually agreed to join for four years instead of three. You got the title, cherry. You earned it. You are the dumbest motherfucker we met in a long motherfucking time."

Everyone was laughing and hollering.

"Levine," an officer called from twenty meters away.

Levine hurried to Lieutenant Bartstell, the platoon commander. They spoke a few minutes then Levine came back to the men.

"Let's get this area cleared out. Choppers will be here in a half hour. Then we all go to the rear where there's hot meals and motherfucking showers. Get to work. "

A shirtless man with a fierce eagle tattooed across his chest hurried to Levine. He was large: six foot two, two hundred pounds of solid muscle. He was squirming and fidgeting.

"What's your major maladjustment, Silver?" Levine asked.

The man grimaced as if in pain. "I gotta take a royal shit," he said with a sheepish tone.

Levine smiled and was on the verge of breaking out with laughter. "Go. Di-di." (di-di-Vietnamese for go or hurry). "Take Reilly and Franks with you."

"Got you Lima Charlie." (slang for loud and clear). He said and ran off.

"Sergeant, do we have to ask for permission to take a shit?" Peyton asked.

Levine's face went from a half smile to narrow eyed fierce intensity in a matter of a second. "No, shit for brains. He listens to orders. When he was a stupid cherry he went to take a shit and got lost. Took us a half hour to find him. So for two months he has to tell me when he has to take a shit and he has to take two men with him in case he gets lost again. In another week his two months are up. "

A cherry named Hart smiled and chuckled.

Levine jumped right in his face. "Shut the fuck up! This group has the dumbest motherfucker we met in a long motherfuckin' time. And, personally, I think this is the dumbest group of cherries I've met in a long motherfuckin' time. Now get your cherry asses in gear and get to work."

While helping others clear a landing zone for the incoming chopper, Fleming felt the sting of the men's laughter and taunting. He had known for a while that he had been duped into joining for four years but it was over and nothing could be done about it. Nothing could be done about the lost orders and the clerk sending him here. It was all just bad luck. His thoughts drifted back to the days before he was about to be drafted – right after he had turned eighteen. A year earlier he had been a star Baseball Pitcher for Archbishop Curley High School in Baltimore, Maryland. After graduation, the Chicago White Sox signed him and gave him a ten thousand dollar bonus. He and Tony Santoro, a slugging first baseman from Mount Saint Joseph, were the only Baltimore high school players pursued that year by big league scouts. But the summer before, when Santoro and Fleming played together for Leone's Baseball club, Santoro told him that he had decided on taking a College Baseball Scholarship and had signed a letter of intent with UCLA. Fleming also had scholarships offers, but he had decided on taking the different path.

His first year in minor league class D ball was a success; winning ten games and losing two with a 2.92 E.R.A. Then he got his draft notice. He took tests and a physical and passed everything with flying colors. The White Sox said they could use their influence and secure him a position in the National Guard. All he had ever wanted to do in life was to face batters in a baseball game and get them out. However using influence in order to shirk his duty to his country didn't seem fair. He didn't want to go to war, but he was not afraid of it. What he feared was being the type of man who was okay with being thrust to the top of the National Guard list. That meant someone would be bumped up the list and drafted in his place; it was a mathematical certainty. What if that someone was killed in Vietnam? No, he decided, no one was taking his place. His Father had agreed with him and said he was proud of him. Since the Civil War, a Fleming had fought in every one of America's confrontations. His Father and his Uncles had all fought in World War II or Korea.

It was now his turn. His ten-year old sister Hope, whom he adored, said he was doing the right thing because her big brother was a hero and heroes always did the right thing. Heroes didn't use tricks and influence to excuse them from serving their country. National Guard service was still serving but being thrust to the top of the list was taking unfair advantage of a favorable situation. There had to be a way to serve and still be able to hone his baseball skills. If he was drafted it was a sure trip to Vietnam. If he enlisted, he had a better chance of being stationed in the States or somewhere overseas where he could pitch and stay in shape. He decided to enlist and let whatever happened happen.

He spoke to a recruiter and learned of the advantages of enlisting for four years in the A.S.A. It was one year more than a regular enlistment but the recruiter told him that since the A.S.A. wasn't in Vietnam he would be stationed somewhere where he could pitch for an Army team during his off duty hours. He could keep his ability sharp, keep his baseball dream alive, and honorably serve his country without someone taking his spot on a draft list. It was a perfect solution to the problem.

Thinking about it now, he should have taken a college scholarship. His friend Santoro was still playing baseball while Fleming was on a hill on the other side of the world with the title of "dumbest motherfucker we met in a long motherfuckin' time." And that wasn't the worst of it; for the next year, people would be trying their best to kill him.

BOOM! BOOM! BOOM!

He is suddenly jolted from his thoughts by the loudest sound he had ever heard in his life.

"INCOMING!" A dozen voices yelled.

BOOM! BOOM!

Get down was his first thought. He fell to the earth and covered his head with his hands.

BOOM! BOOM! BOOM!

Oh, sweet Jesus it's loud, he said to himself.

"GET IN HOLES, EVERYBODY," Levine yelled. "THEY'RE WALKING THEM IN!"

Fleming knew the term from basic training. Walking in mortars meant they were being dropped continuously with approximately twenty meters distance between them until they walked over every bit of the platoon's position.

BOOM! BOOM!

They were coming closer. It was as if a mythical giant or monster was taking thudding, booming, stomping steps across the perimeter.

Oh dear God, make it stop, Fleming said to himself. Make it stop. Suddenly he started coughing, choking and gagging. He lifted his head and spit out dirt from his mouth. He had pressed his face so hard into the earth it was as if he was eating the dirt.

BOOM! BOOM! BOOM!

He rubbed dirt from his eyes and saw that there was no one else on the perimeter. Everyone was in foxholes approximately forty meters ahead of him.

"GET IN A HOLE YOU DUMB SON OF A BITCH! " Levine yelled to him from the safety of a foxhole.

On legs that felt like clay, he stood and started running.

BOOM! BOOM!

He had twenty meters to run before reaching the holes.

Shrapnel whistled past his head.

BOOM! BOOM!

He was within ten meters when a mortar's concussion picked him up and heaved him. He flew through the air, fell to the earth, rolled into a foxhole, and crashed into Peyton.

"Jesus Christ," Peyton said mildly irritated.

Fleming began checking his body to make sure he hadn't been hit.

"Fleming, you okay?" Peyton asked with concern.

"Yeah, I think so."

BOOM! BOOM! BOOM!

The mortars come closer and closer.

Chunks of shrapnel whizzed over their position.

When will it stop? Fleming said to himself, cringing with each booming explosion.

And just then it stopped.

A whistle shrieked a piercing, sharp sound.

"Lock and load," Levine yelled from a foxhole far away. "They're coming through."

Peyton stood up to look out of the foxhole.

A burst of small arms fire struck him in the chest and face. He fell back into the foxhole on top of Fleming. Acting instinctively and revolted by the blood that flowed onto him from Peyton's wounds, Fleming pushed him away.

There was a small hole in Peyton's cheek where a round had entered and exited, blood poured from the wound. A wild look of fear covered his face. "Flem…Flem…" He couldn't speak because of the wound and the broken teeth that fell from his mouth with every attempt to speak. Wheezing and panting sounds escaped his mouth.

Fleming tore away Peyton's fatigue shirt. Blood poured from numerous chest wounds drenching Fleming. The wheezing and panting was pathetic to hear.

I can't take this, Fleming said to himself. Dear God help me. Frantically, he grabbed a bandage from a pouch on his web belt. He pressed down on the wound in an attempt to stop the bleeding. It seemed an impossible task – there was just too much blood; it also flowed from two other chest wounds. He held the bandage down with his right hand and grabbed a bandage from Peyton's web belt with his left.

Just then, Peyton's whole body shook and convulsed. One long sighing breath escaped him. His eyes went wide. His mouth opened and he died.

Literally feeling life leave Peyton's body, Fleming quickly pulled his hands away as if death were some kind of contagious condition. He fell back against the foxhole's dirt wall and stared at Peyton's facial death mask: a frozen mask of surprise, wonder, and resentment, as if he thought it grossly unfair to have only lived eighteen years.

Meahwhile the raging battle continued. Gunfire crackled and hand grenades exploded. Huey gunships darted and dove firing rockets, their automatic weapons unleashed numerous rounds. The thunderous sound was deafening.

Fleming grabbed his M-16 and hugged it against his body. He trembled with uncontrollable fear.

Then the gunfire suddenly grew weaker and soon stopped. The only sounds were wounded men screaming and crying in pain.

Fleming felt a paralyzing numbness. He could do nothing but sit there clutching his weapon to his chest, staring – he didn't know how long – at Peyton's lifeless body.

"Get the fuck out of the hole, you worthless piece of cherry shit!"

Fleming looked up to see Levine staring down at him. With a supreme effort, he stood and crawled out of the hole.

"Why the fuck were you the last man to get in your hole?" Levine asked.

Fleming couldn't speak. He only slowly shook his head back and forth in stunned wonder.

Levine studied a drenched with blood Fleming. He looked at the body in the foxhole. Then he looked back at Fleming, a curious expression on his face. He jumped into the foxhole and checked Peyton's body. He found the two bloody bandages and looked up at Fleming. "You hit?" He asked with a soft almost tender voice tone.

Fleming shook his head no while staring straight through Levine.

Levine studied him for a moment before he said: "Help me get his body outta here." The words were said softly; his facial expression was almost kind.

Fleming dropped into the foxhole and helped Levine lift the body out.

"We'll take him over there with the rest of the dead." Levine indicated an area where a half a dozen bodies lay lifeless.

Fleming grabbed Peyton's feet. Levine took his arms. They carried him over to the dead pile and laid him down. Fleming saw the dead faces of two more cherries, men who were alive and laughing this morning on the chopper coming here.

Doyle and Fields looked down at the bodies.

"That's three," Fields said with a smile. "I told you them dickheads would all be dead in a week."

"Now we're goin to the rear," Doyle motioned to Fleming. "Even the dumbest motherfucker we met in a long motherfuckin' time won't manage to get himself killed in the rear."

"Shut the fuck up!" Levine growled. "And get the fuck outta' here!"

The two men hurried away.

Lieutenant Bartstell called to Levine. Levine ran to him and they began a conversation that quickly turned into an argument. "Fuck you, sir!" Levine screamed, loud enough for all to hear. "We're stayin'! Ain't no way in hell we can leave now!"

The Lieutenant poked his finger in Levine's chest and said in an equally loud voice: "Get the men ready and let's get the fuck out of here, sergeant. That's an order." Then he hurried away from Levine.

"MOTHERFUCKER!" Levine screamed.

What the hell kind of man is he? Fleming wondered. Why would a man argue to stay on the battlefield?

Levine hurried back to the dead men and to where Fleming stood. Face alive with fury Levine grabbed a man who passed by them. "Benson, help this fuckin' cherry get these bodies on the chopper. We're pulling the fuck out. Motherfucker!" He growled.

Fleming sat in a chopper with Levine, Jenks, and a half dozen other men.

Everything about today was another in a never-ending series of mishaps ever since he had gotten his draft notice. His thoughts drifted back to basic training. Every trainee error was met with a drill sergeant's profanity laced tongue lashing on how the trainee was certain to get himself and all his buddies killed in Vietnam if he didn't get his head out of his ass and get his shit together. It was as if drill sergeants wanted everyone conditioned to the fact that Vietnam was every trainee's inevitable destination. But despite it all, Fleming enjoyed basic training. He was in great physical condition so the marching and running were doable for him. Forced marches to and from the rifle range were strenuous but would keep him in excellent condition for baseball. All the push-ups had put five pounds of muscle on him. One weekend, he and another soldier went to the base gym and got a catcher's mitt, ball, and glove. He threw for an hour and felt as if the new muscle had given him a few more miles per hour on his fastball.

He fired at the rifle range and had the third best score in his company. He was so proficient that his C.O. ordered him to act as replacement shooter for one of the ineffective men. The man would surely fail and the company would suffer the indignity of having a man not qualifying at the rifle range. It was done all the time, the C.O. had said. Fleming was proud to have been chosen. He fired for the man and qualified him. It was later, when the man received orders for Infantry A.I.T. that Fleming felt differently. Firing a weapon was an Infantryman's primary duty. Not being able to fire a weapon was akin to a cook not being able to boil an egg. There was a ninety nine percent chance that the man would be sent to Vietnam. What if he died? How many of his comrades would die because of his inability to hit a target? And all the uncertainties boiled down to one: would all the potential deaths be on Fleming's ledger?

After basic he received orders to Fort Devens Massachusetts for Morse Code Intercept School. He was surprised when he learned that practically every graduating Interceptor was sent to Vietnam and every Interceptor had been told, by rercruiters, that the A.S.A. wasn't in Vietnam. He was more than surprised when he learned that the first man killed in Vietnam was an A.S.A. man. It was at Devens when he learned about the great switcheroo – A.S.A. becoming Radio Research.

But none of it mattered. He had developed a fondness for the Army and its strict regimen. It was like being on the ultimate team.

At Devens, he excelled. Because of his Morse code proficiency he received an advanced promotion to P.F.C. and Spec. 4. At

Devens, he put in for airborne training and for Special Operations Detachment or S.O.D. It was a unit attached to the Green Berets. At the very least all the strenuous Special Forces and airborne training would get him in better shape for baseball. At last count he had put on ten pounds of muscle since joining the Army and he was throwing his fastball with much more velocity.

He successfully completed jump school and learned that S.O.D. was being phased out as well as the Green Beret's mission in Vietnam. It was then that he received orders for Vietnam and once there he learned that his orders had been lost and there was confusion to his status. Since he was airborne a clerk decided it was best for him to be assigned to an airborne unit and since all airborne were gung ho, it seemed logical to assign him to a rifle company. Volunteering for airborne at Devens had put him in the position he was in today.

Sitting in the chopper, Fleming looked at his blood caked arms and hands. He could feel the blood and dirt caked on his face.

Despite all his success at baseball, despite his initial success in the Army, he had been a resounding failure today. He was given the title of the dumbest motherfucker the platoon had met in a long motherfucking time. He couldn't deny that during the mortar and ground attack, this dumbest motherfucker in a long motherfucking time felt mind-numbing fear. He had never imagined that fear could be so intense or that such a fear even existed.

He glanced at Levine.

This skinny, short, bespectacled man looked like the most harmless person in the world. Yet battle hardened veterans treated him with the utmost awe and respect. It was a sharp contrast to the ridicule and lack of respect they had for Fleming.

The lessons he learned in sports dictated that any world could be conquered – you just never quit. Try as he might, he could never see himself ever conquering this world of misery and death.

Suddenly the man next to him jabbed him in the shoulder with his elbow.

His thought pattern broken, Fleming turned to him. It was Hart, a man he had come in with this morning.

"Did you get some, Fleming?" Hart asked with an ear-to-ear grin. "You kill any gooks? I got me two of them fuckers."

"No, I didn't get some," Fleming said, disgusted by the question.

Hart turned to Levine and gave him his ear-to-ear smile. "Sergeant, we did good out there today, huh?"

Bespectacled Levine eyed him fiercely, like a rabid Woody Allen. "Shut the fuck up, dickhead! You say one more word you better know how to fly because I am gonna throw you outta this motherfuckin chopper!"

Hart was obviously feeling brave because of the two men he had killed today because he said: "What the fuck is with you? I called you sergeant. I killed two fuckin Gook NVA today. I done good."

Fleming had the ridiculous thought that Hart must know how to fly because he was seconds away from being thrown outta this motherfuckin chopper.

Levine bolted from his seat and started after Hart.

Jenks and two other soldiers had anticipated the move. They were on Levine as soon he neared Hart and pulled him away.

"It don't mean nothin," Jenks said to Levine. "The cherry ain't got shit for brains."

A moment passed. A large African American Soldier held Levine in a bear hug. Levine didn't even try to break free, but he still held his death look glare on Hart.

"What the fuck did I do?" Hart yelled.

"Shut the fuck up, cherry," Jenks warned.

"We fuckin' did good. We kicked those gooks ass. I wasted two of em myself. We done good. I done good."

Jenks placed his face inches from Hart's. "The only thing we did today was fuck up! Silvers, Reilly, and Franks were left behind and we

never do that shit! We never leave men behind! So shut ⟨
we really will throw your cherry ass outta this fuckin' cho⟨

And Fleming suddenly remembered two things instantly. He remembered Levine arguing with the platoon's Lieutenant about leaving the battlefield and he realized why. And he remembered the man who went to relieve himself and the two men who went with him. They were taken prisoner by the enemy. Those poor fucking bastards, Fleming thought. Oh, those poor bastards.

CHAPTER 2

Tiger Cubs

Fifteen-year old Van Phan Duc sat in an underground bunker chamber with his two childhood friends: fifteen-year old Hoi Anh Chanh and fifteen year old Dan Tri Quang. They were waiting for their sergeant to enter and lead them through a training exercise. Van and his friends' faces were filled with fear, the fear of death. In their small village, elders lived eighty, ninety even a hundred years. It was unnatural for fifteen year olds to worry about dying; yet it was a very real possibility that he and his three friends might not live to see their sixteenth birthday.

And what if they survived? From here on out, their primary duty was to kill Americans. They were Buddhists and Buddha forbade the taking of any life form. Would Buddha take into account that it was kill or be killed? Van didn't know. So much was unknown. One certainty rang out; they would suffer. Buddha's first noble truth was: All life is suffering. But this…this went beyond suffering. Suddenly Kim's face appeared in his mind's eye. He drove the vision and the thought away; it was much too painful.

Just then his training sergeant, Nguyen Han Chi burst into the room.

Malevolence glowed in Chi's ugly face: a mottled mess of burned, charred, hideous scar tissue. It looked as if someone had at one time set fire to Chi's head and face. "Dogs, you are fortunate. Yesterday, our forces chased Americans away from one of their mountain outposts. The American dogs ran like cowards and left three of their comrades. We will use these men to make your pathetic fighting spirits stronger and help you become proud warriors of the revolution. Follow me."

Chi, Van and his childhood friends entered another chamber where six armed Viet Cong guerillas sat at a table drinking tea. At the chamber's other side, two armed guerillas guarded three Americans hanging from a beam with a rope tied around their wrists. One man was very muscular and had an eagle tattooed on his chest.

Chi pointed to one of the men. "Take the others away. We will use him."

Four guerillas lowered the muscular man and another man from the beam and led them away.

Chi stepped to the lone American and smiled at him.

The American's lips puckered then tears streamed down his face.

Surprise filled Van. For some reason he thought that Americans didn't cry. They were huge, fierce looking people when compared to Vietnamese.

Just then Van's thoughts were rudely interrupted when Chi's ugly face was inches from his. "Dog!" Chi yelled.

"Yes, sergeant," Van answered.

Chi handed him a knife. "You will have the honor of the first cut. You will stick this knife one inch into the American's stomach. One inch!" Chi emphasized. "We don't want him dying right away. You will then slash sideways for another six inches."

"I can't do that," Van blurted out instinctively.

Chi slapped him hard in the face; it was so fast that Van didn't see the blow.

"SERGEANT!" Chi screamed at him.

"Sergeant," Van answered meekly.

"You will do what I ordered, dog. Or I will have you hung up there."

He had to do it. In his wildest dreams, he couldn't envision himself ever taking a stand against Chi. With knife in hand, Van turned to the American.

The American's face twisted with fear. His eyes darted rapidly inside their sockets.

You must know I don't want to do this, Van said to himself, hoping that somehow the American could read his thoughts. No sane man would ever do this. He wasn't even supposed to be here. He was a poor farm boy drafted into the revolution. But he knew the American wouldn't understand. The American knew one thing – he would soon die and until that time he would suffer horribly.

"You're wasting time, dog. Do it!"

Van touched the knife's blade – it was honed to a keen edge. He thrust it into the man and was surprised at how easily it had pierced the man's mid section.

"Ohh," The American exclaimed, more shocked and surprised than in pain.

Blood splashed onto Van's hand. It was such a rich, vivid red color.

"Dog, continue!" Chi ordered.

Van gritted his teeth. He slid the knife across the American's mid section.

"OHHHH!" This time the American wailed painfully as the knife slid across his body.

Blood poured out of the wound.

Van felt weak and dizzy with nausea. He gagged once and was seconds away from vomiting. With supreme effort, he willed it away. He feared Chi's punishment if he showed any sign of weakness.

"Listen, dog. This is the most important part. Do what I tell you and do it correctly. Push the knife in four more inches and rip it back along the same path only this time slash it along his whole stomach."

He can't be serious, Van thought.

"DO IT NOW!"

Van drove the knife in. Then he ripped it back along the same route and all along the man's stomach.

The American screamed; it was piercing and pathetic to hear. Then everything happened at once. Blood poured from the wound.

Green and brown slimy entrails and intestines exploded out of the man's stomach. Urine burst from his bladder. Liquid like feces poured from his rectum. Van leapt back to avoid the mess, but much of it splashed onto his arms, chest, legs, and feet.

Chi shrieked with laughter – a grotesque, falsetto sound that was as horrible to hear as the Americans screams of pain and horror.

Sick and nauseous, dozens of spots appeared before Van's eyes. He became faint and dizzy. His legs were rubbery and it took effort to stay upright. Bile retched from his stomach and reached his mouth but he held it inside. He swallowed some and spit some out. He wasn't about to vomit and incur Chi's wrath.

A determined look of appreciation slowly crept over Chi's face. "Dog, you did well. You're finally showing courage."

Courage, Van thought disgustedly. How much courage did it take to slit open a helpless man's stomach? The village elders often told tales of the Trung Sisters and how they fought valiantly during Vietnam's many wars with China, their mortal enemy. These were tales of courage. Tales were never told of brutal men torturing helpless victims.

"You are finished for a while, dog."

Van walked back to Hoi and Dan.

Hoi's face was a mask of fear and revulsion. When they were six years old he, Hoi, and Dan were throwing rocks at tree leafs. The object of the game was to knock a leaf from a tree. One time Dan had purposely hit a bird and had crushed its skull. When they went to look at it, Hoi got violently ill. It started that day. From then on Hoi always hated seeing humans or animals in pain.

Van looked at Dan – his face was full of wonder and curiosity. Van didn't know what conclusion could be ascertained from the curious facial expression.

Meanwhile, the American had slipped into unconsciousness. A nurse entered and Chi instructed her to administer just enough aid to keep the American alive.

Fifteen minutes later, the nurse finished and left.

Chi threw a bucket of water in the American's face.

The man awakened, took one look at his hanging entrails, and screamed – a wailing sound rich with fear and pain. It was the sound of suffering personified – a sound that Van would remember for the rest of his life.

The screams invigorated Chi. He leapt high in the air and kicked his feet out with all the agility of a nimble dancer. He landed and began prancing around the room, a high-stepping dance, all the while whooping and braying shrieking sounds of delight.

"Oh, dear Buddha," Hoi said watching Chi's demonstration.

Van could feel his face lose all color, a sick, nauseating feeling. His mouth and eyes were wide open with horror.

Dan watched with the wide-eyed innocence of a child. His face betrayed no emotion, just curiosity.

Chi stopped his prancing dance and rushed to the American. He placed his face an inch from the American and laughed.

The American's lips puckered. Tears rolled from his eyes and down his cheek.

Chi turned back to the three boys.

"Dogs, the American's stomach is on fire. Since he is a soldier I will extend him the courtesy we extend all soldiers. I will ease his pain. I will put out the fire." Chi smiled at the three for a long moment then turned back to the American.

Chi dropped his black pajama bottoms and began urinating in the man's ripped open stomach.

A low wailing sound emerged from Hoi.

Dan still had the same look of child like curiosity. Van had known Dan his whole life. He was always bigger than most Vietnamese. Even at the young age of fifteen, he was physically stronger than most of the village's adults. He liked hearing stories of warriors. Now it seemed as if he had regressed back to when he was a child and Van wondered what it meant.

Chi finished urinating and turned back to the three recruits. "Dogs, I cooled the fire in his stomach with my sweet urine. He will die and because of my golden flow he will die quicker and with greater pain. But I have eased your pain. I am familiarizing you to the horrors of America's war. You can thank me later, dogs."

All of a sudden the American began convulsing. His whole body shook and trembled. He retched and gagged then began wheezing and panting. He sighed, a long wailing sound, then threw his head back and died.

Despite the American's wounds and his ripped open stomach, Van was certain that he died of fear, frightened to death by Chi.

Chi's eyes grew wide with outrage and disappointment. He rushed to the American and checked for signs of life. Finding none an angry, frustrated Chi began pounding the American with kicks and punches. The body swung to and fro, throwing off blood and entrails. Chi punched and kicked him until exhaustion set in forcing him to stop. He bent over for a few seconds until he caught his breath then he looked at the three boys. His face and body was covered with streaks of blood. Bits of intestine and entrails were stuck to his hair and clothing and hung from his body like so many ornaments. "The dog American ruined the whole day," he mumbled. Then he strode briskly to the three boys. "Dogs, follow me."

Minutes later, they entered another room where two Americans sat across from each other at a table, their hands and feet tied. Four men guarded them.

Chi nodded to a guard.

The guard placed his AK-47 barrel against an American's head. Another guard untied the American's hands, then placed them on top of straps attached to the table, and fastened the straps. Then they did the same to the other American.

Chi made eye contact with the American with the large muscles.

The American steadfastly held Chi's gaze.

Chi smiled at him, then grabbed one of the man's fingers and violently pulled it back breaking it.

The American gasped ever so slightly. His face flickered with just the slightest hint of pain.

Chi scowled at him.

The American held the gaze, showing no fear.

Chi's face relaxed into a smile as if appreciating the man's bravado. He turned back to the three boys. "We will break every finger on each man's hand. I have just demonstrated the incorrect way of doing it. I will now show you the correct way."

Chi turned to the American and stared into his face.

The American returned the gaze; small beads of perspiration dotted his forehead.

Chi smiled, a low ominous chuckle came from some place deep inside him. When Chi stepped behind him, the American turned his head to follow him. With both hands, Chi struck him repeatedly on the ears for a long moment. Then Chi reached over the man's shoulder, grabbed his ring finger, and began pulling it back. In a few seconds the finger was at a horrible, unnatural angle and ready to break. A downpour of sweat drenched the man's face.

Slowly Chi inched the finger backward.

The American's face drained of color, yet he continued showing no fear.

POP!

Van jumped at the sound – like kindling crackling in a campfire.

The American moaned ever so lowly; it seemed to go on forever.

A low moaning sound came from Dan. Dan, with the magnificent set of muscles, often removed his shirt to show off for the village women. His sheer beauty and size made him appear older than his fifteen years. Right now he appeared to be a child lost in confusion.

"Dog!" Chi barked, pointing at Hoi.

A wave of dread filled Van. Hoi was sensitive. He enjoyed poetry and singing. When the village elders told warrior tales, Hoi would slip away. But there would be no slipping away from Chi.

"Come here, dog!" Chi hissed.

Fear covered Hoi's face. On unsteady legs he shuffled toward Chi.

Chi placed his face inches from Hoi. "You will have the honor of breaking the next finger, dog. You will do it slowly. Do you understand?"

Hoi looked at the American.

The American glared at him.

Hoi couldn't hold the man's unyielding gaze and looked away.

"Do it, dog!" Chi ordered.

Hoi pulled back on the finger.

"Slower, dog!" Chi barked.

He pulled the finger back, his face a mask of pain as if it is his finger that was about to be broken.

"I said slower you stupid dog! Slower! Do you hear me? Slower!"

Sweat streamed down Hoi's face. Then he let loose of the man's finger.

The American glared at Hoi, as if reproaching him for his failure.

Chi began repeatedly slamming both his fists into Hoi's ribs until Hoi crumpled to the floor. Chi kicked him then grabbed his shirt and pulled him to his feet. "You will do it again, dog! This time it will be done correctly." He slammed Hoi's chest with the palm of his hand.

Hoi grabbed the man's finger.

"Pull it, dog!"

Hoi pulled it back ever so slowly.

"Yes! Yes! Yes!" Chi chanted breathlessly. "That's it. That's good!"

Back went the finger until it was at an unnatural, horrible angle. POP!

This time it sounded louder, like a hefty tree branch being broken across someone's knee.

The American exhaled a pain-filled, booming expulsion of air, which eventually abated to an agonizing moan.

Chi slapped Hoi's back in congratulations. Very good, very, very good. Now you may sit down, dog?"

Hoi's facial expression died right there. All emotion, all pain and fear left, replaced with a horrible expression of nothingness. Van felt as if a critical juncture had just been met and passed and Hoi had lost, as if his spirit, his very soul had been drained from him.

"Your turn, dog!"

Dan stood, looked at Hoi and Van and then made his way to Chi.

"Remember, slowly, dog."

Dan grabbed the finger and yanked it backward breaking it instantly.

The American let out a sharp yelp.

'NO, NO, YOU STUPID DOG!" He rapped Dan on the left ear. There was no time for a second blow.

'GRRRRRRR!" Dan roared savagely.

Stunned and surprised, Chi drew back as if he had been struck.

Dan placed his face inches from the American.

"GRRRRRR!" He roared again.

He grabbed the American's last finger and yanked it violently, breaking it. Then he grabbed the thumb, yanked, and broke it. He interlocked both hands, forming a double fist. He raised his hands high above his head and smashed them down against the American's hand.

The blow was so powerful that the wooden table cracked and the American's hand broke.

The American's face lost all color. His upper body slammed violently forward and he hit his head against the table and was knocked unconscious.

Chi's eyes widened with wonder. He looked at Dan, studying him. Then Chi smiled, his face slowly transforming into a grin of appreciation.

A toothy, narrow smile crept onto Dan's face – the grin of madness.

Dan's behavior filled Van with a cold feeling of dread. He immediately told himself that Dan had been forced into these actions.

It wasn't his fault, he said to himself. But these words brought Van no peace of mind.

For the next hour, the three boys took turns breaking fingers on the American's other hand. The American showed great courage. He stoically endured the pain and never cried out. He brazenly glared at his tormentors. It was different with the other American. When his fingers were broken, he cried continuously; tears streamed down his face.

Finally Chi halted the torture.

"Dogs, if we torture them too long, they become numb to the pain. You did well, dogs. You are free for a while. Meet back here in two hours."

Van stepped out of the bunker complex into fresh air. The sunlight was blinding and it took a moment for him to get used to it. He had always loved the sun shining on and warming his face but his new life demanded that he would spend most of his days in a dark, dank underground bunker complex hiding from Americans.

Van sat on a large boulder. The picture of his friends' faces filled his mind's eye. During the last hour of torture, Hoi had been robotic as if it wasn't him performing the horrific acts but someone else. Dan had been the opposite. He was spirited – roaring war cries and taunting the Americans.

His friends had changed today. His friends were all that was left of a life that had once promised such happiness. Every day, they had all worked alongside their Fathers in the rice paddies. At day's end, Van would meet Kim, the village chieftain's daughter. And every day Hoi and Dan would tease him about Kim. She was his love. The girl he would marry.

Then it all changed.

One night, sitting with Kim at the village gate, the N.V.A. Soldiers came. They were horrible looking men – pieces of human anatomy attached to leather straps hung from their necks. They herded Van and Kim back inside the village where everyone was gathered.

The N.V.A. leader gave a rousing speech about the valiant struggle against the invading Americans dividing the country. The leader wanted the village males to join the struggle to free the nation.

The village chieftain Minh, Kim's Father, politely explained that the village had few men. When asked about Van, Hoi, and Dan, Minh explained that they were too young and knew nothing about soldiering and war. The leader said he understood. Minh invited the leader to share dinner with him and his family. The leader graciously accepted. It was sometime during the night when he had a change of heart.

Bright and early the next morning, the village awoke to see Minh and his family naked and dead, hanging upside down suspended from the village gate. Minh and his son's eyes had been burned out of their sockets and their sex organs had been removed. Kim and her Mother's eyes had also been burned out. Their breasts had been cut off.

Horrified, Van tried to run, but the soldiers stopped him. They held him and his friends at gunpoint.

Then the N.V.A. leader gave another speech. He expressed remorse for killing the chieftain's family. They had no zeal for the revolution and it had to be done. He ended by saying he hoped the three boys would join the great cause.

Van looked at his twelve year old sister Lan and his Mother and Father and realized what the leader would do if he didn't volunteer; his family would be tortured and murdered. Van and his friends enlisted that day.

Van formed a plan for revenge. He would find a way to kill the N.V.A. leader. But the plan never got beyond the planning stage. The next day they were turned over to a different company for basic training – a safeguard protecting recruiters against recruits seeking revenge against those responsible for any such atrocities.

The next two months they marched through the jungle with no destination in mind. It didn't take long to realize that the N.V.A. was breaking them down: body, mind and soul, so they would embrace their new life. Each night they attended indoctrination training. It was just another form of breaking down – brainwashing. Trainees were stripped of personal dignity. Past histories were erased. They were ordered to forget the past and any reference to the past was met with brutal beatings until a recruit actually believed there had never been a past life. The future held only one honorable conclusion – Vietnam's liberation.

Despite it all, Van vowed never to forget the elders' teachings – the past was the future and the future was the past. He would never erase Kim's memory. He would never forget the men responsible for brutally stealing his future.

Van decided to play the game. He gave the cadre answers he knew they wanted to hear. He told them that life was an acceptance of the struggle and that meant fighting and killing Americans.

There was little actual training. Ammunition was scarce and recruits were not permitted to fire weapons. They engaged in a practice called dry fire, which involved sighting targets and squeezing the trigger. But practicing pulling the trigger on an unloaded weapon and firing at imaginery targets was a far cry from firing on an American soldier who was firing back.

After basic training they were turned over to Chi for advanced training. A few hours later, Chi had taken them on an ambush. They sat and waited for an American patrol to wander past their position. When they sighted the Americans, Van knew his duty was to fire on them, but his hands were shaking so badly it was impossible to take aim let alone fire.

At Chi's signal everyone opened fire except for Van and his friends. Seconds later, the Americans were dead. Chi and his men leapt from their positions and began hacking off pieces of the dead soldiers' anatomy. They had looked like wild dogs fighting over scraps of meat.

Afterwards, back at the underground complex, Chi had berated them as dogs in need of more training. Today they had undergone that training; it was conditioning to accustom them to war's brutality and to take further control of their minds. Van would play the game but he'd never succumb to becoming the type of man they wanted. They would never own his soul.

The two hours passed, and they are all back in the chamber with the two Americans.

What more could be done to them? Van wondered. Their hands were swollen and bulbous, a rich collection of colors: blue, purple, red, and black. Their fingers were thick gnarled stumps.

Chi walked up to the defiant American and held his gaze. Then Chi smiled and patted the man's cheek. Then he went to the other American, the frightened one, and smiled at him.

Once again, tears began streaming down the man's face.

A smiling, laughing Chi reached into his pocket and took out a two inch long needle and a bayonet knife and waved it all in the crying American's face.

The man's crying increased in intensity and volume, fearing what new horror would be done with the needle and knife.

An overjoyed Chi turned to the three boys. "Are you ready for some fun, dogs?"

Then Chi placed the needle next to the man's index finger's nail. With the bayonet's handle, he tapped the needle driving it down between the man's thumbnail and skin.

The American bellowed and screamed inhumane sounds.

Chi turned to the boys. "Dogs, I drove it in. Now all you have to do is tap."

Chi turned back to the American and waved the bayonet in his face, taunting him. Then he tapped the needle halfway down into the American's finger. Blood gushed out of the fingernail.

The American convulsed violently in his seat, pain consuming his body. The agonizing screams were accompanied by Chi's shrieking laughter.

When the screaming subsided Chi grabbed the needle with his fingers and began shaking it and the man's finger back and forth.

The American screamed and thrashed. His feet stomped the ground. His knees knocked up against the table. His torso and head jackknifed back and forth.

Chi began speaking while continuing to shake the pin. His voice was heard above the pain filled wailings. "Dogs, all you need to do is tap the needle. When you drive it down far enough just shake the pin."

When Chi finished shaking the pin, the American passed out. He slumped forward, his chin resting on his chest. Then Chi blasted the pin's head with the bayonet and drove it all the way in until the head was flush with the thumbnail. Blood gushed out.

The American's head shot up. A long pathetic scream of pain filled the chamber.

Chi waited until the screaming subsided and the American again slumped over. Chi turned to the boys. "Dogs, who–"

Dan leapt from his seat before the sentence could be finished. He hurried to Chi and looked him in the eye. "It's my turn," he said eagerly and with a conviction that dared to be challenged.

A satisfied smile filled Chi's face. He handed Dan the knife and another needle.

Dan tiptoed silently to the slumped over American. He placed the needle against the man's middle finger's nail. With a quick, hard snapping motion, he slammed the needle's head. The pin travelled down an inch into the man's finger.

Once again, his head shot up and he screamed and bellowed.

Dan and Chi laughed with delight.

Van watched horrified, realizing that Dan had died and a new Dan had been reborn.

"ARRGGGGH!" Dan roared in the man's face. Then he began slapping the American's face until blood started pouring from his nose.

Van could no longer watch. He turned his head and was face to face with Hoi. Hoi stared straight ahead; eyes wide open seeing nothing. He's dead, too. Van realized, not physically but spiritually. He was a living dead man. Hoi had spent only one night and a half a day with Chi and it had killed all of the village elders' spiritual teachings.

Dan and Chi spent the next few hours torturing the American and laughing maniacally. When Hoi was called, he went about the task with the maddening mask of nothingness on his face. When it was Van's turn his hand shook so violently he had to grab his wrist with his other hand to steady it before he could tap the needle – this brought on a round of maniacal laughter from Chi and Dan. Then Chi called a halt to the day's proceedings.

The next day the Americans were taken to the room where the American with the ripped open stomach still hung. The defiant American took one look at the hanging intestines and entrails and tried to run. A V.C. guard butt stroked him in the mid section stopping him.

The other American moaned. His eyes rolled back in his head. A long stream of spittle drooled out of his mouth. Then an insane grin consumed his face. Right before his eyes, Van realized, he has just witnessed a man go insane.

Then Chi had the two men sit at a table. Chi lit a cigarette. Since their hands were bound, Chi held the cigarette to the insane man's lips. The man just grinned. He no longer had the mental capacity to inhale on the cigarette. Chi held the cigarette to the other man. The man eyed Chi warily, not sure what to do.

Chi smiled benevolently and gestured with the cigarette urging him to take a puff.

The American's eyes darted nervously inside their sockets before he warily allowed Chi to hold the cigarette for him and he inhaled on it. Then Chi took a drag. He again gestured with the cigarette and the

American nodded his head yes. Chi placed it in his mouth so the American could inhale on it. Chi removed it then plunged the cigarette into the man's eyeball.

The defiant one finally broke down. He screamed and screamed.

Chi and Dan shrieked and laughed with delight.

When the screaming man stopped, Chi signaled to a guard. The guard left the chamber and returned seconds later leading a hog into the room. The hog took one look at the hanging entrails, hurried to them, and began eating them.

The defiant American, who was no longer defiant, began screaming again. The insane man drooled, the silly grin resting on his face. Hoi sat there emotionless staring ahead, seeing nothing. Dan and Chi laughed with delight. The hog lapped up the entrails. Van watched it all.

Then Chi had the guards hang the Americans on the beam. It was time for a team effort. They would all take turns slashing cuts along the American's bodies. "Not too deep," he warned. "Or they will die right away."

It took two days for the Americans to die. To celebrate training's completion, Chi cut an ear from each American and awarded it to the boys. He ordered that they attach it to a leather thong and wear it around their necks till the ears decomposed.

That night, lying on his straw mat, Van couldn't sleep. His mind was filled with the past few days' horror. He thought of the screaming Americans. Driving that thought from his mind, he then heard Dan and Chi's insane laughter and saw their maniacal faces. He drove the images and the sounds away. For a moment, he thought of nothing, but soon he thought of days working in the rice paddy and Kim.

She's dead, he said to himself angrily. And the village was dead and so was working in the rice paddies. His two friends were as good as dead. He was surrounded by death: mired in a life of pain, misery and suffering, a world where good was dead and only evil, the worst kind of evil, existed. Nothing in the village elders' teachings had prepared him for this. Suddenly he was filled with resentment. Why me? He wondered. He was a devout Buddhist. It wasn't fair that he be thrust onto this life path. He wasn't prepared for all this brutality and death. What man could be prepared?

Suddenly he realized that tears were streaming down his cheeks. Self- consciousness washed over him like a wave. He quickly wiped the tears away. Somehow he would have to learn to survive in this brutal new world. Self-pity would not help. He had to learn survival techniques and learn quickly because for the first time in his life he was without his parents and the bountiful love that had always flourished in his village.

CHAPTER 3

Two Minutes

"Fleming, how do I look?" P.F.C. Hawkins asked, preparing for tonight's ambush.

"Like the baddest motherfucker in the valley." And damn if those words didn't make Fleming feel like the lyingest motherfucker in the valley. The men – the Army generously called them men, but the oldest was nineteen – were the new batch of cherries, replacements that had joined the platoon after last week's mortar barrage. They hadn't seen combat – they weren't bad motherfuckers – and they had no idea what was in store for them. Fleming realized he wasn't exactly a combat veteran but he had seen death and he had heard the sound of falling mortars. The memory of it all haunted his dreams, waking him every night for the past week.

"Man, check my bad self out," an African American named Faison boasted as he primped and preened showing off his combat ensemble.

Fleming couldn't help but think how this all seemed like a sort of macabre game – like football teammates banging against each others shoulder pads; wide receivers blacking their eyes to cut down the sun's glare. Faison's eye black was green camouflage allowing him to blend in with foliage so he could kill human beings. His equipment was the bayonet he had taped to his left leg, the ammunition slings strapped crisscross along his chest, the two grenades hanging from his flak jacket.

"So c'mon, man, how do I look?" Faison asked again.

"Ready, man, like a Goddamn Gook killing machine."

Faison smiled, satisfied. "How about you, man. You ready?"

"Ain't enough Gooks in this country to handle the bad I'm gonna' be dealing. I'm ready to put a damn damn on those rice eaters." And now he felt like the hypocriticalest motherfucker in the valley. But he lied to these men because he liked them. They spoke to him. They deferred to him simply because he had been in country ten days longer. The veterans avoided Fleming and the other cherries like the plague.

"Once Jenks catches your action he gonna' be treatin you better. Ain't gonna' have you burnin no shit no more. Man, you sure smelled bad a couple days there. Ten thousand motherfuckin ambushes got to be better than burnin shit."

"I hear that." Now he was telling white lies. If truth were told he would rather

burn shit for a whole year than go on an ambush. Chances were he would be doing both. Burning shit was the most disgusting detail imaginable; it entailed dumping kerosene into a barrel of human feces and setting it on fire. It was beyond nauseating and, more often than not, he ended up covered in feces. Jenks, his squad leader, had given him the detail every time it was his squad's turn.

This past week had overwhelmed Fleming: the firefight, having Peyton die in his arms, the harassment he had taken from the other soldiers in the platoon, and the shit-burning details. He hadn't signed up for none of this. It was time to take his future in his own hands. Not far from his platoon area the 404th Radio Research Detachment was located. Maybe they could help him out of the horror he found himself firmly entrenched.

He entered the 404th compound. A MP shack was to the immediate left of the 404th's entrance. He went to the shack and told the MP he would like to see the Comanding Officer of the 404th. The MP explained that Shepherd wasn't cleared to enter the area where the C.O.'s Headquarters was located. He would need a Security Badge. Fleming explained his situation to the MP but was again told that he still could not enter the compound unless he had a clearance to do so.

Fleming was completely frustrated. The MP said he would speak with the C.O. and let him know of Fleming's predicament. He told Fleming to come back the following day. When Fleming returned the next day the MP said that he had forgotten to speak with the C.O.

Fleming's first reaction was anger but he calmed himself. Anger would get him nowhere. Right now, the MP was the one person who could help end this nightmare. Fleming asked the MP if he would try again to speak with the C.O. It was then that the MP said that he believed that Fleming wasn't telling the truth. He flat out said that he believed that Fleming was afraid to be in the bush and that he was telling this wild story as a desperate attempt to get out of fighting the enemy. He went so far as to call Fleming a pussy-ass coward.

Again, Fleming had to clamp down on his anger. He assured the MP that it wasn't the truth. He begged the MP to speak with the C.O. Again the MP agreed to do so. He told Fleming to come back the next day.

The following day Fleming was told that the C.O. couldn't take the time to speak with him. The C.O. said that Fleming should leave his name and military serial number and the C.O. would look into it, or so said the MP.

It was not what Fleming wanted but it seemed to be the best he could get. He left his name and number and was told to come back the next day.

The next day he was told that the C.O. sent Fleming's information to MACV but it would take a while to investigate Fleming's claim. The MP told him that he could come back monthly to check his status.

He didn't think he could endure one more day of this let alone a month. To make matters worse, today, again the MP questioned Fleming's bravery when he said: "You sure you're telling the truth. Your story sounds pretty wild. You sure you're not some pussy-ass coward trying to get out of fighting the gooks?"

Again, Fleming assured the MP that he was being truthful. Then he left the 404th area and headed back to his own platoon area. He felt ashamed of himself for having put up with the MP's abuse. However, what alternative did he have? Feeling a twinge of shame was nothing, a small price to pay, if he ended up being rotated out of the field. He decided that he would do his best to adjust to his life as an Infantryman until it was time to do the job the army trained him to do.

The second he entered the company he was greeted by the sight of Levine verbally tearing into another cherry. Fleming was able to slip by Levine unseen.

Levine was always in a bad mood. He was still pissed about leaving the three men in the field. They were listed as missing in action, but a chopper pilot had reported seeing Vietnamese run into the jungle with three American prisoners. The thought of the men being left there angered Levine so much so that he lobbied to have Hart, the man he wanted to throw out of the chopper, transferred to another platoon. The request was granted. To add fuel to the fire, Levine's mood worsened when the platoon lost six veterans. One man was sent home on emergency leave never to return. Three were wounded in the last battle and had been sent to Japan, probably never to return. And two had served their year tour. The platoon was down to thirty-five men, seventeen men under full strength, and only twenty men had experience.

Just then A.F.V.N., Armed Forces Vietnam Network, played a song by the new group, The Jackson Five. Faison danced over to Evans, another African American cherry.

Two Caucasian cherries, Brennan and Hawkins, joined them, boggeying to the beat.

"Faison, you can move, man," Fleming called to him.

"Back home I was king of the dance floor, a Goddamned dancing Machine. Chicks couldn't get enough of my sweetness. I go home with a shitload of medals. I'll take off where I left off. Only I'm gonna be super fine."

When the song ended, Faison went back to turning himself into a human weapon of destruction.

Brennan and Hawkins started a good natured argument over sports then Brennan drove his shoulder into Hawkins' mid section and the two fell laughing onto an Army cot.

Fleming smiled at their antics. Then he heard the sound of an exploding mortar far in the distance, jolting him back to reality. He knew what they still had to learn; they were in a land where death and suffering touched everyone and anyone at any given moment.

"Dog!" A regular called to Van.

Listening intently to a training lesson on field tracheotomies, Van didn't hear him until his teacher/doctor motioned to the regular standing at the hospital's entrance.

"Follow me, dog," the regular ordered.

"Where?" Van asked irritated, wanting to finish the lesson.

"Where?" The regular repeated, outraged. "You're a dog. A dog follows orders. I gave you an order,"

"Sergeant Chi ordered I be assigned to the Doctor. I follow his orders, not yours."

"Van is under my command until Chi returns," the doctor said.

"Chi is back. He wants the dog in the briefing room now."

The Doctor turned to Van. "Go. If you can, return after the briefing."

Van bowed respectfully to the Doctor.

The Doctor returned the bow.

Then Van left with the regular.

The past week had been educational and fulfilling. The day after the tortures Chi had watched everyone go through basic first aid. Then a doctor spoke with Chi and said that Van showed remarkable aptitude for medical work and would be cross-trained as a medic. "It's women's work," Chi had said with a sneer. "I'm not surprised you're good at it. Don't think this will relieve you from fighting. You'll fight. When the fighting is over you'll help the Doctors."

By now, Van knew the correct protocol. "Whatever you say, sergeant. I will do my all for the revolution."

Chi had eyed him warily before smiling and replying: "I will see to it that you do your all for the revolution."

The following day Chi, Hoi, Dan, and a new Dog went on a training mission while Van stayed behind to work with the Doctor. That entire week at daybreak, Van eagerly rose from his straw mat, excited to begin a new training lesson. The Doctors and Nurses marveled at his proficiency – telling him he had learned at least three months of training in only a week. But the wonderful week had finally ended, Van thought, stepping into the briefing room.

The new Dog sat next to Van.

Van was instantly startled by the Dog's appearance. A week ago the Dog had come under Chi's tutelage. He was thirteen years old and had been conscripted from a village. In one week's time he had lost nearly ten pounds and weighed well under a hundred pounds total. Life seemed to have been drained from his face. His eyes were ringed with black circles. What had Chi done to him? Van wondered.

"Dogs," Chi barked. "We have detected a pattern in American movements. Every night a team leaves their compound and follows the same route. Tonight we will ambush them on their way back to their camp. We will be at a location that will allow us ample time to escape through the jungle and return to our complex in case American helicopters arrive. Rest up before we leave. I know you will perform bravely tonight."

"YES, SERGEANT!" Dan yelled. Then he broke out in the maniacal grin that seemed to have become his normal facial expression.

Chi returned the smile. "I know you will do well." He turned to the others. "The rest of you dogs better perform bravely. If not I have special training in mind for you."

It was a win/win scenario for Chi: a stellar performance would gain him much face with his superiors; a bad performance would satisfy Chi's sadistic delight at giving special training.

"Perform satisfactorily and I will reward you handsomely. Now go and rest."

As they filed out of the briefing chamber, Van thought of Chi's offer of a reward. Other soldiers had told Van that Chi often granted leaves as rewards for successfully completing training. Chi would let soldiers visit their former homes. When Van had asked if any soldier had ever deserted he was told that the NVA had a policy of destroying a deserter soldier's village – effectively discouraging desertion.

A warm comfortable glow enveloped Van at the thought of possibly visiting his home. He would dredge up bad memories of Kim's brutal death, but he would also see his parents and his sister Lan. In order to receive such a reward he figured he would most likely have to kill an American. It was against Buddha's law. To compound matters, he held no hatred for them. They had visited his village in the past. They were relatively happy, for soldiers, and they were generous. An Americans soldier had given him his first piece of chocolate and it was delicious. But they wouldn't be handing out chocolate this time. This time they would be trying their best to kill him.

"Dog, you will have the honor of firing an RPD machine gun," Chi said to Dan at the final briefing.

"Yes, sergeant, thank you," Dan replied, bowing to Chi.

"Dog," Chi said, turning to Van. "You will carry medical supplies. But you will also fight, and fight well. I've watched you. You have potential. You can become a fine fighting man. I expect much from you tonight. Understand?"

"Yes, sergeant. I want to do well for the revolution." And he wanted the reward. He couldn't stop thinking about it ever since Chi had mentioned it.

Chi eyed Van for a long moment before turning to Hoi and the new dog. "You two dogs are also expected to perform well."

"Yes, sergeant," they both said.

They'll never do it, Van said to himself, reading their facial expressions.

"Spend time before the ambush checking each others' equipment. Make sure you are well rested. We leave at dawn."

Van and the others left for their quarters to rest.

At 2000 hours the ambush party stood in the company area listening to their platoon commander Lieutenant Barstell's final instructions. Five klicks outside L.Z.

English, they would set up a night laager (position). They would call in a SITREP (situation report) in order to protect themselves from their own artillery fire. At one-minute intervals L.Z. English's artillery shelled the countryside claiming anyone wandering the area whether it was V.C. Guerilla, American G.I., or civilian peasant.

After Bartstell left the staging area, Levine spoke to the men: "People, ambushes have been sent out the past two weeks and they ain't seen shit. It's another night of getting eaten by mosquitoes and ti-ti (Vietnamese for little) sleep. Even though this ambush is a royal clusterfuck, I still don't want any swingin dick jackin off out there. I'm real fuckin short (short – slang for having little time left to serve on a soldier's tour of duty) and I get sensitive when a cherry fuck up puts my ass in the wind."

Cherry is right, Fleming thought. Jenks, Levine and Doc Garret, the platoon's medic, were the only veterans. Garret had recently transferred to the platoon. He had been working at L.Z. English's 25th Evacuation Station for the past month.

"Let's di-di. Jenks, you got point."

As soon as they departed L.Z. English's friendly confines Fleming's mind began working overtime. He thought of all the potential dangers waiting for them: booby traps, enemy soldiers, and a snake, a bamboo viper, nicknamed the Vietnamese two-step. Certain death claimed a victim, two steps after the viper imbedded its fangs into a victim's anatomy. The most insidious terror was constructed in one's own mind. Night sounds had a murderous ring; every shadow was a potential juggernaut from hell.

Then it started raining.

Shit, Fleming cursed to himself. Tonight nature would also be a foe.

All of a sudden hundreds of bats flew by just as lightning flashed across the sky, adding a surrealistic quality to the potential dangers. It was straight out of a grade B horror movie. They were on an unholy mission to kill other human beings and for special effects they had lightning and bats. For a moment the terror was so great, he barely stifled hysterical laughter – sound could mean instant death.

They reached the ambush site, called in a SITREP, placed four claymores twenty meters from their laager, and then set up an L-shaped ambush formation.

The night passed uneventfully. By morning everyone was miserable, wet, and cold from exposure to unmercifully pounding rain. They radioed L.Z. English to tell them they were returning home. They gathered their claymores and began the five-klick hump back to English.

Levine assigned Hawkins point, with Faison immediately behind him acting as slack man. "Stay the fuck alert," Levine warned. "I don't expect trouble but gooks are firm believers in getting up early and the early bird catches the worm. And, gentlemen, I ain't gotta tell ya, we're the fucking worm."

They started out.

The night rain falling on the scorched earth had created a thick fog. That, along with morning mist, made it impossible to see more than a few feet in front of them.

Another grade B movie special effect, Fleming thought. He had a nagging feeling that he would be seeing a lot of grade B movie special effects this next year.

He walked past tree line after tree line in the lush Vietnamese landscape. Birds sat perched on tree branches singing morning songs welcoming in the new day. It was a pleasant interlude from the cold, wet night. And the fog and mist were beginning to lift and visibility was beginning to improve.

Pretty soon he saw familiar landmarks and knew that he was close to home. In less then ten minutes he would be at English where a greasy bacon and eggs breakfast awaited. Afterward he would enjoy blessed sleep.

Last night wasn't so bad, he summarized. Maybe his first firefight was just a tough game. Like baseball, there were tough games and easy games. A few more easy ones, like last night's ambush and he would do fine the next time he found himself in a tough game. He would come back. The mark of a true champion was coming back after defeat, and he was a true champion.

What would it be like to kill a man?

Whoa, he said to himself. Where did that come from? But, for a combat soldier, it was a reasonable, perhaps necessary question. If the situation arose could he kill a man? In a heartbeat, he instantly decided. He would blank his mind and fire. It was the same as throwing a pitch. Decide what pitch to throw, where to throw it, then commit to it – keep it simple. It would be the same with shooting a man. Sure, fear was a factor, but fear was always a factor, even in baseball. The secret was to continue playing even when one was afraid. In this game, all he had to do was successfully and continuously perform the simple act of pulling the trigger.

Let the games begin, he thought. He was ready. He could do it. When the time came he wouldn't fail.

Positioned in the tree line, Van heard the suction like squish-squash sound of feet stepping upon soaked earth. It was the American patrol walking toward them. Soon they would be visible through the fog and mist.

"Ohhh!" The new dog moaned a low, barely audible sound.

Van jabbed him with his elbow, an attempt to silence him.

The dog looked at him. His face was filled with fear but there was also a touch of innocence; it was the facial expression of a young child pleading for help.

Van was taken aback by the look and didn't how to react. All he could think to do was to turn away and look at Hoi.

Hoi's eyes were squeezed shut.

Van jabbed him with an elbow.

Stunned, Hoi turned to him. His face was covered with sweat and was rigid with fear.

Van frowned at him and gestured with his fist, hoping to motivate him and then he looked to the front.

The first American emerged from the fog.

Hot flashes of fear consumed Van. It was like a ghostly apparition of death suddenly appeared on the landscape.

Another American stepped out of the fog.

Hoi started shaking uncontrollably. He buried his face into the ground.

Van grabbed the back of Hoi's shirt and pulled him upright, all the while praying that no sound had been made that would alert the soldiers stepping from the foggy mist.

Soon more of them were visible: huge helmet wearing men loaded down with weapons. They were only thirty-five meters away.

All of a sudden Fleming felt hot prickly needles jab every inch of his body and fear inexplicably washed over him. An errie quiet and stillness seemed to have consumed the land. Something was different, he realized. What? He wondered.

They are thirty meters from the tree line.

"OPEN FIRE ON THE TREELINE!" Levine suddenly screamed. "THERE AIN'T NO BIRDS IN THE TREES!"

That's what's different, Fleming suddenly realized. Earlier, he had enjoyed the birds welcoming in the morning. Now he heard nothing and a quick visual search revealed no birds perched on tree limbs, either.

"FIRE!" Chi ordered.

The stillness and silence was shattered when Dan opened fire with the RPD machine gun and the approaching Americans fired into the trees.

Ambushed, Fleming thought of the irony of an ambush team being ambushed. Then he marveled at the beauty of the green tracer rounds racing towards them, but it was only a moment before the green beauty turned to horror.

Hawkins was literally propelled backward.

Faison performed a crazy, jerking dance as a half dozen green light bolts entered his right leg and groin.

Weapon on automatic, Van squeezed the AK-47's trigger, letting loose a full clip of twenty rounds. He watched the mesmerizing path of green smack into an American's head; chunks of the head flew everywhere.

Fleming had a clear view of Brennan's head suddenly exploding. Then something smashed against Fleming's forehead with enough force to knock him off his feet. He was knocked backward, his rectum landing on the earth with a squishy plop.

I'm hit, he immediately thought. He was dizzy and disoriented. White spots flashed before his eyes. His hands instantly shot to his face. A white and pink spongy matter came off his face and stuck to his hands. Pieces of it were also falling from his face. Oh, Jesus, what is that? He wondered; it was all over his chest and shoulders too. He wiped a gob of it from his cheek. He experienced a fleeting moment of pure joy realizing that he felt no pain, which had to mean he hadn't been hit. But the joy ended instantly when he realized that all the pink and white gooey stuff was brain matter and tissue from Brennan's head.

The sight of the American's exploding head filled Van with disgust. He had committed the dirtiest act possible, a violation of Buddha's most sacred principle. He had destroyed life and not just any life but the life of one of the universe's highest forms, a human being. His stomach rumbled. He turned to his rear and vomitted.

Then he thought of Hoi and the new Dog. He turned to Hoi – who was crying. Van slapped him in the face,

Stunned, Hoi looked at Van.

"Fire your weapon," he said. "So Chi knows."

Realization washed over Hoi. Chi would check their weapons, learn that he hadn't taken part in the ambush, and brutally reprimand him. Hoi nodded his head, understanding. He raised his weapon and fired, sending green tracer rounds soaring over the American's heads.

"AAEEEEIIII!"

The ear splitting scream came from Van's right. Out of the corner of his eye he saw a flashing movement. He turned to see the new dog rush past him toward the Americans.

Dazed and down and trying to pick brain matter from his face and head, Fleming immediately saw the V.C. running toward him screaming inhumane sounds.

Dear God when will the madness end? He wondered, flicking his M-16 selector switch to automatic. He aimed the weapon at the grotesque screaming face only fifteen meters away. Fleming squeezed the trigger and fired a full clip.

Eighteen rounds hit the V.C.'s face and chest and the screaming enemy was no more.

Fleming watched in horror as the body was hurled backward and the head exploded into pieces. He instantly realized his curiosity about killing a man didn't need to be fulfilled – he didn't need a damn bit of this. A mighty clamp seized his mid section. His mouth filled with filthy tasting bile, and he expelled a long stream of vomit.

Van watched as chunks of the new dog's head flew everywhere. His body was propelled backward and fell with a plop on the rain soaked earth.

Suddenly the sound of maniacal laughter filled Van's ears.

He turned to the sound to see Dan laughing and screaming, his face alive with ecstatic joy as he fired the machine gun at the Americans.

Levine grabbed the radio transmitter and called for support.

Faison's cries of agony could be heard above the cacophony of ear splitting noise. "JESUS! OH JESUS!" He wailed over and over again.

"GRRRR!" The medic, Garret, growled, like a rabid dog, while running fearlessly across the field as rounds chewed up the ground all around him. He reached Faison's twitching, squirming, pain wracked body.

From the west Huey gunships approached the battle.

"FALL BACK!" Chi ordered.

They all raced from the tree line and ran across ten yards of open ground before they disappeared into the dense jungle. They ran another twenty meters when they reached the camouflage covering leading to the underground bunker. They removed the cover and hurried inside the tunnel.

The gunships and meda-vac choppers arrived a mere five minutes after the battle had begun. Choppers opened fire with machine guns and rockets reducing the once ominous tree line into broken rubble. Nearly every tree had been hit. Nearly every limb had been severed or broken in half. It was now a place where morning birds would refrain from singing morning songs for a very long time.

Fleming gave Brennan's lifeless body one last glance and decided not to examine him. He had no desire to see what a man with his face shot off looked like. He wandered over to Faison, a few men had already gathered there. A morphine induced Faison had a dreamy, faraway look with a hint of a smile resting on his face.

"He looks okay, Doc," Evans said.

"He can hear you, shit for brains," Garret whispered through gritted teeth so Faison couldn't hear.

"Doc says I'm gonna' be all right," Faison said to Evans. "It don't hurt no more. I don't feel bad at all."

Doc Garret looked back at the meda-vac choppers. "Where the fuck is my motherfucking stretcher?"

Stretcher-bearers had already jumped from the chopper and had started toward Garret.

With scissors Garret cut away Faison's trousers at the crotch.

What was once a human penis and scrotum sac is now a bloody hole. Most of his right thigh muscle has been ripped away and a foot of his femur bone was visible.

Some of the cherries turned away and vomited.

"Get the fuck out of my AO (area of operation)," Garret said furiously. "I need my patient calm." Garret plunged another Morphine needle into Faison's thigh.

Fear flickered in Faison's face. "I'm all right ain't I, Doc? You said I was all right."

"You're fine, man. You're fine. "

Faison made eye contact with Fleming. "Hey, man, I'm fine right? Just like the Doc said right?"

Garret gave Fleming a warning look of reproach.

"Yeah, man. You're fine."

Faison smiled weakly. "Super fine."

Garret and the meda-vac team placed Faison on a stretcher and took him to the chopper.

Fleming walked a few feet away and toward Hawkins' fallen body. He couldn't help but remember Faison's boasts twelve hours earlier. His dancing days were over. He would lose the leg. His ladies' man days were also over – his penis and testicles were gone forever. He would be returning home without a shit load of medals. He'd go home with one, a purple heart. And he wouldn't resume his super fine ways – he'd spend the rest of his life in and out of VA hospitals and under psychiatric care.

Fleming reached Hawkins. He lay dead on the ground. AK-47 rounds had ripped across his mid section and tore open his stomach leaving his intestines next to him, curled like so many snakes. Flies were already feasting on the wound.

Garret approached with the stretcher-bearers. "Get out of the fuckin way, cherry, unless you're Jesus fuckin Christ and you're gonna do a Lazarus miracle on this poor fucker."

Fleming moved away.

Levine ordered the men to form into positions and they started back toward English.

Fleming concentrated on the terrain with a newfound intensity. He wanted no more of this – didn't want any more combat today or any other day for the rest of his life. His questions about playing the game, killing men and being a champion when it got tough had been answered. And it only took two minutes, he thought – two fuckin minutes. His country had called and he had answered the call at a time when most were not, and now he said fuck it! He didn't want it; didn't want to see one more man with his face shot off or one more man with his balls shot off. He was done with it. Except he had three hundred and forty four days left of it; three hundred and forty four more fucking days, he said to himself.

"What the fuck's that smell?" White called out.

And then Fleming smelled it – the odor of urine and feces. And he realized that sometime during all the hell, he had pissed his pants.

"Did you shit or piss your pants, cherry? Jenks fired back.

White gives him a helpless look of realization. "Yeah."

"Don't mean nothing, cherry. So did most everybody else."

That night Van lay on his mat in the underground bunker complex. Right after the ambush, he had gone to the hospital complex and worked with the doctors all day. They were eager to teach him and he was eager to learn. But, today, he really needed to escape his thoughts.

He couldn't stop thinking about the new dog. He died today and no one knew his name or anything else about him. It was terribly impersonal, Van thought, dying in the company of strangers.

If Hoi would have fired his weapon then perhaps Van could have stopped the dog from his suicidal charge. But Hoi wasn't to blame. Even the American couldn't be blamed – he had done what he had been taught, Van realized.

I'm to blame, he said to himself. The elders had said that strong men had an obligation to help weaker men. If Van hadn't been obsessively and selfishly wondering about Chi's reward, then perhaps he would have had his mind free and then he may have realized that the Dog needed protection.

A dull thumping pain began in the middle of his forehead.

Each day this new life revealed horrible realties. What did the future hold? He wondered.

CHAPTER 4

Operation Kansas City

Pacing the squad tent, Fleming looked at his watch: 1100 hours. He hadn't slept at all since this morning's ambush.

White entered the tent – his face filled with remorse. "I can't believe Brennan's dead."

Not now, Fleming thought. The past three weeks he had seen enough death – had thought enough about death. He needed a break from death.

"Man, I liked Brennan," White continued. "I mean…I only knew him a week. But I liked him…. You could tell he was…decent, a real good guy."

"Yeah, well what are you gonna' do,"Fleming replied abruptly, wishing White would shut up. "People die here. It's a fuckin bitch."

"You cherries, all right?"

They turned to the sound and saw Levine standing at the tent's rear. He made his way to them. "You wanna' talk?"

Fleming wanted to hear nothing from Levine. He was an animal. Offering emotional support was a little outside his area of expertise.

"Cherry, you okay?" Levine asked again.

"Sergeant, it's just that Brennan is dead," White answered. "I can't believe it."

"Words can't take away what happened today. It's done. You'll see a lot more dead men before the year is up. Learn to accept it. Don't go flaky, you got a ways to go."

"I hated killing that gook," Fleming snapped back at him.

"That could have been the gook that did Brennan. If you didn't do him, he'd a done you. If you hate it…" Levine paused. His face took on a sad, melancholy look. "If you hate it, it means you've kept your sanity. Some guys go completely ape shit. They enjoy wastin gooks."

Fleming was completely taken aback by the thoughtful expression on Levine's face and that he was capable of showing empathy.

"Levine," A voice barked.

Everyone turned to see Lieutenant Bartstell standing just inside the tent's entrance.

Levine hurried to Bartstell and they went outside. A moment later Levine returned with another man, a P.F.C. The man had a bright white face that hadn't yet been stained with the thin layer of red dust that permeated every man's skin and everything in Vietnam. His fatigues were bright green, not the faded sun bleached color that marked a man who had spent months in country. In short, he had all the earmarkings of a cherry.

"This is a new cherry." Levine smirked at him. "He's a fuckin' idiot."

The cherry's face literally dropped, hearing Levine's assessment of him.

"Introduce yourselves." Levine said. "I gotta' talk with the L T. We're leavin' on an operation tonight that could last awhile."

"Well there it fuckin' is!" White cursed. "Tonight! Motherfucker!"

Oh God tonight, Fleming thought. What are they gonna' make us do tonight?

"Get some sleep. Where we're goin we'll be lucky if we get more than three hours a night."

"Where the fuck we goin?" White asked.

"An area about ten miles east of the Dak To Mountains."

"You've gotta' be shitting me?"

"I'm too short to be going back there. There it fuckin' is." Levine stormed out of the tent.

"What's with that guy?" Allen asked. "All I said was that I was really looking forward to being in the field with you guys and he jumped all in my shit."

"Yeah, well we lost some men today. He's got a case of the ass." Fleming turned to White. "Do you know where this west of Dak To place is?"

"Fuck yeah," White replied. "In 67 they had a big battle there. It's been fulla gooks ever since. It's a stone's throw from Cambodia and Laos where gooks slip into the South. It's a real fuckin' hell-hole. We'll be fighting NVA regulars, son of a bitch!"

"Hey, man," the new cherry offered. "We can take these fuckers."

Fleming and White looked at each other with wondrous amazement and disbelief, as if the cherry had just said that he had foolproof evidence that the Easter Bunny was real.

The cherry offered a handshake. "Name's Jay Allen, I'm from Pottstown, Pennsylvania."

Fleming and White shook his hand and introduced themselves.

For the next few minutes Allen gave his resume.' He was an All State Wrestler and the quarterback of his High School football team. He was looking forward to being a positive influence on whatever squad was lucky enough to get him. "We're gonna' do all right in this Dak To place," he said. "We're gonna' kick some fuckin' gook ass."

White shook his head with stunned disbelief. "You don't know what you're talking about," he said with a smirk.

Allen looked at them as if evaluating them. Then he smirked, as if his evaluation was not at all favourable. "You two seen much action?" He asked in a voice tone loaded with disrespect.

"Some," Fleming replied. "And some is enough for me."

He gave them a smirking chuckle. "I can't fuckin' wait to see action." He smiled smugly. "Nice meetin' ya.' I think I'll catch some rack time."

"Yeah, why don't you do that," White shot back at him.

Allen gave them one more smirking look of disapproval before moving away.

"Do you believe that guy?" White asked Fleming.

"He's a fuckin' dick. We better get some sack time, like Levine said."

They headed to their cots and flopped down on them.

For the next half hour, Fleming tossed and turned. Just as he was about to fall asleep, Levine entered the squad tent. Fleming sat up on his cot. "Sergeant, did you find out anything about tonight?"

"Yeah, I did. Where is everybody?"

"I don't know. Me, White and that cherrry, Allen, are the only ones here."

"I'm awake," White yelled from across the tent.

Allen leaped out of bed and hurried to them. "Me too."

"I'll brief you tonight before we leave. Be in formation at 1900 hours."

"We gonna see a lotta' gooks, sergeant?" Allen asked eagerly.

A sneer resting comfortably on his face, Levine looked at him for a long moment. "Yeah, cherry, we are."

"Good. I came here to kill gooks. I got my shit together, you'll all see."

"All I see is a fuckin' asshole standing in front of me. And I am too tired to deal with fuckin' assholes. I gotta get some sleep."

'Sergeant, I—"

"Shut the fuck up."

Discretion was the better part of valor because Allen needed only to see the rabid Woody Allen look that spread over Levine's face, and the All State wrestler/quarterrback shut the fuck up.

White and Fleming returned to their cots for some sleep.

The upcoming operation was code named Kansas City. Lieutenant Bartstell had just briefed the men on Operation Kansas City's intent. Shortly afterward Fleming and the rest of Bravo Company boarded deuce and a half trucks. They were driven to the flight line where helicopters awaited to take them to their destination. They boarded the choppers. Fleming sat with his squad members: Jenks, the squad leader, Benson, a man who had three months in country, and Allen, White, Evans, and two new cherries, Marsten and Garcia. Forty-five minutes later they landed at their destination, an area ten miles west of the Dak To Mountains.

Once settled on the ground, Levine called Jenks' squad together. "Dig foxholes. We're spending the night here. Military Intelligence reports there's been no enemy activity in this area, but Military Intelligence is wrong more than it's right so keep your shit together. This platoon is loaded with cherries and this squad is the most inexperienced. Jenks is the platoon's best squad leader but no one else here is worth a shit. So–"

"What about me?" Benson interrupted. "I ain't no cherry."

"No, you got three whole fuckin' months in country. You're a baby eating killing machine. I was talking about everyone else."

Benson turned to Fleming and smiled with smug satisfaction.

"As I was saying – since this squad is new, I'm going to keep close to you. Get some sleep and be ready for a rough day tomorrow. There's gonna' be a lot of humping."

"That's marchin," Benson volunteered. "In case all you cherries ain't got our lingo down yet."

"Thanks, Benson," Levine said with a smirking smile. "You're a treasure."

"Just tryin' to help."

"I don't know what we'd do without you," Levine said with a smile. "Now get some sleep. Tomorrow will be rough."

The next morning, Levine stood before the squad.

"We di di in a few minutes. Our Company will sweep the area until we reach our destination. We got about an eight to ten hour hump ahead of us. This squad will head the sweep. Fleming, you got point. I'm gonna' give you a two man point."

Point! Fleming said to himself, shocked. He'd never walked point and for the first time he was walking point in hell. Fleming remembered Levine saying that he had ways of killing cherries and he wasn't afraid to use these ways. Was this one of the ways? Was it a two for one deal? Two cherries dead for the price of one. "Who's walking point with me?"

"I am. Is that okay?"

It was more than okay. "Yes, sergeant."

We don't expect to see any action until we get to our destination. This way, you'll get some experience. Anybody else have a question?"

"How many gooks are out here?" Evans asked.

A frown settled on Levine's face. He took a moment before answering. "There's a battalion of the 92nd PAVN (People's Army Viet Nam) and a battalion of the 44th PAVN."

"We're a fuckin' company!" White practically shouted. "We're goin' after two battalions? That's fucking dinky dau (Vietnamese for crazy). A company against two battalions?"

"I've been assured we'll have air support in no time. Plus two companies of reinforcements can be flown in within minutes. Alpha company is to the east of us. Two companies of ARVNS are north of us and two companies are south of us. We'll have support in less then five minutes. And we don't expect to see any action for a few days."

"But its one company, against two battalions," White pleaded.

"You ever go fishing?" Jenks asked him.

White looked at him, confused. "Fishing…yeah a couple fuckin' times. What's fucking fishing got to do with this?"

"We're the bait. The worm on the motherfuckin' hook. The brass is hoping when the little people see us, they'll hit us with boocoo force. We'll call in air strikes and get a huge body count."

"But what about us?" White demanded. "It's two fuckin' battalions."

Jenks gave him a mirthless, smirking smile. "When you fish, you don't worry about losing bait. You just put another worm on the hook."

"This is the strategy that the high command has chosen to employ," Marsten, one of the newer cherries, said. "Entice the enemy to attack by dangling a carrot. Then attack with overwhelming firepower when they reach for the carrot. It's consistent with their belief of body count or statistical figures as being the way to win this war. We will kill hundreds of them. They will kill fifty or sixty of us."

"That's half the company," Evans blurted out, outraged

"Or half the squad," Marsten replied. "Half of us will die."

"Damn this fuckin' cherry must have college," Jenks said. "The way he talks and figures out numbers and shit. You ever try college, super Jew?"

Levine answered him with a smirking smile and by shaking his head no.

Fleming was shocked that Jenks referred to Levine as super Jew. Could he be Jewish? He wondered. For some reason the revelation was shocking.

'This is suicide," Garcia said with a thick Latino accent. "A company against two battalions…it's no good."

"Enough!" Levine snapped angrily. "I'm short. I got twenty motherfuckin' days left. You think I wanna' do this? The Green Machine says this is the job so this is what we do. Just keep your shit wired tight at all times and your chances of livin are boocoo better. I don't wanna' hear any more bitchin' or I am gonna' start cutting someone a new asshole. Is everybody reading me Lima Charlie?"

Not a word was said.

"Good. Now let's get ready to move out."

"Sergeant, what do you want me to do?" Allen asked urgently.

Levine studied him for a long moment then gave him a thin-lipped smile. "You'll carry the ammo can. We leave in five minutes. Smoke 'em if you got 'em or do whatever you do. The next five minutes are all yours."

Fleming went to his foxhole and plopped down. Bait! He said to himself. Who in the hell came up with the idea of baiting human beings in order to kill other human beings? Despite Levine's assurances of having maximum firepower in less than five minutes, Fleming couldn't help but wonder what two battalions of NVA could do to a company of soldiers in five minutes? It wouldn't be a pretty picture.

Chi stood in front of Van, his friends, and thirty other men in an underground bunker chamber.

"I have good news for all of you. First, my new dogs did well on their ambush. They killed two Americans. It is a good showing for a first ambush. I promised the dogs

a reward. They earned it and they shall receive it. Dan, Van, and Hoi you are no longer dogs. You are now full-fledged members of my regular force. We will celebrate your good fortune after this briefing. We have food and liquor and you will meet everyone in our group."

The regulars in the room applauded and smiled at the three boys.

So this is the reward? Van thought, Chi assigning them to a platoon and they would no longer be referred to as dogs but be called by their names. There would be no leave, no seeing his sister and his family. Nothing!

"There's more good news. Our platoon has been selected for a mission that will bring glory to everyone in this room. American paratroopers are a short distance east of the Dak To Mountains. We have been selected to work with a battalion of the 92nd PAVN. This is a wonderful opportunity. We will bring honor to ourselves working with this elite NVA unit. I know you will all perform well. Enjoy yourselves tonight. We move out tomorrow evening as soon as it turns dark."

Everyone filed out of the room. Van and his friends received the well wishes of other platoon members.

After being congratulated by every platoon member, Van headed back to his quarters deep in thought. The reward was the privilege of going on a dangerous mission near Dak To. A month ago he had never been more than two miles outside the village. He didn't even know there was a mountain range in Vietnam called Dak To. Since being conscripted into the army the name Dak To was the topic of nearly every conversation. It was an entry point from Laos and Cambodia. Countless battles had been fought there, and now Van was to be part of that history.

Living this new life meant violating every one of Buddha's teachings. His whole life he had walked Buddha's golden path and now he was on a path that was the complete opposite – a life filled with suffering and death. Strangely enough, death was an escape. In death, he just might find peace.

Fleming stood next to Levine in front of the company. The plan was to hump in a due west course into Dak To. The journey should be relatively safe. Once they reached Dak To it would become dangerous.

Fleming had developed a love for the sun playing baseball, His hometown of Baltimore suffered through scorching hot summers. But this was different. It was 0600 and the sun was already blazing in the sky. The day's temperature would surely reach one hundred degrees and higher. He had a ninety pounds of equipment on his back, plus his weapon. Just standing here his shirt was already soaked with sweat.

They started out. After three hundred meters, sweat began pouring down Fleming's forehead into his eyes leaving them burning and stinging. He took a towel, draped around his neck, and wiped the sweat away. It was of little help because a moment later he had to repeat the process.

After another five hundred meters, Fleming clothes, even his fatigue trousers, were soaking, wringing wet, and sticking to his body. His rucksack had dug into his sides and shoulders and the pain was excruciating. He shifted the rucksack and felt relief. But pretty soon it once again settled into the original tender spots.

Fifty meters later, he was sure he wouldn't be able to take another step.

"Hold up!" Someone from the rear called to the front.

"Pull up, cherry," Levine ordered.

Thankful for the respite, Fleming immediately took off his helmet. It was beginning to feel like a manhole cover sitting atop his head. It was instant, blessed relief. Then he looked toward the column's rear.

A half-dozen men stood above a sprawled out Allen.

Levine frowned. "He talked a ton of shit and his ass is the first one on the ground. There it fuckin is."

"This is a bitch, sergeant."

"It's a bitch for everyone. That fucker just gave up. You're all right ain't ya?"

"Oh yeah, I'm fine." Fleming saw no point in telling the truth.

Levine grunted a chuckle. "The ammo can is heavy, weighs about twenty-five pounds. It sways back and forth with each step and it throws you off balance. That strap digs into your shoulder. Hurts like hell."

"Sounds like you have first hand experience."

"I carried that thing every day for a week when I first got in country. It tore my shoulder up. It's a bitch but I never passed out like that cock sucker."

Fleming remembered Allen's cocky boasting about his football and wrestling prowess. He was getting what he deserved – what he wanted. He was fighting the Gooks and this was part of the process.

Finally, with the help of some men, Allen got to his feet.

They started out again.

Twenty minutes later, they stood in front of a wooded area.

"Pull up, cherry. We're taking a ten-minute break. Drink some water. We're going into the jungle. Now, it will get real bad?"

"You think we'll run into gooks, sergeant?"

"No, I'm talking about the jungle. You'll see what I mean when we get in there. Stay hydrated, the heat in there will sap you before you know it."

"You mean it's hotter in there?" Fleming asked with disbelief.

"About twenty degrees hotter, telliing you about it don't do it justice. You have to experience it yourself."

"Just what we need a few more obstacles to make this more challenging."

"There it fucking is." Levine answered with a bitter smile and chuckle.

A moment of silence passed then Levine smiled and pointed to the rear.

Fleming turned to see Allen and Benson. Their body language revealed the fact that they were arguing. Allen kept holding out the ammo can to him, an obvious attempt at persuading him to carry it. Benson kept shaking his head no.

The break ended and Levine and Fleming led everyone into the jungle. The temperature did indeed drop. It had to be a hundred and fifteen degrees. Ten minutes later, Fleming could barely breathe. Each inhalation burned. It was like trying to breathe in a steam room. Soon, it became darker and the jungle let off a rotted, rancid odor. The triple canopy above was so dense, sunlight couldn't penetrate the growth and much of the vegetation had rotted and died. Separate and distinct from the rest of Vietnam, the jungle was dark and foreboding. It was one of the most formidable and frightening entities in a land full of formidable and frightening entities.

Twenty meters later, Fleming was gushing perspiration. He was losing body fluid and becoming light headed. His gait was disjointed – he swayed like a drunk. I'm gonna' pass out, he said to himself.

"Drink some water," Levine called to him.

Fleming grabbed his canteen and uncapped it. He poured lukewarm water down his throat. It was gloriously wet. He brought the canteen from his lips and began pouring water over his face. He poured it on the towel around his neck.

"Hey, hey," Levine called. "Save the shit. You're gonna' need every last drop."

Save it, Fleming thought with astonishment. He had four canteens full. He had more than enough water; nevertheless, he capped the canteen, and placed it back on his web belt.

Fifteen minutes later, dozens of spots appeared before his eyes. Vertigo

threatened to overtake him. He was sure he was seconds away from passing out. He desperately wanted to hang on and not be a weak link in the chain.

"LEVINE!" someone screamed from the rear. "TAKE A BREAK!"

Fleming fought back the overwhelming desire to collapse to the ground.

Levine chuckled. "It's that cherry again. He's one fucking pussy."

Fleming turned to see Allen sprawled on the ground. Men were fanning him with towels. Doc Garret hurried to him and started administering aid.

Fleming and Levine sat down.

Ten minutes later, Allen was on his feet. Word came to move out.

They started out again. In a little less than an hour, Fleming had already finished his second canteen of water.

"This is the bad part," Levine said. "Watch for booby traps."

Booby traps, Fleming said to himself. Now he dreaded placing his foot on the ground.

They continued walking. Fleming willed his mind to go blank: all senses vividly aware, ready to intuit or see any change in the landscape, the smallest detail that might indicate a hidden booby trap. His ears strained to hear sound, the click of metal indicating that someone had stepped on a pressure release mine and the next step would bring death or loss of limb.

He was ready to smell any new odor invading his nostrils: 'The air smells different when gooks are near,' Levine had told him earlier. 'Because a gook smells different. You'll know the minute you smell 'em. You can actually feel gooks, even when they're hidden,' Levine had also said. 'You feel their eyes watching you.' Feel, Fleming thought. The feel of a feces dipped punji stick piercing his boot and foot, sending poisons into his blood stream; the feel of a trip wire tenderly touching his ankle and detonating a maiming or killing booby trap.

Ten minutes later, the jungle appeared to be constricting. He felt claustrophobic as if he were suffocating. He plodded on until he felt something tugging at his feet. Trip wire!!! He thought wildly, squeezing his eyes shut and waiting for the explosion. A myriad of thoughts flashed through his mind. Would it hurt? Would it kill him? Would it take off a leg? Or both legs? But mainly he thought of the unfairness of it all: he was a cherry, his third time out, his third day in the bush, and he was walking point. It wasn't fair at all.

But nothing happened except for falling on his face. It had only been a vine that had ensnared his foot and tripped him. The thrill of being gloriously alive sent ripples of excitement through him.

Levine pulled him to his feet, "I told you it's a bitch."

"Ain't too bad, "he said cheerfully and enthusiastically, overjoyed at being alive with all limbs intact. "Coulda' been a lot fucking worse."

Levine's face was a question mark, studying his strange but enthusiastic reaction.

"Let's go," Fleming smiled. "The quicker we get through this the quicker we get out."

Levine returned the smile. "Then let's go."

They started out. But the going got rougher. Thick vines, resembling a mass of electrical wires, had grown from the ground up. The vines seemed to grab onto Fleming's feet and not let go. For the next fifteen minutes he and Levine were taking turns falling down and helping each other back to their feet. Everyone in the company was also falling and helping each other up.

Ten minutes later they made it through the sea of vines only to run into an area replete with thorns that pricked and jabbed at them. Every man was concentrating on getting through this mess and for a moment every man had forgotten about the greatest enemy: another human being.

They finally made it through the thorns only to run into another roadblock. Thick underbrush grew from the ground up and blocked their path.

Levine stepped in front of Fleming and, without a word, began hacking at the growth with a machete. Fleming uncapped his canteen and began gulping water. A half hour later, Levine handed him the machete.

He stepped forward, swung a vicious blow and barely made a dent into the vines. Mindlessly, he hacked away until he felt stinging pain in his right hand. He switched to his left and noticed his right hand was covered with blisters some had already broken open. His right shoulder ached. He could pitch a complete nine-inning baseball game, yet fifteen minutes of this had left his arm dead.

Fifteen minutes later, his left hand was a mass of bloody, oozing blisters.

Levine stepped forward and without a word relieved him.

Ten minutes later, light filtered through the growth. They were approaching the jungle's end. Five minutes later, they had broken through.

Outside the jungle, ninety-five plus temperature felt cool. Fleming gulped in glorious breaths of air – free of the musty odor of jungle decay.

Seven-foot high elephant grass lay ahead of them. It didn't look too bad, but five meters into it, Fleming changed his assessment. Serrated grass edges slashed his arms, leaving bloodless razor cuts; blood washed away by perspiration. They finally made it through. A hundred meters ahead they saw a grove of palm trees. It looked like an oasis.

From the column's rear word arrived for Levine to halt the march once they reached the trees. Minutes later, an exhausted Fleming collapsed inside the palm tree grove. His shoulders stung from lacerations where the rucksack had cut into him. His arms were a mass of cuts. His hands were blistered and bloody, his shoulders stiff and sore all from swinging the machete. Tomorrow he knew that he would barely be able to lift his arms. His uniform was soaked with perspiration, and he guzzled water. He had already drunk three canteens full and had only one left.

All around him, men were cursing and grumbling.

What kind of men are these? He wondered. How could they endure such suffering?

His thoughts were broken when he saw Allen heading toward them; ammo can slung over his shoulder. The can swayed and lurched with each step; Allen swayed and lurched in time with it. He reached them and dropped the ammo can on the ground. "Hey, man," he said pointing at Levine. "I can't carry this thing another fucking step."

"I ain't your man, dickhead. And that sounds like a personal problem to me. Cherries carry the ammo can. It's tradition. You carry it, unless you get someone else to do it for you."

"Don't you think I already tried that? I asked everybody. Jenks, the faggot, said he'd do it if I gave him a blow job."

"Well there it is. Close the deal."

"I ain't blowin nobody. No fuckin' way."

"Then there's no fuckin' way you're getting out of carrying the ammo can."

"I ain't suckin' nobody's dick. I ain't a fuckin' faggot."

"You are a fuckin' pussy though. Bitchin' about carryin an ammo can. What are you gonna' do when you run into a real problem, like the gooks? You can cry all you damn please they ain't gonna' cut you any slack."

Confusion filled Allen's face. He picked up the ammo can. "This fuckin' thing is a motherfucking bitch." He swung the can onto his shoulder. The can swayed and crashed against his hip. Knocked off balance, he performed a slip sliding, tight roping dance on a soggy patch of grass before he flew in the air and fell to the earth with a plop. He had looked like someone trying ice-skating for the first time. "SON OF A BITCH!"

Levine and Fleming broke up in laughter.

Allen got to his feet furious. Without a word, he stormed away.

'He's a dick, but I kinda' feel sorry for him. That thing is a bitch," Fleming said.

"Fuck him. It's the same for anyone out here. He's gotta' learn to quit bitchin' and carry his weight. Carrying the ammo can is boocoo easier than walking point and cutting through that brush like you did."

Fleming felt himself puff up with pride. He had no worries that he wouldn't be able to finish the day, no matter how hard it got. He'd will his way through any obstacle.

Fifteen minutes later, the blazing sun was the only obstacle as Fleming and Levine led the company forward over easy, navigable, flat terrain; however, after ten minutes Fleming's shoulders stung from the rucksack digging into his flesh. A new batch of sweat covered his body.

Twenty minutes later, Levine halted them in front of a rice paddy. "You ready to walk through this slop?"

"Why not walk on the dikes? Fleming asked. The dikes were like lanes or roads across the rice paddies. It seemed a more logical and much easier route to follow than plodding through the muddy water.

"They might be mined. Sometimes they mine the paddies too."

Mined, Fleming thought, staring at the paddy water and dreading placing one foot into it. He stepped in and sunk into the water and mud. Each step his foot plunged into mud up past his ankles and he had to literally pull his foot out, as if little hands had grabbed his ankles forcing him to fight to free himself. It didn't take too many steps before his thighs burned with fatigue. Thankfully only ten meters of rice paddy remained.

BOOM!

Someone had stepped on a mine. The man somersaulted through the air. With a plopping sound he landed in the rice paddy.

Garcia and Marsten were directly behind the man. Levine ordered them to retrieve the body and then instructed everyone to cross the paddy, retracing his and Fleming's steps.

In a few moments Levine and Fleming made it to the other side. An hour later the rest of the men stepped out of the paddy; it should have taken ten minutes but the careful pace was responsible for the added time.

Lieutenant Bartstell immediately called for a medavac.

"Jesus," Allen said, eyes fixed on the man. "Look at his face."

"He ain't got a face, cherry," Jenks answered.

Shrapnel had ravaged every inch of his face. It was a mass of reds and whites and resembled strawberry yogurt. It was impossible to identify him. His nametag said he was Hart, the cherry Levine had had transferred from his Platoon.

Allen leaned over and vomitted.

"War ain't all that it's cracked up to be is it, dickhead?" Levine asked a vomiting Allen. "There ain't no heroes over here. Only dead men and men who survive."

Fear and concern etched all over his face, Allen looked up at Levine.

"Get used to it. It's only gonna' get boocoo worse. And worse is the best you can hope for because it means you're still alive. Get your shit together, or we'll be tagging and bagging your ass next."

Everyone took the opportunity to rest while they waited for the medavac chopper. Five minutes later it landed and they took out the dead man.

Just then, Levine was called to a meeting with all the company's officers and platoon sergeants. Five minutes later he returned and told everyone they were staying for at least another forty-five minutes while the brass decided exactly where they wanted them to stop and set in for the night. Levine showed Fleming how to use C-4 to heat C rations and they both began preparing a C-ration meal.

BANG!

When a single rifle shot rang out, Fleming and the other cherries grabbed their weapons and looked in the sound's direction.

"WHO THE FUCK DID THAT?" Levine screamed out.

He started across the perimeter and was joined by Jenks.

Fleming was shocked by both men's actions. They were experienced combat veterans who were needlessly exposing themselves to probable sniper fire.

"WHO THE FUCK SHOT THEIR WEAPON?" Levine demanded.

"Allen's been hit, kinda," Benson answered looking down on Allen, writhing on the ground.

"What the fuck you mean kinda?" Levine asked.

"He said he dropped his weapon and it went off. He got hit in the foot."

Meanwhile Fleming and others, including Doc Garret, had gathered around Allen.

Levine studied Allen for a long hard moment. "You cherry motherfuckin' cunt."

"I'm hit, man," he whined. "I need a medic."

Doc Garret started toward him but Levine's outstretched arm restrained him. "He's been hit with an M-16 round, his own, in the foot."

Garret nodded his head knowingly. "You cherry cunt."

"I'm hit. I need help."

"And I need to get back to my chow," Garret said. "Before it gets cold."

Fleming wondered why Levine was so angry and why Garret wouldn't treat him.

"I dropped my weapon. It went off. It ain't my fault."

Levine spit on the ground. "Ain't you lucky you got hit in your cherry foot. Now you gotta' get medavacced. You found a way to get rid of the ammo can, didn't you, you gutless cherry fuck?"

Now Fleming understood. Allen had shot himself. It was just yesterday that he worried about not seeing enough Gooks on this operation. Today he made sure that he wouldn't see a one. A self-inflicted wound was considered the most cowardly act a combat soldier could commit.

"It was an accident," Allen mumbled.

"You're a fuckin' accident, cherry."

"I need a medic. It hurts, man."

"Doc's eating. So are the rest of the medics. Sit tight till the medavac comes. I hope the fuck you bleed to death. I hope your cherry foot falls off."

Five minutes later a medavac landed and Allen was taken away.

Fleming and Levine returned to their seats and resumed eating.

"I know I'm gonna turn out sounding stupid but I gotta' ask. Why did you run out like that? How did you know it wasn't a sniper?"

Levine chuckled. "I could tell by the sound it was an American weapon, an M-16. An AK-47 sounds different."

"You can tell what weapon has been fired just by the sound?" Fleming asked with incredulity.

A faraway, melancholy look slowly blossomed over Levine's face – it was becoming a frequent visitor. It was beginning to appear that Levine was filled with haunting memories.

"You hear enough rifles being fired it's easy to do." A moment passed and then he smiled. "Don't worry one day you'll be able to do it too."

One had to indeed worry about hearing enough fired rounds that it was possible to distinguish the difference between a friendly one and one that was meant to kill you just by sound. It was an ability Fleming was not looking forward to acquiring.

Later in the afternoon, Fleming and Levine stood at a river's bank.

"Fleming, can you swim?"

He didn't call me cherry, Fleming thought – and it sent a spark of pride surging through him: Levine thought enough of him to call him by name. "Yeah, I swim pretty damn good." A huge smile rested on his face.

Levine threw off his rucksack and rummaged inside it until he found a rope. He handed it to Fleming. "Secure this on the other side. We'll use it as a safety line to get everyone across."

Fleming shed his rucksack. The idea of immersing his sweat-drenched body into the cool water was damn appealing. He took off his fatigue shirt and placed it atop his rucksack.

Levine handed him his M-16. "You'll need this. There might be Gooks on the other side."

Suddenly the appeal factor pluumented all the way down to pretty damn unappealing. "There're Gooks over there?" He blurted out.

"Gooks are everywhere." He handed Fleming insect repellent. Then Levine secured a rope end to a tree.

"Why do I need insect repellent?"

Levine shook his head chuckling. "I keep forgetting you're a cherry who ain't been to A.I.T. There are leeches in the river. When you get to the other side check for them. You see any on you spray repellent on them. They'll drop right off."

The thought of leeches took away all of his enthusiasm for the swim. Nevertheless, he inserted his muzzle cover on the M-16's barrel tip, an effective way of preventing water from gushing into the barrel. He slung the rifle over his shoulder, placed the repellent into his trouser pocket, tied the rope around his waist then waded in. After he had walked a few feet, he was forced to swim twenty-five meters to the other side.

He climbed onto the river's bank and scanned the perimeter. No Gooks, he thought, relieved. He tied the end of the rope to a tree stump.

The company's men grabbed the line and started crossing.

An inspection of his body revealed two leeches on his left leg and one each on his right leg and arm. He squirted repellent on them and they fell from his body.

Just then Levine stepped from the water after crossing the river. He checked himself, squirted repellent on a few leeches, then checked Fleming's back and found nothing. Fleming found two leeches on Levine's back.

"OH SWEET JESUS!" Someone screamed.

Everyone turned to the sound. Benson stood with his trousers around his ankles. His face was wracked with fear.

Several men, including Fleming, hurried to Benson. A leech, already huge and engorged with blood, was wrapped around Benson's penis.

"Oh sweet Mary, Mother of God, it's on my dick."

"Damn," Jenks remarked in a voice tone loaded with admiration. "That's the biggest leech I ever saw."

"Get it off, Jenks. Please."

Jenks started to do so when a twinkle lit in his eyes. "Whoa, whoa, wait a minute. You got a hard on. That fucking leach gave you a hard on. I ain't gettin near a hard on."

"Bullshit, I ain't got a hard on."

"How can you tell," someone called out. "His dick's about the size of my little finger."

Everybody started laughing.

Jenks looked closer. "The leach does gives your dick some size. You oughta' consider keeping it. You ain't blessed in the dick department, are you, Benson?"

"Bullshit, my dick's as big as yours"

"How you know? You been checking out my dick?"

A few men shouted reprimands concerning Benson's sexuality. Everyone else was smiling and laughing.

"C'mon, quit fuckin' around, get the leech off."

Levine wandered over. "Why don't you squirt repellent on it, Benson?"

"I ain't got none. I lost it."

"That's a serious fuckin' offense," Jenks said with a sense of urgency. "We need that repellent at Dak To. I bet he missed the insect repellent briefing."

Levine's eyes narrowed laser beaming on Benson. "Did you miss the insect repellent briefing?"

Benson's eyes darted nervously back and forth. "Nobody told me about no insect repellent briefing."

"Nobody told me about no insect repellent briefing," Levine mimicked. "Everybody else knew about it. How come you didn't?"

"I don't know, man. But can we talk about that later? This is an emergency."

"And losing your repellent and missing the briefing ain't an emergency, that what you're saying?"

Benson's eyes darted back and forth with utter confusion. "No...I didn't mean..."

"I'd like to help ya,' Benson but I'm afraid my ass would get an Article 15 (an infraction of Army rules usually resulting in a fine and disciplinary action)," Jenks offered with an innocent, almost angelic, look on his face.

"You're Goddamned right I'd Article 15 your ass," Levine said with mock anger. "I should Article 15 your ass, Benson."

Fleming was smiling and laughing along with everyone else.

"Well what am I supposed to do about the leech?"

"Enjoy it," Jenks offered. "It's the closest you're ever gonna get to a blow job."

Fleming broke out into wild, raucous laughter along with most of the gathered men.

"Real fuckin' funny, Jenks. Real fuckin' funny."

"I'll tell you what's real fuckin funny. Leeches don't get that big from just blood. I bet you came in that leech's mouth, didn't you?"

An embarrassed, shocked expression momentarily engulfed Benson's face. He turned to Levine. "Sergeant, Jenks is fucking around will you get the leech off."

"Jenks is in charge of getting leeches off dicks. If you woulda been to the insect repellent briefing you'd know that."

A moment of silence passed as Benson's eyes narrowed, trying to digest this new bit of information. "Well then make him do his job."

Everyone was wildly laughing and shouting comments.

"Benson, you are one dumb motherfucker," Evans said.

"Hey, hey, you can't call me that," Benson replied with righteous indignation. "I been here longer than you." He said, momentarily forgetting about the leech.

"He's right, cherry. Shut the fuck up." Jenks admonished.

Jenks cupped his chin with his hand. Levine stood next to him – they looked like two surgeons conferring on an operation.

"You know," Jenks said. "That leech is big enough. I bet I could shoot him off."

"Jenks, you can't do that. It's my fucking dick."

"Anybody got a hacksaw?" Jenks yelled out. "Or an axe?"

"An axe!" Benson cried out incredulously.

Everyone was doubled up in laughter.

"Levine," Lieutenant Bartstell shouted. "What the hell's going on over there?"

"Nothing, sir."

"Quit the fucking grab assing."

Levine turned to Jenks. "Squirt some repellent on it."

Jenks did so and the leech fell from Benson's penis.

"You're a real asshole, you know that, Jenks?"

"If you were at the insect repellent briefing you'd fucking know that L T promoted me to platoon asshole."

Righteous indignation filled Benson's face. "What else did I miss at that fuckin' briefing?"

"Don't even tell me you missed the order that you gotta pay the leech on dick remover for doing his job."

Benson's jaw dropped open in astonishment. "I gotta pay you?"

"That's right, but not money."

Benson smiled mirthlessly. "I ain't blowin you, like you told Allen to do."

"You gotta dig my foxhole when we set in for the night."

Horror filled Benson's face. "Fuck me!" he cried out angrily.

"Would you rather blow me?"

"No fuckin' way. And the next time somebody better tell me when there's an insect repellent briefin or I'm gonna kick somebody's ass."

The rest of the trek proved uneventful and they reached their objective – five klicks from the Dak To Mountains. Tired and exhausted, they were given only a half hour rest before digging foxholes where they would spend the night. It would be dark in a few hours and the night belonged to the enemy.

Fleming and Levine reclined against their rucksacks.

"How does it feel to be one of the unwilling, doing the impossible, for the ungrateful, ordered by the ignorant, led by the incompetent?" Levine asked.

Not one man wanted to make this impossible march and operation for the ungrateful Vietnamese but was ordered to do so by the ignorant U.S. Government and led by the incompetent army. "I feel unloved," Fleming answered with a grunting chuckle.

"There it is."

"Why does everyone say that?'

Levine raised his eyebrows in surprise. "I keep forgetting how new you are. It's hard to explain. It's like a statement that defines the truth and the truth always comes back to one thing, we're getting fucked. When I first heard about this operation I said: Well there it is. After a while grunts say it for just about everything. Of course, just about everything that happens to a grunt is some kinda screw job."

"There is another thing everybody–"

"How ya gonna act?"

"Yeah, what's that mean?"

Levine thought for a moment. "When Brennan got greased, I heard you got hit by pieces of his brain and pieces of his skull. Then you blew a gook's head off. You saw Faison with his balls blown off. You saw his leg."

Being reminded of it all made Fleming wish he hadn't asked the question.

"You saw Hawkins. You saw that cherry die in front of you that first day. After seeing all that – how ya gonna act?"

Fleming got it instantly. These experiences changed a person forever.

"I've seen that shit too many times. I'm goin home in two weeks. I've killed boocoo Gooks. Suppose somebody pisses me off back in the world. How am I gonna act?"

How ya' gonna' act? Three hundred sixty five days of killing, seeing people die and living like animals all for a war that many believed was immoral. How ya' gonna' act in a society that has seen none of this?

The half hour break ended and the tired, bone weary men started digging five-foot deep, four-foot wide foxholes for protection against mortar or rocket attack. When they finished everyone collapsed in their holes fatigued.

Five minutes later, Levine was summoned to Bartstell's hole.

Ten minutes later he returned to the hole and angrily threw his helmet to the ground. "Well there it fuckin is! We're goin on an ambush tonight."

Shock and disbelief filled Fleming. After the day they put in how were they supposed to pull an all night ambush? All he could think to say was: "Man, I'm so tired I can't even fuckin move."

"We gotta cross a rice paddy a klick west of here. The Colonel thinks the gooks will try and booby-trap it tonight because they know we'll eventually be crossing it. Ten to one it's already booby-trapped." Levine checked his watch. "It's 1600. Get some sleep. We leave at 1900. I'll let everyone else know."

Anger and frustration filled Fleming. They were crossing a possibly booby- trapped rice paddy to set up an ambush deep in the Dak To Mountain area. After all today's back breaking humping how were they supposed to even stay awake? He never imagined that combat could be so difficult. To stay alive a man had to stay sharp. To stay sharp you needed sleep and sleep seemed to be something that was a luxury. How was he supposed to get through this year? This was the army not the civilian world – you just couldn't call in sick. Then an exhausted Flemning fell asleep.

CHAPTER 5

The Justification of Killing

A RICE PADDY DEEP IN THE DAK TO MOUNTAIN AREA

The ambush party consisted of Levine, Jenks, Fleming, Garcia, Benson, White, Evans, and Marsten who was carrying the radio. They stood at the paddy's edge, ready to cross and set up on the other side.

"Once we get in that paddy no one talks," Levine said.

Evans slapped a mosquito on his arm.

Levine glared at him until Evans looked away. "Hopefully all we get tonight is a couple hundred mosquito bites. There are boocoo gooks out here. Make noise and we're zapped. No talking, slapping mosquitoes, nothing, once we leave this spot. If we have to talk I'll do it. If I ask a question you answer in a whisper. Everyone got that?"

"Is there any way to get out of this ambush?" Garcia asked.

Levine smiled mirthlessly. "Step on a mine. The LT says we can abort the mission."

Naturally, everyone's facial expression clearly indicated that that wasn't an option.

Levine made sure everyone had a claymore, grenades, flares, smoke grenades, ten ammo clips and insect repellent. "Keep ten meter intervals. Once we're across we set up claymores and daisy chain them (stringing them together so one clacker detonator set off the string). Remember any noise and we're dead. Got that?"

In their own way everyone acknowledged that they got that.

"Let's go."

They took their intervals and stepped into the paddy's plopping mud. They were in a single, horizontal column with Levine in the middle, Fleming to the right, then Garcia and Benson. To the left were Marsten, White and Evans.

Mosquitoes immediately swarmed on Fleming; biting through his clothing and biting any exposed skin; a few got inside his helmet and bit the top of his head. He was being bitten at least once every couple seconds. He doused himself with repellent but couldn't adequately cover himself unless he stopped walking. The ordeal had to be endured until the other side was reached.

It was a moonless night and he couldn't see more than a few feet ahead of him. The darkness had a bluish tint and a biting edge to it.

The night sounds were ten thousand times different than the night sounds of Baltimore. In the rice paddy the quiet was deafening and sound was magnified: footfalls plopping in the mud, mosquitoes buzzing near his ears.

His mind was working furiously. Any second he expected to see neon green tracers laser-beaming across the paddy. Any second he expected to hear the crack of an AK-47.

And his mind also considered the ridiculous. His heart thump thumped a driving beat in his chest that he thought of Poe's Tell Tale Heart. Could the gooks hear his pounding heart?

Get a fuckin grip, he ordered himself. He was letting his mind go flaky on him. But fear pounded him like a hammer. Damn, if he didn't sense the enemy was near. Levine had told him that the gooks knew where they were at all times; the gooks could always see them and always hear them. As a schoolboy attending Catholic schools the nuns had taught that God sees all, knows all, and hears all. If God could do it and the gooks could do it than didn't that make the gooks God? Or at least God-like, he reasoned.

Suddenly the rice paddy's other side loomed a couple of meters ahead, a wonderful sight emerging from the blue-black night.

Everyone scrambled to the bank. Levine hand signaled them to hit the ground. After ten minutes listening and enduring mosquito bites, they moved forward. They crawled ten meters more before again stopping. They waited five minutes and heard nothing. Levine motioned for them to take out claymores by showing them his own. After moving ten meters, they stopped and listened. Then Levine had each man set up claymores, and he daisy chained them. He placed the men five meters apart and had Marsten click the radio handset, signaling the CP that they had reached the other side safely. Then everyone began frantically dousing his body with repellent.

The night passed by uneventfully until 0100 hours when a distinct whooshing sound was heard, as if something was flying high above everyone's head. Everyone recognized the sound as outgoing mortars. Everyone looked to Levine. He held his fingers to his lips, warning them to keep silent. Then they heard the sound of exploding mortars coming from the NDP (Night Defensive Position). To keep sound at a minimum, Levine grabbed Marsten and they hurried to the paddy's bank where they made radio contact with the company at the NDP. Five minutes later, they returned.

"NDP is being hit," Levine whispered. "Me and Fleming are gonna knock out that mortar."

The hot, metallic taste of fear filled Fleming's mouth.

"Once we knock it out we have permission to abort. When we take it out, we'll throw smoke and di-di like hell back here. Don't fuckin fire at us."

The men nodded their heads in assent.

"Let's go, Fleming."

Armed with hand grenades and smoke grenades, ammo bandoleer and M-16, Fleming left with Levine. It's now two men against two battalions! He thought wildly, crawling through the elephant grass.

Twenty meters later they halted. They couldn't see the enemy but the sound of outgoing mortars had grown louder.

Then it hit Fleming. He could smell them. He thought Levine had been facetious about being able to smell gooks.

Levine motioned Fleming to stay put then he crawled three meters and suddenly stopped. He motioned Fleming forward. He pulled abreast of Levine.

Eight meters ahead, four NVA soldiers were working a mortar.

Levine set his M-16 selector switch on automatic and pulled the pin on a grenade. He motioned for Fleming to do the same.

Fleming did so all the while thinking: this is happening too Goddamned fast! We should wait awhile or something! Think this through!

On Levine's signal, they lobbed grenades toward the NVA position. Then they sprayed the area with a full clip of ammo.

They reloaded immediately and grabbed a second grenade. It wasn't necessary.

Arms, legs, and other pieces of human anatomy were strewn all over the elephant grass. Just a meter away, twelve inches of human arm and hand lay.

Jesus! Jesus! Jesus! Fleming said to himself.

Suddenly Levine's ears perked up like a dog on scent. He grabbed Fleming's arm with a vise like grip.

Fleming immediately heard the audible crack of a tree limb or branch being broken. They're coming, he thought wildly.

Levine threw a smoke grenade among the debris of human parts and enemy dead. "C'mon, let's di di," he whisper shouted.

Rubber legged with fear nevertheless Fleming leaped to his feet and ran with Levine.

Then they heard the chicken squawking sound of Vietnamese voices. They heard the crack of bamboo and branches and knew that the enemy was running toward the smoke.

Fearful that his own men might open fire at the sound of the Vietnamese, Levine yelled: "HOLD YOUR FIRE! HOLD YOUR FIRE!" They reached the others. "Get your shit and don't leave nothin. Di-di outta here fast. Fleming, stay with me."

The men sprinted for the paddy and the CP on the other side."

Levine grabbed the claymore detonator. "I'm blowin the claymores. When we hit that paddy throw a smoke grenade." Levine activated the detonator.

The whining explosion was followed by the sound of screaming men in pain as the NVA were caught in the path of the exploding ball bearings.

Jesus, they were close, Fleming said to himself, just as he and Levine began a mad, thirty-meter sprint for their lives.

They reached the paddy. Both Fleming and Levine threw smoke grenades. They stepped in the paddy's mud and began plowing forward.

The mud tugged at Fleming's boots. He was moving maddeningly slow. Ahead of him other figures were madly dashing for their lives.

Then a man fell face first into the paddy.

Fleming had heard no rifle fire and wondered why the man had fallen? He reached the man and stopped. Seconds later, Levine reached them.

Lying in the rice paddy, White attempted to stand but fell again. "Shit! I think I broke my leg!"

Fleming and Levine each grabbed one of White's arms and the three men hobbled the last ten meters of paddy where they fell in an exhausted tangle of arms and legs. The other men lay exhausted in the grass.

Levine grabbed the radio. Fearful of making sound, he moved twenty meters from the paddy and called the NDP. A few minutes later he returned to the men.

Everyone looked at him with expectant, pleading expression – hoping desperately that they would be allowed to return to the NDP.

"They want us to wait."

Hope vacated every man's eyes.

"Motherfucker for what?" Evans asked angrily. "For the fuckin gooks to waste us?"

"I don't fuckin know," Levine answered irritated. "Marsten, Garcia, take White back."

They agreed eagerly, happy to be leaving.

A few minutes later, the NDP called. Again Levine moved away from the paddy. A few moments later, he returned, the rabid Woody Allen expression alive in his face. "We gotta stay the fuck out here."

The other four men groaned.

"Colonel fuckin Bradford said we done good and we're too hot to stop. He wants us to set up an ambush in case the Gooks try to cross the rice paddy tonight."

"Well at least we ain't gotta cross that paddy again," Benson volunteered.

"It don't mean nothin," Levine countered. "If them little people send sappers across (a suicide squad armed with satchel charge explosives) we won't even see them till they're breathin down our fuckin necks. The point is we're sittin here with our asses in the wind."

Fleming blew out a disgusted stream of air.

"Oh," Levine said as an afterthought. "The fuckin Colonel was happy as a pig in shit cause of our body count. He said get some more."

Everyone cursed at the news then Evans asked: "It's just us four?"

"They're gonna send Marsten and Garcia back. I bet they'll be jumpin for joy when they hear that. Fuck, I'm too short for this shit. Fuck me."

Twenty minutes later, a cursing Garcia returned with Marsten. Levine assigned everyone watch – Fleming had the last two hours. He curled under a tree to sleep and it started to rain.

Tonight he would get two and a half hours sleep and tomorrow would be as exhausting as today. Fifteen minutes later, he was chilled to the bone. The night was warm, about eighty degrees, but after the jungle's stifling heat the temperature drop was approximately forty degrees. And the damn rain only made it colder, he thought.

He wrapped up tightly in his poncho liner and fell asleep.

Sometime later, he heard a sloshing sound and looked at the rice paddy. What he saw made his mouth go dry. His heart pounded in his chest.

Three enemy soldiers approached the men's position. One was headless, dressed in pajamas and carrying an AK-47. Another was missing his right arm and shoulder and the right side of his chest. He was wearing a NVA uniform and he carried an AK-47. The third was missing his right arm and leg. He hopped crazily on his left leg. He was NVA and had an AK-47. Blood flowed from a gaping chest and stomach wound. They continued walking toward Fleming.

Fleming couldn't take his eyes off the man's chest. It appeared as if something was moving inside it. As the man stepped closer, bile churned inside Fleming's stomach.

A huge rat was inside the soldier's chest wound, eating away at the stomach's interior.

Fleming had heard stories of rats nesting in dead soldier's stomach wounds, but nothing prepared him for the shock of actually seeing it.

He turned to the others and tried to alert them but they were laughing and telling jokes. He tried yelling at them but no words came from his mouth. He started jumping in the air and waving his arms but he was ignored.

The unholy trio was only five meters away.

One grinned insanely. The other two opened their mouths and both of them croaked: "We're going to get you for this, Fleming."

Fleming reached for his M-16 but couldn't find it. It was here a second ago, he thought desperately. He turned back to the three NVA.

They were standing above him. The rancid rotten smell of dead, decaying men was overwhelming. The rat hissed, baring its teeth. Pieces of skin, intestines, and human insides hung from his lips and whiskers and were stuck between its teeth.

Fleming screamed.

Levine was on him in a flash, placing his hand on Fleming's mouth, stifling the cries. "Wake up. You're okay. Wake the fuck up."

He looked at the rice paddy.

Nothing was there.

He turned to Levine. "I had a nightmare."

"No fuckin shit. You okay?"

"Yeah, but I ain't goin back to sleep."

A moment of silence passed.

"You okay?" Levine asked again.

"We killed four Gooks tonight," Fleming said. "I figure two were mine. I did that Gook in the ambush. It was gross. His head flew off his body. Jesus!" His face twisted with pain at the memory of it.

"What can I tell you? You just gotta get used to it."

"That's what I'm afraid of – getting used to it. It's an easy thing to do – killing, especially where they're trying to kill you. I've killed three men and I've only been here two weeks. The way I'm going I'll kill seventy two people in a year."

"Don't think too much or your shit's gonna get flaky as hell."

"And if I don't stop doing this, my shit's gonna get flaky as hell."

"Ask to be sent to the rear. I can tell you from experience they'll never let you outta the bush. And, to be honest, we need you. You're a good man."

"Why because I kill men?"

"No, because that first day in the bush you were scared shitless in that ambush, but you tried to save that cherry who died. What was his name?"

"Peyton. Watching him die tore me up."

"Yet you forgot all about that and you tried to help him. I found the two bandages. Not many cherries can get their shit together enough to try and save a dying man."

"So I'm a good man because I tried to save a man's life and failed?"

"That's right."

"I don't know…"

"We're here and killing is going on all the time. If you don't want to do it anymore then the next time we're in a firefight stand up. Let a gook do you. Then your killing days are over."

Fleming grimaced wryly. "C'mon, that's no answer."

Levine removed his glasses and wiped rain from each lens. "Xin Loi, (Vietnamese for sorry about that – pronounced zin loi) man, but that is the answer out here. If you don't do them, they do you – just like that." Levine snapped his fingers for effect. "If we didn't waste those gooks tonight then they'd still be firing those mortars and someone in our company might have been wasted. It's them or us. You have to approach this with the right attitude. Out here you just can't wish for it to go away. The way I see it I'm not killing. I'm saving lives – my life and the lives of my friends."

Fleming thought about it for a moment. It made sense. No one had any idea why they were here but they were and they were here for a full year. One couldn't just pick up and leave. For a moment he thought about all the lies that placed him here. Was Levine's speech any different? He thought about it and realized that he was already neck deep in the ordeal known as Vietnam. Levine advised him on how to get through an already bad situation. It was up to Fleming whether or not to act on the advice. And there was the ring of truth in Levine's words: wrong or not, prejudiced or not, he would rather see the enemy die than his friends. Fleming was beginning to see Levine in a whole new light. He wasn't an animal. He was a man who had learned just how ugly and brutal life could be. Levine had been thrown an awesome challenge and he had met it keeping his morality intact. There was a lot of humanity and goodness in Levine, Fleming summarized.

For the rest of the night the two men talked about their homes, baseball, girls they had known and normal things two young men would discuss. The moral decency or indecency of killing men who were trying to kill you was not brought up again. For a moment the mosquitoes were forgotten, the rain was forgotten and the enemy was forgotten. But tomorrow was another day.

CHAPTER 6

Pawns

The next morning the men returned to the company NDP. Fleming spoke with White – his foot was swollen, discolored, impossible to walk on, and broken. He would wear a cast for two months and would be in the rear for at least that long.

They said goodbye. White hobbled to the chopper and his trip to the rear.

After traveling all night Chi's men arrived at an underground bunker complex. They were still one night's march from their final destination. Van was just entering the complex to sleep the day away when Hoi asked to speak with him. They walked a few meters into the jungle for privacy.

"I've known you my entire life," Hoi said. "You hate this as much as I do. We have to get away."

"How? We are trapped."

"We can run. We can leave today." Hoi's insisted in a voice tone that was loaded with desperation. "Everyone will be asleep in two to three hours. We can just run away."

"If we leave here, the NVA will immediately go to our village."

"We won't go back to the village. We'll go somewhere else – Saigon. It's a crowded city. They will never find us there."

Van shook his head no. "It's not about us getting away. If we desert they will destroy our village and kill everyone. It's how the NVA prevents men from deserting."

Hoi grabbed Van's arm. "They wouldn't do that if just two soldiers left. It's worth taking the chance if we can leave this life behind."

Van pulled his arm free. "They're brutal. Look what they did to make us join their army. And I know they will strike the village. Other soldiers told me that is what they do."

Hoi's eyes darted inside their sockets in desperation. "No one ever told me that."

"You never speak to any of the other soldiers?"

"No one here will talk to me," Hoi said angrily.

"Then you wouldn't know would you?"

Anguish and desperation washed over Hoi's face. "I can't stay here. I will never be able to do this. There's so much pain and suffering…All we ever do is hurt people." Hoi's face was awash with fear and confusion. "We have to find a way to leave. You don't want to live this…this waste of a life, do you?"

"I know how this affects you – how hard this is for you. But I also know you're a good person. You don't want to put the village at risk. We must do what we have to do in order to survive. I don't see that we have any other choice."

"But I'll die here. Chi wants me dead. I know it."

"Not if you do what he says."

"I can't." Hoi's eyes filled with tears that soon come streaming down his face. "I can't."

Van grabbed both Hoi's shoulders. "You will be fine. In time you will be fine."

Hoi broke the hold. "Promise me, you will think about leaving with me. I will find a way to leave so the village won't be harmed."

Hoi would never be able to safeguard the village. But he needed to feel a shred of hope. "If you find a way, I will consider it."

Hoi smiled at him; it was the first time Van had seen him smile in weeks.

"I will find a way, Thank you, Van. You have always been a good friend."

Van touched his arm. "Go inside. Get some sleep."

'Thank you again," Hoi said and left.

Van leaned against a tree. He was disturbed that Hoi had no regard for the village. All that mattered to him was leaving his own troubles behind. It seemed a selfish, self-serving act. But then again Hoi was the last person anyone would expect to embrace a soldier's life.

Van started for the bunker. He was too tired to think this through. He needed sleep.

0900: Fleming stepped into the rice paddy, ready to finish the final leg of their sweep to the Dak To Mountain Range. Fleming was again on point with Levine. Today he was more confident. He had learned much the day before on what was expected of him in the field. Levine's insight was invaluable.

He looked down at the paddy's water. Every step forward brought him closer to a future filled with danger and mind numbing fear. But thinking about it wouldn't help.

After trudging through the slop for twenty meters, the burning sensation attacked his legs. If he kept this up his thighs would grow like tree trunks. He would be able to throw baseballs through walls.

Just then a whistling, whooshing sound was heard.

"INCOMING!" A dozen voices yelled.

Fleming and everyone else dove face first into the paddy.

BOOM!

The mortar's sound was just as loud as he remembered – as if the earth was cracking in two. Terror ran through him just as it had before.

BOOM! BOOM! BOOM!

Three more mortars had fallen in rapid succession.

Each explosion made his body jerk with involuntary spasms.

'WHERE IS IT?" Someone nearby screamed. "OH MY GOD WHERE IS IT?"

Fleming turned to the sound and saw a soldier on his knees. His left arm was missing; blood was shooting from the stump. With his good arm, he was frantically splashing through the paddy water.

"OH, JESUS MY ARM! I CAN'T FIND IT!" He sounded like a crying child who had lost his favorite toy.

"GRRRR!" Doc Garret growled like a dog, running across the paddy, feet plop-plopping in the mud.

"MY ARM! I CAN'T FIND MY ARM! IT'S GOTTA BE HERE SOME FUCKIN PLACE!"

All of a sudden the yelling abated to a sensuous moan, a telltale sign that Garret had reached him and injected morphine into the man.

BOOM! BOOM! BOOM!

Three more mortars fell in rapid succession.

Three Cobra gunships raced menacingly across the paddy and fired rockets. The Gunships M-60 Machine guns opened fire.

"FLEMING!" Levine screamed. "STAY LOW AND GET ACROSS THE PADDY!"

His words were as profound as God's. Fleming would be safe if he listened to Levine. He got to his feet and sloshed through the remaining ten meters of paddy then dropped to a prone position on the paddy bank just as Levine dropped down next to him. Seconds later, Jenks, Marsten and Garcia dropped down beside them.

"Watch for a ground attack," Levine said.

They were there to provide cover fire for the rest of the company. Fleming realized that if they were caught in the paddy, paralyzed with fear because of falling mortars, it would be inviting certain death. But the ground attack never came and the mortars were silenced by the Cobras formidable firepower.

The rest of the company made it across the paddy. Lieutenant Bartstell ordered the squad leaders to set up a defensive perimeter while other men carved out an L.Z.

A medavac landed and took out the man who had lost his arm, along with two other men who had been killed during the barrage.

Levine met with Bartstell while most of the men rested against their rucksacks. Every man was exhausted, their eyes ringed with black circles of fatigue. Most of them instantly fell asleep.

"I'll be dipped in shit!" Evans shouted out. "We bust our asses all day long! We hump through jungles! Rice paddies! Rivers! Ball busting shit, and the only time we get a break is when one of us get fucked up or wasted. Please tell me it's my imagination. Tell me that something is not seriously wrong here."

"Damn, Evans," Benson countered angrily. "We're fightin for freedom against the Commies! It ain't supposed to be easy!"

'What the fuck's that mean – fighting for freedom?" Evans asked. "Whose fucking freedom?"

"For...freedom," Benson stammered. "So people can, you know, be free, so the gooks can be free."

"The South Vietnamese never asked us to fight for their freedom," Marsten said.

"We forced the fight and the freedom on them. Maybe they don't want to be free. Maybe they'd rather be alive than free because we've killed quite a few of them while attempting to free them."

Benson gave Marsten a curious look, not knowing what to say.

Marsten chuckled bitterly. "And Evans is over here trying to free them? Cut me a break! Evans can't even get a hamburger in half the restaurants back home. Yet a Black Man, who has little freedom, is fighting twelve thousand miles from home so yellow Asians can be free? I mean something is seriously wrong with that picture."

"I hear that," Evans said.

For a long moment, Benson stared at Marsten, trying to figure out what to say. "Well what about...If we don't stop them here then we're gonna have to fight them at home. What about that?"

"They can say that about anybody. Tomorrow, they can say the..." Marsten paused searching his mind for an enemy. "Australians are our enemy and we must war with them. Of course, in order to get the people back home on board with their war with the Aussies they might have to make up some lame event like they did with the Gulf of Tonkin Incident just to show how vicious the Aussies are. Then they tell us we have to invade Australia before they invade us. It's how rulers have been doing it since the beginning of time."

Benson's face wrinkled with confusion. "What's the Gulf of Tonkin Incident?"

Marsten groaned. And so did everyone else, except for Levine and Jenks. Fleming had heard of the Incident but didn't know much about it and believed most of the groaning men were just as ignorant.

Marsten explained: "The NVA supposedly attacked two destroyers in the Gulf of Tonkin. However it was proven that one of our destroyers fired first on Vietnamese torpedo boats operating in Vietnamese waters. That sounds to me like we were the ones who attacked and we attacked them in their own country. The point is it was all a big lie. They made up an event then they used their tired old line: we have to fight them over there so we don't have to fight them at home. But, be that as it may, let's look at the facts. In order for the North Vietnamese Communists to invade us...to come over here," Marsten said sarcastically. "They have to cross the ocean. How would they do that? They don't have a Navy or an Air Force – no ships or planes."

"What about them torpedo boats you just talked about?" Benson said smugly.

"It's a boat not a ship. Boats don't make it across oceans." Marsten chuckled as if he had just thought of a good joke. "They also have those wooden sampan boats. Do you think they can make it across the Pacific Ocean, Benson?"

"Well, uh no, I don't think them Gook boats can cross the ocean."

"And if they, by some miracle do, do you really think our Navy is worried about boats?"

Benson is at a loss for words.

"I'll even help you out with this," Marsten volunteered. "Let's give the government a pass. I really don't think they're worried about Vietnam attacking America."

"Not worried," Jenks shrieked. "Then why the fuck we over here?'

Marsten growned at Jenks and ignored his question. He jumped back in to his explanation. "Let's just say, for argument's sake, the Government knows Vietnam will never attack us. It would never happen. What the government is worried about is the spread of Communism. That would make Russia and China move powerful."

"Well…uh, yeah that's right. What about the Russians?" He asked unsure. "Or what about them Chinese?" He emphasized with greater conviction. "What about them?"

"For one the Chinese and the Vietnamese don't get along. They have hated each other ever since the time of the Trung Sisters. That was two thousand of years ago."

"Who are the Trung Sisters?" Benson asked.

"They were warrior women who fought the Chinese two thousands years ago. Vietnam and China haven't seen eye to eye on anything ever since. And the Russians. I donb't believe that they would attack America. If they destroy us with nuclear weapons they know that a second later they would be destroyed and they are not too keen about that happening. After World War II three quarters of their country was destroyed and they are still busy rebuilding it. They're not real thrilled about going through that kind of destruction again. And as far as a ground war is concerned, they don't want that either. They lost like thirty million men in World War II. Thirty million! In short they're not real eager to get into another war. So we're left with one question. Would it matter to the Chinese or the Russians if little Vietnam didn't turn Communist? Would that stop the worldwide spread of Communism? If we win do you think the Chinese or Russians would lose a strategic stepping stone into the United States?"

"Vietnam is too far ain't it?" Benson answered.

"There it is," Marsten replied. "And America is supposed to stand for freedom. That means people are free to choose what kind of government they want in their own country. If the Vietnamese want Communism then freedom means they are free to choose Communism without us attacking them for it."

Benson looked at each man for support. He turned to Jenks. "C'mon, Jenks, help me out. What do you think?"

Without opening his eyes a catnapping Jenks said: "I think that leach sucked out some of your brain, Benson,"

"Jenks, the leach was on my dick."

"Well there it is."

Marsten's simplistic perceptions intrigued Fleming. Fighting a war in Vietnam would do little to affect the fall or rise of Communism around the world. The domino theory was just that a theory. What might or what could possibly happen. And it was a cornerstone principle of freedom, the very definition of the word freedom, that people were free to choose their own type of government.

Levine returned to the group and said: "I got news."

"Oh, Man," Fleming said. "Please don't say there it is."

Levine smiled. "Okay, I won't say there it is."

"Son of a motherfuckin bitch!" Evans cursed.

"Colonel Bradford ordered three platoons back to the other side of the paddy. One platoon is setting up a CP right the fuck here."

Each man cursed or shook their heads in frustration.

A long moment passed.

"Uh, Sarge. You didn't say who's stayin," Benson said softly.

Everyone groaned.

"Well he didn't say. Don't you guys wanta know?"

"We are, Benson," Levine said.

Benson gave a weak smile of victory. "Well…now we all know." A moment passed as he digested this. "Why do we gotta stay? That fucking sucks."

"Why you complaining?" Jenks asked. "You get a chance to fight for freedom against the Commies."

Benson looked at him a long moment trying to think of a response – none came.

"Here's the deal," Levine said, sitting on the ground. "We set up a CP and try to coax the little people into attacking us."

"That should be real fuckin hard," Jenks remarked dryly.

Despite himself, Levine chuckled. "Three companies will be on the paddy's other side. ARVNS are a klick away and will attack from the north and the south. Delta Company is on standby at English and can be here in twenty minutes. Plus we'll have air and artillery support."

"Well we at least have a chance," Benson said cheerfully.

"You gotta get an overhaul on your brain," Jenks said.

"We will have a chance, a good chance," Benson countered. "We got all that help if we need it."

"Jesus, if we have to bring in all those men how many Gooks you think will be hitting us?"

Benson's eyes widened as understanding hit him like a shock wave. "Man, we don't have a chance!"

"No shit, Sherlock," Jenks said.

Levine ordered the men to dig foxholes. Jenks would be taking over temporarily as acting Platoon Sergeant when Levine left Vietnam so Jenks would be in the command bunker along with Lieutenant Bartstell. Martsten and Garcia were paired in a foxhole. Benson was with Evans. Levine and Fleming were together.

"As long as I ain't with Benson," Jenks commented. "I don't want any of his down home intelligence rubbing off on me."

"Fuck you, Jenks. I been doin some thinking on it. All we gotta do is get psyched and we can beat these Gooks."

"Get what?"

"Psyched, man, psyched. S I K E D," he spelled.

Jenks smiled his shit-eating grin. "Maybe I should share a hole with Benson. He can help me with my spelling."

Benson smiled satisfied. "There it is."

A few moments later they all crossed the rice paddy and began digging foxholes. The new assignment concerned Fleming. Each day the odds against them making it through this operation got slimmer and slimmer. Now, they were a platoon against an overwhelming enemy force. He wanted to think about their fate in a`positive light, but realistically their only solace hung on the thin thread of hope that it would all work out in the end.

CHAPTER 7
Human Bait

While Levine was conferring with Bartstell, Jenks helped Fleming dig a two-man foxhole. When they finished, Jenks took Fleming to a nearby bamboo grove where they cut three stalks. With a poncho liner and the stalks, Jenks showed him how to build a hootch for protection against rain. All the while, Jenks continued the on going practice of giving Fleming tutorials on what was to be expected in the bush. With Levine and Jenks' insight, Fleming was gaining valuable knowledge on how to be an infantryman. Then they took seats in the hole. Jenks told Fleming that he was from Philadelphia and had been in Nam for six months.

"Why did you join the Army, Jenks?"

"The same reason you did, the same reason all of us did, so we wouldn't get drafted and go to Nam. The recruiter told me they were only sending draftees and enlisted men who volunteered. I didn't volunteer and look where I am."

Fleming smiled ruefully. "Recruiters aren't really truthful people."

"There it fuckin is. Joining the Army was never in my life plan. I had a good gig back in Philly. I mean I wasn't no big time ballplayer like you."

"Really? What did you do?"

"I sold hot dogs on Market Street."

Fleming's face dropped. "You mean you had one of those hot dog carts?"

Jenks laughed. "Everybody gets that look when I tell them I sold hot dogs. It's one of the best gigs in Philly. My old man ran it for years so it was an established business. All you need is the cart and an umbrella in case it rains. There's little overhead and you work for yourself. When I was old enough, my old man retired and gave it to me. You had to bust your ass but you gotta' bust your ass in any job. I made thirty-five grand my first year then Uncle Sam fucked me up. I had it dicked and now I'm getting dicked. This war really fucked up my day." Then Jenks pointed to Levine, who was making his way to them. "Here comes the Super Jew."

"He's Jewish?"

"Yeah and he's one fierce motherfucker and a real good dude."

"Who's a real good dude?" Levine asked reaching them.

"The recruiter that lied to you and sent your ass over here."

Levine chuckled and sat on the foxhole's rim. "I was taught all through grade school and high school that a man should be above board in all life dealings. My old man told me, my Mom, all my aunts and uncles, teachers in school. Rabbis told me. Then the first time I have a serious life dealing it's with a recruiter employed by the fuckin United States Government and I get lied to and I end up in a really fucked up war."

"Same thing with me," Fleming said. "Except I'm Catholic. I heard it from the Nuns and Priests."

"Me too," Jenks said. "Obviously recruiters' parents don't tell their children diddly squat about truth and shit. What did the L T want?"

Levine smiled bitterly. "Bradford wants a two hundred man body count. L T says we ain't leavin' till we get it."

Jenks groaned. "Operation Canyon Falls all over again."

"There it is," Levine replied.

"What's Operation Canyon Falls?" Fleming asked.

Levine looked at him a long moment. "I don't want you getting wrong shit in your head about the people in charge. I can't tell you."

"I can," Jenks said with a smile. "Two months ago, a platoon of Alpha Company was on a CP just like this one. Bradford gave them a hundred-man body count quota before they could return to the rear. That night they were hit. Alpha kicked ass. A thirty-five-man platoon and air and artillery killed one hundred and fifty Gooks. Alpha lost six men, ten wounded. Next day Bradford sent in reinforcements, sixteen men, ten cherries. Bradford kept Alpha there. He said they were on a roll. He wasn't going to bring them in when they were on a hot streak. That night they were hit again. Only this time they weren't so lucky. They killed seventy-five Gooks. Alpha lost twenty men and ten wounded. Bradford took them out. Five men walked out of that operation – five fuckin men."

"Jesus!" Fleming exclaimed.

"Fuckin Bradford got a bronze star for his successful, strategic handling of the operation. His command capabilities got two hundred and twenty five gooks killed. By the time it made it to division it came out to four hundred and thirteen. He only lost twenty-six men," Jenks said.

Fleming looked at Levine.

Levine nodded his head yes.

"Bradford's killed more Americans than the gooks," Jenks said bitterly. "And this wasn't the first time he lied his ass off about a body count, the fucking lifer ass puke."

"This shit goes on a lot? Fleming asked.

"Boocoo. It ain't just Bradford. All the fuckin pukes lie about their body counts. And when some poor farmer or mamasan gets zapped, and that's happened boocoo times, the lifers just say they were V.C."

"How is Captain Wiggins?" Fleming asked. "Is he an asshole too?" Wiggins was their Company commander.

"No, he's got his shit together," Jenks said immediately.

"Wiggins is okay," Levine concurred. "He's been over here a while though and he's getting burned out, but he's seen it all. He's won boocoo medals when he was a field commander and he actually earned them. He was out here with the grunts fighting the gooks. He's been wounded three times too. He's seen the shit. But I think working behind the scenes is fucking his mind over."

Jenks smirked. "Any decent officer who works closely with Bradford can't help but get his shit fucked up and his mind fucked over."

Fleming shook his head in disgust and frustration. "This is one fucked up war."

Jenks smiled at Levine. "Tell him about the Doughnut Dolly affair?"

"Doughnut dollies?" Fleming asked surprised. "Red Cross girls?"

"Jenks, I told you, I don't know if that's the truth or not," Levine said.

"What about them?" Fleming asked, dying to know just who was or wasn't telling the truth.

Jenks was animated, eager to tell the tale. "Doughnut Dollies go to bases all over Nam to cheer the troops up. They play games with us lowly grunts." He smiled surreptitiously, his facial expression strongly declaring that his hard won knowledge, provided by a lifetime of street experience, couldn't be fooled by the word games – there was more to games than just games. "Officers get different treatment, if you know what I mean. First, let me tell ya about the games. These Doughnut Dollies came to English and had this trivia contest. This chick had tits, I sware, Fleming, they were as big as melons. She was fine." Jenks leered as if he was mentally reliving the moment. "Three buttons on her blouse were undone. One more button and, bang, them melon tits would have been freed for all the world to see. She knew she was driving us out of our fuckin minds. I mean we ain't seen round eyed pussy in fuckin ages. Anyway, she says we're gonna have a contest and the winner would get a prize. I figured maybe she'd let the winner see her tits, or maybe even touch them."

Levine laughed. "You're too fuckin much, Jenks. Touch her fuckin tits."

"Well the way she was fuckin standin there. You could tell she was proud of them tits and I don't blame her. If I was a chick, I'd be damn proud, poud as hell to have tits like that."

"You sure you wanta listen to this guy, Fleming? There's some deranged shit goin down here."

"Tell me more," Fleming replied with a smile. He was more than eager to here some more deranged shit go down.

"The first man to get three questions right wins the contest. The first question," Jenks paused for dramatic effect. "What were the names of Donald Duck's three nephews?"

"Donald Duck had three fuckin nephews?" Levine asked.

"Huey, Dewey and Louie. I nailed that one."

Levine and Fleming looked at each other and broke up with laughter.

"The second question: Who were Rocky and Bullwinkle's arch-enemies?"

"I know that one," Fleming replied excited. "It's that small dude with the mustache and that tall chick with long black hair."

"Yeah but to get it right you gotta know their names."

"Fuck, it's on the tip of my tongue."

Jenks smiled a shit-eating grin. "On the tip of your tongue ain't gonna get ya to see melon tits." He paused for effect. "And the winning answer is: Boris Badinoff and Natasha."

"Damn, I almost got that one."

A wide smile rested on Levine's face. "Jenks...it figures some swingin dick like you would know shit like that."

"I like to keep up on current events."

Levine and Fleming exchanged smiles.

"We got one more question. I get it right, I win, hands down."

"Why in the hell would you care about winning a contest like that?" Levine asked.

"Ain't you been payin attention? She has tits like melons. I thought I made that clear," he emphasized in a mildly pissed-off tone of voice. "I'm hopin to see em or maybe even touch em."

Levine nodded his head, a solemn expression on his face. "You're right. I'm wrong. To tell you the truth, I might a' done some wild-assed shi, too. I mean, Goddamn, anybody, and I mean anybody, wouldn'ta minded winning that prize their own self."

Jenks smiled with satisfaction. "The third question: Who is Scrooge McDuck's arch enemies?"

"Who the fuck is Scrooge McDuck?" Levine practically yelled out.

"The fuckin rich guy in the Donald Duck comics," Jenks answered, shocked. "I can't believe you didn't know that. You knew didn't you, Fleming?"

"Nah, I can't say I did. I guess I had no chance at seeing them tits."

"Jesus." Jenks is genuinely surprised at their ignorance. "Anyway, Scrooge McDuck's arch enemies were the Beagle Boys."

Levine grunted out a laugh. "Oh good Christ the Beagle Boys."

"Well, a good story is only a good story if it has a happy ending. This story has a somewhat happy ending. I won the contest. I beat the other guys. They were pissed. That's happy."

"There's fuckin justice in the world," Levine commented.

Fleming smiled. "Did she show you her tits?'

"Almost."

"How do you almost see tits?" Levine asked.

"The chick calls me to get my prize. I fuckin' practically run to her. She gives me this big smile and I sware shit was growin.' She gets real close, looks in my eyes and smiles. She wasn't that tall so all I had to do was look down and, damn, she had some fine cleavage. I looked at her and she knew I was checkin her out. And I knew she was testing me to see if I would check her out. I can tell by the look on her face, she's glad I'm checking her out. Now I am really starting to grow. I'm ready to bust right through my O.D. fatigue trousers. I just know I'm seconds away from seeing fabulous melon tits. She says in her best sexy voice. Let me give you your prize. She gives me this great big smile. At this point my dick is so hard it could cut diamonds." Then Jenks frowned. "She reaches into her pocket and hands me a Tootsie Roll Pop."

"That's it," Levine blurted out. "A Goddamned Tootsie Roll Pop."

"Yeah, and it wasn't even a Chocolate one. Everyone knows Chocolate is the top of the line when it comes to Tootsie Roll Pops. I get an Orange one which everyone knows is a bottom line fuckin Tootsie Roll Pop."

Levine nodded his head agreeing. "I never liked them Orange ones either.

Chocolate is definitely top of the line."

"There is fuckin is," Jenks said emphatically.

A wide smile split Fleming's face. "A Tootsie Roll Pop!"

"Yeah and I did all that thinking and wracking my brain and all I get is a bottom line, Orange, fuckin Tootsie Roll Pop."

"That truly sucks." Fleming said matter of factly.

"There's more to this story," Jenks looked at Levine. "Tell me, do Doughnut Dollies give Bradford a Tootsie Roll Pop?"

"I told ya, Jenks. I don't know if it's true or not."

"Well tell me and Fleming what ain't true or not."

Levine gave Fleming a long look.

Fleming nodded his head yes at Levine.

Levine frowned then said: "I was driven to this awards ceremony a couple months ago by Bradford's driver."

"Yeah, the Super Jew won a bronze star. I'm telling ya cause he won't."

Levine smirked at Jenks. "Shut the fuck up." Levine looked at Fleming, took a deep breath then blew it out, reluctant to tell the truth. "The driver told me that Bradford and some other officers were fucking Doughnut Dollies. He swore that Dollies spend the night in Bradford's quarters and Bradford has some nice quarters. It's like a house with sofas, stereos and shit. He has a movie projector. Anyway, the driver takes the Doughnut Dollies to the chopper pad the next fucking morning. He says they count their money right in front of him."

Fleming looked at Jenks. "He's right, that's not real proof that they're fucking officers."

"Tell him about L T Chalice."

A fond, yet sad smile engulfed Levine's face. "L T Chalice was our last platoon commander. He was a good fuckin guy…. He's dead now…One night I got drunk with him. That's what I mean by him being a good guy. He was a good combat leader was real good with the men. No officer would ever drink with an enlisted man but L T Chalice did. Not all the time, he was cool about it. He'd drink with you if you got promoted or got a medal or if you did something important, you know. Anyway, he told me that Bradford and some of the other REMF officers bragged about banging Doughnut Dollies. Rumor control had it that some of these chicks are making boocoo bucks fuckin all the high ranking officers in da Nam."

A silent moment passed.

Levine looked at his watch. "I gotta check on the other guys. You guys wanna' come?"

Jenks stood. "I do. I wanna fuck with Benson."

Fleming went with them. Doughnut Dollies were young girls who cared enough about spreading goodwill and charity that they spent one year tours in Vietnam in order to bring a taste of home to young American combat soldiers. To think that some of them were acting as prostitutes was beyond belief. But ever since he had been involved in this thing called Vietnam he had felt the pain and disappointment of many of his most sacred beliefs being shattered to bits and this was the demise and the shattering to bits of just one more.

It was going to be a tough year in more ways than one, he decided.

The squad members were all gathered at Marsten's and Garcia's foxhole.

"But, Sarge," Benson said. "We're just gonna wait for them to hit us?"

"Why you freaking out now?" Jenks asked. "It's what this whole operation's been about from the beginning. It's what this war is all about. We wait for them to hit us."

Benson's brow burrowed, deep in thought.

"Oh, Man," Jenks admonished. "Quit thinking, you're gonna hurt yourself."

"No, no, I'm thinking good. We've been doin okay. If we're doing the same thing we've always been doin then what we're doin should make the same things turn out the same way…if we keep on doin what we've been doin. Know what I'm sayin?"

"Know what you're sayin," Jenks said exasperated. "A fuckin genius couldn't understand the shit that just came outta your mouth. All I know is now we're a platoon instead of a company. And that makes it worse."

Benson's brow furrowed again and a painful expression filled his face.

"I told you quit thinking. Now you're hurting me. The reason it's worse is there's less of us."

"What do you mean less?" Benson asked. "We ain't lost any men, have we?"

Jenks rolled his eyes. "If you're a gook, or if you're a grunt in any army, what would you rather hit a company or a platoon?"

Benson's eyes widened with realization. "That's right. There ain't as many of us as there is of them. We're gonna' get murdered, sarge."

"We'll be all right," Levine assured him. "Jenks, quit fucking with him."

"He ain't fucking with me, sarge. I figured it out my own self and he's right."

Jenks rolled his eyes at Fleming.

Fleming smiled at his frustration.

Benson, let's talk about something else," Jenks said slowly and patiently, attempting to assuage Benson. "How about home?" he asked with a smile. "You're from Oklahoma, that's back in the World ain't it?"

Benson eyed him warily and his face set in determination. "It's just as much back in the World as fuckin' Philadelphia,"

"I didn't know that." Jenks smiled his impish grin. "See, you're teaching me."

For a moment, Benson warily eyed Jenks then Benson smiled satisfied.

"What did you do back in the World?" Jenks asked.

"I worked on my Daddy's farm."

A light sparkled in Jenks' eyes. "You're Daddy, huh? Not your old man, your Daddy?"

"That's right, my Daddy. We had a sideline too. It was bad ass."

"Did you and your Daddy sell Peach Preserves your Mommy made? Maybe sold your Aunt Petunia's honey, too?"

"For one thing my Ma didn't make no peach preserves. For two things, I ain't got no Aunt Petunia. And for three things none of that is bad ass."

"Okay, so what did you do that was so bad ass?"

"We raised fightin' dogs." Benson smiled smugly at Jenks. "Pit bulls."

"Wooo, that is impressive. What did you do? Walk the dogs when they had to take a do do or a pee pee?"

A few of the men snickered and chuckled.

"You can't fuck with me on this, Jenks. I had a real important job. I was in charge of the breedin."

"Breedin' fightin' dogs! And you the main man. That is impressive."

"Damn right, an important job and a bad ass business. We had some fine fightin dogs too. We used to make boocoo money sellin the dogs I bred. Everybody wanted them."

"People only want your shit when you put out good shit. Your fighting dogs musta been somethin."

Fleming knew enough about Jenks to know that Benson was being set up. It was only a matter of time before the hammer fell.

"Damn right, Jenks." A wide smile lit Benson's face. "You sold hot dogs, but I was the one who really sold hot dogs." Benson chuckled. "Get it?"

Everyone groaned.

"No, I thought that was fucking funny," Jenks said to the other men with a tone of mock indignation. "You guys just don't appreciate a good joke."

Benson gave him a smug smile of satisfaction. "I know what you're doin.' You're tryin' to get on my good side cause you ain't got nothing smart ass to say do ya, Jenks?"

"Not a fuckin' thing. I just wanta' learn from a pro who obviously knows the score. What does a man in charge of the breeding do?"

The smile vanished from Benson's face with lightning like speed. "Huh?"

Jenks knew that he had struck a nerve. "What do you do if you're in charge of breeding? You pimp for dogs?"

Some of the men began to chuckle.

Benson couldn't make eye contact. "No, I didn't…." Confusion lit his face.

"What does pimp for dogs mean?"

"I don't care if you been here longer than me or not," Evans protested. "You are fuckin dumb. Don't even know what pimp means."

"Pimp is probably one of them city words. I ain't no city boy like you two boys. I don't know city words."

"Pimpin' means you went out and found the dogs a piece of ass. That's what you did right? You got your dogs pieces of ass."

Benson smiled confidently. "No, I didn't get them pieces of ass."

"Well then how did ya breed them? How did ya get other fightin dogs? Even in Oklahoma a dog's gotta fuck in order to get puppies."

The smile on Benson's face grew larger. "That how much you know, Jenks. Our dogs were so damned mean they wouldn't even fuck. And anyway that woulda been a waste of dog cum."

"How the fuck you waste dog cum?"

Fleming was wondering the same thing.

Jenks shook his head with confusion. "How did ya' get puppies? The cums gotta' swim to the egg or some shit like that. I took enough biology to know that."

"First of all, ya' artificially insert the cum into the bitch's pussy. Do that you can get about ten bitches pregnant with one load of dog cum from one dog." Benson said puffing up with superiority. "A dog cums boocoo more cum than a human cums. If them dogs would fuck, you'd be wastin boocoo cum. Damn, Jenks, you don't know jack shit."

"I gotta admit I don't know as much about dog cum as you do. You're an expert when it comes to dogs cuming."

Again the men started snickering and chuckling.

"Tell me this. If the dog don't cum in the girl dog then how the fuck you get the dog cum so you can shoot it into the bitch's pussy?"

Benson's took a long slow breath. His eyes darted back and forth in their sockets looking at each man.

"Come on, man, enlighten us. How ya get the dog cum? You gotta know. You were in charge of the breedin.'"

A sick expression settled on Benson's face.

"You don't know, do ya?' You were in charge of the breedin' and you don't even know how to get dog cum."

"I know," he snapped brusquely. "I fuckin' know."

"Then tell us. We don't know."

"Maybe I don't wanta' fuckin' tell ya.' Did ya' ever think of that?"

"You don't fucking know," Jenks replied.

Benson's face puckered into a pout,

"Tell us," Jenks demanded. "I mean if you were in charge of the breeding you are the man. You gotta know. You were the one and only man who could know. So tell us or we're all gonna think you're just talking shit."

"He is talking shit," Levine said. "Or else he'd tell us."

Benson nervously licked his lips. "Uh, you, uh…you massage the dog till he cums and then you collect it. That way you save the cum."

A long moment of silence passed. Everyone in the squad exchanged eye contact, not really believing what they had just heard.

"Massage a dog till he cums…" Jenks said softly, knowing what he's heard, knowing what it meant yet still having a hard time registering it. "Does that mean, no…that can't…did you beat the dogs off?"

"Uh, kinda," Benson mumbled inaudibly.

"Ya gotta speak up, Benson."

"That's what it means."

Again a long moment passed; the realization of what has been said is so shocking it still hasn't quite set in.

"Jesus, Benson," Jenks said with genuine shocked surprise. "You used to beat dogs off?"

Again everyone just looked at each other in shock. Then Evans started laughing and that set off a chain reaction. The whole squad exploded with laughter.

"It's scientific," Benson pleaded. "It's how all breeders get cum."

"Scientific or not you're still beatin a dog off," Jenks said, laughing.

"We needed the cum!" Benson insisted.

Evans fell to the ground laughing and kicking his feet into the air.

Levine shook his head in wonder. "Jesus, Benson. How could you do that?"

"I know boocoo dudes got bitten by pit bulls," Garcia offered. "But I ain't never met a dude who whacked one off."

Fleming and Marsten are laughing so hard they are close to tears.

"You need help, Benson," Jenks said. "Lesson number one, it's more fun to sexually play with women than it is dogs."

"I like women," Benson shot back angrily. "I got a girl." He took out his wallet, removed a picture, and handed it to Fleming. "She's hot huh, Fleming?"

Fleming looked at a picture of a too heavy girl wearing bib overalls. "Uh, yeah, man. She's pretty nice." Fleming handed the picture to Levine.

"She's hot," Levine said too quickly and not too convincingly.

Marsten looked over Levine's shoulder at the picture then quickly eyed Benson. "She's very attractive."

Benson smiled with appreciation mixed with a dash of modesty.

Jenks snatched the picture from Levine, looked at it, and handed it back to Benson. "You shoulda stuck with the dog."

Benson gave Jenks a heated look.

A new round of laughter consumed the men. When it subsided, minutes later, Levine ordered the men back to their holes.

Then it started to rain.

The rain pounded everyone as Van stepped carefully through elephant grass, walking point. Hoi was behind him as slack man. All night long, the thirty-man V.C. platoon had traveled at a blistering pace but they were still a short distance from the underground complex that would serve as headquarters. Now, at daybreak, they were conspicuously in the open. Nevertheless, Van slowed the pace, wary of running into an American patrol. They were twenty minutes from their final destination when a foul odor filled the air.

Americans, Van thought. When Americans first entered the village, he had questioned the elders on their unique smell and was told their different diet caused their body odor to smell differently.

Van stopped. He held up his hand, halting the squad. Slowly and carefully, he inched forward twenty meters.

Ten meters in front of him, eight Americans were in an L-shaped ambush position.

Van hand signalled Dan and some others to move north forming a flanking maneuver, giving them a clear firing line on five Americans. This would leave Van and Hoi responsible for killing three men. The Platoon consisted of twenty-two other men, but Van feared that moving them could create noise and the Americans would be alerted. Then they would call for air and artillery support and Van and the others would be caught in the open. They had to kill the Americans before they radioed for support.

A last check of the men told Van that everyone was in perfect position. The ambush would go off flawlessly. But when Van looked at Hoi, Hoi immediately looked away and Van knew he would be useless. There was no time to motivate him. There was only time to eliminate the Americans. Van took aim and opened fire on full automatic, spraying the rounds.

Van's rounds hit the three Americans and killed them instantly.

Almost simultaneously Dan and the others unleashed a murderous volley. Every American was killed.

Van quickly exchanged weapons with Hoi. He grabbed Hoi's shirt, and pulled him along until they reached the dead Americans. He fired a full clip into their bodies and again exchanged weapons with Hoi.

Meanwhile, Dan and the other men began hacking off pieces of the dead men's anatomy.

Chi led the rest of the men forward and they quickly stripped the American bodies of intelligence and supplies. Then Chi quickly gathered the men and headed them out with Van again taking point.

Van set a blistering yet careful pace to the compound. The Americans surely heard the ambush and would be sending out patrols and helicopters to search for them.

They reached the complex and once inside they were safe for one more day.

"Hoi, did you fire?" Chi asked.

"He fired, sergeant," Van insisted.

"I asked him," Chi shot back.

"I was right next to him, I know. Just check his weapon, you'll see."

Chi glared angrily at Van.

His ugly face still filled Van with icy shudders of dread.

"Leave. Go to your quarters and get some sleep," Chi said to Hoi. "Van, you stay."

Hoi hurried away.

"I can no longer put up with Hoi's attitude. Can you understand that?"

"No, sergeant, I don't understand," Van said. "I don't understand any of this. I don't understand why we are at war. I don't understand why we must kill Americans."

"You are to follow orders, not ask questions."

"I follow orders. I've killed Americans. I would like to know why I kill them."

Chi's face softened. "We kill Americans because they are here. We kill them because they interfere with our country. We kill them because of their arrogance to think they can come here and tell us what to do. We kill them because they kill us. Is that enough reasons for you?" Chi spoke calmly and patiently as if he sincerely wanted Van to understand.

"Some of our country's leaders asked them to be here."

"Some of our leaders are corrupt and want American money. America bought their support. Some of our leaders were paid handsomely. Ninety Nine per cent of our people will suffer so one percent can prosper, that is the American way. We don't want that for our country."

"So because of politics we are odered to kill them? Killing people because we are told to do so is no answer. We need a stronger reason."

"You want a stronger reason? Chi asked his one good eye filling with hate. "You really want to know why we kill them? We kill them because of my face!" Chi placed his face inches from Van's. "See it! They did this to me! And I am only one of tens of thousands that they have hurt. This is why we kill them."

Shock ran through Van. The hideous burnt mass of facial scar tissue was a burden no man should carry.

"My village was the most peaceful place on earth," Chi said emotionally. He was doing all that was possible trying to maintain control. "It stood for centuries. Then one day American planes dropped napalm on us. Most in my village died that day. I lived, but look at me. LOOK!"

Van looked away.

"I spent a year in an American hospital. They tried to fix my face. I asked everyone why my village had to be destroyed. No one knew. They said it was a mistake. The napalm was dropped on the wrong location. Finally, an American official gave me money and apologized for America. I left the hospital and had nowhere to go, no family, no friends, no village, nothing. I gladly joined the revolution."

Van was filled with a surge of overwhelming empathy. "I'm sorry for what you had to go through."

The anger left Chi's face; his features softened. "You are a good person, Van. You have a good heart and you use your head and think. Think about this, if the Americans had never come to Vietnam all this death and destruction would have never happened. I would be in my village. You would be in yours. But they came and they won't leave. They have placed us in the position where we have to force them out so we can once again be free and live in peace."

Van nodded his head yes.

"Get some sleep. You are tired. You marched all night and you fought this morning. Think about what I said to you."

A silent moment passed.

"I know you care about Hoi. He is your friend. Make him understand what we are trying to do and his life will be easier. Unfortunately, we are in this struggle to the end. It's what America forced on us. Hoi must do his part."

Van left Chi and walked to his assigned quarters. Chi's hatred for America was understandable. He felt a kinship with Chi; they both had been forced to become soldiers because of what had been done to their homes, their beloved villages. Why are they here? Van wondered. What could Americans possibly want in Vietnam that was worth all this destruction? These questions continuously haunted his mind. He wondered if an answer would ever surface or if there even was an answer.

Fleming awakened and looked at his watch: 0600. Levine was at a morning briefing with Lieutenant Bartstell. Fleming removed his helmet and started scooping shin deep high water out of the foxhole. The hootch he and Jenks had built couldn't stand up to the rain that had fallen continuously for ten days. Water gathered in the poncho liner roof causing it to collapse and flood the hole. Rain and dropping temperatures made nights unmercifully cold. Fleming's jaw chattered unceasingly and tired because of it. He never before even imagined that a man could suffer from jaw fatigue. This was the operation's twelfth day. Some of the men had the beginning stages of immersion foot, an infantryman's worst nightmare. Their feet were constantly wet, causing the skin to crack and peel. Keeping their feet dry was the only remedy but it was impossible: they were rained on constantly; they stood in puddles, sat in puddles and even slept in puddles.

Just then Levine returned to the foxhole. He had a canteen full of C-Ration coffee and without a word poured some in a canteen cup and gave it to Fleming.

"When you leavin?" Fleming asked.

"I don't fuckin' know. I gotta' be in Saigon in four days for processing so I can catch my flight back to the World. They'll probably keep me out here another three days."

"That's cutting it short."

"Xin loi, (pronounced Zin loi-Vietnamese loosely translated to mean sorry about that), Bradford is gonna bleed me until we get our body count quota. He wants to look good to the Saigon high command and he needs the numbers to do that."

"Sometimes I wonder if we are fightin a war on two fronts. I know the Gooks are trying to waste us but sometimes I think the brass is too."

"There it is. I guess it all works out in the end though." Levine's eyes took on a desperate expression of hope. A moment passed before he said: "I still got things to do before I leave, gotta' make sure the platoon has their shit together. Make sure Jenks is ready. He's takin' over for me."

"Jenks is a Spec 4,' Fleming pointed out. "A Spec. 4 is takin over as Platoon Sergeant?"

"He's all we got. He'll probably be replaced back at English after this operation is over. That should be in a week to ten days. It's only temporary till we get another Sergeant." A smile suddenly appeared on Levine's face. "Jenks was one scared cherry when he first got here. But now he can take care of himself in a firefight. He's still a wise ass, that'll never change. But for all his shit he really cares about the other men."

"I know. I saw him putting salve on Benson's feet the other day. Of course that was after he gave him his new nickname."

Levine smiled. "This has gotta be good. What's he call him?"

"Hand Job."

Levine and Fleming broke out in laughter.

"Then the whole time he was putting the salve on his feet," Fleming said while laughing. "He was telling Benson he hopes he wasn't turning him on too much because there was no way he was letting him give him a hand job."

"That's Jenks," a laughing Levine said.

A moment of silence passed.

"I hate to see you leave, but I'm happy you're getting outta' this place," Fleming said. "We're gonna' miss you, sergeant."

"Cut the sergeant shit. Call me Levine or sarge, or even Super Jew. You ain't gotta call me sergeant no more."

"Sarge it is. I like sarge."

Levine yawned. "I'm fuckin beat. I'm gonna catch some Z's. Wake your sarge up in an hour."

Fleming smiled. "You got it, sarge."

Levine placed his helmet over his face and reclined in the muddy foxhole.

Fleming looked at him for a long moment. Two sets of personalities and values existed in Vietnam. There was Levine, unselfishly giving of himself for the men's welfare. There was Colonel Bradford, selfishly using men to attain personal gain. Fleming couldn't help but wonder about himself. What kind of man was he? He knew instantly how he wanted others to think of him. He wanted to be thought of as unselfish, like Levine. And at that moment he realized this mattered more to him than anything in life. Even baseball, he decided.

CHAPTER 8

The Tiger Takes The Bait

Everyone was gathered at Benson and Evans' foxhole. Jenks was attempting to remove Benson's boots.

"Oh, shit! Goddamn, Jenks, it ain't gonna' work!" Benson cried in pain. "My feet are truly fucked!"

"Shut the fuck up, Hand Job." Jenks placed his hands on Benson's boot heel and pulled ever so slightly.

Benson pulled his foot away. "Oh, Jesus no, Jenks! They ain't comin off!"

Jenks turned to Levine. "His feet are fucked. The skin's stuck to his socks and boots."

"Who else is having trouble?" Levine asked.

Everybody confessed to his feet being in some sort of disarray.

Last night, Fleming had taken off his boots. His feet were wrinkled, pasty-white, and puffy. Blisters were forming and he would soon be in the same condition as Benson.

"Benson, you been taking care of your feet?" Levine asked.

"There ain't much I can do. It ain't stopped raining in over a week. Jenks has been helping me. He was putting salve on them but now I can't even get my boots off. My feet are just fucked."

Levine shook his head in frustration. "Two fucking days and a wake up and I'm dealing with this shit."

"How are your feet, Super Jew?" Jenks asked.

Levine smiled like a little boy whose hand has been caught in the cookie jar. "To tell you the truth I ain't no better than you guys.

Another day of this and they're gonna' have to carry me to my Freedom Bird. But I'm your sergeant, and I gotta' beg on your asses."

"I gotta' tell ya,' sarge," Benson said softly and emotionally. "Jenks has been helping me boocoo. He ain't such an asshole all the time."

Jenks turned to Levine. "Doc Garret told me dog cum cures immersion foot. Maybe we should take out a patrol and find a village with dogs. Hand Job can jack off a couple." Jenks smiled at Benson. "I gotta' tell you, buddy – I'm really looking forward to seeing your work."

Everyone has wide smiles on their faces except Benson.

"You're a fuckin' asshole you know that, Jenks."

"How many times I gotta' tell you the L T promoted me to platoon asshole. I gotta' do my job, don't I?"

"Yeah, well, you're doin' it real good. L T sure picked the right guy."

"Listen up," Levine said. "Yesterday a squad from Alpha got zapped not far from here. Bradford thinks the gooks are ready to do battle so we got an ambush today. Hand Job, Evans, you're excused cause of your feet."

"Yes, sergeant," Evans said. Both men have wide smiles on their faces.

"I'm glad you both approve. Since you can't go on the ambush, you got the L.P. tonight and tomorrow night."

The smile left both men's faces.

"We gotta go out during the day?" Garcia asked. "Every Gook from here to Hanoi will see us."

"If the fish don't come to the bait," Jenks said. "The bait goes to the fish."

"Why don't they just split us all up into four different squads," Marsten said facetiously. "Then the enemy can choose who they want to hit."

"Funny you should mention that. High command is a step ahead of you. Three squads are going on ambush in three different directions. That leaves one squad here at the CP."

"Jesus Christ, we'll be spread out all over the fuckin' place," Jenks said angrily and spit on the ground. "I mean they're just askin' the Gooks to waste us all."

Garcia breathed a heavy sigh. "I'm from San Antonio. This place reminds me of home."

'Man, San Antonio must be one fucked up place," Benson said.

"The Alamo is in San Antonio." Garcia explained. "This place is like the Alamo."

"Oh yeah, the Alamo, where Davy Crockett and Jim Bowie fought," Benson said excitedly. "We should call this place the Alamo. I can dig that."

Jenks gave him a bitter smile. "Davy Crockett and Jim Bowie died at the Alamo."

Realization washed over Benson's face. "Maybe we can think of a better name."

Jenks smiled mithlessly. "Maybe we should, Hand Job. Maybe we should."

However, in the next few moments they all agreed to nickname the CP the Alamo. Then Levine said to be ready to leave in two hours. Levine and Jenks would be in the command bunker studying maps of the area.

Seeking shelter from the rain, Fleming and the other four men took seats under a tree. Within minutes, the exhausted men fall asleep.

That afternoon, ready to leave the Alamo's perimeter, Fleming wondered if they had enough men. With Benson and Evan's excusal, the squad was down to five live bodies. The other two ambush teams had nine. Immersion foot had decimated the platoon and Bartstell wanted to break up the squads so they would each have an even number of men. But each squad leader and Levine argued vehemently against it. They were used to working as a team. Breaking them up would only hamper their effectiveness.

"Listen up," Levine said. "I figure the Gooks are watching this position as we speak. They'll see us leave the CP and watch us the whole way. Jenks and I found another route to our position. It's a trench south of here. It zig zags around the Alamo and the Gooks will never suspect it."

"What's the drawback leaving from that position?" Marsten asked.

Levine gave him a smirking smile. "Ya' had to figure out that there would be a drawback didn't ya?" Levine eyes Marsten for a moment before speaking: "It will take an extra hour. So that means we leave an hour ahead of everyone else."

"You're the platoon sergeant, why didn't you order the other squads to take the same route?" Marsten asked.

"I left it up to their squad leaders. They wanted to follow the conventional route."

"So we leave earlier and hump an hour longer?" Marsten asked.

"Yeah and there's more. No doubt the trench is flooded from all the rain. The water is probably about shin to waist high."

"Our feet are already fucked up from being wet," Garcia complained. "Now we're walkin through water when we ain't gotta?"

"Would you rather be wet or dead?"

Garcia said nothing. He looked away from Levine's penetrating gaze,

"People, I ain't asking for permission. This ain't no thing we're gonna vote on. This is what we're doin.' Ya' got that?"

Nobody said a word.

"Good, now that that we all agree, we move out in ten minutes. Oh, if you got an extra pair of dry socks bring them. We'll change when we get to the ambush site."

Everyone looked at each other and frowned.

"None of us have dry socks," Fleming said.

"I didn't think so. I don't either. We leave in ten minutes."

Levine and the squad reached the ambush site at the designated time. They were wet from walking in the ravine and tired from humping an extra hour. They begin grumbling and complaining until Levine ordered them to shut up.

They were positioned in a fruit tree grove two klicks from the Alamo. Levine ordered the men to set up and daisy chain claymores then he assigned positions and told Jenks to call in a SITREP.

"There it fuckin is," Jenks cursed. "This fuckin Army radio ain't working."

This was exactly what they didn't need, Fleming thought. They wouldn't be able to call in a SITREP and they wouldn't be able to call for support if the situation demanded it.

"Is it the battery?" Levine asked.

"I switched batteries before we left and I brought an extra one. I tried them both. It ain't fuckin' workin.' And before we left I checked it out just like you told me to. It was working perfectly."

"Awright,' we ain't got a radio. Just keep cool. We'll be okay."

They wait in silence for an hour, eyes glued to the terrain in front of them.

Suddenly one hundred meters away a NVA soldier, the point man of an attacking force, emerged from a tree line. More NVA soldiers soon followed until approximately forty-five appeared.

Oh my God, Fleming said to himself.

Then men from a second platoon exited the tree line.

"Jenks," Levine whisper shouted. "Get that fuckin' radio working."

"I can't. I been tryin." Jenks whisper shouted back. "I can't will it to work."

The nauseous sensation of fear swept through Fleming.

Garcia, next to him, was mumbling the Lord's Prayer.

"Listen, people," Levine whisper shouted. "They don't know we're here. They saw first and second squads go to their positions. They're gonna try to waste first and second squads."

"What are we—"

"Shut up!" Levine snapped at Garcia. "Nobody talks but me. We're gonna take out those two platoons."

Five men, Fleming thought wildly. Five men are going to take out two platoons.

"Stay cool," Levine said in a soothing tone. "The way I figure it they'll come within fifteen meters of us and turn east. Keep your shit together, fire accurately and we'll get these fuckers." Levine handed Marsten the claymore detonator. "Everyone, give your grenades to Fleming. Fleming, throw them motherfuckers at that second platoon. Use that pitching arm and be on target. You're pitching for your life now. Got it?"

Fleming nodded his head in assent. He got it and he immediately understood Levine's strategy. The claymores would take out most of the first platoon. If the grenades were on target, and he threw them quickly enough then he would take out much of the second platoon. If the other men were accurate with their fire they would decimate many of the remaining soldiers. The key to it all was timing. They would have to wait until the NVA were nearly on top of them before they opened fire.

The NVA were seventy-five meters from their position.

Taking the alternate route allowed them to reach the ambush position unseen. If they successfully ambushed the NVA platoons then they would save first and second squads. There was a better than good chance that if they let the NVA pass by they would not see Levine's squad, but then first and second squad would be slaughtered. By taking action Levine's squad would burden all the danger. They had to be successful.

The NVA were twenty-five meters away.

Fleming organized the grenades in front of him and held one in each hand. He had to heave them approximately thirty meters to reach the second platoon. It wasn't a long throw but grenades were much heavier than baseballs and the throwing motion was completely different. Accuracy was crucial – he had to throw strikes.

The NVA approached within fifteen meters and turned east.

"Go. Now." Levine whispered to Marsten and Fleming.

Marsten clacked the detonator.

Fleming heaved the grenade. He immediately knew he had thrown a strike. He pulled the pin on the second grenade as he switched it to his right hand and threw a second strike.

The Claymores exploded and the ball bearings cut a deadly swath through the approaching NVA. The grenades fell within a second of each other and shrapnel shredded men in the second NVA platoon.

Levine sprayed the two platoons with the 60 just as Garcia and Jenks opened fire with M-16's. Martsten grabbed an M-79 grenade launcher and fired a grenade round at the second platoon.

Fleming had two more grenades in the air when the first two exploded. He picked up two more and threw them.

Everyone had performed flawlessly and with precise timing. The NVA were decimated. Approximately forty-five men had fallen. The others turned and ran back to the tree line.

"Let's go," Levine ordered. "Di di! Remember to take your shit and leave nothing."

"Well there it fuckin is," Jenks called out. "This fuckin Army radio is working now."

Levine hurried to it. "Six actual, this is rolling hills, over."

"Roger, six actual, over."

"Roger, we engaged with two platoons of NVA at our pos. We are coming in. Have the other two squads abort also. Be advised NVA ran into a tree line a hundred mikes from my pos, over."

"Will do, rolling hills, we'll light them up. Good job, over and out."

"Let's go. Garcia on point and double time."

Garcia took point and the men started running on sore feet back to their base camp.

When they reached the Alamo, the men fell to the ground writhing in pain and cursing their feet. After a few moments, Levine and Jenks stood and limped away to report to Bartstell.

Fleming limped to his foxhole and sat.

Soon, men from the other squads came to his hole and thanked him. Two men, Doyle and Fields stayed behind. They all sat on the foxhole's lip.

"You saved our butts today, cherry," Doyle said. "And to think, I bet that you'd be dead in a month. You're the only fucking cherry ain't been greased. Ya cost me fifty bucks, but ya' helped save my ass."

"You won me fifty bucks," Fields said with a smile. "And saved my ass."

Fleming wished they would leave he disliked both of them. "Four of us are dead. White broke his foot. He's in the rear for a couple months."

"He's one lucky fucking cherry," Fields said.

Doyle nudged Fields with an elbow. "Maybe this cherry wants in on the bounty."

Fields draped an arm around Fleming's shoulder. "Me and Doyle started a bounty on that fuckin puke Bradford. It's up to two grand. You wanna' put in?"

"A bounty for what?" Fleming asked.

"The fucker's been trying to get us all wasted ever since we got here," Dolan replied with a surprised tone, as if the question needn't have been asked. "We're collecting money so somebody will do him. You wanna' put in?"

"I don't think so."

"Maybe you wanna' collect," Doyle said with a smile. "His chopper will be here later. He's gonna' count them dead gook bodies from the air. Shoot his chopper down, you can make two grand."

Fleming shook Field's arm from his shoulder. "I said I don't think so."

"It's two grand," Doyle emphasized. "You can buy a car with two grand. You're gonna' make boocoo friends you do that beggin' ass puke, cherry."

"You know what – quit calling me cherry."

Doyle and Fields looked at each with surprise.

Fields nodded his head and smiled. "All right, whatever you say. You earned it. Take it light".

"Thanks again," Doyle said and grabbed Fields' arm. "Let's di di outta here." They walked away.

Just then Benson and Evans hobbled over and sat with him.

"How you two holdin up?" Fleming asked.

Evans frowned. "Feet hurt, I'm tired as shit, and I'm worried I'm gonna get wasted any minute now, other than that I'm fine as wine."

Benson's eyes narrowed. "You better get some sleep before tonight."

Evans sighed. "I know. We got the listening post. I hate listening posts."

Fleming chuckled. "Ever notice how we hate pretty much everything we do?"

"Ever notice how pretty much everything we do pretty much sucks?" Evans replied.

Helicopters suddenly arrived at the ambush site. One of the choppers flew low to the ground while the others circled it.

"That's Bradford's chopper. The low flying one," Benson said. "He counts the bodies."

"No fuckin' way!" Evan blurted out.

"Well not him personally. He's got an aide doin' it. He counts 'em for the body count number. It don't mean nothing, he's gonna' make up his own number anyway. How many did you guys zap?'

"About forty, maybe forty five," Fleming answered.

"Bradford'll stretch that to sixty-seven," Benson said knowingly.

"Sixty-seven!" Evans said. "Why not say seventy?"

"They always pick an uneven number. That way it looks more real."

Just then a man from first squad rushed from a foxhole and fired at Bradford's helicopter. Two other men grabbed him. They argued for a moment before they pulled him away.

"That happens boocoo," Benson said. "More G.I.'s have tried to do Bradford than the gooks."

"You're flaky," Evans said. "He wasn't shooting at Bradford's helicopter."

"What the fuck was he shootin at then?" Benson asks.

"I don't know. But he wasn't trying to do Bradford was he?"

"Fields and Doyle were just here. They tried to talk me into doing Bradford," Fleming said. "They said I'd get two grand. I guess they found a guy."

"You mean to tell me," Evans said, shocked. "Americans are trying to do other Americans and they get paid for it?"

"Damn right," Benson said. "The shit over here is real. You fuck up, or some officer is gung ho with your life, it pisses boocoo people off."

"Fuck!' Evans said.

Fleming sat alone on the foxhole's rim when Levine and Jenks returned and took seats next to him.

"You did good today," Levine said to Fleming.

Fleming smiled at him, nodding his head. A moment passed with Fleming deep in thought.

"Something bothering you?" Levine asked.

"Doyle and Fields were here. They wanted me to put in money for a bounty on Bradford. They even asked me to waste him."

"Those two are assholes," Levine said. "But somebody's gonna' do Bradford. The fuckers wasted too many Americans."

"Some cherry from first squad was shooting at Bradford's chopper. Some other guys stopped him."

"You know why?" Jenks asked.

"Cooler heads prevailed. You can't go around wastin your own people."

"You are way off. The man flying Bradford's chopper is a pilot named Douglas. He's goin' home in a few days. Two weeks ago he was flying medavacs. His whole tour he flew into boocoo hot L.Z.'s, took out boocoo wounded G.I.'s. He risked his life boocoo times for us. You don't waste a man who saves lives because you're trying to waste a man who has taken them."

"Yeah, but killing him. It's a bit radical ain't it?

Jenks' laugh is more a grunt. "Fleming, sometimes you're one dumb fuckin new guy. Bradford's the enemy. You kill the enemy."

"You wouldn't do him, would you?"

"No, I ain't waistin him, but that don't mean I wouldn't mind seeing him wasted. Fuck, I threw fifty of my own money in the bounty."

Midnight: The rain had abated to a fine drizzle. Earlier, Fleming and Levine had dug holes into the foxhole's north and south walls. Then they ran bamboo poles from hole to hole; giving them raised platforms allowing them to stand out of the water.

"Man, you saved everybody's ass today," Fleming said. "I mean everybody was scared shitless, but you were cool. You knew exactly what to do. You even knew we should take that alternate route."

"I came up with the plan. You guys did the rest. That second platoon would have had us in deep shit if you weren't on target with them grenades." Levine paused then frowned. "Unfortunately, all we did today was piss the Gooks off. They're gonna' come back on us. They're gonna' hit us soon and hit us hard."

A long moment passed while Fleming digested this information. "Let's change the subject. I'm tired of talking about death. I don't know much about you. I know you're from New York. What did you do back there?"

A curious expression settled on Levine's face. "You mean what kind of work dud I do?"

"Yeah. "What was your job?"

Levine looked at him for a long moment. "I tell you, you can't tell anybody."

"I won't say anything."

Levine studied him for a long moment. "I sold ladies shoes in Brooklyn."

"Ladies shoes!" Fleming blurted out.

Levine chuckled at his reaction. "I was fuckin good at it, too. Made boocoo money, boocoo commission." He sighed and the melancholy look that Fleming had been seeing quite frequently filled his face. "I enjoyed it. I just hope I can go back to it."

"Sure you can. Why not?"

Levine's eyes assumed a faraway unfocused look. "I killed boocoo gooks. I seen boocoo people die, seen boocoo bad shit. I'm here this week and next week I am back selling ladies shoes. It seems like a big jump. It's scary."

"This is scary – this shit here. You're getting out of it."

"Selling shoes, it seems like someone else did it. This shit here, where we are now, I can do this. I know how to sit in a flooded foxhole wirh a thousand gooks out there wanting to kill us."

"A thousand gooks!" Fleming blurted out, stunned. "That many? A thousand?"

"It's why Bradford is trying so hard to get them to hit us. Intelligence has confirmed it and Bradford's got a hard on dreamin about his body count."

All of a sudden they heard the whoosh of a mortar going over them.

BOOM.

The mortar hit about twenty meters outside the south end of the Alamo's perimeter. That night eighty mortars fell inside and outside the Alamo's perimeter.

Van awakened refreshed and rested. Last night was the first night in a week that he hadn't marched through jungles and impossible terrain in order to reach this underground bunker complex.

Just then Chi entered along with Dan and Hoi. Van left with them for a conference toom where they took seats alongside the other thirty men of Chi's platoon. This was the official end of their one-day vacation. Today they were to meet the fearless commander of the 92nd PAVN Colonel Nguyen Cao Quoc. A few moments later Nguyen Cao Quoc entered the room. His appearance belied the fact that he was the fabled commander of the 92nd PAVN – a man others had spoken of with reverence. Dressed in a green t-shirt, he was frail with thin as matchsticks arms and a concave, sunken chest. His long fingers and smooth skin give his hands an effeminate appearance. They were the opposite of a typical soldier's rough calloused hands. His pale complexion lent evidence to the fact that most of his time was spent inside the underground complex. He looked nothing like a soldier.

Quoc smiled. "I am happy that you brave fighting men have made it here safely."

Van was taken aback at this effeminate man's deep, rich voice tone; it was commanding, yet pleasant to hear.

"To free the country of our birth, the country we all love, we have a long struggle ahead of us. Tens of thousands of our fine young men, men like the ones gathered here today, have been slaughtered by the American aggressors. The Americans are strong and rich. They have many terrible weapons. Their airplanes drop death on our people in many horrible ways. They have planes that fire so many rounds it equals the firepower of one battalion of our soldiers. However, the Americans lack one weapon that we have a thousand times demonstrated – a weapon that will defeat them. That weapon is you, the individual Vietnamese soldier; the young man who grew up working next to his father in the rice paddies: a man with will and indomitable spirit, a determined man with strong faith who believes in our country and our cause. Americans are soldiers fighting with no motivation, no cause. We will beat them because they are a corrupt people from a corrupt culture sent on a corrupt mission. We will beat them because they are not as strong as the men sitting before me today. We are better people, and better people will always win out over the decadent and the evil. I have been to America. I studied in France and I know the Western mind. Last night I made a move. The Americans didn't retaliate. Tonight I will make a second move. Tomorrow this platoon will have the honor of striking the first blow against the Americans. You will rest for the remainder of the day. Tonight I will brief you on your role in the operation. Thank you and know that I am honored to have met brave young men like you."

The men cheered wildly for Colonel Quoc.

Chi and Quoc exchanged salutes and then Colonel Quoc left the room.

Soon afterwards, the gathered assemblage left after him. They were all excited and eager about tomorrow's mission.

Van stayed behind in the conference room. Quoc's words were strong and inspiring. But Van understood what hadn't been said. The village elders had taught that men who spoke and inspired others to perform heroic deeds were often men who feared doing the same deeds themselves. Quoc wanted them to go out and die while he sat safely in an underground complex. His pale complexion was undeniable proof that he was never out in the sun; it literally screamed that he had never commanded troops in battle.

Van stood and started out of the conference room. What was he to do? With each move he was becoming firmly entrenched in a life that promised suffering, pain and eventually death. And tomorrow it would only get worse.

Levine leaped into the foxhole after his morning briefing with Bartstell and said: "Bartstell asked for reinforcements and Bradford puked all over him. He said reinforcements would discourage the NVA from attacking. Bartstell told him he didn't have enough men to defend. And Bradford reminded him he was Airborne and to hang tough."

"Yeah and Airborne Bradford is hanging tough thirty miles away from the combat in an air conditioned room," Fleming said with a smirk.

"There it fuckin is."

A few minutes later, Levine left to check on the other men. Fleming stayed back at the foxhole. To his left two dead men, victims of last night's mortar barrage lay covered with poncho liners, waiting for their helicopter to the rear. It was the only way out, Fleming realized. The other alternative was for the enemy to attack in force, kill enough of them to reach the body count quota, and win a trip to the rear. Of course a successful body count would be won only if a high price was paid; it was plainly evident that the high command was more than willing to turn living men into dead men in order to reach a quota. They were the bait, and the bait always died.

The tragedy in this bazaar of tragedies – the men, the ones who would die, would suffer up to the moment of death. Immersion foot had decimated the platoon. Fleming's feet were raw and blistered. Every step felt like nails were being driven into his feet. And every man in the platoon was in the same condition. How could thirty-three crippled men defeat a force of a thousand?

The only consolation was that it would be over soon and their suffering would come to an end. But would all their lives end soon, too? Fleming wondered.

All of a sudden thunder cracked in the sky. The fine drizzle picked up in intensity and pretty soon the rain pounded the men.

Levine and Fleming sat in their rain-flooded foxhole watching the land in front of them.

"Why are we in Vietnam?" Fleming asked.

"I got no idea."

"Gooks are getting wasted. Our friends are getting wasted. We're sitting in the rain in a foxhole, you'd think we would know why we're doin it. You'd hope it's for a good reason – not because somebody ordered us to go out and waste some fuckers."

Levine chuckled bitterly. "That's the only reason – some shitbird said go out and waste some fuckers and we're waistin' them. I don't buy that bullshit that if the gooks go Communist then we'll have to fight Communism at home. Leaders have been saying the same thing for centuries to fire up the people for war. Like Marsten said they can bring that line out any time they want to go to war."

"The only way we'll know is if we lose in Vietnam."

Levine gave him a dubious smirk. "Us lose. Whatta ya mean?"

"If we're fightin them here so we don't have to fight them at home then it stands to reason we have to win here. If we lose then what...are we gonna have a war with Communists in the States? It sounds pretty wild. "

Levine nodded his head in understanding. "Yeah, but we ain't gonna lose."

"These people...they don't care about Communism or Democracy. They're farmers. They care about getting rice from the fields so they can eat. Boocco people are suffering for no reason."

Levine removed his glasses and wiped rain from the lens. "Yeah and all this suffering and dying is being done so the one percent can live good."

Fleming cocked his head in wonder. "What do you mean the one percent?"

"The one percent – the control freaks, the people who run shit and everybody's lives. One percent in Saigon don't want the country to go Commie. One percent of our Country agrees with Saigon. All these one percenters are sitting in air conditioned offices in Washington and Saigon getting rich, smoking cigars and drinking fine liquor, and the ninety nine percent are sitting in places like this."

Fleming made a show of looking around his rain-flooded foxhole. "Well there it fuckin is."

Levine puffed his chest up in a mock imitation of a politician addressing the people. "We both know this to be true and these truths to be self evident. So I ask you – how ya gonna act?"

Suddenly the whooshing sound of incoming mortars was heard followed by explosions inside the Alamo's perimeter.

"Here we go again," Levine said.

"Same old shit again," Fleming sang, mimicking a cadence song from basic training.

It was evident to all the Alamo's defenders that the mortars were being fired from a tree line to the North. Yet American artillery didn't fire back. Fleming wondered what had happened to all the support they had been promised. But he knew that support would only come when the position was about to be overrun. He knew that it was a designed ploy to feign passiveness in order to tempt the enemy into attacking. If support were offered too early it would discourage the enemy from attacking. Suddenly the barrage ceased.

Shifting uneasily in the foxhole, Levine suddenly stood and surveyed the perimeter. "Why the fuck they stop? They saw the medavac this morning. They know they hurt us last night and tonight they drop only ten mortars. Why?"

"I don't know. Why would you stop?"

Levine's face illuminated with the light of understanding. "Keep your eyes open," he said with a sense of urgency. "You see anything out of the ordinary waste it. It'll be a Gook. I gotta let everybody know. I'll be back in ti ti time." Levine grabbed an ammo bandoleer.

"What the fuck's up?"

Levine climbed out of the foxhole. "I think we got sappers in the perimeter." Levine sprinted toward the other holes to warn everyone of the possibility of sappers.

Fleming had the sudden realization that the mortars could have been dropped to provide cover fire for sappers. He watched the perimeter with recharged intensity. Just then he saw movement. A shadow, he thought. But a shadow of what, he immediately asked himself.

The shadow moved again.

The hot taste of fear immediately filled his mouth. He aimed his M-16.

The shadow moved again. This time he saw that the shadow was wearing black pajamas.

He fired and the shadow dropped dead to the ground.

Out of the corner of his eye he saw a flash to his left. He turned just in time to see a crouching black pajama clad figure run across the perimeter. Fleming squeezed off two rounds and the sapper was hit in the back – he was propelled forward as if a train had hit him.

Gunfire exploded behind Fleming.

All of his muscles knotted with tension, an involuntary reaction caused by the gunfire's close proximity. Simultaneously he heard a thump to his right. His head snapped around toward the sound. He was face to face with the wide-eyed stare of a dead sapper.

Levine stood a few steps from the foxhole, his M-16 smoking. It was Levine who had killed the sapper thereby saving Fleming's life.

A tremendous blast exploded nearby.

Levine turned to the sound and saw a sapper running from the foxhole where he has just delivered his satchel charge. Levine squeezed off six rounds and blew away half the sapper's head and face. "Fleming, out of the hole. They ain't got AK's, only them satchel charges. We're safer in the open."

Fleming exchanged a spent magazine for a fresh one. He scrambled out of the foxhole just in time to see a sapper throw a satchel charge into another foxhole. Fleming fired two rounds into the sapper's chest.

A sapper appeared out of nowhere and leaped on Levine's back, knocking him to the ground. The sapper raised a knife high over his head ready to plunge it downward.

Fleming emptied the remainder of his clip into the sapper's chest and head. Chunks of the man's anatomy flew everywhere.

Fleming ejected a spent magazine from his weapon.

From a prone position, Levine fired multiple rounds into another sapper charging Fleming's back. Then Levine changed magazines.

Satchel charges exploded everywhere, rocking the perimeter.

Fleming and Levine ran to foxholes and screamed for the men to get out into the open.

Garcia and Marsten exited their foxhole.

A sapper leapt on Garcia's back knocking him down. He plunged his knife towards Garcia's face. Garcia caught his wrist. Bigger and stronger, Garcia easily twisted the man's wrist and forced him to the ground. He rolled on top of him and drove a punch into his face instantly crushing his cheekbone and knocking him unconscious. He grabbed the man's knife and plunged it into his chest. Blood spurted upward and splashed into Garcia's face.

Ten meters away two knife wielding sappers charged Garcia's exposed back.

Swinging his M-16 in a six-inch horizontal line, Marsten opened fire.

The rounds passed a foot over Garcia's head and struck the sappers in the chest propelling them four meters backward.

Garcia turned and saw the two dead men.

Marsten hurried to a bloody faced Garcia. "Are you hurt?"

Garcia somberly shook his head no then smiled weakly at Marsten. "You saved my ass, amigo."

Marsten extended a hand to him and helped him to his feet.

The firing and the sounds of explosions were now coming with much less frequency.

Levine and Fleming approached Garcia and Marsten. "Get back in your holes we—"

Levine's words were cut off by the sudden thunderclap of AK-47 fire. Neon green tracer rounds raced through the black night in a relentless search for targets. The AK fire was instantly met by M-16 fire. The red and green tracers intersected. Flares ignited high in the air – the light show and explosions could have easily resembled a fourth of July celebration if it wasn't for screaming men in pain.

Rounds zipped inches past Fleming's ear; it sounded like a swarm of bees had just passed by him. He dropped to the ground for cover. He crawled ten meters into a vacant foxhole. Blood and pieces of human anatomy hung all over the foxhole's dirt walls.

Levine picked up an M-60 machine gun from a dead man, and then jumped into the same foxhole as Fleming.

A high pitched whistle shriek filled the air; for some reason it sounded much more threatening than anything Fleming had so far heard this night. The sound was a signal for hundreds of NVA soldiers to rush from the trees and charge the Alamo's perimeter.

Levine fired M-60 rounds into the pressing horde.

NVA soldiers swarmed from the tree line into the perimeter like so many Soldier-ants.

A Chicom grenade flew into the foxhole next to Fleming and Levine. It exploded, killing its occupants instantly.

Agonizing cries of wounded men mixed with the sound of explosions and fired rifle rounds. The smell of Cordite filled the air.

Suddenly four choppers appeared over the Alamo's perimeter. The men hunkered down in their holes as the gunships' door gunners opened fire with M-60s.

Ten NVA soldiers opened fire on a low flying chopper.

Rounds riddled through the chopper's cockpit, instantly killing the co-pilot. A round pierced the pilot's throat. He gurgled and spit blood. His last act on earth was to steer his aircraft toward the ten NVA and crash into the middle of them. The aircraft burst into a ball of flames, engulfing ten other NVA. The human torches rushed through the perimeter screaming in agonizing pain until they fell dead to the ground.

The crashing chopper and the continuing fire from the door gunners decimated the NVA ranks. A few retreated and made it out of the perimeter but most were cut down by the gunfire.

Levine dropped in an exhausted heap into the hole.

Adrenaline fueled Fleming during the battle. Now that it was over he suddenly felt a rush of fatigue. He slumped backward exhausted against the foxhole's wall.

Doc Garret and another medic rushed and administered aid to screaming wounded men, but it was impossible to adequately treat everyone.

The smell of Cordite was thick and intermixed with the nauseating stench of burning flesh.

Bile rushed from Fleming's stomach. He leaned his head out of the foxhole and spouted out a huge flow of vomit. Then he sat in the foxhole next to Levine. With a dirty forearm, he wiped away beads of perspiration dotting his forehead. His body alternated between hot and cold flashes. "Damn," he cursed. "They never show puking in war movies."

An exhausted Levine stood and gazed out at the carnage.

Fleming stood up beside him. "How do you do it?" He asked. "You always got your shit together. I've never seen you puke. It's like it doesn't bother you.'

Levine gave him a weak smile. "It bothers me. And I've done my share of puking. I think I used up all my vomit my first few months in country." Again the sad expression fell over his face. "The day you stop puking, shitting, and pissing your pants is the day you wonder if you lost your soul. That was one scary fucking day." Levine shook his head as if clearing cobwebs. "Come on. We're gotta' get Jenks, Marsten and Garcia. We got an ugly job ahead of us...I think they should be with us."

They climbed out of the foxhole. Fleming feared asking about the ugly job. Levine wasn't prone to exaggeration and somehow he knew it would indeed be ugly. It would be best to take all the ugliness in one fatal dose.

CHAPTER 9

The Bait Always Dies

THE LISTENING POST

Levine, Jenks, Fleming, Garcia and Marsten stood fifty meters outside the perimeter, five meters from the listening post.

When they had initially entered the area, Evans and Benson hadn't challenged them and Fleming knew it was a real bad omen.

The bad omen became reality: Evans and Benson lay face down in the foxhole in an enormous pool of blood.

"Garcia, cut me a bamboo pole from that thicket over there," Levine motioned at the thicket. "Make sure it's long and sturdy so I can turn their bodies. Be careful. The thicket could be booby trapped."

Garcia returned shortly with the pole.

A visual inspection revealed no sign of wire or booby trap. Their bodies could be rigged to detonate a booby trap when they were turned over so as a safeguard Levine used the pole. He stuck it into the foxhole, placed it underneath Benson's body and rolled him over.

"Jesus Christ," Jenks said disgustedly.

Marsten vomitted and Fleming and Garcia turned away.

Levine then turned Evans body over. "Them motherfuckers," Levine muttered.

Evans and Benson's fatigue trousers were ripped open. Their testicles and penises had been hacked off and had been stuffed inside their mouths. Their lips had been crudely sewn together so their sex organs would remain inside their mouths.

"Damn, Hand Job," Jenks pleaded. "All them times I fucked with you, it don't mean nothin, man."

"Get them the fuck outta' there," Levine said harshly. "And take that shit outta' their mouths."

Marsten, Garcia and Fleming removed the sex organs and stuck them inside the dead men's pockets. They removed the bodies and Garcia and Fleming carried them back to the perimeter.

Back at the Alamo, the men went about the gruesome task of inspecting bodies and wrapping dead Americans into poncho liners and body bags. They searched the dead NVA for intelligence purposes. They found pictures of family and sweethearts but nothing of military importance. The personal pictures brought forth the realization that the Vietnamese were human beings with family and sweethearts back home who would mourn their deaths. It was just another reminder of war's insanity.

Just then Jenks rushed over to Levine and Fleming. He was holding a bulging poncho liner that was apparently filled with various items. He glared angrily at them then dumped the liner's contents on the ground: bandages, first aid kits, hand grenades and numerous other articles of Army equipment fell onto the ground. "Guess what? They all have red magic marker markings on them."

Fleming picked up a grenade and saw a red magic marker circle around the grenade's neck.

"There if fuckin' is," Levine said softly.

"What?" Fleming asked.

"We took all this shit from dead Gooks," Jenks said savagely.

It was plainly evident that all the weapons, medical supplies; everything lying on the ground was all American made. "How did they get all this stuff?"

"Oh, we know how they got it," Jenks replied angrily. "That's what's frosting my balls! We're getting zapped by our own shit." Jenks turned to Levine. "Tell him! He's got a right to know!" Jenks stormed away.

"What the hell was that all about?" Fleming asked Levine.

Levine looked at him for a long moment. "We've been finding Gooks with American supplies for a long time now. A couple months ago, Jenks figured out that we captured most of the stuff after we gave it to ARVN battalion commanders. He got with a supply sergeant and they came up with the idea of putting magic marker markings on everything we gave the ARVNS. Jenks and the supply sergeant put different color marks for each battalion commander. We had about ten different colors going. We started capturing stuff with magic marker markings within a month. Jenks asked a Kit Carson scout about it (a former NVA soldier who defected to the Americans). The scout said that the ARVNS have been selling them the supplies for a long time now. He said the NVA buys supplies from the ARVNS in every province in Vietnam."

"You gotta be shitting me."

"It gets worse. Jenks and the supply sergeant went to the brass about it. It made it all the way up to Bradford and he took it to MACV (Military Assistance Command Vietnam). A few weeks later, we were told to forget about it. Our mission was to fight the gooks not to conduct investigations. They said that the Army would take care of it."

"What happened?"

"Nothing. The Army didn't take care of it. We kept marking the supplies and

capturing the stuff. As far as we know the brass is just ignoring it."

For a long moment, Fleming could only stare at Levine. "Nothing? They're letting them get away with selling our shit to the gooks?"

"There it is."

Fleming could think of nothing to say.

"I gotta run, gotta talk to Jenks," Levine said. "We're meeting Bartstell and I gotta try to calm his ass down."

Fleming nodded his head. As much as he respected Levine and Jenks Fleming found it impossible to believe that the high command would ever ignore the fact that their chief ally was selling American supplies to kill Americans. What was the motivation? Levine and Jenks couldn't have possibly gotten the full story from MACV. It was all just too wild to believe, but it greatly disturbed Fleming nonetheless.

After conferring with Bartstell, Levine and Jenks returned to the squad and told them the bad news. They had lost fourteen men leaving them with only sixteen defenders. Replacements, ten cherries, were to arrive within the hour. The good news: gunships were patrolling the area offering protection and support for the remainder of the night. Bradford had offered his congratulations on a job well done. They had killed two hundred and forty men on the operation. Since they had reached their body count quota, they would be choppered back to L.Z. English tomorrow.

"I'll bet my ass, and I love my ass," Jenks said. "That body count total will be close to four hundred Gooks once Bradford gets through with it."

When it was pointed out that they had reached their quota yet they were still in the field, a smirking Levine said that the brass thought it would be too dangerous to risk choppers at night in an effort to bring them out. Levine also said that Bradford was so happy with the performance that he wanted the men to know that he would be personally coming to the Alamo at 1100 hours the next morning to congratulate them. "He said we should be proud," Levine finished.

Everyone saw the lie immediately. If it was safe enough to chopper in replacements than it was safe enough to relieve the men as promised. Despite it all, Fleming was relieved to be leaving, even if he had to wait till the next day. He felt no pride. The war and the operation's butchery left no room for pride. The human carnage had left him feeling ashamed to be a human being.

"Men, just an hour ago our Army attacked the Americans and killed many of them." Chi said, exchanging smiles with Colonel Quoc sitting in a chair to the side of him. "Tomorrow, we will finish the job."

The thirty assembled Viet Cong cheered.

Today, a North Vietnamese soldier had told Van that only a few

Americans were at the position. It was impossible to kill many when there were only a few. How many Vietnamese were killed? He wondered. But here he sat among smiling, cheering men. Why were they so eager to believe? Were they gullible or were they afraid of the truth? Were lies easier to believe when truth was so horrible?

"We have been given a great honor," Chi said. "We will strike the first blow. As I speak, many of Colonel Quoc's soldiers are hidden in the jungle near the American site. Tomorrow, I will be positioned with Dan and Hoi." Chi turned to Hoi, purposely making eye contact. "You will fire an RPG at the American Command Bunker. It will be a signal for the rest of the men to attack. This is a great honor. Your aim better be true."

Hoi's facial expression was one of wide-eyed fear.

Van knew he couldn't do it: did Chi choose Hoi to disgrace him then punish him later? If so, there was a twisted reality to the scenario – if Hoi performed poorly Chi's leadership ability could be questioned. The elders had said that hate often blinded men. Chi's lack of vision could cause Chi more shame than Hoi.

Van stood and with righteous indignation said: "Sergeant, I demand the honor of firing on the Americans. I am a better soldier than Hoi. I would be a wiser choice."

Chi glared at Van, shocked at his insolence and his audacity to question him. "Orders have been given. Orders will not be changed."

"I want us to succeed. If Hoi fails it will bring bad Karma to the mission. I don't mean to question Sergeant Chi or belittle Hoi but the simple truth is he is not ready for this honor and I am."

"Why isn't Hoi capable? Colonel Quoc asked.

"Sir, I have known him all his life. He is a gentle soul and is slow in learning the ways of a soldier. Sir, he is improving – the other day he killed two Americans during an ambush, but he is not ready. If we want success, I should take his place, sir." Van knew that he had brought attention to Hoi's lack of ability and Chi's judgement in selecting him. Hoi's probable failure would reflect unfavorably on Chi.

A moment passed. Quoc motioned for Chi. They spoke for a few moments then Chi returned to the front of the room to face the men. "Hoi needs more experience and training. Van has shown great potential and will take his place."

Hoi was visibly relieved at being replaced.

"Thank you, Sergeant," Van said. "I will not let you down. My aim will be true."

Chi smiled evilly at him. "It better be."

For a brief moment Van questioned his actions. A less than perfect performance would incur Chi's wrath; however, Van was supremely confident of his abilities to perform the task. He would steady himself and his aim would be true. It would be a simple task and that concerned him; taking human life was becoming easier and easier.

05:30 Hours: "GOOD MORNING VIETNAM!" Levine yelled out happily. "I AM SO FUCKING SHORT, I GOTTA REACH UP TO TIE MY BOOT LACES!" The jubilant yell could be heard all over the Alamo.

Fleming was happy that Levine was finally going home after a year of war. But he had grown close to him and would miss him.

Lying hidden with Chi and Dan in a bamboo thicket, Van held a RPG. From his position he watched the Americans going about their morning tasks; however, he was fixated on the Command Bunker, his target. His aim had to be true. A successful performance would motivate the others to overtake the position before the dreaded gunships arrived.

"Fleming, pass me some C's. I'm so short I can't reach 'em myself." Levine said with a wide smile on his face.

Fleming gave him the C-rations.

A long moment passed as Levine studied the weak smile on Fleming's face. "Fleming, I was thinking. Maybe I could write you. You can let me know how Jenks is running the platoon."

Fleming was instantly filled with a warm glow. "You'd actually write me, a fucking new guy cherry?"

"You're no fuckin new guy cherry. For a fucking grunt that ain't been to A.I.T. you're one fuckin capable grunt."

"Thanks, man, thanks."

"Make it out of here alive, you hear. That's an order."

"I will. I always follow orders."

"There it fuckin is! You make it out alive, come see me back in the World in Queens, and I'll buy you the biggest and best steak that New York has to offer."

"We'll make it a tradition. Every time I come to New York and pitch in Yankee Stadium you get a steak dinner and box seat tickets to every game."

Levine smiled. "You're on. But I'll only root against the Yanks when you're pitching." He climbed out of the foxhole. "Stay here. I gotta say goodbye to Jenks. I need to do that alone. I'm gonna give him orders to keep you alive. Jenks is another grunt that always follows orders."

"Then, by all means, please go and give him that order."

Levine left and Fleming dropped down into the foxhole. And then, miraculously, the rain stopped, bringing an even wider smile to his face. It was the start of a promising day.

Van was about to let loose the rocket propelled grenade at the American's command bunker when Chi placed a restraining arm on him.

"Wait," Chi said. "A helicopter is coming."

The sound of the approaching aircraft signified a dangerous threat. The gunship's door gunner could fire at them from the air and from that advantageous angle the gunfire would be nothing less than fatal.

Levine had returned a few moments ago. He and Fleming were sitting on the foxhole rim looking out at a radiant beautiful sun when

Fleming pointed to the approaching chopper. "There's your bird. How come they're sending a special chopper for you?"

"L T Bartstell set it up, pulled some strings, called some people. I catch a flight to Saigon and it leaves English in two hours. I don't make it I have to wait till tomorrow and then I'd miss my flight home."

A moment passed.

"My last night in the bush was one to remember. I'll never forget that shit."

"We'll never forget you, none of us will. You saved boocoo lives. I only hope one day, I can do the same."

Levine's eyes narrowed in protest. "Fuck that shit! It don't mean nothin.' Don't go lookin' to save lives, save your own. You owe it to yourself. The name of the game is survive three hundred and sixty five days, nothin' else."

"I don't plan on dying."

"No John Wayne hero shit, you hear me. Remember you got a New York steak waitin' on you and I wanna' see you pitch in Yankee Stadium."

"No hero shit, I promise."

When the helicopter landed, the door gunner leaned out of chopper. "We wanta' di di outta' here real fuckin' fast. Whoever's Levine, I need you aboard my bird in about two minutes or xin loi, motherfucker, cause we're booking out."

Levine chuckled. "He sounds serious. I'd better go."

Just then Jenks, Marsten and Garcia arrived at Levine's foxhole. "We came to watch you leave, Super Jew," Jenks said.

Levine embraced him. Then he embraced Marsten, Garcia, and then Fleming.

"No hero shit, none of you guys." Then Levine ran off to the waiting chopper.

Chi, Van, and Dan were positioned within fifty meters of the Alamo's perimeter, perfectly concealed in the bamboo stalks. Van again positioned the RPG launcher on his shoulder. His mind raced furiously and he kept reminding himself to aim and just pull the trigger.

Levine's chopper took flight. It hovered in the air just above the Alamo.

Van took aim on the Command Bunker.

Chi touched his shoulder. "Fire on the helicopter," he ordered.

Van adjusted his aim and fired. The rocket zoomed forward and slammed the chopper's side. The bird instantly exploded into a flaming ball of orange.

The explosion sent everyone scattering for fighting positions except for Fleming. His eyes were glued on the fiery ball that was once a chopper. It didn't happen; it couldn't have happened were his first thoughts. It was an illusion. His mind was playing tricks on him. The orange ball of flame mushroomed across the sky. The smell of cordite and burning gasoline filled his nostrils and realization finally set in. His face twisted into a mask of agony. Fiery chunks of helicopter steel fell to the ground. The orange flame turned into a black cloud of smoke.

Van's eyes were transfixed on the lone American soldier watching the fiery helicopter. What is he doing? He wondered. Suddenly American rounds riddled through their position. Then an exploding M-79 grenade landed nearby. The concussion threw Van, Chi, and Dan ten meters away; the three men lay there barely conscious. The RPG lay bent and damaged a few yards from Van; it was no longer usable as a weapon.

Fleming felt someone grab him and whirl him around.

"Fleming, you asshole!" Jenks yelled at him. "Move your cherry ass!" Jenks started pushing Fleming, prodding him along.

Still feeling dazed, Fleming began running across the perimeter with Jenks. They leapt into a foxhole."

"My fuckin feet!" Jenks screamed in agony. "Goddamn you, you made me run on my fuckin' feet!"

"Jenks, they wasted Levine," Fleming said

"It don't mean nothin!" Jenks hissed at him.

"But he's dead. Guys like Levine ain't supposed to die."

A wide-eyed Jenks screamed at Fleming: "You stupid Motherfucker! Don't go flaky on me! We gotta fight!"

The word fight was like a ringing alarm clock in Fleming's head. He wanted to fight; kill every one of these gook motherfuckers, he thought. It was payback time. He opened fire at the NVA who were already running through the perimeter. A half dozen NVA Soldiers fell. He quickly changed magazines and fired again, swinging his 16 in an arc – eight more soldiers fell.

Jenks clacked a claymore detonator and a dozen NVA were shredded by the murderous ball bearings. Other men detonated claymores and approximately fifty enemy soldiers were caught in the deadly path. Yet the NVA continued charging from the jungle.

His M-16 in hand, Lieutenant Bartstell and his radioman raced from the Command Bunker, headed for the nearest foxhole; an AK-47 round pierced Bartstell's forehead spilling his brains all over the radioman's face and chest. Then numerous rounds ripped through the radioman's upper torso, killing him instantly.

The charging, swarming NVA have forced the Americans to retreat, limping toward the rear in search of foxholes where dwindling American forces had bunched together. Providing cover fire for the retreating men, Fleming furiously fired his 16 at the charging NVA.

Screaming, charging enemy soldiers forced Marsten and Garcia out of their foxhole.

Fleming fired, quickly exchanged magazines and fired again, killing or wounding a group of NVA who were dangeroulsly close to Marsten and Garcia.

Garcia, who could barely walk, helped a limping Marsten back toward the rest of the men; their pace was agonizingly slow.

Desperately laying cover fire for Garcia and Marsten, Fleming continued firing at the never-ending horde of NVA charging from the tree line.

Gunfire hit Marsten in the back, propelling him forward. Garcia limped to him.

Fleming ejected his last magazine from his weapon. "Jenks, I'm out. I'm gonna' help Marsten and Garcia. You got any grenades?" Fleming had two grenades of his own.

Jenks handed him two more. "Go, I'll cover you."

Fleming climbed out of the foxhole and ran toward Marsten and Garcia; it felt like he was barefoot and running on glass. He started throwing the grenades, one after another, at the NVA approaching Garcia, killing or wounding all the enemy soldiers; however, more would be coming from the tree line at any moment.

Fleming reached Garcia. They each grabbed one of Marsten's arms, and the two men limped away with him. Marsten's legs dragged helplessly behind him. He kept saying thank you to Fleming and Garcia over and over again. It seemed like it took forever to reach the Command Bunker. Once inside, they lay Marsten down.

A drenched in blood Doc Garret closed the eyes of a dead soldier and hurried to Marsten.

"I can't move my legs," Marsten said in a pathetic tone. "Dearest God, I am hurt bad. I know it."

Garret slammed a morphine syringe into Marsten.

"You'll be all right, amigo." Garcia cried, tears streamed unashamedly down his face.

"We gotta go, Garcia," Fleming said. "Jenks needs help."

Marsten smiled weakly at Garcia. "Go, I'm all right." He grabbed his arm. "Be careful, okay?"

Tears streamed down his face preventing Garcia from speaking. He nodded his head yes.

"Check those fuckers out," Garret said motioning to the bunker's farthest corner.

Fleming saw two men. He moved closer and saw that it was Doyle and Fields. "What the fuck are you doing?"

"We ain't goin out there," Doyle said. "I don't care what you say."

Fleming grabbed the 16 lying by Doyle's feet and his ammo sling. "You gutless fucking pricks!" He turned from them and limped away with Garcia.

Garcia and Fleming stepped out of the bunker and into the battle.

Numerous NVA were fighting from vacant American foxholes; others were running wildly through the Alamo.

A NVA soldier charged Garcia and thrust his bayonet at him. Bad feet and all, Garcia managed to sidestep the move. He drove the butt of his M-16 into the enemy soldier's face.

A NVA soldier charged Fleming. Fleming fired a full clip into the man's face and head pulverizing it.

A second charging, screaming NVA thrust his bayonet at Fleming. Fleming barely evaded it. He swung his 16 like a baseball bat crushing the man's head and shattering the M-16 stock. In all his baseball years he could never remember such a sweet swing; that sense of satisfaction all ball players felt when the bat's sweet spot crushed the ball.

Fleming threw the broken rifle away and reached down and grabbed a 16 from a dead American.

Garcia reached into a foxhole and grabbed a dead man's M-60 machine gun and belts of ammo.

Fleming arrived at Jenks' foxhole and leaped into it next to Jenks.

Garcia leaped into the adjacent one.

Firing his weapon, Jenks said: "Where the fuck you been?" Then he saw Fleming's face – covered with blood from the men he killed. "You okay?" he asked.

Fleming ignored him and fired his 16 at the endless horde of men rushing through the perimeter.

From a concealed position inside the bamboo grove, Dan, Van, and Chi sat dazed and disoriented. Confusion didn't prevent Van from seeing the American's mad, killing frenzy. Earlier, when the man was watching the burning helicopter, Van had missed a golden opportunity to kill him. If he had done so then many Vietnamese would have been spared death. And in that instant Van realized there was a way for him to make sense of the war and justify it to Buddha. If he could save lives he could wash away guilt for taking lives. Killing the American now, he could begin saving lives now. He aimed his weapon. He had the American perfectly in his sights. It was the first time his hands didn't quiver; the first time he didn't feel pangs of guilt for pointing his weapon at another human being with the intent to kill. Just as he squeezed the trigger another M-79 grenade exploded nearby and the concussion jerked his body. His round found a target, but it was the wrong American.

Something crashed against Fleming's back. He turned and saw Jenks at the bottom of the foxhole, blood gushing from his chest. Fleming dropped down to him,

Jenks eyes were wide open in confusion, as if he didn't realize what had just happened to him. Blood gushed from his chest. Fleming tore away Jenks' fatigue shirt. He grabbed a battlefield dressing, placed it on the wound, and applied pressure.

Jenks gurgled horribly. A huge splotch of blood popped out of his mouth, splattering Fleming's arms, face, and chest. Jenks' body heaved and convulsed. The sucking sounds coming from his chest and mouth were pathetic to hear.

"Hang on, Jenks," Fleming pleaded. "Don't give up." Please God let him live! Please! He said to himself.

But God wasn't listening. Jenks shivered for a long horrible moment. He heaved a tremendous cough, stiffened, choked, and died.

Fleming held Jenks' dead body close to him, feeling the horrible stabbing sensation of utter grief.

Another explosion lifted Van, Dan, and Chi and sent them crashing through clumps of bamboo. They fell dazed to the ground. Van tried standing and got halfway up when the world spun before his eyes; his legs turned rubbery and he crashed to the ground face first.

Garcia, Fleming suddenly remembered. He took one last look at Jenks' dead body, straightened to full height, and saw that Garcia was out in the open limping forward firing his M-60 from the hip.

Why isn't he in his foxhole? Fleming wondered, firing his 16 at the NVA infesting the perimeter.

Garcia limped forward firing the 60 cutting a murderous swath through the NVA.

Fleming reloaded just as five NVA soldiers emerged from the elephant grass on Garcia's right.

Fleming jammed a magazine into his weapon and chambered a round.

The five NVA opened fire on Garcia.

Garcia jiggled and jerked as if a basket of live wriggling snakes had been dumped inside his shirt. Then he fell to the ground dead.

Fleming sprayed his M-16 fire into the five men killing or wounding them all.

A series of continuous explosions suddenly fell on the Alamo perimeter's eastern sector.

Fleming turned to the sound.

American soldiers were crossing the rice paddy firing M-79 grenades into the perimeter's eastern sector where the majority of NVA had taken occupation of American foxholes.

A prop plane and gunships rushed toward the Alamo. The prop plane unleashed a tremendous blast of min-gunfire into approximately one hundred NVA swarming from the tree line, killing them instantly.

Dazed and confused, Van stood on shaky legs. Blood flowed from his nose and ears, a direct result of the blast's concussion. Chi and Dan were sitting on the ground disoriented, blood also flowed from their noses and ears. Van virtually willed himself to stand. On shaky, unsteady legs he wobbled over to Chi and Dan and helped them to their feet.

"We have to get back before the Americans find us." On shaky legs Chi started walking toward the underground bunker complex.

Van grabbed his arm. "No, we will be killed if we go that way. I know another route. Follow me."

Still confused, Chi nodded his head in assent. He and Dan followed him.

Fleming stood and looked out of the foxhole at the Alamo's perimeter. Four others crawled from foxholes. Only four, he said to himself with wonder, that's all that's left. He recalled Jenks' haunting words: they were the bait, and the bait always died.

Doc Garret ran toward Fleming to help the wounded. He took one look at Fleming's blood stained face and stopped. "Is that you, Fleming?" he asked with a tone of disbelief.

Fleming nodded.

"Jesus, all that blood, I almost didn't recognize you. You okay?"

"I'm fine. The blood is everybody else's."

Garret studied him a long moment, trying to determine if he had heard the truth. "Okay, if you're all right. I gotta' go. I got work to do."

You ain't got shit to do unless you're fucking Jesus Christ and you can do a Lazarus thing and bring back the dead, Fleming said to himself, remembering the words Garret had spoken to him after his first ambush. He could only nod his head to Garret.

Garret nodded his head in assent and then ran off.

Fleming crawled out of the foxhole and walked through the perimeter. It was a stroll through hell. American soldiers were going through the perimeter firing rounds into every wounded enemy soldier they found, killing them. To his left, a man without a face thrashed his arms and wildly kicked out his legs while men attempted to hold him down. To his right a red headed soldier with a freckled face – that looked like it belonged on a Norman Rockwell poster – sat with his arm around a dead NVA soldier's shoulder. The redhead couldn't be more than seventeen years old. He took a drag from a cigarette, and then placed it into the dead soldier's wide-open mouth. The kid smiled insanely until he saw Fleming staring at him. Then his eyes narrowed and his face took on a deranged expression of hate

"Don't get any fuckin ideas," the kid said. "This is my fuckin gook. I killed him and he's mine." Then he placed the cigarette in the Gook's mouth. He smiled a hideous grin.

All around him wounded men wailed and screamed with pain. The sounds were maddening to hear.

Marsten, he suddenly remembered. He turned and headed for the Command Bunker. He reached the entrance – Doyle and Fields were urinating in the wide-open mouths of dead NVA Soldiers.

Fleming entered and immediately went to Marsten. "You okay, man?"

An unfocused stare sat on Marsten's face. "Doc was here. He shot me full of morphine. I feel fine."

Fleming smiled weakly. "That's good."

Fear suddenly lit Marsten's face. "I can't move my legs, Fleming. I'm so scared."

Fleming couldn't think of anything to say.

Marsten's eyes widened, as if he's just been struck by a sudden realization. "Where's Garcia? He's still alive, right?"

Fleming didn't know what to say. "Yeah, he's okay. He's wounded, a ti-ti wound."

Marsten slowly nodded his head and smiled. Then he fell into unconsciousness.

Fleming left the bunker. Once outside he heard the sound of an approaching helicopter. In moments, it landed – Colonel Bradford, a General, and two other Colonels hopped off. They were dressed sharply in crisply starched jungle fatigues. They wore helmets and their ensemble consisted of combat web gear. Three men followed them off the chopper. They were dressed in civilian clothing and carried cameras. Two other men followed after them: they were obviously reporters; they carried notebooks and were furiously scribbling in them.

Garret, one of the walking surviviors, was furiously working on wounded men along with other medics. The seven other walking battle survivors huddled together and watched the show.

And Bradford and the other officers did put on a show; they took turns posing with dead NVA soldiers. The civilians followed them, snapping pictures. Then Bradford placed his foot on a dead NVA soldier's chest and held an M-16 across his own chest; the classic pose of a big game hunter with his dead prey. The cameraman snapped the picture. The other officers insisted on having the same picture taken. The reporters wrote incessantly in their notebooks.

"Look at them fuckin assholes," one of the survivors said. "All dressed up for Halloween."

For fifteen long minutes, the officers continued posing, pictures continued being snapped, and reporters continued writing in their notebooks.

Soon Bradford and the others returned to the chopper where they popped open a champagne bottle and toasted themselves.

Meanwhile, reporters wandered over to the battle survivors and tried talking to them. Fuck you and get the fuck outta here were the most popular responses to their questions.

Many American lives could have been spared if they had been choppered out last night when they reached their body count quota as Bradford had promised. For a few damn pictures, Fleming thought. Levine, Jenks, Garcia, and all the others would be alive if it wasn't for Bradford's lust for putting on this show.

Bradford summoned a Platoon Sergeant from Alpha Company. He hurried over to Bradford. They spoke a few moments then the

Platoon Sergeant took a position near the Command Bunker and in his best parade ground voice barked: "SECOND PLATOON FALL IN!"

That's our platoon, Fleming thought.

"You gotta be shittin me," a soldier said loud enough for everyone to hear.

The seven other men broke up in laughter and took their time falling in.

Alpha's Sergeant barked: "PLAATOONNN ATTTENCH-HUT!"

The seven men smiled insolently and slowly assumed the position of attention.

Wearing a stone faced, warrior's expression, Bradford strutted up and down the line of men looking each man in the eye. "At ease, men," he ordered.

The men relaxed.

Bradford clasped his hands behind his back in a stilted, modified parade rest position. "Gentlemen, I am proud of you. I am proud to be your commander. The freedom loving people of South Vietnam are proud of you and grateful for your sacrifice. Your country is proud and grateful. The President is proud of you. You faced the enemy today and you defeated him. We will continue defeating Communists and Communism wherever and whenever it rears its ugly head. This was a tough operation. You lost friends. Rest assured they didn't die in vain but died bringing liberty to the oppressed freedom loving people of South Vietnam."

"Jesus," someone mumbled loud enough for everyone to hear.

Everybody began snickering, trying to stifle outright laughter.

Taken aback, Bradford paused a moment then continued: "You honored yourself today. You honored your unit and you should be proud. Thank you," he said hurriedly and awkwardly then motioned to the Sergeant.

"PLAAATOON ATTEN-HUT!" The Platoon Sergeant barked.

The men came slowly to attention.

Colonel Bradford performed a crisp right face and marched back to the other officers. The Platoon Sergeant dismissed the men.

The men moved far away from the officers then sat on the ground and lit cigarettes.

Just then two companies of South Vietnamese soldiers were seen in the distance marching toward the Alamo.

"Ain't that just like the Marvin the ARVN," a soldier said contemptuously. "They show up after we done all the fightin."

Fifteen minutes later, choppers landed and the men boarded the flight back to English.

Once in the air, the door gunner said: "Man, I'm tired of this shit. I been here eleven months and I seen the same shit over and over. You guys fight, die, and leave. I bet my ass you'll be back here in six months fighting the same battle all over again."

Fleming smiled weakly at him. His feet were killing him and he was incapable of speech or thought. He was feeling unbridled grief over the death of his friends. Right now, he didn't care one way or the other whether or not the battle was replayed months down the road. He knew he would probably feel differently about it later but all that mattered to him was right now and right now sucked.

It don't mean nothing, he said to himself. Not a fuckin thing.

CHAPTER 10

The Business Of War

Two hours after the battle, Van hurried to the underground bunker's hospital section. The agonizing screams and cries of wounded men were heartbreaking to hear, but he was soon so engrossed in helping the doctors that it wasn't a distraction. He was more than surprised that over fifty percent of the battle dressings, morphine and other medical supplies that they used were American made.

Hours later, the medical personnel finished. Some lives have been saved, many men have died, more would die later, but they had accomplished all that could be expected. Exhausted, Van left the treatment area for another room and stretched out on the floor. Minutes later he was joined by a doctor named Phan.

"You should wash off," Phan suggested. "You're covered with blood."

"I will. I am just so exhausted. It has been a long day."

Phan sat on the floor next to Van. "You performed well today. If you could somehow get more education, you could become a fine doctor."

"I like the work."

"Maybe after the war." Phan's face sagged, his eyes sad. "But that won't be for a while."

"Most of our supplies are from America, the enemy. How did we get them?"

"America supplies the South Vietnamese then they sell to us."

"But the South is their ally."

"The South is corrupt. It's the business side of war."

"But they're allies," Van insisted again. This time his voice tone was filled with wonder, outrage filled his face. "They're cheating their allies and selling to us?"

The doctor smiled, a patient, patriarchal expression as if he were speaking with his young son. "The Americans don't care. In some ways they encourage it, all in the spirit of capitalism I might add."

It seemed inconceivable and Van wondered if he had heard correctly. "What do you mean they don't care?"

The doctor's face tightened, an expression of deep thought, as if he were searching for the appropriate words to explain this seemingly unbelievable scenario. "Americans want to win. Their culture is based on winning. But for them they win here in Vietnam even if they lose the war."

Van was shocked. "Explain what you mean."

"Americans have a saying: actions speak louder than words. Actions explain this scenario. The way they are fighting the war – they allow us free rein in Cambodia and Laos, free rein in the North. They fight to fight, not to win."

"But we are killing their people."

"People who are expendable. People they're willing to let die."

"I don't believe this," Van said horrified. "No one would believe it."

The Doctor grinned mirthlessly. "That's why they get away with it because no one would ever believe that any government would ever do it. But governments have been doing it since the beginning of time." Doctor Phan sighed. His brow furrowed. He knew his explanation was inadequate but it was a difficult thing to explain. "All governments are treacherous, every government. They all end up cheating the people. America's government is dualistic; it is a Capitalistic Democracy. Democracy means freedom and equal government for all. Capitalism means making money any way possible. Their Capitalism overrules their Democracy. Their strategy is to prolong the war. The war would end in weeks if they chased us and fought us in the North and in Laos and Cambodia but their profit from the war would also end in weeks. Think of it, why would any country adopt a strategy that guarantees that a war would not be won quickly? It makes no sense unless there is motivation to do it. They're Capitilists. Money is the motivator in a Capitilistic society. If the war goes on forever then they make money forever."

"How can you say these things? I know you wouldn't just make rash statements like that."

"I was educated in France. I interned in one of America's finest hospitals, John Hopkins. I spent five years in America. I know their Capitalistic system and their people. They are warm, friendly, kind, and generous. They are the finest people you could ever hope to meet. But they are gullible. They would never ever consider that their leaders would lead them to war unless it was a righteous war. They were warned of it but they ignored the warnings, not out of stupidity or because they are brutal, uncaring people. They are simply gullible."

"How were they warned? Who warned them?"

"Two of the past three American Presidents warned them about war profiteering, the business of war, and they still don't believe. One was a man named Eisenhower. He was retiring from politics so his words carried much substance but little weight. But the second man his name was Kennedy he was a sitting President. He warned about war profiteering and how secret societies were trying to take over America. He said he was determined to crush them and crush their war machine. He even promised to stop the war in Vietnam."

"What happened? Why didn't he stop the war?"

"He was killed. Another American shot him with a rifle."

"Businessmen who wanted war killed their country's leader?"

"No, Americans arrested one man and said he was responsible. No one knows exactly why he did it. All that the American public knows about him was that he was insane and he was working alone."

Confusion filled Van's face. "What do you mean, no one knows. If they captured the murderer he had to have said something. What did he say?"

"No one knows. The law authorities had him in custody for a few days but kept no record of his interrogation. That in, itself, is very unusual, not keeping notes regarding the interrogation of the man who was accused of assassinating the country's leader. The alleged murderer did say on American television that he was innocent of the shooting. He was killed a few days later. A man came into the police station and shot him. That insured that no one ever heard what he had to say about the assasination."

Van's face is locked in a maze of confusion. "He just walked into a Police station and shot him?" he asked amazed. "A police station?" he emphasized.

The doctor nodded his head yes.

"That sounds…" Van is at a loss for words. "It's in the past. Nothing can be done about it. How does America make money from this War? How can they possibly make money? The South is cheating American businesses."

"No, they are cheating the American people. American taxpayers pay the bill. It doesn't matter who receives the goods. The more the South wants, the more they get. The more their goods are in demand the more money the businesses make. They are supplying their own Army, the South Vietnamese Army, and to a great extent, their enemy, us. The businesses can't help but win and it's very profitable. I believe America will be in the war business for a very long time. Eventually, they will be in a constant state of war. I believe they will go so far as to supply their enemies with war materials then declare war on that very same enemy. It is the wave of their future."

"American families send their sons to fight for this corruption? Doctor, what you're saying…it is very hard to believe."

Doctor Phan smiled at him. "I said it earlier. It's how they get away with it. The bigger the lie the more the people will believe." The Doctor suddenly stood. "Please excuse me. If you like I will speak with you about this later. I am exhausted. I need sleep."

"Thank you, Doctor. I am tired too."

Phan walked away.

What the doctor had just told him couldn't be true. He liked Doctor Phan, but he was from the North. Many from the North hated the Americans so intensely that they would say anything about them. Obviously Doctor Phan was blinded by this hate.

Van yawned. He was exhausted and thinking rationally was becoming impossible. He needed sleep. He stood and started toward his quarters.

The choppers landed at L.Z. English and deposited dead, wounded, and survivors.

Each step off the aircraft was agonizing. During the battle, Fleming was high with adrenaline and hadn't felt the pain so intensely, but he was feeling it now. After walking a few feet he had to stop. Even standing was painful so he opted for sitting on the ground. The chopper's door gunner approached him. "C'mon, man. I'll give you a hand." The door gunner helped him to his feet. Fleming hopped on his back, piggyback fashion. The man started off.

Three weeks ago forty men set out eager to meet and defeat the enemy and to hell with anyone who stood in their way. They had passed through impenetrable jungles. They had been pelted by rain, had slept in rain filled foxholes and crossed rivers and booby-trapped rice paddies. They met an overwhelming enemy force, a suicidal attack, and bravely withstood it all. And now the forty strong men were reduced to a handful of survivors who had to be carried on stretchers or helped by others the short distance of two hundred meters so they could reach the primitive comforts of their tents. Their once steely eyes were now haunted and soulless, as if they had seen all life had to offer, and, frankly, they had had enough.

Back in his tent and sitting on his cot, Fleming stared at his combat boots. They hadn't been off in at least a week and he dreaded removing them. He reached down, untied the laces, and began loosening them from the top down to his toes. Then he pulled the boot flaps back and wasn't at all prepared for the incredible pain. It felt as if someone had rested a hot steam iron on his foot. He crossed his right leg over his left and placed his hand on his right heel. Then he pulled ever so slightly.

"Son of a bitch!" He hissed through gritted teeth, the pain so incredibly sharp that it took his breath away. It felt like he was peeling his heel from his foot. He shook his head in frustration and disgust. He grabbed his right leg with both hands, uncrossed it, and placed it slowly and gingerly on the ground. Fuck it! He said to himself. He took his bayonet, stuck it between his wide-open boot flaps and started cutting away at the boot. Each sawing attempt brought searing pain to his feet as if someone was dropping hot cooking oil on an open wound. He gritted his teeth and decided to just hack away. Take the pain all at once, he decided. He sawed away violently for a few seconds and the sharp pain brought tears to his eyes.

"Fuck this!" He said aloud, defeated.

Just then a medic walked into the tent. Without a word he used scissors to cut away the sock and canvas boot parts that weren't stuck to Fleming's foot. Fleming grimly endured it all. He didn't want to let the medic know he was in pain – only an occasional gasping moan escaped his lips.

Each moan brought a glance from the medic. Finally the medic reached into his bag and pulled out a pint of Jack Daniels whiskey. "Take a really good hit. From now on it's gonna hurt boocoo."

Although not a drinker, Fleming eagerly grabbed the pint bottle and took a long gulp. The hot taste was comforting but left him coughing and choking. The medic had cut away as much boot and sock material as possible. Now he would have to rip the remaining material from Fleming's foot; pieces of skin, a quarter inch deep was also being ripped away. It was like husking corn. It took a half hour more of cutting and ripping and husking before the boots and socks were removed. Fleming's feet were streaked with lines of quarter inch deep, one to two inch long patches of bloody hamburger meat. The intact skin was wrinkled and pasty white. What was almost as bad as the pain was the nauseating stench that rose from his feet; it smelled a lot like a rotted, rain drenched cellar.

The medic washed then placed a generous coating of salve on both Fleming's feet. Before leaving he gave Fleming a pair of rubber sandals and told him to stay off his feet and rest. Then he offered him another shot of whiskey. Fleming took a long healthy gulp and gave the bottle back. The medic left.

I need a shower, he thought. But he hadn't had more than four hours sleep a night for the past three weeks and he realized how tired he was. He lay his head down on the cot for what he intended to be only a moment and fell asleep almost instantly.

"Fleming, you up, man?"

Fleming opened his eyes.

White was looking down at him.

Fleming wiped sleep from his eyes. "White, how ya doin?"

White smiled weakly at him.

"What fuckin time is it?" Fleming asked.

"Seven in the morning."

"I slept for…eighteen hours."

"My first day back, I slept thirteen." White looked down, not making direct eye contact. "The other guys…they all bought it, huh?"

Fleming's face dropped into the expression of unbridled grief. "Yeah…even Levine." A flicker of hope suddenly entered his face. "You hear anything on Marsten?"

White shook his head back and forth while grimacing. "He's paralyzed, man. Shipped out for Japan last night. He can't move nothing from his waist down. And I mean nothing, to put it nicely."

"Fuck nice. It don't work over here. You mean he can't ever fuck?"

"For the rest of his fuckin life. He's fuckin twenty-two. He's got a degree from UCLA and he can't walk or fuck."

"Fuckin hard core, man." Fleming looked at White's cast and motioned to it. "How's your foot?"

White tried hard to suppress a smile. "It's good." But the smile won out. It lit up his face. "Actually, it's great. I've been helping the company clerk. He di di'ed back to the World a couple days ago. The first sergeant gave me the job permanently. I don't have to go out there again."

"Good. You owe it to yourself.'

A moment passed and White studied Fleming. "You're, uh…not pissed at me? I mean for getting such a dicked job? For skatin out on you guys?"

"You skated out on nobody. All the guys got wasted. I'm the only fucker left. I ain't pissed. Like I said, you owe it to yourself."

"I gotta tell ya, man. I was only out there ti ti time, but, man, I could smell death out there. It was like the fucking devil stepped outta hell and let out one badass fart. I mean I was so fuckin scared. I know I woulda bought it, this broken foot saved my ass."

Eyes unfocused, like he is lost in the middle of a bad dream, Fleming nodded his head yes.

"How you doing, man?" White asked softly and with genuine concern. "I knew you were taking it pretty hard after you killed that Gook."

Fleming looked at him. "What fuckin Gook? I've killed boocoo Gooks."

White's eyes widened with surprise. "The one you did in the ambush, when Brennan bought it."

Fleming had completely forgotten about that. It was only a few weeks ago. He remembered that the taking of the life shook him to his core. How could he so thoroughly forgotten about it? What is happening to me? He wondered. "Man, that seems like it was years ago."

The look on Fleming's face concerned White. He waited a few moments before asking: "You okay?"

"What can I tell ya. I don't feel much…This shit, this war, it's…I mean I'm nineteen years old and…" All of a sudden he stands. "I gotta take a shower."

White nodded his head, still concerned about his friend. "Yeah, you smell pretty rank." It was all he could think to say.

Fleming grabbed a towel and limped to the shower.

White was waiting for Fleming when he returned from showering. "I've been thinking – you gotta lighten up." A smile appeared on White's face. He inched closer to Fleming as if he's about to reveal a secret. "The platoon's getting boocoo cherries because…well… because everybody is dead. But you got skate time. You can't go on details cause of your feet." He smiled. "We're gonna parrrtyy! It's what you need to mellow out."

"Party! I hardly drink.'

"Fuck booze. We're goin to the head shed. Do some dew."

"What the fuck is dew?"

White cocked his head back, studying him. "You're fuckin with me, right?"

"I got no idea what you're talking about."

"Herb, man. Grass. Weed. Marijuana."

"Man, I don't know about that. I never smoked that stuff. " Fleming had smoked cigarettes for a six month period while in High School. It was after the baseball season and he started smoking out of an adolescent desire to be "cool." He realized the foolishness of his decision and quit when baseball season began and hadn't smoked since.

"Man, the weed is what you need. Everybody's doin it.

"Everybody I know said it's bad for you."

"And who's these everybodies that told you that bullshit? The same everybodies that told ya comin to the Nam was the honorable thing to do."

A smile slowly crept onto Fleming's face. "That's exactly who told me that shit. I just got the sudden, irresistible, uncontrollable urge to do some dew."

White smiled. "Then let's go do some dew."

"Now, in the day?"

"Day or night, anytime is the right time to get your head to see the light."

"Don't you gotta do your clerkin duties?"

"It's fuckin Sunday. The C.O. and First Sergeant are sleepin off hangovers." White stood. "C'mon, man. We're gonna get stoned."

"It ain't too far is it? I ain't walkin too good."

"It's just two tents over. A ti ti walk."

Fleming stood. "Fuck all them everybodies. Let's get stoned."

The head tent held fifteen men. The actual part where marijuana was smoked was an area separated by hanging blankets fastened together and serving as walls. One blanket was left unfastened and acted as an entry-way. White and Fleming entered. A stereo was playing Jimi Hendrix's Rainbow Bridge. A table sat in the room's middle with a bong and marijuana atop it. There were about six men inside; two were Doyle and Fields. They exchanged momentary eye contact with Fleming before looking away.

"White," Doyle called out, an awkward tone to his voice. "You brung us a new head."

"Yeah, man, this is Fleming."

Fleming nodded to them.

They returned his nod with a weak smile and a nod of their own.

The other four men all wore fresh new uniforms and had the fresh facial expressions of men who were about to embark on the great crusade of liberating Vietnam, and they were ready for it. They were cherries, Fleming thought, and cherries didn't know shit.

Fleming and White took seats at the table. White grabbed some paper and rolled a joint. He lit it, took a few long, deep hits, and passed it to Fleming with instructions to take a small hit, hold it in his lungs, and try not to let any smoke out. Fleming took a hit and held in the smoke. He knew how to inhale and it was similar to inhaling a cigarette, except for holding the smoke in and not letting it out.

'There ya go," White said. "That was perfect. You don't need much. This shit is potent and will knock you on your ass."

Fleming took a few more rapid deeper hits.

White's eyes widened; then he started laughing at the huge amount of smoke Fleming had inhaled.

"What's so funny?" Fleming asked.

"Nothing, man, nothing. Feel anything yet?"

"Not a thing."

"You will, man, you will."

Jimi Hendrix's Star Spangled Banner began. Fleming never liked the rendition – it lacked respect. But soon he found himself listening intently to the music. The crashing guitar sounds reminded him of bombs. It paralleled Fleming's thoughts about America's involvement in Vietnam and how America was crashing. People were in the streets protesting against the war and it seemed like a part of America was dying because of it.

White nudged him, breaking his train of thought. "How ya feeling, man?"

Fleming giggled. White's voice tone had slowed a speed and he sounded comical. "Hendrix's, man. The guy is deep."

White laughed. "Boocoo people are gonna start soundin deep. You're digging this, ain't ya?"

Fleming smiled contentedly. "I feel fucking good."And he did, too. He felt like the only thing that mattered was this moment in time and at this moment he was relaxed and at peace. And he hadn't felt relaxed and at peace since coming to Vietnam.

"FUCK THAT SHIT!" Doyle suddenly yelled.

"Damn right fuck that," Fields chimed in.

And suddenly all Fleming's drifting, the digging it, was about to come to a crashing halt.

"Let me tell you how it is, cherry," Doyle said. "You take life for what it is – a fuckin shit pit. There it fuckin is. You're ahead of the game when you know that. And how ya gonna act when you live in a shit pit. You watch out for number one, that's how ya fuckin act. There it fuckin is!"

"What do ya mean, man?" One of the fresh-faced cherries asked.

Chest puffing with pride, Doyle basked in the attention. "You watch your ass. Don't expect others to watch it – you watch it. You're in a firefight watch your own ass. Cause anything else is suicide and suicide is against God's law. I ain't even gonna break one of God's fuckin laws. A-fuckin-men."

"Damn right," Fields chimed in. "No one watches your ass for ya. You do it your own self. Me and Doyle been here longer than anybody in this sorry assed platoon. We know what we're talking about. We been here four fuckin months and it takes one thing and one thing only to get through four months of da Nam."

"What's it take, man?" Another fresh-faced cherry asked.

"A huge set of fuckin balls," Fields replied.

"There it fuckin is," Doyle said.

A moment of silence passed.

"I guess them huge fucking balls weighed you the fuck down at the Alamo, huh, Doyle? " Fleming asked. "Same with you, Fields? Couldn't move is that it?" Images of Levine, Jenks and the rest of them flashed in Fleming's mind's eye. These were men with huge sets of fucking balls.

The cherries looked at Fleming with curious wonder.

"You fuckin dicks," Fleming said to Doyle and Fields. Fleming turned to White. "I'm outta here," he said then he stood and rushed out of the tent. Once outside he pulled up in pain. He leaned against a sand bag emplacement to take pressure off his feet. He had gotten so angry he had forgotten all about his feet and that he had to walk carefully.

A second later White rushed out of the tent.

Fleming was leaning against the sandbags, face wracked with pain.

"You okay, man?" White asked.

"Fuckin feet," Fleming said, grimacing.

A moment passed until White was sure Fleming was all right then he asked: "What the fuck went down in there?"

"Let's get outta here. Go somewhere so we can talk."

"Let me give you a hand."

Fleming placed an arm around White's shoulder and they hobbled away.

Five minutes later they were sitting in a bunker. White took out a joint held it up with a flourish and smiled. "For the pain. Weed's one of the best pain killers in the world." He lit the joint, took a hit and handed it to Fleming.

"Take small hits," White instructed. "You don't wanna get too fucked up."

Fleming took a small hit, held it in and handed the joint back to White. White took two big hits. "What's all the shit with Doyle and Fields?" White took two more hits and handed it to Fleming.

Fleming took a hit and handed it back. "They hid in the command bunker when we we're fightin that last battle at the Alamo. I'm telling ya, White, that last fuckin firefight was ten thousand times bad. And them slimy ass bastards hid."

White handed the joint back to Fleming then reclined against the bunker walls and sighed. "I've known dudes like that my whole life. They always get away with shit. It ain't fair...But you ever think they may be right, man?"

"Whatta ya mean by that?"

"They watched out for number one and they're alive. All the other guys are wasted."

"They're alive but they got no kinda' life. They're always bitchin. Living, for them is pure hell. Levine, Jenks, you could just tell by the way they acted they enjoyed life. Doyle and Fields, for them the world is a shit pit cause their world really is a shit pit."

"Kinda' sounds a bit like…" White paused, his mind searching for words. "I don't know what it sounds like. I'm stoned."

"It's common sense. For one thing, there's boocoo we don't know. Maybe there is life after death. I don't fuckin' know. Maybe what we believe in life…what we believe about life is all true. If we believe life is a shit pit, which, by the way, is a real easy thing to do, believe life is a shit pit. If we believe that, than when we die we go to a shit pit. If we believe life is good, which is pretty damn hard to do because it takes balls to believe that, but if we do believe it than when we die we go somewhere good. Levine, Jenks, the dudes who bought it, they liked people. Maybe right now they're sitting some place with people they like, doin' things they like. One thing's for sure, you don't live life real fuckin' long, even if you live to be a fuckin hundred. If you die and…you are like…in eternity, well eternity is forever. If that's the case, then dying and doing it right, is a lot more important than livin life like it's a shit pit watching out for only number one."

"Damn, I must be fuckin stoned cause some of that kinda' made fuckin' sense."

"And I must be fuckin' stoned cause I got no idea where the fuck that come from."

They both started laughing.

White took a big hit of pot, held it in and exhaled a small amount of smoke. "When we were on that ambush, near the rice paddy, Levine said you and him were knockin out that mortar. I was scared shitless, like he asked me to do it. I was glad he didn't, but I woulda' gone. And then I got real fuckin' calm. I knew I was ready to die. And it wasn't scary any more. If I was gonna' die, I was gonna' help my friends till the gooks did me. It was fuckin weird. Then you guys came back. Levine said we were gonna' run across that rice paddy. I just knew I was gonna' get shot in the back and get wasted, so why bust my balls runnin' in that mud. But I figured if I lived and got across that paddy, I could put down coverin' fire for you and Levine if you needed it. I had to get across so I could help you and Levine. I was runnin' for everything I was worth. I was goin' so fast I stepped wrong and broke my foot but it saved me. I was saved right there, saved from getting wasted. It was like somebody just snatched me outta' there. It was fuckin' weird."

"You knew you were gonna' buy it?"

"I know it sounds stupid!" White said sharply. "But I fuckin' knew."

"No, no, sometimes you just know shit. You were ready to die and you accepted it because the world is a shit pit."

"YYeeeah," he said cautiously. "What the fuck's that mean?" He demanded.

"This world is a shit pit. But it's a test for the next one. The next one is only a shit pit if you live like this one is."

White took a moment to contemplate what he had just heard. "That's some heavy fucking shit, man. I never thought about it like that."

"You don't think about it because deep down you know it. Doyle, Fields, they think about it all the time. They worry about how they're gonna' get over on people. When they act like that they're holding on to their little piece of shit in their shit pit world because they know when they leave they're goin to a worse piece of shit."

"Now I know I'm stoned cause that made fuckin sense."

"When you were in the bush, right before you broke your foot. You were thinking about getting across the paddy and laying cover fire. What you were doing was looking out for number one."

Anger erupted on White's face. "What the fuck you mean? I just fuckin' told ya' I was—"

"Lookin' out for number one in the bush is lookin' out for your friends like you were doin.' If we all hid in the bunker like Doyle and Fields, the Gooks could just walk in and kill us all, no fuckin problem. Lookin' out for your buddies gives you a chance because we're all lookin' out for each other. So lookin' out for everybody is lookin' out for number one, the only real way you can look out for number one."

White's face was tight with thought, pondering on Fleming's words. Then he smiled. "Far fuckin' out! I think I got all that.

"The shit pit's a test to see what we can make outta' shit."

"Well we got a helluva' opportunity to do that. A year in da Nam you get boocoo oppurtunities to see what you can make outta' shit?"

"There it fuckin' is!" Fleming said.

A moment passed.

"Father fuckin' Fleming. It's Sunday and that's was the best sermon I heard in a long time because it's the only sermon I've heard in a long time that made any sense."

Fleming smiled with mock reverance. "Father fuckin' Fleming of the order of dew smoking priests, ministers, and chaplins. Right now Father fucking Fleming feels real fucking good, like he ain't got a care in the world. And he started the day with boocoo cares. It feels good to let them go, even if it's just for a little while."

Exhausted from another day at the hospital, Van entered his sleeping quarters and was about to lie down when Hoi approached.

"I haven't slept all night," Hoi said.

It was apparent. His eyes were ringed with black circles. His complexion was dull and lusterless. "Neither have I. I was at the hospital all night."

Hoi began nervously gnawing on his lower lip. "You're more tired than I am. I'll let you sleep."

"No, what's on your mind?"

"What's on my mind?" Hoi snapped. "I can't do this. That's what's on my mind. I can't live this life. I can't stop thinking about what we did to those Americans. I dream about it every night."

The tortures, Van thought. It seemed so long ago.

"I don't hate Americans," Hoi pleaded. "That day, when I broke that man's finger, he looked at me. His eyes...they spoke to me. They asked me why do this to each other. Why kill and hurt each other?" Tears started rolling down Hoi's face. "I'll never forget that face, those eyes."

"I don't know why we kill them. If we don't kill them, they kill us. Killing is the nature of things today in our country."

"There has to be a way out of this," Hoi pleaded. "You said if I found a way out you would be willing to help me."

There was no way out. Hoi needed to accept his fate. "We're stuck. We can't go to the village, or to Saigon or anywhere."

"I read a leaflet, distributed by the Americans. We can desert. We can defect to the Americans. They will relocate our families to a protected village."

"My family, your family, no village family would ever agree to be relocated. All our families have lived in our village for the past five hundred years. Our ancestors are buried there. The village is our soul. None of the villagers will agree to leave. You know that."

Hoi's face tightened in anguish. "I know, but I have to get away. I can't do this."

"Why do you believe the Americans? What if they are lying about relocating our people?"

Hoi grabbed Van's arm. "But what if it's true?"

"I would never make a move unless I'm a hundred percent certain that the village would be safe. And there is no way we will ever know that."

"There is a way. I know there is. I will find it. Just don't give up on this. We're getting closer. I can feel it. Just don't give up."

Van was too tired to debate. And Hoi still needed to have hope. In time, he would become more adjusted to the life they had been forced to lead. "I won't give up."

Hoi's face broke into a huge smile. "Thank you. I'll let you sleep I know you're tired. Soon I will find a way out of this. We will be working for the other side,"

Van nodded his head yes and Hoi left.

Van lay on his mat. Why would the Americans help them? Why would they trust two men who had switched sides in the middle of a war? Why trust two men who had betrayed their comrades? What use would they be to the Americans if they defected? There were too many unanswered questions.

And then Van was fast asleep.

The next day Fleming awakened at 0600 hours. He felt great after ten hours sleep. He was starting to feel more aware and refreshed after the last operation's exhaustion. Breakfast, he thought. It was supposedly the most important meal of the day. And L.Z. English served a damn good breakfast: eggs so greasy that if you weren't careful they would slide down your throat into you stomach before you could put one bite into them, burnt hash browns or home fries, bacon and sausage lathered with grease. And if he was really lucky they might have pancakes. And the toast, the toast was always perfect. One thing Army Cooks knew how to do was to throw bread into the toaster and cook a mean piece of toast. It was hot food and better and tastier than anything he had eaten in weeks.

The mess hall was a five-minute walk but on his hobbled feet it took twenty.

Once inside he got breakfast with all the trimmings. And it was a lucky day because they did indeed have pancakes, although they had no syrup. He lathered them with butter and jam and they were bone dry but edible.

When he finished eating, White arrived. Fleming nursed a cup of coffee and sat with him while he ate breakfast.

"You got mandatory duty today," White said. "In fact we all do."

"Not with these feet. They can stick that work detail shit up their ass."

"Relax, man. It's a good detail. Fuckin round-eyed pussy, man! Doughnut Dollies are visiting English. It's mandatory we go and see their show. We're gonna' catch some round eyed fuckin pussy!"

"I got shit to do. I wanna' write my parents and my sister. I'm her hero brother. I don't write her it'll break her little ten-year-old heart. Then I wanna' smoke the joint I was gonna' bum from you, and then I was gonna' take a nap. I got boocoo sleep to catch up on. I got teeth to brush. Like I said, I got shit to do."

"No can do, G.I. I mean I'll give you a joint, but ya gotta see the Dollies first."

"No fucking way."

"It's mandatory, man."

"Fuck 'em. What are they gonna' do send me to Nam?"

"The first sergeant says everybody's gotta' go. If they're nice enough to come here, we should be nice enough to go see them."

"The first sergeant said that?"

"Actually that's from Bradford. He wants everyone to go and that means the first sergeant wants everyone to go."

"Fuck 'em all!"

"You just can't say fuck 'em all. Why make trouble on something like this? It's dinky dau. You're gonna' get your ass in a sling because they're making you go see round eyed pussy? Pussy is pussy, man, even if it's only pussy you can just look at. Besides, use your imagination a little and that pussy can come in handy later."

"You're one sick motherfucker, ya know that?"

"I'm horny. Horny always turns a man into a sick motherfucker."

Fleming gave him a smirking look. "I guess I'll go see round eyed pussy." If truth be told, Jenks story had intrigued him. He wanted to see the Doughnut Dolly show for himself. "You know, Jenks told me those chicks are selling their round eyed pussy to officers."

"That ain't exactly earth shattering news, everybody knows that."

"Shit like that pisses me off. It makes me not wanna' go."

"It ain't like Bradford's orderin' you on one of his suicide missions. This is dicked compared to the other shit he makes you do."

"Yeah, I guess it's better than being bait for the Gooks."

"There it fuckin' is."

Fleming was lying on his cot when White rushed into his tent.

"C'mon, Man. Let's go so we can get a good seat. They'll be here soon."

Fleming got up from his cot.

White had a wide smile on his face. Excited, he grabbed Fleming's arm. "Round eyed fuckin pussy man! Round eyed pussy!" White looked like a kid at Christmas.

They left the tent and a few moments later entered a hootch that acted as company club. It had a bar; beer and soda was sold for only a dime. Every night a movie was shown.

"What's playing tonight?" Fleming asked.

White frowned. "A Disney flick about a squirrel."

"Why can't they ever show us something decent, something adult?"

"They say they don't want to show us indecent, immoral movies. Tbey said it'll ruin our minds – like killing Gooks every day ain't ruinin' our minds."

Pretty soon there were seventy-five men in a club that held sixty. Many were standing. Some sat on top the bar; anywhere they could find a seat. Then someone rushed into the club and yelled: "Bradford's driver just pulled up. They're here."

A few moments later three attractive girls, between the ages of eighteen and twenty-one, entered the club. The buttons on their blouses were unfastened just enough to strategically reveal cleavage. And every man in the room stared at them with mouths agape and wide-eyed wonder. It was as if some species that had long been thought extinct had suddenly reappeared.

A Doughnut Dolly stepped forward. She was bra-less and one unfastened button away from having her bounty spilled out for the entire world to see. "It is so nice to see you all," She squealed enthusiastically with the slightest trace of a Southern accent.

"You don't know how nice it is to see you," someone shouted back.

The three Dollies laughed along with the gathered men.

"My name is Kandi," she said. "That's Kandi with a K. And this is Misty and Wendy."

"Hi," Misty and Wendy said in unison.

"Is everybody ready to have fun today? Yay!" Kandi squealed. Misty and Wendy pitched in with their own yaying squeal.

All the men cheered with approval.

"We will play a game," Kandi said with a smile.

Fleming felt hot flashes of anger. Everything, so far, was exactly the way Jenks had described it.

"We will ask three questions. Whoever gets the most correct answers will win a prize. But you must raise your hand, like you were back in school. If you shout out the answer it won't count even if it's the right answer. Is everybody ready?"

The men all answered in the affirmative.

"Wendy will ask the first question. Wendy."

Wendy stepped forward. "Hi!" she said cheerfully.

The men all acknowledged her with whistling and cheering.

She smiled, basking in the attention. "Who was Donald Duck's girl friend?" Wendy asked.

"Daisy Duck!" a cherry yelled out as fast as he could, just as four men raised their hands.

Everybody groaned and shouted catcalls at the cherry. A few men started beating on him with their hats and with open palm slaps.

"You're supposed to raise your hand," White called out. "Dumb ass cherry."

"That's right," Wendy scolded. "You must raise your hand." Wendy turned to the two other Dollies. "I think this is a smart group. We better ask tougher questions."

"Yeah, we got our shit together," someone shouted.

"What was the name of Tarzan's chimpanzee and what was his favorite command to him?"

Three hands shot up and one of them was White's.

She pointed to one man. "You raised your hand first. What is the answer?"

"Uh, Cheetah?"

"Correct. What was the command?"

"A command? He had a command?"

Everyone booed the man and shouted catcalls at him.

She pointed to Doyle.

"Cheetah. He used to say to him. Cheetah, ongowa," Doyle said with a big smile.

"Almost," Wendy replied. "But there is more." She pointed to White. "Do you know?'

White stood and smiled. "Tarzan used to say: Cheetah, ongowa simba."

Wendy, Misty and Kandi started clapping enthusiastically, as if White had really made their day. "Correct," Wendy said.

All the men groaned at White and shouted disparaging remarks at him.

White whispered to Fleming: "I got this shit covered, man."

"Maybe you'll win a Tootsie Roll Pop," Fleming shot back at him.

White frowned and whispered back: "Get the fuck outta here. A Tootsie Roll Pop?"

"Let's hear it for Misty," Wendy said while clapping her hands.

All the men cheered and whistled for Misty.

Misty flashed a radiant smile. "Roy Rogers horse was named Trigger. What was Dale Evans' horse's name and what was the name of their sidekick's jeep?"

White raised his hand. It was the only hand raised.

"No one else knows?" Misty asked.

No one says a word.

Misty smiled at White. "This is a hard one. You need both answers to get credit."

White smiled confidently and stood. "Dale Evans horse was Buttercup and the jeep was named Nellie Bell."

Misty, Kandi, and Wendy enthusiastically clapped their hands. "Very good," Misty said with a wide smile on her face.

White beamed with satisfaction.

Another man mumbled: "Fuckin White. He's gonna win the prize."

Fleming's anger was nearing its boiling point. Sitting through this was borderline offensive.

Kandi stepped forward. "The winner is the first man who gets three questions correct. The rest of you men better put on your thinking caps or this man will win."

"Uh, White…ma'am. My name is White."

Kandi with a K smiled. "Private First Class White, this is a toughie. I need the first name, the middle initial, and the last name of both of the next two answers. Are you all ready?" She asked cheerfully.

Everyone said that they were ready.

"Here we go. What two heroes made Frostbite Falls Minnesota their home?

White was the only one to raise his hand.

Kandi smiled. "Remember it's the first name, middle initial and last name. Do you know it?

"It's Rocky and Bullwinkle, them cartoon guys," another man mumbled. "But who the fuck knew they had last names and initials and shit?"

Sandy smiled at White. "Do you know the full answer?"

"Yes I do," he replied.

"Fuckin White, he's got his shit together," someone mumbled.

"Their names are Rocky J. Squirrel and Bullwinkle T. Moose."

"And we have a winner," Kandi smiled as she, Misty, and Wendy smiled and clapped their hands.

Fleming had seen enough. "I gotta go," he whispered to White.

"Wait, see what my prize is," White insisted.

But Fleming didn't wait. He maneuvered his way through the men, and rushed out the door. Once outside he pulled up, wincing because of his feet. Fuck this fuckin shit! He said to himself. Vietnam, Doughnut Dollies and all this bullshit was just too much. Three days ago they had asked him to kill gooks; asked him to act as bait for an enemy who was determined to kill him. Today, they said it was mandatory to take part in games where he was asked: who the fuck lived in Frostbite Falls. Who would believe this shit? He asked himself. They were ordered to perform acts of unspeakable brutality and once it was done they were ordered to take part in games that a ten year old would enjoy.

And the real tragedy was he was being forced to endure this treatment for a whole year with no foreseeable way of changing the future. He felt a desperate need to find some way to take control of this world instead of always being at the mercy of men who were either trying to drive him crazy or get him killed. Fuck it! He thought. Fuck it all! He hobbled back to his tent where he was determined to smoke the joint he had bummed from White and take a nap.

CHAPTER 11

Promotions

The next morning Fleming returned from breakfast and ran into White. He learned two things: White's prize was three Superman comic books and that Fleming was to report to Captain Ronald Wiggins, the Company C.O. at 0900 hours.

Fleming saluted. "Sir, Specialist Fleming reporting as ordered, sir."

Wiggins returned the salute. "Take a seat, Fleming. How're your feet?"

Fleming couldn't help but notice that Wiggins seemed distracted and his voice tone had a weary edge to it. His face was lined with worry and the lines made him look older. But his eyes laser beamed with intensity, as if he were trying to read Fleming's mind, an attempt to assess his character. It all validated what Levine said about Wiggins being burned-out but also being a strong leader because Fleming could sense that Wiggins possessed an unlimited reserve of strength. "Sir, my feet are coming along. In a few more days they will be good as new, sir."

"I'll get straight to the point, your platoon is in bad shape, but I guess I don't have to tell you that."

"Yes, sir, I mean no, sir, you don't have to tell me we're in bad shape, sir."

"You'll get new replacements today. You'll also get a new platoon guide and a new platoon sergeant."

Everyday someone new, Fleming thought. The supply of men seemed inexhaustible.

"The company is operating under staffed. Your platoon lacks men and leadership. I took men from the other platoons and put them in yours. At least you'll have three experienced squad leaders. To make a long story short your former platoon sergeant Levine and Lieutenant Bartstell spoke highly of you as did Garret and White. I want to make you squad leader of fourth squad."

Fleming was stunned. "Sir, I...I've only been here six weeks. I'm too inexperienced. I don't want men dying because of it, sir."

"It's either you, Fields, or Doyle. From what I've heard I'd rather go with you."

Fleming was shocked that these two men would even be considered. "Sir, it's between me, Doyle, or Fields?"

Wiggins' eyes seemed to gather fire and burn more intensely, studying Fleming. "Yes, is that a factor?"

"Sir, uh, no sir, but I'll do it. I'll be squad leader, sir."

For a moment the intense look on Wiggins' face reached a fever pitch then he smiled weakly, as if smiling was a skill he had once possessed and was trying to relearn. "Well, outstanding. I think you'll do well," he finally said. "Just use what experience you've gained from your first six weeks."

"Sir, yes sir."

"You've had it tough. You've proven you can take care of yourself. Now you have to take care of your men. You do that and they'll take care of you."

Fleming instantly liked Wiggins. He seemed to care. "Yes, sir, I will. I'll do the best I can, sir, I promise you that. I don't want anybody wasted cause of me, sir."

"When it comes to good leadership concern for your men is half the battle. I wouldn't have picked you if I didn't think you could handle it. But, Fleming..." Wiggins squirmed uncomfortably in his seat. "At the risk of contradicting myself...don't care too much."

"Sir?" Fleming said confused.

Wiggins' eyes filled with compassion. "Some of your men will die. Don't let the deaths affect you or your judgment on how to lead or more will die. You must be strong. I know I'm giving you a tough job, but I believe you can handle it."

"Sir, thank you. I hope I can measure up, sir."

"You're the best we have."

Fleming smiled weakly. "Sir, I'm all you have."

Wiggins also smiled weakly. "True. But you're still a good man."

"Sir, thank you."

"One more thing. You're the most inexperienced of the new squad leaders. I thought it would be a good idea to assign Doyle and Fields to your squad."

Fleming could feel his jaw drop.

"Is there anything wrong with that, Fleming?"

Should he have them in the squad? He wondered. They were gutless, but he knew what he was getting. And they were better than two cherries. "Sir, nothing's wrong. They are experienced so they should help."

"I'm not going to strap you with men you don't want. I can put them in another squad."

"No, sir. It will be all right for now, sir."

"If you have any problems, you can talk with me. I'll have an open door policy with you. See me whenever you like."

"Sir, thank you. It makes it boocoo easier knowing I can talk to you about it, sir."

Just then White stepped into the room. "Sir, uh, the new Lieutenant is here."

"Send him in. Fleming, I'll introduce you to your new Lieutenant."

"Yes, sir." Fleming couldn't help but wonder if he was ready for this new position. He was nineteen years old and had six weeks experience. He wasn't sure if he could take care of himself, let alone take responsibility for a squad. But then he thought of all the tutorials given him by Levine and Jenks. They had taught him what was expected of an Infantryman and a leader in Vietnam, as if they had known that one day he would be in this position.

The new Lieutenant, Daniel Ryerson, reported in then took a seat.

"Lieutenant Ryerson this is one of your squad leaders, Sergeant Bill Fleming." Wiggins looked at Fleming. "I'm making you an acting sergeant. I forgot to tell you that."

"Yes, sir. Thank you, sir."

"Don't thank me. An acting sergeant has the responsibility of a sergeant but not the pay. But in six to seven months, I am sure I can get you real stripes."

"Sir, I appreciate it."

Lieutenant Ryerson offered Fleming a handshake. "It's a pleasure, sergeant."

Fleming shook his hand. "Sir, thank you. It's my pleasure."

"I'm sure we'll work well together out there," Ryerson said with a smile.

Fleming returned the smile. The new Lieutenant had no idea what waited for him out there. He had the dedication and eagerness of a cherry. He looked capable at six feet tall and a powerful one hundred and ninety pounds; however, his small, almost delicate mouth and nose gave him the appearance of a choirboy. His wide, brown eyes made him look as innocent as Bambi.

"Sir," Fleming said to Wiggins. "Maybe I should leave, sir, so you and Lieutenant Ryerson can talk."

Wiggins nodded his head yes. "Remember, it you ever need to talk, I have an open door policy with you."

"Yes, sir. Thank you, sir."

Ryerson smiled at Fleming. "Sergeant, I am looking forward to working with you. We'll give them more than they can handle."

"Yes, sir." Fleming said, realizing the severity of the situation. Ryerson was naïve, like any other cherry, except he was in charge. Fleming saluted both officers and left.

Yesterday, he had a desire to take some control of his life and today they put him in a position of authority – a classic case of ask and you shall receive.

Walking through the company area, he wondered about the new Lieutenant. Did he know that nothing in his life experience had prepared him for what was waiting for him in the bush? Was Captain Wiggins telling him that the platoon had been literally wiped out in the last operation and lacked sufficient men with field experience? Did he know that the platoon couldn't keep a commander? He was the platoon's third Lieutenant in the last six months. The other two had been killed in action. Did he know that the Army was mired in a piss poor losing streak in Vietnam and was hell bent on continuing the streak because it was following the very same strategy that had proven disastrous time after time? Did he know that the enemy was anywhere, everywhere…nowhere? Did he know that the game had one rule – to kill? Did ayone tell him that the killing would go on and on, but the game would never end and he'd never ever understand the game? Did he know that he'd spend weeks, maybe months, in the field with men so unlike any he had ever known? Men, who for the most part, were poor and ignorant: some had chosen Vietnam over a jail sentence; men who had been driven to the brink of sanity and were inches from plummeting over the edge. Would Captain Wiggins tell him any of this? And if so, would the new Lieutenant listen? Of course there was the slimmest chance that Ryerson would be a fearless leader of men and a lion in combat, but if that were true there would certainly be a learning phase. There were a lot of questions that needed answering. But one question was always a constant: how many men would die during the new Lieutenant's question and answering phase?

Fleming stood in formation with the rest of third platoon. As Captain Wiggins had promised the platoon had been reinforced with veterans giving them ten men with combat experience including three experienced squad leaders. Raines, the fourth squad's leader had been transferred from second platoon. Ramirez, first squad's leader, was also from second Platoon. Pierson, an African American, was from first platoon and was second squad's leader.

Although his feet were responding to treatment, Fleming was still wearing sandals. A cherry from first squad pointed at him and laughed.

Ramirez, the squad leader, placed his face inches from the cherry. "What the fuck you laughing at, you cherry cunt? That man got his feet fucked up on an operation and he still killed twenty gooks. You wanna go over and fuck with him, cause I can get that shit arranged?"

The cherry lowered his head. "No, sergeant."

"You're lucky I don't let him loose on your sorry cherry ass."

Fleming held back a smile. He understood a veteran's insolent sense of pride when a cherry invaded his world. A veteran wore his filth and wounds like a badge of honor; a symbol of a man who belonged to an elite club or fraternity. Cherries weren't shit, he realized, until they had suffered.

Many of the new cherries were either Black or Latino. Most of them were posturing with the attitude and bearing of inner city toughs. Most of them were from poor disadvantaged backgrounds. It was the new equality. Levine had compared it to polo. The poor would never play polo, he had said, and the rich would never play Vietnam.

Just then Lieutenant Ryerson approached the formation. "Men, I'm your new Platoon Leader Lieutenant Dan Ryerson. I am as new as some of you men. Captain Wiggins has assured me that we have excellent squad leaders. Our new platoon sergeant, Frank Lebeau has had a previous combat tour and should fit in nicely. We will all do fine."

Fleming couldn't help but notice that Ryerson's voice lacked confidence. He sounded different a short while ago when Fleming had met him in Wiggins' office. Captain Wiggins must have set the Lieutenant straight about what to expect in Vietnam, Fleming thought. Then Fleming's thoughts drifted toward Lebeau. He wondered how he would stack up when compared to Levine.

Sergeant Lebeau approached Ryerson and performed a snappy parade ground salute. Then Ryerson moved away.

Lebeau began pacing up and down the front line of men warily eyeing each one. "I'll keep this short. What I see before me is a slack, undisciplined platoon. I will change that. Welcome back, troops. You're in the Army again. I want all the squad leaders to report to Lieutenant Ryerson's tent. The rest of you people are dismissed."

Ten minutes later, everyone was gathered in Ryerson's tent. Lebeau stood in front of the men. "I ain't pulling any punches. I don't believe in that. You squad leaders are in positions of respect and authority, employed by the United States Army. You need to look like men who deserve to be treated with respect and authority. Look llike men employed by the United States Army. Every one of you needs a haircut. You're wearing unauthorized jewelry. Some of you got writing on your helmets. I want all the shit cleaned up. You start looking sharp, you'll act sharp and so will the men under you."

"We ain't never had to do this before," Ramirez said. "Why now?"

"It's simple. There's a new sheriff in town and he demands it. Don't fight me on this. I can guaranfuckintee' you I'm gonna' win. You'll get haircuts, the peace signs will be taken off your helmets, and you will throw the love beads away. I hope that came in loud and clear. Now get outta' here and the next time I see you, you all better look different."

Lebeau's words had filled the men with tension; it was evident in their body language as they left the tent. They were good men, Fleming thought, or Captain Wiggins wouldn't have picked them for their positions. They could handle themselves in the field and that was their most important duty. Today's soldiers were not fighting for God, the flag, Mom, or apple pie. No one had ever told them why they were fighting. They were just ordered to fight. No one had given them a sensible strategy for winning the war. They were just told to go out and kill. They were all putting their lives on the line for a war most of them didn't believe in. It stood to reason that a price had to be paid for that kind of sacrifice. Being allowed to wear hair a bit longer than regulation or to write a few slogans on helmet liners seemed a ridiculously small price to pay.

Eagerly anticipating the upcoming day, Van leapt from his sleeping mat and quickly dressed. The past week had been spent in the hospital learning from the doctors. Even though the hours were long and the work was never ending, he felt exhilarated at day's end.

Just then another man in his platoon approached him. "Van, Chi wants to see us all in a conference room. He sent me to get you."

Van accompanied the other man. Everyone in the platoon treated Van with respect. Chi and Dan had spoken highly of his actions during the last firefight. Everyone also appreciated his skill as a medic. They knew they could count on him during battle and if they were ever wounded, he might be the difference between life and death.

A few moments later Van and the platoon were seated in the conference room. Chi and Colonel Quoc were there.

Chi's face broke into a huge smile that still sent chills through Van: mere words could not describe Chi's ugliness, especially when this horribly scarred man smiled.

"Colonel Quoc has seen fit to upgrade our platoon's status. I am being put in charge of a small company. In a few weeks we will be getting fifty new men bringing our total to eighty. I have already promoted three men and am ready to announce promotions for two more." He smiled at Dan and Van. "Dan, Van, you are now squad leaders. I would not have attained my position if it weren't for each and every one of you. Tonight we celebrate. Some of the local villagers will be bringing us food and liquor. Colonel Quoc has arranged for thirty women to be brought in for our pleasure. Have a great time tonight. We have also been given responsibility for a new operation. I will have more word on that later. For now, you are dismissed. Enjoy yourselves tonight."

Everyone rushed to Van and Dan to offer more words of congratulation. Van accepted the praise while rushing through the wellwishers and out of the room to catch up with Chi.

"Sergeant Chi," Van called to him.

Twenty feet ahead of Van Chi stopped and turned to him.

"Sergeant, I don't want this promotion. I am grateful for your trust in me, but I am too inexperienced. I want no one dying on my account."

For the first time, Van saw compassion light on Chi's face. "You are wrong and you judge yourself too harshly. That day when we fought the Americans you saved my life. You saved Dan's. We were disoriented and confused and would have been killed but you were aware enough to know that we had to wait before returning back here. You keep your wits about you when others lose theirs. If you're a squad leader, men won't die because of your inexperience. Men will live because of your poise under pressure. You can refuse the position, if that's your wish. But you will be saving lives by accepting it. Think about it and talk with me later." Chi left.

Van started back to his quarters. A part of him had always known that he was strong during pressure situations. Faith in Buddha gave him strength. He had no fear of death and having no fear left his mind clear to think rationally. If he could help others stay alive then it was his duty, what Buddha demanded of him. Van turned and went in the opposite direction in search of Chi to tell him he had decided to accept the position.

Fleming studied the faces of the men standing before him. Earl Vines: a six foot two, two hundred pound African American with raven black skin. Everything about Vines exuded power, confidence, and quiet dignity.

Ted Carter: a two hundred pound Caucasian with milky white skin, rosy tinted cheeks and reddish blonde hair. He was big and soft, the exact opposite of the muscular Vines.

Leon Carlyle: An African American, five foot ten, one hundred forty-five pounds with skin the color of coffee with cream. His hair was styled in an Afro, bordering on the extreme length Army Regulations allowed. His eyes blazed with a fierce intensity.

Jerome Washington: Another African American, he stood six foot one and weighed about a hundred and eighty. He had a long, muscular build. His smile was so open and friendly that Fleming was instantly warmed by it.

Gonzalo Rojas: A Puerto Rican stood five seven and was a muscular one hundred and fifty pounds. Rojas kept his eyes peeled to the ground and Fleming thought him insecure and introverted. It took only one time for Rojas to look him in the eyes for Fleming to know the truth. Rojas exuded strength and an acute sense of his own self worth as a human being. Fleming felt no hostility in him.

And then there was Doyle and Fields. Fleming could only hope they would be no trouble.

"I'm your squad leader, Bill Fleming. We got one mission, to stay alive and keep each other alive. Spend any time here and you learn the only thing you need to know about Nam – you are here to survive three hundred and sixty five day and go home, nothing more, nothing less. Every man will do his part and maybe we'll all get through this. No one skates when it comes to the team's welfare."

Then Fleming assigned Vines, the strongest man, an M-60 machine gun. Since the squad was under strength he wouldn't be assigned an assistant-gunner as was normally the case.

"I appreciate you giving me this bad motherfucker," Vines said. "I plan on going home in one piece, sergeant."

Being called sergeant was strange; it was what Fleming had called Levine. "My name is Fleming. I want everyone to call me Fleming, not sarge or sergeant, it's Fleming, got it?"

Everyone answered in the affirmative. Then Fleming assigned Carlyle an M-79 grenade launcher. Carlyle gave him an unbridled look of hostility and Fleming knew he would be a problem. Fleming excused everyone and took Carlyle and Vines to supply for their weapons. Then they went to a practice range to fire them.

At the practice range, Vines fired the 60 with deadly accuracy.

Fleming was awe-struck at how quickly Vines took to the weapon. Fleming needed to see no more. He excused Vines and he headed back to the company area.

It was now Carlyle's turn. He fired and was way off target. After a few more tries he failed to improve.

"Man, you ain't even close. Take your fuckin' time. It's like you ain't even aiming."

"Guess this black boy can't get the hang of this thing."

"Cut the fuckin shit and just fire the fuckin weapon?"

"Yes, Massah."

"I said cut the fuckin shit. I ain't gonna tell you again. You wanta play games, you'll be dead in a month. Listen to those who know more than you, if you want your cherry ass to stay alive."

Carlyle studied Fleming for a long hard moment then aimed the weapon and fired. This time he was a few feet away from the target. After a few more tries, he was hitting the target every time.

"Good, you done good. Let's call it a day."

They left the range for the company area. On the way, nary a word was spoken by either man.

That night Fleming sat on his cot reading and writing letters to his family and his sister Hope. She had written him at least once a week, always saying how proud she was of him. It brought a smile to his face when she wrote that her teacher let her read his letters to her fifth grade class. Now all her friends knew that her big brother was a real live hero, she had written. Then he read a letter from his mother and he learned that his cousin, Dan Shepherd, had enlisted and was in Vietnam as a Ranger with the 101st Airborne. His mom asked him to write Dan and keep in touch with him. Fleming had always gotten along with his cousin and truly liked him. He would write the letter, only because of his mother's request. But Fleming had already written him once, when was in basic training and he had never written back. And his cousin had promised to write. And he loved to write, Fleming thought. Dan was always writing stories and one day wanted to become a published author.

He finished the letters to his sister and cousin then one of the cherries, Ted Carter, approached and asked to talk. For the next hour

Carter rambled incessantly about how much he enjoyed the Army. He seemed like a genuinely nice person minus the misguided, gung ho bravado of most cherries. During the whole conversation, Carter munched on candy bars and often spoke about his weight problem. He said this would be his last night of indulging his sweet tooth and that he was determined to lose weight.

The only other person in the tent was Rojas, who was also writing letters. Everyone else had gone to the club for a few beers and to watch the movie. At 2100 hours the three of them went to bed.

"ARRRGHHH! OH MY GOD! SOMEBODY HELP ME!"

Fleming awakened. He sprang from his bed and started toward the screams coming from Carter's cot. He reached Carter the same time as Rojas, the only other man in the tent.

The scream was now one long agonizing wail.

Fleming ripped away Carter's mosquito netting. "Jesus Christ!" he said staggering back.

Rojas uttered a string of Spanish.

A rat the size of a small terrier dog was gnawing on Carter's face. Blood was pouring down his lips and chin.

Instinctively, Fleming reached for the rat but pulled his hands back in disgust. He had to remove the rat from Carter's face, but he hated rats.

Rojas didn't hesitate. He shoved Fleming away. In one blurring motion, he dropped to one knee and shot out his right hand at the rat.

The rat's body arched backward.

Rojas withdrew his hand – the rat was somehow attached. He placed the rat and his hand on the ground and stepped on the rat with his left foot. He removed six inches of bloody switchblade.

For a moment Fleming forgot about Carter and stared with wonder at Rojas. Then he looked back at Carter.

The rat had eaten away most of Carter's lips and much of the skin around his cheek and chin.

"His face," Rojas said with a soft tone of disgust and wonder.

"We gotta get him to the aid station," Fleming said. Then Fleming saw a stain on Carter's bed sheets and like a key fitting a lock the mystery of the attacking rat was solved.

Rojas and Fleming helped a moaning Carter to his feet and then helped him dress. Then they quickly dressed and led Carter out of the tent.

A half hour later, after depositing Carter at the Evacuation station, Fleming and Rojas started back to the company area.

"You were quick with that knife, Rojas," Fleming said.

"It came in handy back home. I'm from New York, Spanish Harlem."

"How didja' learn to use that thing?"

"I didn't want to join a gang so I took up boxing– "

"Boxing," Fleming interrupted impressed. "Were you any good?"

"I was New York State's lightweight Golden Gloves champ two years in a row."

"That's damn good. Do boxing gyms teach you how to use a knife?"

"I learned that myself. Once I learned how to punch, it was pretty easy to learn how to fight with a knife. Basically, just box and stab."

"You gonna' continue with boxing?"

"I wanna' go to school but I don't have the money. I figure with what I save here and the G.I. Bill I can go to college when I get home."

"So you enlisted?"

Rojas looked at him for a long moment, studying him, wondering whether or not to speak. He decided to speak. "I was kinda forced to enlist."

"Whatta ya mean?"

"One night I was jumped by four guys. I beat up two of them. The other two took out knives. I took out mine. I cut them up pretty bad. The cops asked no questions. They took me to jail. I told them I was innocent but they hear that a lot in New York City. A public defender took my case and worked out a deal. If I pleaded guilty the judge would let me off but I had to join the Army. So here I am."

Rojas told the story without the slightest trace of anger or bitterness. "You're a tough guy. Hopefully you make it outta here in one piece and go to college."

"It's tough here, huh?"

"There it fuckin is. The gooks are everywhere. The Army sends you on some hairy operations. The last one was real bad." A sad, melancholy expression filled Fleming's face. He paused for a moment, thinking of Levine and the others. "It's hard to talk about. Some real good guys got wasted. That's why I'm a squad leader, everyone else is dead."

"Bad shit," Rojas said. "Real bad shit."

"There it is."

For a few moments they walked in silence. The night was alive with exploding rockets, mortars and small arms fire. It was all coming from way outside L.Z. English's Perimeter: however they could see tracer illumination lighting up the sky.

"Do rats attack like that all the time?" Rojas asked.

Fleming frowned. "Carter was eating in bed. I saw chocolate stains on his sheets. The rat smelled the food on his face and I guess it thought his face was food."

"Man, that's gross."

"That's da' Nam. You're gonna' see boocoo worse than that. Boocoo worse."

"Fuck," Rojas replied.

"Goddamnit, Fleming, wake up!"

Fleming opened his eyes to see Doc Garret's snarling face standing above him.

"Get your lazy ass up, you cherry fuck!"

Fleming wiped sleep from his eyes. "Damn, good morning to you, too, Garret."

"Fuck you and fuck your good morning, you dumb ass cherry!"

"What the fuck did I do?"

"What the fuck did I do?" Garret mimicked. "Why didn't you call me last night? One of my men goes to the hospital and I gotta' hear it from some other medic? You made me look bad. You're a squad leader. You should know better."

"I didn't know it was a squad leader's job to tell the platoon medic that one of his men got bitten by a rat."

"You're a dumb ass you know that? He's my man too. He's my responsibility."

Fleming got out of bed and put on his fatigue trousers. "Okay, the next time someone gets bitten by a rat, I'll let you know." Fleming said in a placating tone.

"What, you're fucking with me? Now you're fucking with me?"

"No, seriously, from now on, I tell you if one of my men gets hurt. No problem."

Garret studied him for a long moment. "You're entitled to a mistake." Then his eyes narrowed fiercely. "You owe me one."

"What do I owe you?"

"It don't mean nothing. I'm gonna' ask your sorry ass for a favor one day! One! Just one fuckin favor! It ain't no big thing. You got a motherfuckin' problem with that?" Garret said with a rapid fire, staccato tone.

"Okay, Christ, okay."

Garret nodded his head yes. "Is this rat bait new guy all right?"

"I don't know. I'm gonna check him out this afternoon." Fleming smiled. "You're so concerned. Why don't you come along?" He purposely used a voice tone that was confrontational and challenging. Let's see Garret put his money where his mouth is, he thought.

Garret smirked, his eyes shined like two pieces of flint. "All right, when you going?"

Fleming had the distinct impression that he had just been hustled. "Uh, this afternoon," he said, taken aback by Garret's attitude.

A moment passed. "I'd like that, like to see how the fuckin cherry's makin out. When exactly are ya' leaving?"

Fleming warily eyed Garret. "About a hour from now."

"Come by and get me. And, Fleming," Garret said with a smirking smile on his face. "Make sure you don't fuck this up." Then Garret left.

Fleming knew that he had been set him up. But set up for what? He wondered. They were visiting a man in the hospital.

Just then White walked into the hootch. "How're your feet?"

"Coming along." He motioned to his feet with a hand gesture. "I'm wearing these sandals another day or two then I'm gonna try boots."

"Captain Wiggins wanted me to ask you about the new guy, the one that got bit by a rat. He gonna be all right?"

"His face is pretty chewed up. Me, Rojas and Garret are goin to see him in about an hour. I guess we'll find out more then."

"This Rojas guy, he stabbed the rat with a switchblade?"

"He was like lightning with that thing. That knife shot out and came back with a rat attached to it."

"What is he? Like some kinda psycho, bad ass, gang dude or something?"

"Nah, he's a good dude."

"I saw Doc Garret leavin here. What did he want?" White asked.

"He was super pissed cause I didn't let him know about Carter getting bit. He was about ready to kick my ass."

"He is one crazy motherfucker. You know he re-upped?"

"No fucking way. He doesn't seem like a lifer type."

"He re-upped for another tour of duty in the field. He had six months left in Nam when they assigned him to the Evac.Station. They do that to all of the medics. All of them get flaky. They think they're invincible and try to run through bullets to get to wounded men. Doc

Garret's the worst. He's got two Bronze Stars, an Army Commendation Medal and two Purple Hearts. He's flaky. He carries just two canteens of water so he can carry extra plasma bottles. He steals medical supplies so he has extra in the field. The dude that bunks next to him says he has a medical catalogue. He sends away for his own medical stuff – spends his own money, too. He said that Garret complains that the Army doesn't give him enough equipment to do his job. He re-upped for six years and another tour in the Nam so he could get back in the field. Says he wants to be where people really need him. He's flaky."

"Damn," Fleming replied. "That's either super dedicated or super flaky fuckin' crazy."

"He's super flaky fuckin' crazy," White said.

That afternoon, Fleming introduced Garret to Rojas and the three of them started toward the Evacuation Station.

"Remember, you owe me," Garret immediately said to Fleming. "Cause of – what was that fucker's name – Harper?"

"Carter. His name is Carter. What this I owe you shit?"

"You're freakin' the fuck out over this? One day I'm gonna' ask you to do me a favor. It don't mean nothing."

Fleming gave him an acidic smile. "Don't mean nothing? Why you keep bringin up this favor thing if it don't mean nothing?"

"Maybe you worry too fuckin much. Whadda' ya think?"

"Maybe you're the type of dude that makes a man worry too fuckin much – whadda' ya think?"

Garret smirked at Fleming then turned to Rojas. "You got an excuse, you're a cherry and cherries don't know shit. But you still fucked up. You owe me too. You got that?"

Rojas looked at Fleming for help.

"He's a weird fucking dude," Fleming said. "But I been tryin' and I can't figure out how owing him a favor is such a big deal."

"That's what I've been saying," Garret said enthusiastically agreeing. "What can it hurt?"

Ten minutes later, they arrived at the 25th Evac. Hospital – a two-story building with sandbags atop a corrugated tin roof.

"That's one fucked up looking hospital," Fleming remarked.

"It may not look like much," Garret said. "But if you're ever treated in there, you'll get the best medical attention available. There's some dedicated dudes in there."

Fleming gave him a weak smile. "I think me and Rojas would rather just visit. We ain't interested in findin' out how good your buddies are."

They entered the hospital and were taken to see Carter's Doctor. They learned that he had been medavacced to Saigon. From there he would be sent to Japan where they would attempt to rebuild his lower lip. The Doctor was sure Carter would be sent home, ending his Vietnam tour.

Then Garret said he wanted to visit some friends and asked Fleming and Rojas to accompany him to medical supply. Suddenly Garret called out to a man walking in the halls. "Wait here," Garret said to Fleming and Rojas. "That dude owes me boocoo favors." Garret hurried over to the man.

"What are these favors Garret keeps talking about?" Rojas asked.

"I don't know, but now I'm startin to worry."

Garret smiled at his friend and they began speaking. Soon they were arguing. When the man's body visibly sagged and he nodded his head meekly, it was apparent that Garret had won the argument. Garret smiled triumphantly and vigorously shook the man's hand.

"Garret just conned that guy into something," Rojas said.

Fleming nodded his head in assent. "I'm getting a bad feeling about this."

Garret hurried back to them and smiled. "Follow me."

"Follow you where?" Fleming demanded.

"It's time to pay back that favor."

"The favor again – we ain't doin shit till you tell us what's up." Fleming insisted. "You're up to some kinda shit and we ain't getting dragged into it."

The other man called to Garret: "If we're gonna do this we do it now or we don't do it at all."

"You heard him. We gotta go. I'll tell you on the way." He grabbed Fleming's arm and pulled him along. "I'm picking up a few things – that's all. What I'm doing is good for you, your squad, for the whole platoon, for the whole company for that matter."

"Fuck you. My old man told me to watch out for people doing things for my own good. What are you doing for my own good?"

"Picking up supplies, I'm requisitioning provisions we'll need in the field. The Army gives us diddly-squat. The ARVNS get boocoo more than us, so I gotta find ways to get my own shit."

For a fleeting moment Fleming wondered if he should ask Garret if he knew anything about the South selling supplies to the North but now was not the time for it. "So what you're saying is we're stealing supplies?"

"Stealing is a real fucking ugly word…but, yeah, I guess if you gotta' use a word that's the word you'd use."

"Stealing fucking supplies, Garret? That's a federal offense or some shit. I mean we could end up in L.B.J. (Long Binh Jail)."

"Sometimes you gotta go the extra mile to get shit done. You're a sports guy. You know all about that, goin the extra mile. We're goin the extra mile."

"By fuckin stealing?"

"What can I do if they don't give me enough supplies? We need this shit."

Fleming's face tightened with determination. "I ain't going to fuckin' jail, you can bet your ass on that. So find another way to get your shit."

Garret gave him a bitter smile. "The next time we're on an operation and men are getting all fucked up and I ain't got enough shit to treat them, we'll all know whose fault it is. Men will be lying around dying, fucking dying, cause you didn't have the balls to help me. And, Fleming." A thin, evil smile spread on Garret's face. "I'm gonna remind you of this day. You can bet your ass on that."

Fleming had a vivid mental picture of wounded men lying in the field without plasma bottles attached to them. "Oh, Man," he muttered. "I can just see that shit happening, too."

"You'll help me then?" Garret asked quickly.

"Yeah, yeah, I'll help," Fleming said with a defeated tone.

Garret grabbed Fleming's arm and pulled him along. "I knew you cared, Fleming. I just knew it."

They reached medical supply where Garret's friend waited. They nervously scouted the area before opening a door and then everyone rushed inside. Then Garret's friend quickly locked the door. Garret greedily grabbed plasma bottles, bandages, endeotracheal tubes, scalpels and anything he could lay his hands on. He filled a laundry bag then began stuffing supplies into everyone's fatigue pockets.

"Here, put this under your arms." He handed Fleming and Rojas each two plasma bottles.

"How in the hell we supposed to walk with these things under our arms?" Fleming asked.

Garret rolled his eyes. "Jesus, Fleming, like this." Garret stuck a plasma bottle under each arm and demonstrated; it looked as if his arms were tied to his side and he couldn't swing them naturally. Consequentially he walked with a stiff, almost effeminate gait.

Rojas found the sight comical and chuckled.

"Man, you look like a fairy walking like that." Fleming said with a smile.

Garret returned the smile. "It's okay, I ain't gonna be walking like a fairy, you two are."

"Why are we gonna—"

"I ain't got time to answer bullshit questions," Garret interrupted." We gotta hurry."

"You're taking too much," Garret's friend protested. "If you get caught, I am truly fucked."

"Don't worry about it," Garret said. "It don't mean nothing." He grabbed Fleming's arm. "Let's go."

"How the fuck you gonna' get by the MP'S?" Garret's friend demanded.

"MP'S!" Fleming shouted. "You never said dick about MP'S. I ain't – "

"What are they gonna' do – send us to Nam?" Garret countered. "Just trust me. I got a plan."

"That's the problem," Garret's friend said with a bitter smirk on his face. "You always got some kinda' plan."

Garret grabbed Fleming's arm and pulled him along. They exited the room, hurried through supply and stopped outside, thirty feet from a shack that housed the MP'S.

"Listen up," Garret said.

A wide-eyed Fleming and Rojas stared at Garret.

Garret took one look at their ultra serious facial expressions and started laughing.

"What the fuck's so funny?" Fleming demanded.

It took effort before Garret could stifle his laughter and he said: "Just follow my lead. I'll go first. I'll set it up for you two. You just walk real fast by the MP'S. Try and look scared." Again he studied their faces. "You're gonna do real good in that department." He looked back at the MP'S then gave Fleming and Rojas one last look. "Let's do this."

Garret hurried to the MP'S waving his arms wildly. "HEY! HEY!" he screamed. "Call somebody, fast!"

A MP, engrossed in reading a Playboy, looked up from the magazine at Garret.

Fleming and Rojas started away – walking with their strange gait.

"I'm a medic," Garret said. "I was visiting one of my men when this dude pulled out a frag! I just did get out of there. He's holding everyone prisoner. He's gonna' pull the pin. You gotta' do something! Call somebody!"

The MP reached for a field phone.

Rojas and Fleming slithered past.

"Christ, fourteen days and a wake up and I'm dealing with this shit! I'm too short for this!" Garret protested then he hurried away. He quickly caught up with a running Rojas and Fleming. "Just walk. It looks suspicious if you run. It looks funny."

Looks funny, Fleming thought angrily. Walking with plasma bottles stuck under both their arms he and Rojas couldn't look anything but funny.

Five minutes later, they approached their company area. They hurried inside the compound and scurried inside a bunker for concealment.

"Jeezzzusss!" Fleming cried, removing plasma bottles from under his arm.

All three men gave each other a series of solemn glances. Then they broke up into wild laughter. They began clapping each other on the back.

Garret was laughing so hard he could barely speak. "T-T-That was e-easy as hell," he sputtered out. "We'll go b-b-back tomorrow, do the s-s-same thing."

A new round of laughter erupted from them.

"N-N-No way,' Fleming said still laughing so hard it was difficult to speak. "We're p-p-paid up. We d-d-don't owe you s-s-shit."

A few moments later when the laughter subsided, Fleming thought it was time to broach the subject that had been nagging him. "Did you enlist in the Army or were you drafted?"

Garret's expression immediately turned fierce. "I enlisted. What the fuck's wrong with that? You enlisted."

"Mellow out. I'm just asking a question. It don't mean nothing."

"Damn right, it don't mean nothing."

"I'm just talking, trying to get to know you better. Why did you enlist? Did you always wanna' go in the Army or something?"

"Fuck no, I didn't always wanna' go in the fucking Army." A moment of silence passed. "When I was in high school, I couldn't control my temper. My chief claim to fame was getting into fights."

"God, I would have never guessed that," Fleming remarked sarcastically.

Wondering if Fleming was ridiculing him, Garret studied him for a long moment before continuing. "I was in reform school for awhile. All them shrinks said I was anti-social that I'd never amount to jack-shit. Senior year in high school I got in a fight with the school principal. The bastard said I had bad upbringing. I had no upbringing. When I was three years old my old man went out for a pack of smokes. The son of a bitch never came back. My mom brought me and my younger brother up alone. The dip-shit principal knew it too. I figured he was cutting on my mom so I cold-cocked the sucker, broke his jaw. The bastard expelled me."

"The bastard had no sense of humor," Fleming said wryly.

Again, Garret warily eyed Fleming before continuing: "I was walkin' home from school feeling real shitty cause I knew my mom would be upset. Then I saw a recruiting poster. You know the one – the dude's face is all camouflaged. He's got a Ranger tab on his arm. It was a bad-ass poster. I walked into a Recruiter's office and tried to enlist. I was seventeen, expelled from school so the Army looked pretty damn good. The recruiter said I was too young but I could get in if my mom signed the papers. She didn't want to do it. Didn't want me goin to Nam. I told her the Army would straighten me out. I didn't wanna cause her no more trouble with my fights. She signed the papers. The only reason she did it was because she knew I really wanted to go. She's a good lady." Garret chuckled. "I went in and started fucking up right away. I got in about four fights in basic training. I thought I was gonna' get kicked out. Then I got orders for medic's school. For the first time I found something I really dug. I did real good too. Then I got orders for the Nam and there it is."

"Okay, you enlisted. But I heard that you just re-enlisted?"

Garret studied him, his face undergoing various stages of rage. "Yeah, Motherfucker, I re-enlisted. You got a problem with that?"

"Settle the fuck down. It don't mean nothing."

206 | TIM DAVIS

"Yer Goddamned right. Don't mean I'm a lifer or nothing."

"I ain't calling you a lifer. I heard you did it to get back in the field. I'm just wondering why the fuck anybody would do that shit. I mean you know enough about the field to know it is a real easy place to get wasted."

"I wanna' be where I'm needed, where I do my best work. I wanted back in the field so I re-upped. I figure it would be better for everyone. I got a ten grand re-enlistment bonus. I can save at least another six grand spending two years here. When I get out I can go to College. I'll have sixteen grand, the G.I. Bill. I can study to be a doctor. I'll make good bread. I'll be able to take care of my mom."

"I hate to point out the obvious. Two more years in the field, there is a real good chance you could get wasted. How you gonna take care of your mom then?" Fleming knew it was bad luck to talk about getting killed, but he had asked anyway.

Garret looked at him for a long hard moment. "I thought about it, thought about it boocoo. Men have always shit on my Mom…my old man, even me, with my fights. I buy it over here my Mom gets my sixteen grand and the ten grand from the insurance policy. A man will finally do something nice for her. She deserves it."

Rojas and Fleming both look at him with wide-eyed wonder.

Garret stood. "I ain't talked this much in ages." He gave them a weak smile. "Gotta' run. I had fun. We'll have to do it again sometime." Without another word Garret gathered his booty and left the bunker.

Fleming turned to Rojas. They stared at each other for a moment, both shocked at what Garret had just told them. They said nothing. They stood and walked out of the bunker and to whatever destiny fate held for them.

CHAPTER 12

Going Home

Van sat next to Hoi in a conference room waiting for Colonel Quoc to brief them on an upcoming operation. Today, like every day, his mind was filled with thoughts of medicine. He wondered how he, a farm boy could be so skilled? The elders had taught that in desperate times Buddha always provided. If man kept faith in Buddha and in himself then man would always reap Buddha's harvest. Medicine was Buddha's gift during these desperate times.

Just then Quoc entered the room and Chi called the men to attention.

"NVA command will undergo a major troop infiltration from Cambodia and Laos," Quoc said. "This will conclude in a major operation. We will need a few months to infiltrate equipment and personnel into an area east of the Ngok Kam Leat Mountains in Kontum Province. Once this is accomplished a massive offensive will be launched against American bases operating in the area. Four Companies of Viet Cong, including this company, will play a major role in the operation's infiltration phase. Your mission will be to gain support from villagers in the area and to divert American patrols from the infiltration points. You're to harass the Americans by employing snipers, mortar attacks and hit and run missions."

Quoc moved to a wall and removed a bamboo cover to reveal a map. Then he turned to the men. "Sergeant Chi's Company will operate in this area." With a pointer, Quoc outlined an area on the map.

Van nearly jumped from his seat. Quoc was outlining the area near Van's village.

"We will win the support of the villagers in this area, and we will operate near this village."

Van tingled with excitement. Quoc had just pointed to Van's boyhood home.

Quoc continued: "We need the local villagers' support. This is always easy to gain because of atrocities committed by Americans."

Quoc failed to mention the North's atrocities against this very same village, Van thought. However, there would be no resistance from the village. It was only six months ago that the NVA had brutalized the village. They would never forget the consequences of incurring the NVA's wrath.

Quoc continued speaking but Van's mind was filled with thoughts of returning home. Time passed and suddenly everyone stood and began filing out of the room. So engrossed in his own thoughts Van had missed most of the briefing. He stood and left with the rest of the men.

Once outside, Hoi grabbed Van's arm. "We are going home," he said with a huge smile. "We can finally put our plan into action."

Van had no idea what he was talking about.

Hoi noticed the vacant look on Van's face. "Our plan," he emphasized. "We can talk to the village about letting the Americans relocate them. Then we can defect."

Now he remembered. He hadn't really given much thought to Hoi's scheme; it hinged on the belief that the villagers would relocate. No Vietnamese would ever leave the village of their birth.

A childlike confused expression settled on Hoi's face. "You still plan on going with me to the American side?"

"I won't put the village in danger. Their safety is my first priority."

"Mine, too. I would never put the village in harm's way."

"What do you think the Americans will have us do if we defect?" Van asked.

Hoi's facial expression was blank. "What do you mean?"

It was just as Van had expected. Hoi had put no thought into this. "If we go to the Americans we will fight for them. It will be no different than what we're doing now."

Hoi's eyes darted back and forth in fear and confusion.

"Other soldiers told me Americans use our soldiers for combat. I can work in a South Vietnamese hospital. What can you do? If I am in a hospital you will be alone."

Hoi's face seemed to die. The anguish in his expression filled Van with empathy. "If you start helping me in the hospital, you can acquire basic medical skills then you may not be forced to fight."

Hope immediately filled Hoi's face. "I will. I will help you."

For the next few moments they walked in silence until Hoi said: "What will you tell the villagers about the American atrocities we've seen?"

"What atrocities?" Van asked.

"Chi said we are to tell the villagers that we have witnessed many American atrocities. Then the villagers will sympathize with us."

Now he realized what he had missed during the briefing. "I don't know. We will talk about it later."

They reached their quarters and went their separate ways.

Van lay down on his mat. Chi wanted them to lie to the villagers. If he refused he would be disobeying orders. A soldier could be put to death for disobeying orders. Lying to the villagers to get their support could only have one purpose – Chi wanted to involve them in the war. Van could think of nothing to do but pray to Buddha for guidance.

A grim faced Fleming made eye contact with an equally grim faced Rojas.

Rojas smiled weakly at him.

A blast of air hit Fleming's face as the helicopter took flight and whisked away. They were being flown into an area east of the Ngok Kam Leat Mountains as part of a battalion size operation attempting to stop the flow of NVA Regiments infiltrating into Vietnam from Cambodia and Laos. Military Intelligence had intercepted both Morse code and voice radio transmissions reporting heavy V.C. guerilla movement during the past week.

B Company along with Charley and Alpha were to patrol an area two miles from the Cambodian border. D Company was a mile east of the three companies. Further east, Third Battalion was laagered at the Battalion CP. Two battalions of Vietnamese Rangers were also along to offer assistance if needed.

From the operation's sheer size it was evident that the Army expected huge results.

Less then a half hour later, the helicopters touched down and the men disembarked. Their initial mission was to sweep to a hamlet and question villagers on V.C. and NVA activity.

Sergeant Lebeau and Lieutenant Ryerson ordered Fleming to report to them. When Fleming reached them they were kneeling on the ground studying a map.

Squinting from the sun, Lebeau looked up at Fleming. "Your squad has point. Put that new guy, Hamilton, on it."

"That ain't how it works," Fleming protested. "I know the men in my squad. You tell me we have point, I pick who's walking it."

"Well, we're making a change. Put Hamilton on point."

Hamilton had been Carter's replacement. He was an eightteen year old and had been in country for a week. "This is his first time in the field. He's the last guy I'd pick to walk point his first time in the field."

"You ain't picking him. I am. And I really don't need you telling me how to run a platoon."

Fleming realized Lebeau's motivation. He was picking the point man because he wanted to make sure the platoon knew that the new sheriff in town was indeed in charge. "I ain't telling ya' how to run the platoon. I'm telling ya' this man is way too new."

"Everybody in your squad is way too new, including you, shit for brains. Put him on point."

"I don't like it. I don't like it at all."

"And I don't like arguing with no acting jack sergeant about who's walking point." Lebeau stood and placed his face inches from

Fleming's. "I was here in 65 when you were in high school trying to cop your first feel on Mary Jane Rotten Crotch's tits, so don't tell me how to run a platoon, asshole. Put Hamilton on point."

Fleming turned to Ryereson. "L T, do I gotta do it?"

"The Lieutenant ain't got time to settle debates. I ain't telling you again!"

"Fleming," Ryerson said. "The Sergeant gave you an order. Follow it."

"This is a royal fuck up," Fleming cursed before walking away.

Fleming stood in front of the squad. "We're moving out in five. Hamilton, you got point."

Hamilton looked up at Fleming with wide-eyed wonder. "Point! This is – "

"You got point," Fleming interrupted him.

The expression on Hamilton's face was a curious mixture of fear, wonder and confusion.

"There's one simple rule – you see anything out of the ordinary open fire," Fleming said. "You'll have plenty of support. Just pay attention. Keep your shit together."

"Do I really gotta do this?"

"Yeah, you really gotta do this."

Lebeau called for them to move out and Fleming ordered them to leave.

They started toward the village.

Fleming knew that the V.C. and the NVA were watching them, simply because the V.C. and the NVA were always watching them. Normally they wouldn't attack in broad daylight but a hit and run ambush was always a threat. All in all, Fleming's greatest fear was Hamilton opening up and killing an innocent villager.

Watching Americans advancing forward, Van lay hidden in a tree line thinking of the past week's events. He and the others had been restricted to an underground bunker complex two klicks from the village. Yesterday Chi had put him in charge of this ambush, consisting of Hoi, four others and a second squad. Presently, Chi and Dan were in the village infiltrating three North Vietnamese women among the villagers. The women were to act as spies in an effort to discourage villagers from divulging intelligence to any American soldiers who entered the village. It would only take minutes to place the women. Chi and Dan certainly had time to do that and take part in this ambush. Simple hit and run operations always satisfied their blood lust. Why would they choose to stay with the villagers when they could kill Americans? Van wondered. But then seeing that the American had gotten closer he shook himself from his thoughts and concentrated on the job at hand.

Moving forward, Fleming knew there was absolutely no chance of Hamilton firing on an innocent civilian. The entire NVA Army could walk right by him and he'd never even notice. Cherry Hamilton was walking point with cherry expertise. He constantly looked backward, checking to see if the men were following; when he wasn't doing that, he was dabbing sweat from his face with a towel or drinking water from a canteen. He was doing everything but looking out for the enemy.

Van mentally rehashed the ambush plan. The two teams were in a classic L-shaped ambush position. They would open fire then flee to an underground bunker; it was a standard hit and run ambush that would kill some Americans. A mine had also been placed in the American's path. If it were tripped it would kill or maim more Americans. The Americans would then enter the village frustrated and angry. Van could only pray that they wouldn't vent their anger on the villagers.

Van aimed his weapon.

Fleming shook his head in frustration and wonder as he watched Hamilton gulp water from his canteen. He was paying no attention to the terrain and what was in front of him.

Van and the others opened fire on the point man. The men on the flank opened fire on Americans on the right flank.

Fleming dropped down instantly.

Frozen in place, Carlyle stared aimlessly in Hamilton's direction.

Fleming scrambled to his knees, grabbed Carlyle's rucksack and pulled him violently to the ground.

Carlyle landed with a resounding thud.

AK-47 rounds whistled over Fleming and Carlyle's head.

"VINES, WASHINGTON," Fleming yelled. "PUT FIRE ON THE TREELINE IN FRONT OF US!"

Rojas crawled toward the downed men on the left flank and found one man alive. "MEDIC!" he screamed. "I NEED A MEDIC."

"GRRR!" Doc Garret growled doglike as he ran toward Rojas.

Fleming slapped Carlyle's helmet. "You okay? You got your head outta your ass?"

"Yeah, I'm fine," Carlyle answered, sounding a bit shaken.

"Lay cover fire on that tree line." Fleming fired a burst of M-16 fire at the tree line.

Carlyle fired his M-79, dropping grenades in the same location.

Garret reached the wounded man and began working on him while Rojas provided cover fire.

All of a sudden mortar rounds begin falling inside the platoon's position.

"Son of a bitch!" Fleming cursed. "Stay here!" he said to Carlyle. "Keep your fucking head down. And keep pouring on that cover fire."

Carlyle nodded his head yes. He continued firing his M-79.

Fleming removed his rucksack. He stood and began running across the perimeter toward the rear. Mortar rounds fell near him and shrapnel whizzed past him. He passed Sergeant Lebeau who was heading in the opposite direction.

"Where you going, dipshit?" Lebeau yelled.

Fleming ignored him. In a few seconds, he reached the platoon's radioman. Lieutenant Ryerson was sitting next to him. Fleming grabbed the handset from the radioman.

"What are you doing, Fleming?" Ryerson demanded angrily.

Fleming yelled into the handset: "Adjust your fire. Adjust your fire. Short rounds. Put them two hundreds meters north. That's two hundred meters November. Over."

The artillery fire stopped and resumed seconds later. The rounds fell in the tree line.

"Outstanding. Right on target."

Fleming turned to Ryerson. "Sir, whoever called in that fire called in the wrong fuckin' coordinates. The rounds were right in our perimeter."

Horror filled Ryerson's face. "I called it in," he mumbled

"Sir, they were wrong," Fleming said. "You dropped the shit on your own men."

A vacant look on his face, Ryerson just stared at him.

Just then Ramirez came running up to them. 'Who's the fuckin' dipshit that called in them coordiates! The rounds are in our fucking pereimeter!"

Fleming clearly saw embartassment and despair alight on Ryerson's face. "The L T fixed it," Fleming said quickly to Ramirez, covering for Ryerson. "He's on it. Can you figure the coordinates on that tree line on the right flank. I gotta' get back to my men."

"Yeah, sure, man," Ramirez replied.

Fleming hurried off.

American mortar fire started falling near Van's position. He and the others started back toward the underground bunker's entrance when shrapnel hit one of the men. He fell to the ground screaming and writhing in pain.

Van started toward him when another soldier grabbed him. "We have to go or we'll be killed." Both Van and the other soldier instinctively ducked as shrapnel whistled by them and mortars exploded all around them.

Van shook himself free of the man's grip and ran back to the downed man. He picked him up in a fireman's carry, and hauled him away.

All enemy firing had ceased. American artillery fire still pounded the tree line and the right flank.

Fleming made it to Doc Garret just as the wounded man was being loaded onto a chopper. "He gonna' be okay, Doc?"

"It looks bad. Hamilton is dead. We got three dead and one wounded. What was with the short rounds?'

"The new L T called in the wrong coordinates."

"There it fuckin is! All he's gotta do is figure out coordinates and he fucks that up." Garret motioned toward Rojas. "He laid down cover fire and then helped me work on the wounded man. He's a cool customer."

The sound of Sergeant Lebeau's booming voice, barking out orders, was heard all over the perimeter. Fleming pointed to him. "He had to be there when the L T called in the coordinates. He's supposed to be experienced. He shoulda caught it"

"There it fuckin is. We got a shitty L T and a shitty platoon sergeant. That adds up to a real shitty time."

Twenty minutes later, all the men have been medavacced and the platoon was about to start forward.

Lebeau stood in front of Fleming. "Colonel Bradford wants us in that village to question the villagers. Saddle up your men and lets go."

This time Lebeau didn't pick the point man. Fleming gathered his squad then took Rojas off to the side. "You're on point. I'll be right behind you. Chances are they won't ambush us again but watch for booby traps. Remember, the Gooks gotta' know where the booby traps are so they leave markings, a bent twig or bush. Look for anything out of the ordinary."

Rojas nodded his head in understanding and they started out.

They walked two hundred meters when Rojas called to Fleming. He pointed to two broken limbs on two small bushes. "Is that what you mean by out of the ordinary?"

The broken limbs were arranged in such a way that it might indicate a mine had been placed between the limbs. It would be easy for any villager to notice the markings if they knew what they were looking for, an effective safeguard protecting villagers from inadvertently stepping on a mine meant for an American. Fleming smiled. "That's exactly what I meant."

Fleming took out his bayonet, dropped to the ground, and probed with it. Rojas did the same. All of a sudden Fleming's bayonet struck metal. He called for an EOD man (explosive expert). "Good work, Rojas," Fleming said with a smile.

"I was motivated," he said, returning the smile. "I'm allergic when it comes to mines."

"I got the same allergy."

A half hour later the mine was disarmed and they started out again. Fifteen minutes after that they entered the village. Ryerson instructed a Vietnamese Soldier named Bac, a Kit Carson scout, to interrogate the villagers. Bac ordered all the villagers to gather together. Ryerson ordered some of the squad leaders to have their men search the villagers' huts.

Ryerson, Lebeau, and the other squad leaders huddled near the villagers while Bac questioned them.

The villagers' facial expressions were a mixture of hatred and fear.

"These are the people we're helping," Ryerson said, astounded. "They're looking at me like I'm Atilla the Hun."

"They're gooks, sir," Lebeau said. "You can't figure a gook. They ain't like regular people."

"They say no villagers be V.C.," Bac translated. "They say everybody hate V.C."

"But we saw V.C. near the village," Ryerson said. "Tell him that."

"I already say. They say they hear guns they hide. They see nothing, only hear guns."

"They are all saying the same thing?" Ryerson asked, his face filled with confusion.

"Yes, they all say same-same."

Ryerson shook his head as if clearing it. His face took on a look of utter frustration. "What do you think? Do you believe them?"

"They all lie."

"Well tell them, Bac. Tell them we know they are lying."

Fleming knew they would hear nothing substantial. He wandered over to Vines. "Let's go check some of these hootches."

He and Vines made their way to some hootches. Vines went in one hootch and just before entering another Fleming heard what sounded like muffled cries. He stopped, listened, and heard it again. He chambered a round in his M-16. He carefully and silently opened the hootch's door and entered.

A girl was spread eagled on a straw mat, a towel stuffed in her mouth. Fields held her down while Doyle straddled her, moments away from unbuckling his pants and raping her.

The girl couldn't be much older than Fleming's own sister and this mental reference filled him with rage. He dropped his weapon, rushed forward, grabbed Doyle by the hair, and pulled him off the girl. Doyle fell to the floor on his knees. Before he could stand, Fleming kicked him in the chest knocking him down.

"You son of a bitch," he yelled at Fields. Then he punched Fields in the mouth, knocking him down.

The girl hopped off the mat and ran out of the hootch.

"You bastard!" Doyle cursed. He had fallen near his M-16. He grabbed it, chambered a round, and pointed it at Fleming. "You've been out to get me ever since we met!"

"Waste his ass!" Fields yelled, wiping blood from his lip.

The hootch's door flew open. Vines entered. Weapon at his hip, he fired a volley of M-60 rounds above Doyle's head, "Drop the weapon, Doyle, or I waste your ass."

Doyle gave Vines a long hard look. Then he dropped his weapon.

An evil smile slowly crept over Doyle's face. "What the fuck's with you two? She's only a Goddamned gook."

"And I'm only a Goddamned nigger, right?" Vines replied with a smile.

Doyle looked away.

Vines aimed his 60 at Fields. "What about you, Fields?"

"Hey, man. I got no problem with you."

Vines turned to Fleming. "You okay?"

"Yeah, man." Fleming turned to Doyle and Fields. "Get your weapons and get the fuck out there with the rest of the men."

They grabbed their weapons and hurried out of the hootch. Fleming and Vines left a few moments later and rejoined the platoon. Lieutenant Ryerson was on the radio.

Lebeau moved to Fleming. "What was that shooting about?"

"Nothing, a girl was scared. She started running. I fired some warning shots and she stopped. I told her to get out here with the rest of the villagers and she did."

A solemn expression filled Lebeau's face. "Do you think she's V.C.?"

"Who knows. You ask her she'll say no whether she is or not."

Lebeau smiled at him. "These people have no concept of the truth."

Fleming smiled and nodded his head as if agreeing. Lebeau had to be brainless, Fleming thought. These people wanted to stay alive, and people with fierce weapons had just invaded their village and had asked questions. The truth to them was saying anything that prevented them from being shot.

Then Ryerson wandered over to them. "They want us to set up for the night about five hundred meters outside the village. Once we get set up I'll let everyone know what tomorrow's plan is. Let's move out. Fleming, your squad still has point. You pick the point man." Ryerson smiled at him.

Fleming returned it and nodded his head at the L T. He returned to his squad and called Doyle and Fields aside. "We're setting up outside this village. Doyle, you got point."

Doyle nodded his head without making eye contact.

"I covered both your asses with Lebeau, but I ain't doing it again. You got that?"

With the slightest bit of reluctance they both gave head nods of assent.

"Get your shit together. Let's go."

They formed up and Doyle led them out of the village.

Van sat in a conference room waiting for Chi and Dan to return from the village. They had gone there to speak with the three women spies about the villager's behavior while the Americans were in the village.

Just then Chi and Dan entered. Dan sat next to Van and patted his leg affectionately.

Van wondered why. Dan was not one for sensitive gestures.

Chi stood in front of the men and spoke. "The villagers told the Americans nothing of our mission. The American dogs tried to rape a twelve-year old girl. She managed to escape. She is Van's sister Lan." Chi made and held eye contact with Van. "Tonight we get revenge for you and her. We will strike the Americans. We will protect the villagers to the best of our ability. Today, Dan and I gave them identification cards, identifying them as South Vietnamese. Hopefully it will protect them from further incidents, but the Americans are brutal. We can only pray that Buddha will look after them. Everyone, get some rest."

The men filed out of the room. Nearly all of them had given their condolences to Van. Then Hoi approached.

"Van, I'm sorry about Lan."

"Thank you. I don't want to speak about it. I need time alone."

"Don't let this affect our plan to–"

"Leave," Van snapped. "I said I want to be alone."

Hoi frowned, nodded his head and left.

A clear picture of huge Americans atop his sister was a horrifying image in Van's mind. She knew nothing about men. She was only twelve years old, he thought angrily.

He stood and started pacing the room. Try as he might the picture of grunting, groaning Americans atop his sister wouldn't go away.

The platoon's NDP was just outside the village in an area surrounded by bomb craters and near two large hills. The squad leaders were at the CP being briefed by Ryerson and Lebeau. Tomorrow morning they would be assigned an area to patrol. So far none of the other companies had made contact with the enemy. When the briefing ended, Lebeau ordered Fleming to stay behind.

The rest of the squad leaders and their men went about the task of digging foxholes. Fleming had instructed Rojas on where the men should dig their holes. Rojas was to share a position with Vines. Carlyle and Washington would share a position and Doyle and Fields would share one. Fleming told everyone to make sure their holes held three people. Since the squad had an uneven number of men he would take turns, throughout the night, sharing holes mainly with the inexperienced squad members.

"Fleming, what happened on that ambush?" Lebeau asked. "Why didn't your point man spot the gooks?"

"You can't put that on me or him. I told you he wasn't ready to walk point."

"The Lieutenant and me already know that." Lebeau answered in a condescending parental tone. "We wanna' know what happened."

"Number one, the gooks are good. They set up an ambush they're hard to spot and Hamilton was a cherry. He didn't know what to look for. He wasn't payin' enough attention, I mean what can I tell you. He made a ton of cherry mistakes. Maybe he would have been a good soldier, given enough time, but we will never know that."

Ryerson lowered his head. "I'm sorry we made you put him on point."

Lebeau blew out a disgusted stream of air. The new lieutenant was apologizing to an enlisted man. Good officers didn't do that.

"Sir," Fleming said. "To be honest, there's a good chance none of my men would have spotted that ambush. The point is I'm the squad leader, I choose who in my squad walks point. If not, then you need to replace me. I woulda picked anyone but Hamilton."

"We read you loud and clear," Lebeau replied. "Let's not beat this to death."

"Fair enough, as long as history doesn't repeat itself."

Lebeau thrust his face inches from Fleming's. "You got a smart fuckin' mouth. This is the Army and in case you ain't learned, acting sergeants treat platoon sergeants with respect." He put sarcastic emphasis on the words acting sergeants.

"If the gooks woulda waited, they mighta got boocoo more of us. We were lucky. They were out to get just a couple men then beat it outta there before any of their men got hit. It's how they fight. Platoon sergeants should know that shit," Fleming put sarcastic emphasis on the words platoon sergeants.

"Motherfucker–" Lebeau started but was stopped be Ryerson's restraining hand on his arm.

"Why fight like that?" Ryerson asked, interrupting Lebeau.

For the past few moments, Lebeau and Fleming had been maintaining eye contact, their faces only inches apart. Fleming finally broke the intense gaze to look at Ryerson. "Our airpower, sir. And our artillery. They need to escape before we hit them with the big guns."

Ryerson shook his head with frustrated disgust. "And then I call in the big guns and we hit our own men."

"Sir, that was a mistake, but just like Hamilton needed time to learn, you do too. Everyone does. Everyone in the bush has to go through a learning experience."

"Well, I'm glad my mistake didn't kill anyone."

"Okay, Fleming, you've made your point," Lebeau said. "Get back to your men."

Fleming gave Lebeau a long hard look then left. He was making an enemy of Lebeau but he was beyond caring. He was surprised at Ryerson's behavior. His question concerning the enemy's fighting tactics showed he wanted to learn.

Chi led the men out of the underground bunker complex. They silently and quickly started toward their assigned ambush positions.

"They tried to rape a girl?" Rojas asked in disbelief.

"She looked like she was about ten," Vines said. "It was gross."

"I got pissed and started beating on them," Fleming said. "Doyle pulled his weapon on me. Vines saved my ass."

"Do you really think he woulda tried to do you?" Vines asked.

"He was pissed. There's bad blood between us. He may have fired. I dunno."

"What's the bad blood?" Rojas asked.

Fleming debated whether or not to tell about them hiding in the command bunker and decided against it. "It don't mean nothing. It's a personality clash. We just don't get along."

KABOOM!

The men duck down in the foxhole at the sound of the exploding mortar.

KABOOM! KABOOM! KABOOM!

The mortars began falling with frightening frequency.

Twenty-one men had been ordered to assault the American position. Chi, Dan and two squads were positioning themselves to probe the LP in order to learn their exact location. Van's squad was one hundred meters west of Chi and would ambush any Americans sent to aid the LP. Hiding behind the tree, Van clearly saw that the mortar fire was coming from the village. Why would Chi do that? He wondered. The Americans would surely learn of the mortar's location and would want revenge.

"Those mortars are coming from the village," Fleming said.

'The villagers are shooting at us?" Rojas exclaimed with skepticism.

"No, the V.C. or NVA are in the village doing the shooting," Fleming answered.

"They gotta know we're dug in," Vines said. "They don't get any of us unless they get a direct hit."

A moment passed with Fleming deep in thought. "I think I know what they're doing. They're keeping us pinned down so they can take out the LP."

"This sucks," Dodson, a Cherry on the LP, said. "We're out here all alone and now we're being hit by mortars."

"Just keep your shit together, Dodson," Myers warned. He was one of the experienced men who had been transferred to Bravo.

"This is fuckin scary," an African American cherry named Grady said. Fear consumed him and motivated him to instinctively stand and look out of the foxhole.

"GET THE FUCK DOWN!" Myers yelled.

The sound of a fired AK-47 rang out.

Grady was hit. He fell down into the hole.

Myers grabbed him and quickly examined him. A round had entered the left side of Grady's neck and had exited. The wound was bleeding profusely. "Dodson, put a dressing on him and stop the bleeding," Myers ordered.

Dodson placed a dressing on Grady's neck and applied pressure. His head only a few inches above the foxhole's rim, Myers surveyed the situation.

Just then a squad of V.C. ran across the landscape toward a knoll.

Myers grabbed a claymore detonator and activated it.

The Claymores exploded.

Two V.C. were hit but at least a half dozen made it successfully behind the knoll.

Myers dropped down into the foxhole. "They're probing us. Don't fire your weapon."

"Don't fire my weapon!" Dodson literally squealed. "How am I gonna' fight if I don't fire my weapon?"

"Throw grenades!" Myers said angrily. "You fire your weapon they'll see the muzzle flash and put an R.P.G. in here."

"They already know we're here. It's how they got Grady?"

"They ain't fixed us yet."

"How do you fuckin' know that?"

"Cause we're still alive, ain't we?"

"Motherfucker! We're fucked!"

"Don't go flaky on me, you cherry cunt." Myers grabbed the radio and spoke into the transmitter. "River Bravo Six, this is Pirate Leader. Gooks are all over us. We got a wounded man. He don't get help he'll bleed to death. We'll all be dead unless we get help. Our shit's in the wind out here, over."

"Roger, we'll get somebody to you. Hold tight Pirate Leader, over and out."

Dodson threw a grenade. "Jesus Christ!" Dodson squealed with a fear-filled, falsetto tone. "A bunch of Gooks got behind that hill over there."

Myers looked – the hill was only fifteen meters away. "They're close enough to lob grenades in here."

Unbridled fear filled Dodson's face. "Let's go back to the platoon," he said with the pleading tone of a child.

"We won't get two steps before the gooks put a bullet in our backs. We ain't running. And what are we gonna do with Grady, just leave him here?"

Dodson's eyes darted to and fro. "There's gotta be something we can do."

"Do you know the Americans' location?" Chi called out to one of his men probing the Americans.

"Not yet. But they're close," the man called back from his location twenty meters away.

"Damnit, Myers, they're talking to each other. What did they say?"

"I don't speak fuckin gook. How the fuck would I know. Just keep cool. Until they actually get us we got a chance. The CP will send some men."

Garret ran across the perimeter as mortars fell all around him. He finally jumped into a foxhole.

Garret's trying to get to the LP," Fleming said. "Somebody has been hit."

Then Garret, Raines and a Cherry ran out of the foxhole and sprinted through the perimeter while the mortars continued falling; miraculously they were not hit. Finally they jumped into another foxhole.

"They're definitely heading for the LP," Rojas said.

BOOM! BOOM!

Chi-com grenades fell within meters of the LP's foxhole.

Dodson grabbed Myers' arm. "We are fucked, Myers! Dear Jesus, we are fucked!"

"They don't know where we are," Myers shot back. "Keep your fucking shit together."

Suddenly to the right of the hole a shadow of a man scurried by them.

"Did you see that gook? We gotta' start shooting. We can't let them get behind us or we'll be cut off."

"Don't shoot your fucking weapon unless I tell ya' to shoot! I ain't telling ya' again."

Another V.C. ran by them.

"Oh fuck, there's another one. The CP ain't gonna send anyone. They're pinned down by the mortar fire."

"They'll send somebody. I'm telling you."

Lieutenant Ryerson jumped into Fleming's foxhole. "The LP needs help. Somebody named Grady has been hit. He'll die if we don't get him out of there. They'll all die."

Fleming understood the unspoken command. "Sir, we only gotta' run thirty meters and we'll be outta' the mortars line of fire. We can make it. The odds are pretty good."

"You sure you want to try it? It's dangerous."

"What over here ain't dangerous, sir?" Then Fleming looked at Rojas and Vines.

Their faces were knotted in fear, but they nodded their heads yes.

"We'll go, sir." Fleming said.

Ryerson nodded his head yes. "Be careful."

Fleming turned to Vines and Rojas. "We need Carlyle. I'll get him. When I leave his hole, follow me."

Fleming jumped out of the hole, ran a few meters, and jumped into Carlyle and Washington's foxhole. "Carlyle, we need your 79. The LP's about to be overrun. Some cherry named Grady's been hit. He's gonna die if he ain't medavacced."

"I know Grady. He's a friend. I came in country with him."

"Let's go." Carlyle and Fleming climbed out of the hole. Rojas and Vines left their hole and they all ran across the perimeter.

Forty meters away, Van saw the running Americans. He ordered his men to open fire.

Bullets whizzed past Fleming's ear.

He and the other four men dropped to the ground and crawled behind a huge tree that provided excellent cover.

Van silently cursed his luck. They had missed their chance to stop the Americans.

At the LP the Chi-com grenades exploded all around the foxhole until one made its way inside.

In one fluid motion, Myers scooped it up and threw it out.

The grenade exploded five feet from his right hand, shearing off three fingers. He dropped into the hole. His arm was shredded by pieces of shrapnel.

"Oh my God we are fucked!" Dodson screamed.

"Shut the fuck up you cherry dip shit! I ain't even dying in this hole!!" Myers began applying a dressing to his arm while holding his fingers up, elevating them in order to slow the blood flow.

Small arms fire forced Garret, Raines and the Cherry to seek cover behind a large boulder ten meters from the LP.

Garret attempted to charge from behind the rock but small arms fire forced him back. "Damnit!" he swore. "I gotta' get up there."

"Don't even think of it, Doc," Raines warned.

'MYERS!" Garret yelled. "IS GRADY STILL ALIVE!"

"YEAH, BUT WE DON'T GET HIM OUTTA' HERE SOON, HE'LL DIE. I'M HIT TOO."

"Shit!' Garret cursed through gritted teeth.

Fleming grabbed Carlyle's arm. "Did you see where the gooks are firing from?"

"Thirty five meters away, near that hill," Carlyle answered, pointing in the direction.

"Drop a couple rounds in there. Then a crystal." A crystal was a tear gas projectile that would force them out of the position or disorient them enough so Fleming and the others would be able to get by them. "Be on target. We gotta get to that LP."

Carlyle nodded soberly then fired a round.

The M-79 grenades fell near Van's position. The concussion lifted him and threw him five meters backward. He fell unconscious.

Gunships arrived and unleashed a fierce barrage into the V.C. position, allowing Garret to run from behind the rock and to the LP.

Carlyle fired a crystal round and they all sprinted toward the LP.

Chi saw the Americans running from their position and ordered his men to open fire.

Small arms fire forced Fleming and his men to again hit the ground. They crawled fifteen meters to the large boulder where Raines and the Cherry were located.

"Thanks, for coming out," Raines said. "My men are on the LP." He chuckled. "Actually, Garret got me to come out here. He reminded me of a favor I owed him."

Fleming looked at Rojas. "I think everyone in the 173rd owes Garret a favor."

"That wouldn't surprise me," Rojas said with a smile. "He's an expert, getting dudes to owe him favors."

"There it fuckin is," Raines said with a smirk.

Van regained consciousness. Dazed and disoriented, he lay in a wet, sticky substance. Left of him, he saw a man lying there with a missing leg and a huge chunk of his stomach was split open. Van realized he was lying in the man's blood and his intestines.

He instinctively scrambled away while gasping in horror.

Tear gas fumes instantly filled his lungs. He choked and retched. Every breath was burning agony. Tears fell from his eyes.

He hurried to his feet. Mucus and snot flowed from his nose. The tear gas haze had made seeing almost impossible. Groping his way through it, he saw severed limbs and body parts of other men. Despite his agony, he checked each downed comrade. Three were dead. A fourth man was alive, but barely breathing.

Then he realized that he hadn't seen Hoi. He frantically scanned the area until seeing his downed body. He rushed to him and was grateful to find him alive but unconscious. Van slapped his face until reviving him. He helped him to his feet and then made his way back to the wounded comrade. He hoisted that man on his shoulders and, while supporting a dazed Hoi, he slowly and agonizedly made his way through the tear gas fog and toward the village.

A murderous round of gunfire from the Americans on the ground and the gunships in the air forced Chi to rally his men together and flee the area.

Wary of enemy fire, Fleming and the others made their way to the LP. Helicopters hovered, vulture-like, over the area, offering protection. Fleming and his men helped Garret take the wounded to the NDP where a helicopter waited to medavac Grady and Myers back to the rear. Raines and the Cherry stayed with Dodson at the LP.

Carlyle dropped down on one knee to speak with a conscious Grady. "You gonna be okay, bro. You outta the shit now. You goin to Japan."

"Take care of yourself, blood," Grady said with a smile. "Thanks for coming out for me."

"No sweat, brotha."

"I feeeel good, now I knew that I would, yeah," Myers suddenly sang out in a poor imitation of the James Brown song.

Garret turned to him. "What the fuck's with you, Myers? You lost three fucking fingers and nearly got your arm blown off."

"Oh, Doc, your shit's in the wind. I ain't never comin' back here. My trigger finger is missing. I can't pull the trigger on a weapon if I ain't got a trigger finger. This is a million dollar fuckin' wound, man. I'm goin' back to the world."

Men hoisted Grady's and Myers' stretcher and started away.

"Mamas back in the world grab your daughters cause I'm comin home horny and I feeeel good."

They are loaded into the chopper and shortly afterward it took flight.

Ryerson moved to Fleming. "You did good out there."

Fleming smiled at him nodding his head. Then his eyes narrowed. "They fired from the village, sir. They retreated back there, too. I saw them."

"I know. I'll tell Wiggins when I talk to him in the morning. Again, good work tonight." Then Ryerson left for the command bunker.

Just then Carlyle approached Fleming. "Mind if I talk to you?"

"No, what's on your mind?"

"You saved my life today."

"When did I do that?"

"That first ambush. You pulled me to the ground. If you didn't do that I'd be dead."

"Maybe. You froze, a cherry mistake. Keep your shit together it won't be long before you'll know how to handle yourself."

Carlyle nodded his head, deep in thought. "I don't like white people, least I never have. You know that don't you?"

"I knew the first day I met you. You wouldn't speak to me. The way you looked at me. It wasn't hard to tell."

"I gotta tell ya, this shit over here…it ain't no picnic. It's a war and it's a brutal war. Yet with all this savagery, I see people trying to help each other. You saved me. Tonight a bunch of white boys and a Puerto Rican all put their asses on the line to save one Black man's ass." Carlyle chuckled. "Me and Vines, we was the token niggers."

"The only way we can get through this and go home in one piece is if we all help each other. We fight each other our chances of getting fucked up get boocoo better."

Carlyle shook his head confused. "I get sent to a war and I find people that care about each other. Can you believe that shit?"

"What's this all mean? Why you telling me this?"

Carlyle gave him a long hard look, studying him. "I don't know. I guess I'm sayin I'm gonna listen to you. I'm gonna take orders from you. I just thought I should tell you."

"You're a good soldier, Carlyle. You proved that tonight. Good soldiers mean boocoo other good soldiers get to go home alive."

"So my job over here is to keep men alive?"

"That's it." Fleming thought of Levine and a haunted, melancholy look filled his face. "Another good soldier once told me that."

Carlyle nodded his head, understanding. They shook hands and Carlyle went back to his foxhole.

Fleming watched him as he walked away. Just one month ago he needed to hear the same words he had just told Carlyle. How did he get from being that man to the man he was today? He had no idea.

Entering a village hootch, Van placed his wounded comrade down and learned that the man had died. Then he placed a bandage on Hoi's head laceration.

Exhausted, he dropped to the floor. He immediately thought of the day the NVA had entered the village and committed the atrocities that placed him in the position he was in today. He drove the thought away but then thought of his sister and the rape attempt. He looked at the dead man, lying on the mat. His beloved village now held so many horrible memories for him.

Suddenly he heard footsteps outside the hootch. Instinctively he reached for his weapon.

His sister Lan entered the hootch.

Van placed his weapon down and embraced her.

She immediately saw that he was covered with blood and some of it has gotten on her. "You've been hurt."

"No, I'm fine." He pointed to the dead comrade lying on the mat. ""It's his blood. I'm fine, really."

Her face was a mask of horror. "It's so much blood." She took a moment to examine him.

He moved to hug her again but stopped when he noticed that some blood had gotten on her. "I am fine. How are Mother and Father?"

"They're asleep. They haven't been sleeping well. They've been worried about you. I can wake them if you want?"

"No, I'm covered with blood. It will only worry them more. Let them sleep. I have to report back to my unit soon anyway. I can see them another time."

Lan smiled at him. "When I heard you were in the village I had to come see you."

"I am glad you did."

She made eye contact with Hoi and smiled at him. He only gave her a head nod. Then he walked outside the hootch leaving Van and Lan alone.

Confusion filled Lan's face. She thought Hoi might have said something to her. She looked back at Van and smiled at him. Fully knowing she risked staining herself with the dead man's blood, she grabbed her older brother and embraced him again.

Holding her brought back warm memories of their childhood when there was no war, no revolution, and no complex questions about right or wrong. Then he remembered that she had been attacked. He broke the embrace, held her at arm's length, and looked deeply into her eyes. "How are you? I heard an American attacked you." He purposely avoided using the word rape.

"I am fine."

"How did you get away? Americans are so large and you're a small girl?"

Her face tightened and she pouted. "I am almost a woman."

Her determined, scowling facial expression made him chuckle. "Then tell me how woman managed to escape from an American?"

Her brow wrinkled with confusion. "You don't know? Didn't your Sergeant and Dan tell you? They know."

"No, they said nothing."

"An American saved me. He fought the two men who attacked me. If it wasn't for the American I don't think I would have gotten out of there."

"They never told me that."

"He kicked them and hit them. He was so angry. I couldn't believe the look in his face, the fire in his eyes. I was so surprised that he helped me. When Dan and Chi came to the village they said the Americans committed many atrocities in Vietnam. Dan said he had seen them do horrible things. He said that the NVA had done the right thing that day when they had taken you from the village; that everyone had a duty to fight the Americans."

Now he understood why Dan and Chi were not on the ambush. They were in the village telling tales of American atrocities and justifying the horrors committed by the NVA. Chi took Dan because he would do whatever Chi ordered and who better to convince the villagers than someone from the village. It would also explain why they planted the booby trap. Chi wanted to provoke the Americans into committing an atrocity, proving that he was telling the villagers the truth. It was all done to win the village's loyalty and to justify the NVA's crime against this very village.

"The American who attacked me grabbed his weapon and was about to kill the man who saved me, but a black American saved him. Have you seen the Americans commit atrocities in other villages?"

"No, I haven't."

"I wonder why your sergeant told us that. Why did Dan?" Just then she yawned. "I am tired. I haven't slept well. We are all so worried."

"Go back to bed. I will have time to come back and visit in the next day or two."

She nodded her head in assent. They spoke a few moments longer then she kissed his cheek and hurried off. Van grabbed the dead man then he and Hoi started back to the underground complex.

Van's mind was awhirl with thoughts. He remembered a month ago when he missed an opportunity to kill an American, a butcher of a man responsible for killing so many Vietnamese. Now, today, a good American had saved his sister from rape. It was just as the elders had taught: there was good and evil in all nationalities. His thoughts drifted to Chi and Dan. He understood why Chi had lied to the village. He hated Americans and wanted to repay them for what they had done to his village and to his face. But Dan had grown up in the village – his ties were strong. He knew that Dan had changed but could he have changed so radically? He thought of Hoi. He believed that defection was the way out of the war. But there was no escape until the war ended. Just then it occurred to Van that defection might be an answer for his family and the villagers. They could be relocated to a safer village instead of where they were now, geographically located in an area that was amidst some of the war's fiercest fighting. But getting them to move from the village they loved would be near impossible.

CHAPTER 13

Losing A Part Of One's Self

The next morning the high command ordered Ryerson to have his men re-con the area of last night's firefight in order to get an accurate count of enemy dead so they could be added to the day's statistics as confirmed kills. Afterwards they were to interrogate the villagers about their part in last night's action.

At the ambush site, the platoon found dead dismembered Vietnamese: arms, legs and other pieces of anatomy lay everywhere.

Ramirez, second squad's leader, whistled in appreciation. "They're yours, Carlyle," he said with a smile and a chuckle. "Every last motherfuckin Gook piece."

A visibly upset Carlyle gave him a weak smile and turned away from the sight.

An inspection of the tree line near last night's LP found two more dead enemy soldiers plus blood trails – telltale signs of enemy being carried away by comrades.

An inspection of the third enemy position revealed three dead soldiers, blistered and charred black, obvious victims of napalm.

Vines stared, transfixed at the bodies, and said: "They're like burned hot dogs right off the grill."

Some of the men, mostly the cherries, giggled excitedly; there was a forbidden mischievous tone to their laughter; they sounded like teenaged boys getting their first look at nude centerfolds.

Ramirez tugged on a burned corpse's arm and it came off in his hand. "Like breaking off a chicken leg," he said with a smile. "Anybody want a bite? A gook's a mighty tasty meal, only problem is it's just like all chink food, you're hungry again an hour after eating."

Practically every man broke out in laughter.

Pierson, another squad leader, walked closer to the gooks. "Worst case of sunburn I ever seen."

Someone threw a container of Coppertone lotion and hit the corpse in the chest.

Everyone was laughing and smiling.

Fleming wondered why anyone would bring sun tan lotion to the field; it was extra weight and although it wasn't heavy combat soldiers always avoided carrying extra weight.

Pierson moved closer to the dead men and sniffed them. "They're rank, too. Anyone got deodorant?"

No one threw deodorant, but everyone was laughing and enjoying the whole affair.

Before Nam, Fleming would have never believed that he, or anyone else, would be reduced to poking fun at the dead; however, when one found oneself in a world where death was always waiting around the corner poking fun at death made it seem much less real.

Just then, Carlyle bent over, retched, and vomitted.

Ramirez turned to Fleming. "You got some weak ass cherries, losin their lunch over a few crispy critters?"

Carlyle looked at Rojas and pointed at his vomit. "K-K-Kinda reminds ya of that shit you guys eat," Carlyle said while gagging. "You wanna dig in?"

Rojas laughed with disgust.

"Get your shit together and let's get the fuck outta here," Fleming said with a chuckle. "We got more to do then watch cherries puke all day."

"I'm ready," Carlyle said. "As soon as I finish makin y'alls lunch."

Everyone let out a disgusted groan and then they all lined up and started toward the village.

Once in the village, Lieutenant Ryerson ordered the men to inspect the hootches.

Just then the village leader came running toward them, waving his arms, and rattling off an endless string of Vietnamese.

Bac turned to Ryerson. "Papasan, say no V.C. be here. You come yesterday. Why come back today?" Bac smiled a mirthless grin. "Papasan boocoo bullshit."

"Tell him we know they were firing mortars from the village last night," Ryerson snapped frustrated.

Bac and the Papasan again engaged in heated conversation. Papasan emphatically shook his head no. His arms and hands fanned out in a universal gesture of pleading and supplication. Finally, with a huge smile on his face, Papasan reached into his pocket and pulled out a card and waved it in Bac's face.

"Papasan say he no V.C. He say he hear big guns everyone in the village hide. They say they see no V.C. here." He hands Ryerson papasan's card.

Ryerson looked at the card.

Papasan smiled at the other G.I.'s. He waved his finger in the air gesturing that the G.I.'s were number one.

"What the hell is this?" Ryerson asked.

Fleming looked at the card and scoffed in disgust. "Sir, it's a Can Cuoc card. It's an identification card issued by the South Vietnamese Government. A villager has to buy one to prove he ain't V.C. The card costs boocoo and the villagers can't afford them. The only people who buy them or have them are V.C."

"They issue a card to prove someone isn't V.C. but the only people that have it are V.C.?"

"There it is, sir. Typical Vietnam bullshit."

Just then Vines rushed up to them. "Sir, we found something in a hootch."

They followed Vines to the hootch. Once inside, Vines pointed to a blood stained mat. "Sir, we figured they treated some of the men we wounded last night in this hootch."

"Well lookee here," Carlyle screeched. He held up two U.S. Government issue battle dressings. 'This is some kinda hospital and the bastards are usin our shit to treat their wounded."

Garret grabbed the bandage. "The South Vietnamese sells this shit to the enemy. MACV (Military Assistance Command Vietnam) knows about it too. They just don't do diddly squat about it."

Fleming thought back to the day at the Alamo when Levine said the same thing.

Ryerson smirked at him. "C'mon, Garret. You actually believe our allies are selling supplies to the enemy? And if by some chance they are we're not doing a thing about it? Please don't tell me you believe that?"

"It makes no fuckin sense, sir, but it's the truth. We even proved it." Then Garret told the story about the magic marker markings.

Ryerson shok his head in disbelief and scoffed: "I find that hard to believe."

"I ain't lying, sir."

"I'm not calling you a liar. I just said I find it hard to believe."

It mirrored Fleming thoughts to a T: it was just too unbelievable. But now Garret was saying it and Levine had said it and Jenks had said it. These were men who didn't make rash statements.

Meanwhile Bac and Papasan both rattled off a string of Vietnamese. Then Bac turned to Ryerson. "Papasan say no V.C. be here. No one stay in this hootch. Mebbe V.C. come here he don't know, he no see. Papasan number one bullshit." Ryerson and Bac continued speaking meanwhile Carlyle stepped up to Papasan and smiled.

Papasan looked at him cautiously for a moment before he slowly broke into a huge grin and smiled back at Carlyle.

Carlyle began nodding his head and smiling. "Bac says you number one fuckin bullshitter." Carlyle says in a soft, non-threatening tone, all the while smiling and nodding his head yes. "He's telling the truth ain't he, Papasan?"

Having no idea what has been said, Papasan continued smiling his toothless grin and nodding his head, mimicking Carlyle.

A smiling, head nodding Carlyle said: "Papasan, you lying motherfucker. I oughta take my 79 and blow your dick and balls right off huh, Papasan?"

A smiling Papasan nodded his head agreeing. He raised his index finger in the air and rattled off his entire vocabulary of the English language: "G.I. numbah one."

Ryerson stormed out of the hootch. "I'm calling Wiggins. See what he has to say about this."

Once outside, Ryerson called Wiggins. He spoke for about five minutes then had Lebeau gather the squad leaders together. "Wiggins says we're to sweep the valley east of here for approximately five klicks and see what we can find. Then we're to come back here tonight and set in at the same CP and observe the village's actions."

"There it fuckin' is," Fleming said with a mirthless chuckle. "They don't know what to do so they're sending us out to patrol." Fleming smirked. "Our mission is successful if we can get the V.C. to hit us."

Ryerson sighed wearily. "Get your men together. We move out in fifteen."

They left the village heading northeast. All day they humped the area, laboring in one hundred degree heat. They found no signs of enemy movement or activity. Tired and frustrated, they returned to the same CP at 1800 hours.

Every man fell to the ground exhausted.

"Take ten," Fleming ordered. "Then get started digging new foxholes, before it gets dark."

"Bullshit," Carlyle fired back at him. "I got me a perfectly good foxhole I dug yesterday. I'm sleeping in there."

Fleming smiled at him. "Remember that Papasan you were fucking with this morning?"

"Yeah, what's he got to do with me digging a foxhole?"

"While you were out there humpin all day, he was out here. He either booby trapped your hole or marked it off. You're either gonna set off a booby trap or tonight when the V.C. start dropping mortars they gonna send you an air mail package."

Carlyle threw his helmet on the ground. "Everything in this place is guaranteed to kill you or make you work your ass off."

"Look on the bright side. If you work your ass off you might just save your ass."

Carlyle rolled his eyes at him. "Look on the bright side? In Viet-fucking-nam? Shut the fuck up, Sergeant Sunshine."

Fleming smiled and laughed and Carlyle gave him a mirthless smile.

That evening at a briefing, Chi ordered Dan to take a five man patrol ten klicks north. With a high-powered lantern, Dan was to flash signals to a squad placed in the village. The hope was that Americans would send a patrol to the village. Chi had another squad in position ready to ambush them if that happened.

When the meeting was dismissed Van approached Chi. "You're using the village. Throughout this operation you have made them a participant in the war."

"The minute an American boot stepped on Vietnamese soil they became a participant."

"They aren't soldiers. They– "

"Today, in our country, everyone's a soldier."

"If you flash signals from the village, the Americans will harm it."

"And if my plan works we kill more Americans. We gain a victory."

"At the expense of the village."

"Van, I truly hope the village suffers no harm. There are no weapons in the village, so the Americans shouldn't harm the villagers. If I send the signals and the Americans investigate, and we kill some of them, I have done my job. I have killed the enemy."

"Sergeant, please–"

"I understand how you feel. I am sorry it has to be this way but this is war. Everyone in our country must pay a price to drive the invaders from our land. I won't speak about this any longer. It is not my fault the way things are in our country. Go back to your quarters and rest. I may have a job for you on tonight's operation."

"I won't take part in this. This is my home. I won't hurt my home or my people."

Chi gave him a long hard look. "You're a good soldier. But you are walking a thin line. This is war and it requires sacrifices from everyone until the Americans are driven from our land. Now, I haven't the time to debate with you on this. I have much to do concerning tonight's ambush." Then Chi turned and walked away from Van.

Van plopped down on a chair in the vacant conference room. Frustrated, he understood Chi's position about the war and how everyone had to pay a price. But the village had already paid a huge price. Why were the Americans here? He wondered once again. The question would not stop nagging at him. America was strong with many weapons; it would be years before they would be driven out of Vietnam, if that were even possible. How many villages would be destroyed because of this war? Whatever the Americans wanted in Vietnam was it worth all the innocent lives that would be lost? If the villagers survived this operation, it would only be a matter of time before they would become a casualty of war. Hoi's idea seemed to be the only sensible option. In order to insure the safety of their families and friends they somehow needed to convince them to defect to an American protected village. But the same obstacle loomed large – how do you convince people to leave a village that had family ties that went back centuries?

Sharing a foxhole with Rojas, Fleming prayed for an uneventful night. The platoon was exhausted. They hadn't a peaceful night's sleep in four days and being cherries they weren't used to the pace they were being asked to endure.

Fleming had the last watch so he lay down in the hole and was soon asleep. It seemed like it was only minutes later when Rojas awakened him. Fleming looked at his watch: it was 2100. He had been asleep two hours.

Lieutenant Ryerson was standing outside the foxhole. "The LP says flickering lights are coming from the village," Ryerson said. "Lights are also coming from a tree line about ten clicks away. They're signaling back and forth. Let's check it out."

Vines, Fleming, Rojas, Ryerson and a radioman hurried to a trench on the perimeter's outskirts. They had a clear view of the village and saw that flashing lights were indeed being sent from the village to someone in the tree line.

"I'm calling for illumination," Ryerson said. 'Then we're going to hit that ville. See what happens."

SOP demanded that an Officer had to call in for permission before opening fire on a village. It was a lengthy and time-consuming procedure. Permission had to be granted by the high command and that could go all the way to the top. In fact, President Lyndon Johnson once boasted that not even a Vietnamese outhouse could be hit unless he ordered it. It was all designed to protect Vietnamese civilians, but in many situations it also put American soldiers at a very high risk. Sometimes situations called for action to be split second. Calling the president to ask permission was not split second and the huge number of civilians killed by American bombing negated the saving innocent lives argument. "Sir, ain't ya' gonna' call it in first?" Fleming asked.

"I'm not blowing the village up. I'm putting small arms fire on them. I want to see what happens if we hit the hootch that is sending the signals."

Illumination was requested. In seconds the area was lit like it was daytime.

Rojas pointed at the hootch. "There, see the lights."

Everyone saw the flashing lights coming from the hootch.

"Light them up, Vines," Ryerson ordered.

Vines opened fire wth his 60 until Ryerson ordered him to stop. Within seconds illumination from tracer rounds accidently caused the hootch's straw to catch fire.

Weapons-bearing men came running out of the burning hootch.

"Open fire," Ryerson ordered.

Everyone fired on the fleeing men. Most were cut down, but some get away. Ryerson ordered the men to cease-fire.

"There it fuckin is," Fleming said. "Let's see Papasan say there's no V.C. in his village now."

"Let's get back," Ryerson said. "Tomorrow we're going to the village and finding out what the fuck is going on."

"Papasan, lai dai," (Vietnames for come here) Bac screamed.

"Something is wrong," Ryerson said. "Papasan has always greeted us when we came before."

Bac smiled evilly. "He be here, or we kill Papasan last night. Papasan, lai dai!"

Ryerson ordered Lebeau to have the squads search the hootches. Minutes later, Fleming exited a hootch accompanied by Papasan. Papasan was wearing a long sleeve shirt. He shuffled nervously toward Ryerson and Bac.

Bac exploded into a machine gun rattle of Vietnamese.

Papasan, wearing the same innocent expression that everyone knew so well, began his familiar whining spiel.

"Sir, when I found him he was wearing a short sleeved shirt," Fleming said. "He put that long sleeved shirt on before comin out here. Check out his arms, sir."

Bac ordered Papasan to remove his shirt.

Fear immediately engulfed Papasan's weathered face. He tried to explain why he didn't want to remove his shirt.

Bac made a show of chambering a M-16 round and pointing the barrel at Papasan's chest.

With pleading eyes, Papasan turned to Ryerson.

Ryerson also chambered a round and pointed his weapon at Papasan. "He's lying," he said to no one in particular. "And I am getting real tired of it. Today we get to the bottom of things."

Reluctantly, Papasan finally removed his shirt.

Fleming pointed at Papasan's arm. "His arm, sir. See what I mean?"

Ryerson rudely grabbed Papasan's wrist.

An angry red burn ran from his wrist to his elbow.

"Sir, I'll bet my R and R he was in that hootch when it caught fire. The bastard was probably the one sending the signals."

All of a sudden, Rojas approached with Vines, Carlyle, and two Vietnamese women. "Sir," Rojas said. "Carlyle found these women. We think they're V.C. Their teeth are white. They don't chew betel nut. They're the only women in the village with white teeth."

Betel nut was a seed and a mild stimulant that gave the user a heightened sense of awareness. It also stained the users' teeth black. Village women principally chewed the nut so that meant the women Carlyle found were probably from the city and most likely V.C. One thing was certain; they were not from the village.

"Look at their hands, sir," Rojas said.

Bac asked the women to show their hands.

They responded with a venomous look of hatred and malice.

Carlyle grabbed both women's wrists and twisted their arms violently, exposing their palms.

Rojas pointed at their hands. "No calluses, sir. They don't work the fields like the other women."

"They V.C. for sure," Bac hissed.

Ryerson nodded his head in assent. "I'm calling Wiggins and telling him we have a suspected V.C. village and three suspected V.C."

Carlyle smiled at the women. "I bet one of you cunts shot my bro Grady."

Stone-faced, the women gazed right through Carlyle.

Carlyle smiled angelically. "Hard core cunts, huh? I wish I'da seen you bitches last night. I woulda blown your V.C. snatches all the way back to Hanoi."

"Knock the shit off, boy," Lebeau ordered.

A flicker of rage flitted across Carlyle's face for a fleeting second. Then he smiled. "I's sorry, Massah. Don't beats me, I be good."

Lebeau glared at him. "I told ya to knock it the fuck off. I ain't tellin ya again."

Carlyle was about to say something else when he saw Fleming surreptitiously shaking his head no at him.

Meanwhile, Ryerson returned from radioing English. "We're sending Papasan and the women back to English. Military Intelligence will deal with them." Ryerson turned to Lebeau. "Sergeant, get the men together. We've been ordered to burn the village."

Fleming wasn't ready for this. They had caught the two women V.C. He would bet that the remaining villagers were innocent victims caught in the middle of war. Burning their homes was too radical. Levine had told Fleming that all Vietnamese revered their village; it was part of their soul and was regarded as a sacred, holy place.

"None of the villagers are to be harmed," Ryerson said. "They can remove their belongings, but watch them. If anyone removes a weapon, they will be taken in for interrogation."

"Sir, we can't burn this place down," Fleming protested.

"We're following orders. I don't like it either, but there is nothing I can do. At least no more Americans will be ambushed from this village."

Bac translated Ryerson's orders. Immediately the villagers erupted into a string of Vietnamese that didn't need translation. They were protesting the loss of their sacred home. Some of the older women began crying.

"Out with the Zippos!" Lebeau shouted. The smile on his face betrayed the fact that he was enjoying this. He handed Fleming a lighter. "Get your ass in gear, Fleming."

Fleming hesitated. He was here to fight the enemy not this.

"Take the fuckin lighter, troop," Lebeau sneered. "Start burning down these fuckin huts."

Fleming took the lighter. "Thanks," he said with a mirthless smile. Lebeau smiled at his discomfort. "Get to fuckin work."

Fleming stormed to a hootch. This was dirty. He didn't sign up for this. He took one last look at the crying faces and torched the hootch. The straw quickly ignited. The fire spread rapidly.

A few moments later he heard human sounds coming from inside the hootch. Instinctively, he switched his M-16 selector switch from safe to semi-automatic. He chambered a round and carefully looked inside.

A Vietnamese woman was rummaging through some items. Concerned that she could be searching for a weapon, Fleming carefully entered the hootch and saw that the woman was crying. "Mamasan, di-di," Fleming said.

She turned to him. Tears were streaming down her face. She turned back to the task at hand.

Fleming hurried to her. "Mamasan, di-di." He said, touching her arm.

She slapped his hand away and grumbled a long tirade of Vietnamese. She glared at him and it reminded him of the look his own Mother gave him when he had done something wrong. Then she went back to rummaging through her items.

"Jesus," he mumbled. Without the slightest idea of what he was looking for, he began searching with her.

Suddenly, she let out a triumphant yell. She turned to him, a smile on her face, and held an old, decrepit teakettle in the air.

A teakettle, he said to himself, astonished. He was risking burning to death for a teakettle! But then he realized that it was so old it probably had been handed down from generation to generation and it held much sentiment for her. He grabbed her arm and gently pulled her away. "C'mon, Mamasan. Di-di."

As soon as they exited the hootch a crying girl, the same girl Fleming had saved from being raped, ran up to the woman. Mamasan embraced the girl. Fleming assumed the woman was the girl's mother or at least a very close relative.

Recognition of Fleming flooded the girl's face. Their eyes met and they shared a moment. The girl spoke to the woman who then turned to Fleming and smiled. She patted his arm affectionately. A warm glow filled Fleming's whole being. He smiled back at them before hurrying over to Ryerson.

"Get your men together," Ryerson ordered. "We're moving out."

"What's happening with these people, sir?" Fleming asked.

"They're being relocated to a government sponsored village. They'll be safe."

Most of the women were wailing and crying. The older men wore heavy, sorrowful facial expressions.

"Where are we going next to win the hearts and minds, sir?"

Ryerson frowned. "We're humpin northeast in no particular direction, destination, or goal in mind."

"Sir, we hump till we get hit, then we know we're headin in the right direction."

"There it is," Ryerson said, shaking his head in frustration.

Hours after the Americans had left the burning village; Van and Hoi were amidst the smoldering ruins. Van stood before a mound of ashes that used to be the hootch where he had slept as a child, where members of his family had slept since the time of the Trung sisters. The village had withstood countless hurricanes and monsoons, had withstood the day the NVA had changed it forever. It only took one week of American presence and this village that had stood for a thousand years had been wiped from the face of the earth forever.

Six months ago, Van's world revolved around family, Kim, and the village. Today it was all gone: Kim was dead, the village was dead, and he had no idea what had become of his family. He had started this mission with a sense of hope. At the very least, he thought he would be able to visit with his family. Except for a few fleeting moments with his sister, that dream had also been dashed.

"Van," Hoi said softly, breaking Van's thoughts. "The village is gone. There is nothing holding us back."

"Hoi, our village has just been burned down. Our families have no home. I have family who were buried here for hundreds of years and now they have no one to pray over their graves. Do you really want to join the people responsible for it?"

"My family is buried here too. But our living family is safe. We both saw the American helicopters taking them away. They took them to a protected village."

"They could have taken them to a prison, or executed them for all you know."

"We both know that Americans don't do that."

"I don't know that. I do know that they destroyed my home and took my family."

"And you also know that Chi was responsible. He conducted operations from the village. The Americans reacted the only way they could have."

It was exactly what Van had argued with Chi about. Chi had forced the American's hand.

"Van, I know this hurts. It hurts me. You know I'd loved the village just as much as you, but it is gone. Nothing can change that. And you know as well as I that Chi is to blame. But all of that is in the past. We look to the future now. There is nothing holding us back. We can leave this life."

"I need to figure out the right thing to do."

"You need to be practical. Even when you were a child you always worried about right and wrong. Sometimes there is no right or wrong there is only what has happened. Life is a matter of choices. Life has a flow. The elders taught us that – following the flow. That means we move forward. Moving forward means moving to the Americans."

Deep in thought, Van looked at him for a long moment. "I need time to think. This has just happened. I can't make any move until I think this through."

For a long moment, Hoi studied Van's face before smiling weakly. "I understand," he said in a voice tone loaded with patience. "Take time to think."

A moment passed as the two boyhood friends' eyes locked.

Compassion filled Hoi's face. "I am sorry about the village," he said softly. "I will pray to Buddha that your family and your ancestors are safe."

"Thank you," Van answered. "I will also pray for yours."

They both started back toward the underground bunker complex.

Hoi had spoken truthfully and practically. It couldn't be denied that Chi had forced the Americans' hand. But the Americans had committed the act. Why are they here? This question just would not stop haunting him. Nothing made sense in his new world, except for one thing – he hated this soldier's life; it was his life's one, true certainty. He hated it with all the intensity he could muster. He would do anything to leave this perverted life, this war.

Fleming sat on his helmet, eating breakfast. The past week the platoon had marched in endless circles three miles from the Cambodian border. Every day they set up a CP then patrolled the surrounding area. The next day they would leave the CP only to continue with the same routine a few miles away.

For a moment, his attention was drawn to a C-123 plane. The plane was a crop duster and it was dropping its load – a trail of some silver colored substance. He had seen this same sight a couple of times in the recent past.

He finished his meal, wiped his plastic spoon on his shirt, stuck it in his shirt pocket and rubbed his hands together eagerly. He placed his empty C-ration can next to him, grabbed his bayonet knife, touched the steel blade, and decided it was hot enough. Earlier, while his meal had heated, for sterilization purposes he had also heated the knife.

Then he looked lovingly at a huge sore on his arm. G.I.'s called them gook sores. A week ago he had cut into it with his bayonet and drained enough pus to fill a six-ounce C-ration can. A month and a half ago, Jenks had told him that the record for gook sore pus draining was a helmet full. Fleming wanted that record. He knew the record wouldn't be broken today but he was eager to see how much he had progressed.

Prodding the sore with his knife, he had a fleeting moment to think of the absurdity and lunacy of this exercise, but when the pus started draining he forgot all about absurdity and lunacy. He grabbed the C-ration can, and let pus drain into it.

Just then a helicopter landed at the CP.

Three ounces, he said to himself, high with anticipation.

Carlyle wandered over. He looked at Fleming then looked at the pus draining into the can. "What the fuck you doin?"

"Goin for the record," Fleming replied, gritting his teeth and squeezing the sore. "In the next couple days or so this baby is gonna give it to me."

"That's sure one ugly lookin baby." Carlyle pointed at the sore and shuddered. "How the fuck did you get that?"

Engrossed in his work, Fleming took a moment to look up at Carlyle. "I cut my arm on some elephant grass. An ant or some bug probably pissed in it." He smiled. "Left me with one hell of a Gook sore." Then he looked back at the sore, intent on the operation.

Carlyle grimaced as if in pain. "Yeah, that's one hell of a sore. You sure your ass ain't pregnant?"

"Sure the fuck hope not. Lousy world to bring a kid into."

"There it fucking is."

Vines wandered over to them. For a long moment he looked at Fleming then turned to Carlyle. "What the fuck's he doin?"

"Playing with his son."

"Damn, Fleming, your arm oughta be donated to medical science." Vines grimaced as if in pain. "Better make that science fiction."

Fleming gritted his teeth and squeezed the sore. He looked like a housewife squeezing the last drops of juice from a lemon. "Fuck!" He yelled, disappointed. "Only six ounces." Fleming held the can out to them so they could see.

Vines jumped back, as if some pus-demon would leap out of the can. "Damn, you sure you're awright? Maybe I oughta' get Garret."

"Shee-it," Carlyle exclaimed. "Fleming digs hard-core shit like this."

Fleming thought a moment before smiling at Carlyle. "I do kinda' dig this."

"No really," Vines said concerned. "Maybe I oughta' get Garret."

"Nah, it's fine." He eyed both men. "Don't worry, when you two cherries finally get some time in country, you'll get one too."

"Can't wait," Carlyle said facetiously.

"I'm not worried," Vines added. "And I can wait."

Fleming rubbed some salve on the sore. "What's up?"

"Ohhh," Vines said. He reached inside the pocket of his fatigue trouser. "I almost forgot. The chopper left some mail. You got some." He handed him two letters.

Fleming took them and read the address. A wide grin split his face. "Thanks, it's from my sister and my Mom. My sister's ten. She thinks I'm a hero. She says her whole fifth grade class thinks I'm a hero too" He mentally noted that he hadn't received a letter from his cousin Dan Shepherd, a ranger in the 101st. But as long as Fleming had know bim, his cousing had always been an asshole about some things.

"Read your letters, hero," Vines said. "Me and Carlyle will get the squad ready."

They left and Fleming opened the letter from his sister. It was brief but alarming. It simply said. I still love you even if you have changed, but I hope you haven't. Love, Hope. What the fuck was that all about? He asked himself. Every letter from his sister was only a few sentences but this one was strange. Then he opened the other letter. His mother wished him well, told him to be careful and to take care of himself. He'd always been a fine, kind son and she emphasized that she would never believe he would do anything immoral or wrong.

What the fuck? He thought. Where the hell was all this coming from?

She went on to say that the other day Hope had come home from school crying because people in her class said that her brother was a baby killer, that all Vietnam soldiers were murderers. She said that some of the other students' parents had complained to the school that Hope was reading letters from her soldier brother and since a lot of the parents didn't believe in the war she was now forbidden to read them. His mother went on to say that the newspapers and the evening news had been full of reports about atrocities committed by American soldiers. She repeated that she knew he would never do anything like that. She asked that he stay the same happy go lucky boy she had always known and loved. She asked that he write and tell her that he had done no wrong and if he couldn't honestly tell her that, then she knew that extenuating circumstances pushed him to it. Above all, she wanted him to come home alive and in one piece.

Angry and frustrated, he didn't know what to think. Did she really want the truth? Sorry about that, Mom, but your son has done a lot of killing. What do you think, Mom? Should we tell Hope that her hero big brother is one hell of a gook killer? I'm not bragging either. I'm good at it. I'm the best of the best. The past two months, Mom, I've wasted at least twenty to thirty men. Don't know for sure on that figure, Mom, I done lost count after about fifteen. And the other day, I set the night on fire. I burned down a whole village. I left all these old men, women, and little children homeless. It's freedom, Mom. We're setting these people free even though they don't want or need our concept of freedom. But they're dumb gooks, Mom. We must show them what's best for them.

He stood, seething with anger. He flung his precious can of pus across the perimeter.

He sat back down and placed his head in his hands. I can't believe this shit, he said to himself. Fuck the Army! Fuck the War! Fuck the News! Fuck the newspapers! And fuck the motherfucking parents who hurt my sister's feelings! What the fuck did they know? How many of them were ever in a situation where they wondered if they were about to spend their last minute on earth? Were they ever so scared they shit and pissed their pants? Did they ever laugh with a friend then the next minute that friend was dead? And not just dead either, disintegrated into a broken mass of severed arms, legs, and human insides. Did they ever play mind games with themselves so they could forget that they ever knew the men who had died? Because if they didn't they would just sit down and cry their eyes out at the absurdity of it all. Did they ever wrack their brains wondering how shit like this happened? Did they ever try to justify why it was happening?

They sent me here, he said to himself. Every last swinging dick was responsible for him being here and now they were feeling dirty because this shitty war was so fuckin' immoral they needed someone to blame and they weren't about to blame themselves. It was easier to strike at the very people who had been forced to carry out their filthy war.

"Fleming, you okay?"

Fleming looked up and saw Ryerson standing above him. Fleming said nothing.

"We're moving out and your squad has point." Ryerson moved closer and whispered. "You look like shit. Like you lost your best friend."

"I lost enough of them, ain't I?" he shot back.

"Yeah, you have, but we haven't the time to get into that right now. We have to move out. Are you all right? I can put another squad on point."

Fleming looked at his men: a filthy, ragtag collection of nearly every ethnic, minority group in America. They were all young, vulnerable, mostly teen-agers, men who desperately wanted to live at least until they turned twenty. They tried to hide their fear behind the masks of bravado that they all wore. It was then that Fleming realized that there was one thing he feared more than the bullets and the death and the unwarranted reprimands. He wasn't about to be the type of man who let his men down. They depended on him. He was their leader. His skin suddenly tingled and broke into gooseflesh. He felt the hair on his arms rise. He grabbed his gear and put on his helmet.

"I'm all right, L.T." He walked over to his men. "Let's move the fuck out. I got point."

Every man's face broke into a childlike grin. For a short while their fear was gone.

CHAPTER 14

Somewhere in the Central Highlands

THE NEW CHERRY

Fleming gazed out at the dark night. The past two months the platoon had humped Kontum Province's impossible terrain without incident.

Lieutenant Ryerson jumped into his foxhole. He pointed at Fleming's arms – a mass of inflamed, blistering gook sores that slowly oozed sticky thick pus. "That looks bad."

Ryerson wasn't looking so good himself. His fatigues were ragtag and ripped. Torn trousers exposed much of his right leg and the red rash that ran all along his inner thigh. His left leg was in the same condition.

"I'm one big gook sore," Fleming said. "I got crotch rot on my legs and it itches like hell until we hump and I start sweatin, then it burns like hell. I got the runs so bad that when I shit it's like Niagra Falls. I'm pretty fucked."

"Everyone's fucked," Ryerson replied. "We lose any more men we'll be in a world of hurt."

That was Fleming's only consolation. There were more men in worse condition than he. The past two months they had lost ten men to malaria, heat exhaustion, hookworm, ringworm and dysentery. "We're still getting cherries tomorrow, ain't we?"

Ryerson chuckled mirthlessly. "Yeah, and that will bring the platoon to close to three quarters strength. We lose more men to sickness then we do to the gooks."

"Sir, cause we ain't seen the gooks yet. When we do we'll still be fucked up, only we'll be dodging bullets and losing more men."

"Sometimes I wish they'd hit us. It would break up the monotony." Ryerson looked at his watch. "I'd better run. Gotta check the other holes." Ryerson climbed out of the foxhole. He turned back to Fleming. "We got a good platoon. They're humping motherfuckers." Then Ryerson hurried off.

They were indeed humping motherfuckers. They had also become close to each other, huddling like wild horses before a storm.

He glanced at Carlyle, sleeping in the same foxhole. Carlyle had a sharp wit and a biting tongue and was totally unpredictable, yet he fit in with the squad like a greased gear meshing with a similar gear.

A klick away a flare illuminated, lighting the pitch-black night and countryside like it was daytime.

Carlyle taught Fleming to see things with a newer, fresher viewpoint. One time Fleming made a reference about colored people. Carlyle had asked: "Who are colored people?" Fleming felt foolish with his reply that Carlyle was colored.

"No, you are," Carlyle countered. "You're white. No, Luke the Gook is colored, he's yellow. Rojas is colored. He's...I don't know what color he is but he ain't like you or me. We all got a little color in us."

Fleming had never thought about it before. "Tell you what," he said. "From now on, I'll call all the white dudes colored – kinda even up the score for you a bit."

Carlyle smiled at him. "You ain't that fuckin dumb for a white motherfucker."

Fleming smiled back. "For a colored motherfucker."

Most of the men clung to the members of their squads almost exclusively, but everyone respected both Garret and L T Ryerson. Ryerson was a born leader. He always sought a second opinion before issuing orders. Then he formulated a plan and took responsibility for it. He was from Seattle, Washington, the son of a successful lawyer. Ryerson had political aspirations and that was why he volunteered for Vietnam. He believed that a leader of a city, state, or a country should know how to lead and the only way to gain that skill was to actually lead. "My Father didn't want me coming here," Ryerson had told

Fleming. "He said I would be with low life Infantry types. He's pro Vietnam. It's okay for others to come here but not his son."

Everyone had seen Doc Garret literally run through enemy fire to help a wounded man. Everyone owed him a favor and he wasn't shy about collecting. Of course payment always came down to a unique way to keep men alive or to save lives.

Sergeant Lebeau got along with no one. He constantly argued with the men for wearing jewelry, love beads, peace signs, black power medallions and helmet graffiti. Washington had written 'God is my Pointman" on his helmet cover and Lebeau argued furiously with him about it until Ryerson was forced to intervene.

Doyle and Fields clung exclusively to each other and rarely spoke to Fleming or the other squad members. But since the rape, they had been on good behavior.

At 0300 hours, Fleming woke Carlyle for the final four hours of watch. Fleming then snuggled into the foxhole's corner for some sleep. In Vietnam he was a member of a community working toward the brotherhood and well being of other community members. Each day they were learning to ignore fear, hardship, and prejudice. Before falling asleep he wondered what tomorrow's cherries would be like.

Four hours later, Fleming awakened to the sound of choppers landing at the CP. Cherries were deposited; two were assigned to Fleming. He took them off to the side to speak with them in private. "What's your names?" he asked.

"Carson," a tall blonde said with a smile. "Carson from Connecticut. He held his hand out to Fleming and shook hands with him vigorously. "It's sure a pleasure meeting you, sergeant." His smile was warm and friendly.

"Call me Fleming.

"Okay, Sergeant Fleming," Carson said enthusiastically, his ever present smile resting on his face.

Despite the minor sergeant faux pas, Fleming couldn't help but smile back at him. He turned to the other cherry: he was skinny, wore glasses, and had curly black hair. He stared straight ahead saying nothing.

"What I gotta ask twice?" Fleming asked. "What's your name, cherry?"

The man heaved a heavy sigh, a look of revulsion on his face as he scanned the perimeter. "This can't be where you reside. This can't be what we're all dying for?"

"We don't talk about dying, cherry. We like to think this is what we are living for."

The cherry rolled his eyes skyward.

The gesture angered Fleming. "I asked you your fuckin name. You ain't told me yet."

Again he rolled his eyes skyward and pointed to his nametag.

"I can fuckin read," Fleming shot back. "Tell me your fuckin name," he said each word slowly and distinctly.

"Rodgers," he answered brusquely. "Ryan Rodgers."

Fleming gave him a long hard look then ordered Rodgers and Carson to follow him. He took them to the squad's fighting position. The other men were busy preparing their gear for the day's march.

"Well I'll be dipped in shit," Carlyle said, shaking his head and groaning. "We got ourselves two brand new chucks." (Chucks-slang for Caucasian).

"What's a chuck?" Carson asked.

"Colored guys like us," Fleming answered.

Carson's face tightened with confusion.

Carlyle, Washington, and Vines had wide smiles on their faces.

Carson saw their smiling faces. "What? Did I miss something?"

"You and me," Fleming explained. "We're colored guys. That's all you gotta know."

"Okay," Carson said uncertain. "I guess…. I can be a colored guy. I'm Carson from Connecticut." He introduced himself while shaking each man's hand.

Rodgers didn't make eye contact with anyone. He scanned the perimeter, a bored expression on his face. Then he walked about twenty meters away, placed his rucksack on the ground and sat on it.

"Let me check your rucksack, Carson from Connecticut," Carlyle offered. "I don't want your cherry ass passing out. It'd be just my luck they make me hump some of your shit."

"Sure," Carson said, smiling; his smile was rivaled only by Washington's. "That's awful nice or you. I sure appreciate it." He handed Carlyle his rucksack.

"Get your shit together," Fleming ordered everyone. "L T says we're moving out within the hour." Then Fleming walked over to Rodgers. "Are you a hardass, or are you just fuckin dumb?"

Rodgers rolled his eyes once again. The eye-rolling trick was getting old fast, Fleming thought.

"I have never been called a hard ass. And my hearing is fine so I am certainly not dumb. If your meaning was am I stupid? I'm not that either. Most people I know think I am a rather interesting, intelligent person."

"And I am one of those people," Fleming snapped sarcasticly. "That's why I'm taking the time to impart words of wisdom. Your stuck up prick attitude ain't gonna fly. Why the fuck didn't you introduce yourself like Carson did?"

"I am sure I didn't offend anyone's feelings. They look like the sort of men who wouldn't be offended by a mere lapse in social protocol."

Fleming eyed him for a long moment. "You're a cherry in Vietnam. That makes you the lowest and dumbest motherfucker on the totem pole in a place where you really don't wanna' be the lowest and dumbest motherfucker on the totem pole. So I'd try and get on everybody's good side. They'll keep you alive. I mean that's what I'd do if I was you."

Rodgers wore a bored facial expression during Fleming's speech. "You're not me."

Again Fleming was angered by the attitude. Before he could say anything Rodgers asked: "Isn't it appropriate for an Army squad to consist of approximately thirteen men? With the addition of myself and Carson it brings our squad's total to nine."

"It is appropriate for an Army squad to consist of thirteen men," Fleming replied. "But thirteen man squads is a luxury we ain't never had."

"Great," he snapped sarcastically. "Are you finished speaking with me?"

"Why, you goin somewhere?'

Rodgers stared at a spot somewhere above Fleming's head, clearly making a show of ignoring Fleming.

"Listen, asshole. We're gonna' start over. Where you from?"

"Los Angeles."

"Carlyle's from L.A." Fleming replied in a matter of fact tone.

Rodgers frowned. "So what's that supposed to mean, I know him. Maybe you failed to notice but Carlyle is obviously from the inner city. My Father was rather wealthy. I doubt if Carlyle and I traveled in the same circles."

"You're a real asshole. It's surprising because you talk like you're educated. You'd think you'd know how to treat people."

"Your insulting assessment of my lack of social grace aside, I am educated. I've been to college. I attended Berkely."

"I shoulda' fucking known. That's where they're doin all the war protesting."

"They're protesting everywhere. Berkely is more vehement about it so it receives most of the attention."

"What's an educated, important guy like you doin in the Nam?"

Rodgers shifted his body, an uncomfortable expression rested on his faces. He began fidgeting with his hands.

Fleming knew that his words had struck a nerve. "You quit college, didn't ya? Or you flunked out?"

"I decided to drop out for a semester. Then I had the misfortune of being drafted."

"I can tell you ain't real thrilled with being here."

"Quite observant of you," Rodgers answered sarcastically, rolling his eyes again. "The war is immoral and wrong."

"Then why didja' drop outta' school? And why didja' volunteer for airborne? They don't draft you into that. You're rich. You drop outta' college. You had to know you'd be drafted. They're drafting like everybody. Didja' think Daddy's money was gonna protect you from the draft?"

Again Rodgers shifted nervously. "This is really starting to sound like the third degree. I don't believe I am required to answer all these questions."

"You don't have to answer shit. You do have to listen to every word I say or you and I have a real problem and that can only turn out bad for you. I'm one guy you don't want to piss off."

Rodgers again looks at a spot directly above Fleming's head.

"Get your shit together, cherry. We're movin out in about five minutes." Fleming turned and started away. There was no way Rodgers would fit in with the other squad members. And Fleming's job was to make sure that he did. So far being a squad leader had been simple. Now wasn't the time to think about Rodgers. They had patrol. He needed to focus on the enemy.

"All right, troops," Lebeau yelled. "We're climbing that hill."

The hill was sixty feet high. It went straight up at almost a ninety-degree angle.

"Why are we attempting to climb that mountain?" Rodgers gasped to Fleming. "Why can't we just bypass it?"

"An hour ago a chopper spotted the NVA in this area. That means they know we're here and we're on their asses. They gotta' slow us down. There's a better than good chance that they've mined everything around this hill. Somebody steps on a mine and blows himself to hell, we gotta' find the pieces. That will slow us up. That's what they're countin' on. That's why we take the harder route. That's why we gotta' go up the hill."

"I believe climbing the mountain will also delay us?"

"Yeah it will. Either way the gooks win. But the hill is safer. We go around it you might be the one who steps on the mine and we have to look for your pieces."

Rodgers frowned.

They started up the hill. Each step was energy sapping. Rodgers' breathing came in gasps. Sweat streamed down his face.

Half an hour and thirty feet later, they were half way up the hill. It was so steep that Fleming could see the tread of the man's boots above him and nothing else.

"Oh my God!" Rodgers suddenly screamed. He began swatting at his fatigue blouse. Then he lost his balance and started sliding down the hill.

Fleming just barely managed to grab Rodgers' rucksack slowing him down. Rodgers grabbed a small bush breaking the fall.

"Something's biting me!" Rodgers screamed at Fleming.

Fleming wedged his foot against a shrub and opened Rodgers' blouse.

Ants swarmed all over Rodgers' chest. The second Rodgers saw them he started swatting at them.

Fleming produced a bottle and squirted insect repellent on Rodgers'chest. The ants fell off. "You'll be okay. Now get your ass in gear and let's go."

An hour later they reached the hill's top where it leveled off to a plateau. Ryerson ordered the platoon to break for chow.

Everyone removed rucksacks and flopped on the ground exhausted.

"Carlyle," Vines said with an impish twinkle in his eye. "Rodgers is from LA. You're practically neighbors."

"Really" Carlyle said unemotionally. "Where in LA?"

Rodgers gave him a mirthless smile. "Brentwood."

Carlyle frowned. "He's from the other side of the universe. I'm from Watts." He smiled mischievously and grabbed his crotch. "We were so poor if I wasn't born a boy I woulda' had nothing to play with."

Most of the men grunted out a chuckle.

"That's what I like about you guys, you're always joking. Kinda' takes the edge off what a bitch this shit is," Carson said laughing and smiling at Carlyle.

Wide smiles spread across everyone's face. Carson's smile was contagious.

Rodgers shook his head in disgust at Carson. Then he opened his canteen and started pouring water on his hands.

"What the fuck you doing?" Washington yelled grabbing Rodgers' hand and stopping him.

"Washing my hands. Before eating I always wash my hands."

"Damn, cherry, you need that water. You can't waste it like that." Fleming reached down, grabbed Rodgers' canteen, and screwed the cap back on. "You'll fucking dehydrate. Water is like gold out here."

Washington shook his head at him. "For a smart guy, you're one dumb motherfucker."

"No, no," Carlyle protested. "The cherry's got his shit together. I gotta' tell ya, I'm getting tired of all ya'all's filthy asses. In fact, fuck all ya'all, I'm washin' my hands too." Carlyle dropped his fatigue trousers and began urinating on his hands while going through the motions of washing.

Everyone started laughing except Rodgers.

"Now I shall towel off," Carlyle said in a pretty good imitation of a British accent. He wiped his hands on his shirt, sat down, and held his C-Ration spoon with his pinkie finger extended.

Most of the men were roaring with laughter. Vines laughed so hard tears rolled down his cheeks.

"That's what I mean," Carson said laughing. "You're always doing some really funny shit."

Rodgers watched them with a look of disgust written all over his face.

A few moments later everyone is settled down.

"Hey, cherry. You're a smart motherfucker. Why we in the Nam?" Washington asked.

Rodgers frowned at him. "So corporations can make money, why do you think? This country is engaged in a civil war. Political Science rule number one is to stay away from involvement in foreign civil wars. Yet we're here. And, to compound matters, America is responsible for the civil war. The people back home are protesting our involvement. The Vietnamese, the ones we are allegedly helping, want us to leave. Yet we are here. Our Politicians disguise our true motives with speeches, pontificating dubious claims about democracy and the honorable goal of spreading freedom, setting people free. But a Texan President has granted a Texas Company, Halliburton, and their subsidiary Brown, Root, and Kellogg the majority of the defense contracts and they are reaping a fortune. Does that tell you anything?"

"Who the fuck are Brown, Root, and Kellogg?" Washington asked.

"Kellogg," Carlyle said. "Ain't they the people who make Rice Krispies? Rodgers is right. We got the Krispies, we're over here getting their rice."

Rodgers smirked at them, shaking his head back and forth. "They are defense contractors, like Boeing, who makes helicopters, and makes billions from this helicopter war. The bottom line: our true motive isn't freedom for the Vietnamese but monetary gain for these corporations and a dozen others like them. Our ultimate aim in this fruitless endeavor is most assuredly one that is aimed to facilitate business conglomerates back in the U.S. And corporations are quite frank about stating their goals. Profit, money, is all that concerns them."

Washington stared at him with open mouth wonder. Then he jabbed Carlyle with an elbow. "He talking English?"

"No, it's foreign. Irish, I think."

Carson beamed his smile. "See what I mean – Irish. I like that."

Everyone was smiling and laughing except for Rodgers and this time Fleming. He didn't like the conversation's tone. He didn't want the squad split and this kind of talk and behavior could create a rift between Rodgers and the other men. Rifts had a tendency to grow and he didn't want dissension in the squad.

Vines whistled, a loud shriek of mocking appreciation. "That white motherfucker can talk, and he got all the answers. I'm looking forward to him teaching my dumb Black ass."

Rodgers looked at him. "We speak on different levels. I sincerely doubt that you would gain any intellectual stimulation by conversing with me?"

"Say what?" Washington asked with genuine confusion.

"Ain't nobody gonna understand this honky talk cept when we get in a fire fight," Carlyle said. "And he yell for help. Then he'll find the power of the black man intellectually stimulatin' when we pull his lilly white ass outta' the shit."

"Enough!" Fleming growled. "I don't want to hear any more of this shit from any of you. Lay off this dip shit cherry." He intensely gazed at Rodgers while pointing a finger at him. "Lighten the fuck up. You don't know shit. I don't wanta' say it again. Everybody shut the fuck up." Frustrated, Fleming stood and walked to the other end of the plateau. Frustrated he sat on a boulder.

Seconds later, Rojas took a seat next to him. "Man, you're about to have trouble."

"I know. This cherry is fucked. What can I do?"

For a long moment Rojas studied Fleming's face. "We ain't worried about him. We're worried about you. He's white, you're white."

"I ain't prejudiced. You guys all know that."

"My whole life Whites have called me Rican, Spick Dick, shit like that. The Brothers have had it even worse. This Rodgers is an asshole. You're trying to get him to fit in with us but it ain't gonna happen unless you get all up in his shit. You don't, the other guys might start thinking you're sidin' with the white man."

"So you think I need to be tougher with him?"

Rojas stood. "That's it. I know you're trying to be a nice guy, but it ain't up to you to make sure he fits in. It's up to Rodgers to fit in." Then he walked away.

Rojas's logic was simple and concise. Fleming hadn't the time to hold Rodgers' hand through a tour in the Nam. And it was a cherry's job to fit in, not the other way around.

Fleming stood and hurried back to the men. "Rodgers, straighten out your college, rich boy ass or I'm gonna do you and I am gonna do it legally. You are to listen to every one of these men. If they tell you what to do, do it. I catch you fucking up one time you go on permanent point till you get wasted. Now do you understand what I just told you?"

Rodgers said nothing. He just stared into Fleming's eyes.

"You got two seconds to answer or you're on point."

"I understand," he replied instantly.

Fleming turned to Carlyle. "Gimme' some fuckin' skin." He holds his palm out.

Carlyle looked at the outstretched hand for a moment. "I got piss on my hands."

Fleming frowned at him. "Do you really think a colored guy is afraid to get a little pee pee on his hands?"

Carlyle's smiled at him. Chuckling he held his palm to Fleming.

They gently rubbed palms together while the rest of the men watched smiling.

"You really are some funny fucking guys," Carson laughed and smiled.

Van sat with the rest of the men in the underground bunker complex's conference room. The past few weeks had passed uneventfully. Patrols were intelligence-gathering missions to learn if a pattern could be detected in American movements. Standing orders were to engage if the Americans were near an infiltration point and only during an infiltration. It was fortunate it never happened; it was then that the Americans called in airpower and artillery.

Chi stepped in front of the gathered men. "I know all of you are thirsting for action. We have finally been ordered to engage the enemy. An American Platoon is getting too close to an infiltration point. It is only a matter of time before they learn that we are bringing men into South Vietnam at this location. We will harass them and slow their march. It is a hit and run tactical operation that we do so well. We go out tonight." Chi then adjourned the meeting.

As they were leaving Hoi rushed up to Van and stood by him until they were out of earshot of the others. "When are we going to defect?" He whispered.

Van had known that Hoi would bring this up the minute Chi had explained the mission's intent. Hoi had never gotten over his fear of combat. He had hardly mentioned defection when they were only patrolling. "When I am sure it's the right thing to do."

"It's the right thing to do. We were forced into this life – against our will!" Although Hoi was whispering he was livid with rage, small beads of spittle sprayed from his mouth when he spoke. "The Americans had nothing to do with forcing us to live this…this perversion of life!"

"Why are they here, Hoi? Their being here forced us into this life."

"You don't know that! You're a farm boy! You don't know the affairs of government! Maybe they are here to truly help us. And the Americans didn't kill Kim? They didn't kill her parents either. The North did!"

It was why Van could never give full allegiance to the North, but he couldn't give allegiance to America either. Whoever started this war was responsible for the unspeakable suffering in his homeland. But determining the guilty party seemed impossible. "I am not moving from a bad situation only to end up in a worse one."

Hoi grabbed Van's arm tightly. "The South is better than the North. I know it is." On the verge of tears, he let go of Van's arm and looked away. "I can't serve with the North any longer. I can't hurt people. I surely can't kill them…. I can't"

"Maybe both sides are wrong. Maybe we won't have any type of life until this war is over. Maybe it is our karma to go through this."

"I can't fight. I can't go on one more mission. If we defect and refuse to fight they will give us other jobs. It's worth taking the chance. Here we have no choice but to fight."

"Sometimes you have to fight in order to survive."

Hoi's jaw set stubbornly. "I can't do this any longer."

"I will make a decision soon. Just promise me that you will take care of yourself."

"I hate this. I can't kill human beings. I won't kill." Hoi turned and walked away.

Hoi was the last link to the village and Van had to protect him. However, Van was also a squad leader and couldn't put the lives of his comrades in danger in an effort to protect Hoi. It was an unwinnable proposition. He knew only one thing – for everyone's sake, he had to soon make a definite decision about defecting.

CHAPTER 15

Playing The Game

Rojas relieved a tired Fleming who then curled in the foxhole's corner for some much needed sleep. The past three weeks they seemed to have covered every square inch of the Central Highlands and found no trace of the large enemy force supposedly infiltrating the area.

It was a numb, exhausting ordeal: humping all day, stopping at dusk to dig nighttime foxholes and then every fourth day going out on an all night ambush. Every squad was operating at less than full strength which meant that night time watch hours were longer than usual; the men were only getting four hours restless sleep a night. The next day the same exhausting routine was repeated. Some of the men were literally so sick they were running fevers; however, MACV'S policy clearly stated that a sick man's body temperature had to be at least 102 degrees for a period of two days before he would be allowed back to the rear for rest and treatment. All of the men were physically exhausted. Because of the enemy's inactivity the men, mostly cherries, were not getting any combat experience. There was no way to gauge how they would perform in a firefight.

Rodgers was a mass of rashes and sores and constantly complained about everything. Fleming had told him he'd eventually get used to the routine. "I realize this," he had said. "In time, a person can become accustomed to anything. I need to know why I am being made to suffer. What's the reason behind it? Where is the justification in it? Is this a government sponsored, macabre endurance experiment to see just how much a man can endure?"

Thankfully his bitching and negativity didn't affect the squad. But it did have a ring of truth. No one could come close to explaining why they were enduring such hardship or justify why they were suffering.

Rodgers remained a mystery. Fleming learned nothing about him, except that he was twenty-four, a few years older than most of the men, and that he had attended college for four years but hadn't yet graduated. His Father owned a huge advertising agency and had been a standout football end at Stanford. Naturally, Rodgers hated football. Piecing together bits of information, Fleming concluded that Rodgers frittered his way through college, using his Father's money while harboring hostility toward him.

His last thought before falling asleep was of Rodgers. Fleming wondered how he was going to turn him into a soldier.

0600 hours, underground bunker complex: Chi stood before the platoon. He spoke: "Three squads will attack the Americans. Van's squad and a squad led by me will follow and harass by doing what we do best – hit and run. Our job is simple. We slow their march. If they become frustrated and careless we will kill more of them. Our first priority is to slow them and divert them from the infiltration point."

A moment passed, as everyone digested the information.

"Let's move out," Chi ordered.

Fleming called the men together. "People, we gotta turn around and march in the direction we just came from."

"Well there it fuckin is," the normally taciturn Rojas cursed. "Why the fuck we turning around – military intelligence fuck up again?"

"They intercepted voice communications just twenty minutes ago. The Gooks are only one to two klicks behind us."

Rojas blew out a tired stream of air. "That ain't too bad, two klicks."

"Hey, cherry," Carlyle called to Rodgers. "Maybe we'll finally see some action. You can show us how you "get some." Maybe you'll even win a medal."

"Oh, I can hardly wait. That would be a momentous feat in my military career, winning a medal for gallantry."

"I don't care what any of you say," Vines said. "He says things in the prettiest way."

"Let's go," Fleming ordered.

"I think the Gooks done gone home," Carlyle said. "They know we got Rodgers and they scared of this super honky."

Carson flashed his smile. "You got that right. They're afraid of all us super honky colored guys."

Carlyle threw an arm around Carson's shoulder. "Don't he just remind you of your little brother."

Carson smiled at him. "Do I really?"

"Well, yeah, except for one thing."

Carson pondered for a long moment. "What's that?'

"My little brother's black you're white.

Carson flashed his brilliant smile. "No, I'm colored."

"There it is," Fleming said. "Now that it's established that Carson's a colored person can we move out?"

Rojas moved the men forward.

After walking a klick, the sound of a single fired AK-47 round pierced the morning stillness.

A cacophony of M-16 fire followed almost immediately.

"CEASE FIRE!" Fleming screamed, hearing no more enemy fire. "CEASE FIRE! BUT STAY DOWN!"

Everyone followed the order. Silence ruled for a long moment.

"I NEED A MEDIC!" a voice suddenly screamed out.

Seconds later, Doc Garret's was seen running across the perimeter.

Minutes later, gun ships arrived and unleashed a bevy of rockets and machine gun fire at the enemy position.

Rojas and Fleming made their way to Garret. Fields was lying on the ground, blood pouring from a hole in his chest. Doyle was sitting next to him, a bloody bandage in his hand. Garret looked up at Fleming and Rojas and shook his head no.

"Is he dead?" Doyle asked.

A moment passed.

"Is he fuckin dead, Doc?" Doyle snapped.

"Yeah, he's fuckin dead," Garret snapped back.

Five minutes later, a chopper landed and took Fields' dead body. Minutes later the men resumed their march.

Ten minutes later, they approached a heavily wooded area. It was like a mini jungle; it lacked triple canopy growth, but the vegetation was thick and rich enough to provide ample ambush sites.

Lebeau, Ryerson, Fleming, and the other squad leaders gathered together to confer. Ryerson studied a map. "According to the map after three hundred meters we come to a clearing. Going around this little jungle would add an hour to our time and they want us near the infiltration point ASAP. So we go through the jungle."

"If we get ambushed at least we'll have the little people trapped in there," Lebeau offered. "They gotta di-di out in the open and the choppers will get them. With luck we'll get Colonel Bradford a decent body count."

Fleming and Pierson exchanged glances.

"What?" Lebeau asked. "You against getting the Colonel a decent body count?"

Fleming shook his head no. "If the Gooks got the balls to hit us they probably got an underground bunker complex in that jungle. It would take a month to find them."

Lebeau thought about it for a moment. "You're probably right. I wish just one time they had the balls to stand up and fight us."

Fleming wondered if Lebeau would have the balls to stand up and fight without the huge advantage of superior artillery and air power. "They're gonna have to grow them balls, Sergeant. And we ain't got the time to wait on that."

Lebeau chuckled. "We finally agree on something,"

Fleming turned away from Lebeau and rolled his eyes at Pierson.

Pierson gave him a surreptitious smile.

Then they moved into the jungle.

Inside the jungle, Chi was with four other men on the flank of an L-shaped ambush. Dan was with another squad directly in front of the American's path. This was the first part of a two-part attack plan. Each part was designed to slow the Americans march toward the infiltration point so soldiers could safely slip into Vietnam from nearby Cambodia and Laos.

Rojas led them fifty yards into the jungle. He intently studied the terrain directly in front of him. He, Fleming, Vines, Washington, and Doyle were acting as a team. Fleming was to the left of Rojas and ten meters behind him. Fleming's job was to watch everything at eye level to the left of Rojas. Vines, thirty meters to Fleming's immediate right, studied the terrain at eye level on the right flank. Between the three of them they were effectively covering all the terrain for an area of thirty meters, east to west, in front of them. Behind them Washington and Doyle were scanning the treetops. Thwarting an ambush depended on a lot of luck and each man's ability to maintain focus on their specific assigned areas.

One of the newer men in Dan's squad raised his head ever so slightly above a clump of vegetation.

Rojas saw the slightest flash of a human face. Acting on sheer instinct, he squeezed his weapon's trigger while dropping to the ground. Fleming and the others immediately opened fire while falling to the earth.

The American point man's rounds hit the V.C. soldier in the face and a huge splotch of blood spurted into the air. Dan and the other men fell flat to the ground in order to avoid the American onslaught of M-16 and M-60 fire.

When the initial American onslaught subsided, Chi ordered his men to open fire on the flanking Americans.

Buzzing rounds whizzed past Carlyle. He dropped to his hands and knees and crawled, advancing toward the flanking enemy.

Carson advanced forward but was stopped when a round pierced his neck. He staggered backward then fell at Rodgers' feet. Rodgers took one look at Carson's blood gushing neck wound and vomitted. Desperate and scared, revolted by the bloody wound, he ran behind a tree five meters from Carson's downed body.

Unaware that Carson has been hit, Carlyle continued crawling toward the gunfire on the flank.

A V.C. raised his AK-47.

Carlyle rolled behind a tree just as the V.C. let loose a burst of AK-47 fire.

Fleming, Rojas, Vines, Doyle, and Washington continued firing at the enemy in front of them and were unaware that there was a battle on the flank.

Dan and his squad were armed only with AK-47's and were completely outgunned by the Amercans on the point. They were putting up a fight but the M-60 fire was devastating.

"Rodgers," Carson moaned in a gurgling choked tone. "Help me, please."

Rodgers wanted to run out and pull him to safety. But he was petrified with fear.

Pinned down by AK-47 fire, Carlyle clearly heard Carson moaning and calling to Rodgers. He saw Carson lying on the ground, blood gushing from his neck. "Rodgers, get Carson," Carlyle screamed. "I'll cover you." Carlyle knew the general location of the V.C. firing the AK-47. If he fired a grenade in that direction; it would allow Rodgers ample time to rescue Carson.

"Rodgers.... Help me...please," Carson moaned.

Rodgers closed his eyes and placed his hands against his ears to drown out Carson's helpless, pathetic moaning.

Carlyle fired his M-79.

Chi heard the blooping sound of a fired M-79 round and knew a grenade would soon fall near his position. "DOWN!" He yelled. "GET DOWN!"

The grenade fell twenty meters away. Shrapnel whistled just above everyone's head, but no one was harmed.

"Rodgers...please," Carson moaned.

Frustrated, Rodgers pounded his fist against the earth.

Carlyle looked back and couldn't believe that Carson was still lying out in the open. "Rodgers, I'm covering you. You'll be okay, I promise! Get Carson!" Carlyle fired another M-79 round.

Again Chi ordered the men down. This time the round fell closer to them

Blood gushing from his neck, Carson continued moaning and pleading for help.

Rodgers wished that Carson would shut up. Rodgers wanted to help him but he just couldn't make himself run out there and grab Carson.

"Motherfucker!" Carlyle yelled, frustrated. "Get him! Don't let him die!"

The M-60 fire and the American onslaught forced Dan and his men to retreat. They backed out, laying suppressing fire as they made their way back toward the underground bunker complex and safety.

Weapons' blasting away on automatic, Fleming realized that the V.C. intended to retreat. He ordered the men to push forward relentlessly.

Carlyle finally realized that he would have to pull Carson to safety. The enemy position was thirty meters in front of him. He fired his 79 then slung the weapon on his shoulder. In an attempt to reach

Carson, he ran from behind the tree all the while throwing hand grenades.

Chi saw that Dan and his men were retreating. The mission had been successful; they had seriously wounded an American and they had bought time for the infiltrating soldiers. He ordered the men to leave. Crouched low he and the other men started away. One man stayed behind and took aim on Carlyle.

Carlyle threw a grenade just as the V.C. fired his weapon. The grenade exploded. A chunk of shrapnel imbedded itself in the V.C.'s leg. The fired round penetrated the side of Carlyle's helmet, knocking him to the ground. Overcome with pain, the V.C. fell to the ground unable to retreat from the Americans.

Chi and his men scrambled behind a thick area of underbrush and trees. The temporary cover allowed them to stand erect and sprint toward the underground complex fifty yards away. They arrived shortly after Dan and his squad.

With the V.C.'s retreat, Fleming and his men headed toward the right flank and found the V.C. that Carlyle had wounded. They see a bleeding Carlyle sitting on the ground, dazed. "Washington, check on Carlyle," Fleming said.

Washington started toward him and saw a body lying on the ground. "Fleming, somebody else has been hit."

"Fuck," Fleming growled. He was sick and tired of losing men and then having the enemy run away. "Vines, Doyle, watch this Gook motherfucker."

"I'll watch the bastard," Doyle cursed. He fired a round into the man's head spilling his brains all over the ground. "There, he's watched."

"Damn, Doyle," Vines said, shocked.

"That coulda been the Gook who wasted Fields! Fuck that motherfucker!"

A silent moment passed.

"C'mon let's check on that body," Fleming said.

Just then Garret began examining Carlyle while Fleming and the others started toward the soldier lying on the ground.

"Jesus Christ, it's Carson!" Vines said. He and Fleming hurried toward the body.

Carson lay in an enormous pool of blood. His eyes and mouth were wide open in death's eternal stare. Fleming bent down, checked his pulse, and felt nothing.

It is then that Vines noticed Rodgers behind a tree. "Rodgers," he called out, surprised.

A vacant, stunned expression on his face, Rodgers sat there clutching his knees to his chest in a seated fetal position.

A moment of silence passed.

"What happened?" Fleming asked.

"I'll tell you what happened," Carlyle said approaching them along with Garret and Washington.

A generous amount of blood covered the right side of Carlyle's face. "Carlyle, you okay, man?" Fleming asked. "That's boocoo blood."

Carlyle wiped at the blood. "I'm fine. It's a scratch."

Garret shook his head in wonder and disbelief. "Bullet entered his helmet and scraped the side of his head. He is about an eight of an inch from being dead."

"You one lucky fuckin nigger," Vines said.

"What happened with Carson?" Fleming asked.

Carlyle's face tightened with anger, pointing at Rodgers. "He let him die. He coulda helped him and he just let him die."

With a blank facial expression Rodgers looked up at Carlyle.

"Why didn't you help him? Why?" Carlyle pleaded.

Garret dropped to his knees and examined Carson's dead body.

"What happened, Carlyle?" Fleming asked.

Carlyle related the story of Carson being shot. "He was begging you to help him. You were safe. I was laying covering fire. You just let him die."

Rodgers said nothing.

"Rodgers, is that how it happened?" Fleming asked.

"Damn right that's how it fuckin happened," Carlyle emphasized.

"Let him speak," Fleming said softly. A moment passed. "Rodgers, speak."

Rodgers looked in each man's eyes. "That's how it happened."

"You, Motherfucer!" Garret started toward him. "I'm gonna kick your fucking–"

Vines grabbed Garret in a vise like bear hug.

"I can't do this!" Rodgers yelled at them. "I'm not wired for combat. I wanted to help. He begged me to help him." Rodgers placed his hands against his ears as if he was reliving the event and he wanted to block the sound out. "I wanted to but I couldn't move."

"That don't cut it, you worthless piece of cherry shit!" Garret yelled while Vines had his clamp like hold on him. "You help men–"

Fleming grabbed Garret's arm and pulled him away from Vines. He ushered him away until they were out of earshot from the rest of the group.

"What the fuck you doing, Fleming? I need to set that cherry straight."

"That's my job."

"Then do your fucking job."

"You examined Carson. If Rodgers woulda got him could you have saved him?"

"It don't mean nothing. He let him lay there. I saw Carlyle run out there laying covering fire. He ran at them throwing fuckin frags for Christ sakes. Rodgers didn't do jack shit. Carlyle took a fucking round to the fucking head to help Carson, but Rodgers didn't–"

"I asked if you coulda saved Carson?"

A moment passed. "He bled to death. If Rodgers would have pulled him outta there he might've stopped the bleeding."

"That's a maybe. Would Carson have lived?"

Garret's face was alive with fury. "He woulda probably bled to death."

"So there it is."

"But he just sat there. He did nothing. He coulda helped–"

"It don't mean nothin. It wouldn't have mattered in the end."

Garret said nothing for a moment. "Everyone knows what that fucker did. They know they can't count on Rodgers. How ya gonna deal with that?"

"Man, I don't know, but it's my problem."

"He coulda at least tried. He didn't do jack shit. He just let that man die." Garret said while they walked back to the rest of the men.

"Carlyle, how's your head?" Fleming asked. "You okay?"

"My ears are ringing, but I'm all right."

"I can medavac you outta here," Garret offered. "It might be a good idea to get checked out back in the rear."

"I'm okay. I don't need no meda-vac."

"All right, let's di-di outta here." Fleming stared at Rodgers for a long hard moment. "Rodgers, carry Carson's body."

Rodgers nodded his head yes. They assembled and started away. This time Pierson's squad was on point.

Ten minutes later, they cleared the wooded area. Within five minutes a chopper landed and they loaded Carson's body.

Ryerson went to Fleming. "Sorry about your man. He seemed like a nice kid." "Eighteen fuckin years old and he's dead," Fleming replied. "Eighteen years old.

It's a fuckin waste."

"Boocoo good men are dying for some dubious reasons. But I do have some good news."

"I could use some good news."

"We're heading back to the rear. We finish this sweep, and then they are pulling us out, back to English for some hot chow and showers."

"Well, damn, that is pretty good news."

They spoke a few moments longer then the platoon started away and toward a huge patch of elephant grass.

Inside the jungle Chi and his men exited the underground bunker complex. The plan's second phase called for them to follow the Americans through the elephant grass until they entered the clearing then they would open fire on them. Directly in front of the Americans to the North was an ambush party. East of the Americans, Van, Hoi, and another man were in the jungle manning a mortar. The Americans would be hit from three sides.

Van sat next to a mortar with Hoi and another man. The ambush was safe for Chi and Van's team but dangerous for the men in the trench. They were directly in front of the Americans. One mistake could prove fatal to them. If the American helicopters came the men would be easy targets. This morning Chi had ordered them to camouflage their position with shrubbery and vegetation. It looked unnatural and Van pointed it out but Chi disregarded it.

It wouldn't be long now, Van thought. Any moment he expected to see the Americans emerge from the elephant grass.

The platoon exited the grass. They were close to finishing the sweep then hopping on a helicopter and a trip to the rear for showers, a hot meal, and a couple weeks rest.

Up ahead, Fleming saw an uneven line of shrubs and vegetation. It looked unnatural.

Rojas made his way back to him and pointed it out. "That looks out of place."

"There it is. I was thinking the exact same thing."

Suddenly small arms fire erupted from the shrub line, killing the point man and three other men.

In the Jungle, Van, Hoi, and the other man fired a mortar round.

"INCOMING!" A dozen American soldiers screamed simultaneously.

Fleming along with most everyone else hit the ground and started crawling toward bomb craters pockmarking the area.

Two Americans rushed back toward the elephant grass. They were cut down from small arms fire coming from inside the grass.

Fleming saw them fall and realized that they were taking fire from the North, South and the East.

Doyle was weaving drunkenly in front of Fleming. Most of his right arm was missing. The stump was flip flopping crazily, shooting blood as if it were a fire hose. Fleming stood and ran toward Doyle. He tackled Doyle around the waist. They tumbled into a bomb crater already occupied by Rojas and Carlyle.

Barely conscious, Doyle babbled incoherently, a dreamy faraway look filled his face. Fleming turned him on his side, elevating his blood-spewing stump. Doyle began screaming in pain. Fleming slammed a morphine shot into his leg. He fixed a tourniquet to his arm to stop the bleeding. "MEDIC!" Fleming screamed.

'I'M IN THE CRATER NEXT TO YOU!!" Garret yelled back. "I'M COMING. LAY DOWN COVER FIRE."

Fleming scrambled to the crater's top. He, Rojas, and Carlyle provided cover fire.

"RRRR!" Garret growled. He ran a few feet and leapt into the hole.

Hovering thirty feet in the air, gunships fired down into the trench. A second gunship, on the opposite side also began firing, trapping the enemy in a murderous crossfire.

A running Chi and his men arrived at Van's position. Simultaneously the tree line erupted into a fiery inferno of orange flame as the American planes dropped Napalm.

Instinctively, Chi's hand shot to his scarred face. "RUN!" he yelled.

Van grabbed his arm. "We have to check the trench. There might be wounded men in there."

"They're dead. You saw the gunships. They're dead."

"We have to check," Van insisted.

Fear was written all over Chi's face. "We have completed our mssion. We've stalled the Americans. Now we must leave. This whole area will be on fire soon."

"I'll help you," Dan offered.

Since they hadn't spoken in months Van was completely surprised but he welcomed the offer. Without another spoken word, he and Dan head through the jungle toward the trench's entrance.

Soon all firing ceased

Slowly the rest of the men exited the bomb craters. They started checking downed bodies for signs of life.

The gunships flew from the trench area and hovered above the jungle searching for the enemy mortar team.

"Where's that cherry motherfucker?" Carlyle yelled out.

No one had to ask whom he meant.

Just then Rodgers emerged from a bomb crater.

"Hey, cherry, you get some?" Carlyle snapped at him, still angry because of Carson.

Rodgers looked down.

Fleming rushed toward him, snatched his weapon, and sniffed the barrel. He threw the weapon back at Rodgers hitting him hard in the chest. "You got this fuckin thing so you could fire it! You gotta fuckin help us!"

"I can't do this!" Rodgers fired back. "I'll never be able to do this. I didn't ask to come here. This is not my war."

Rojas poked a finger into Rodgers' chest. "None of us asked to come here. And we sure as hell ain't gonna do your fightin."

Van and Dan reached the jungle's edge and were a short distance from the trench. They dropped to a prone position and slithered unseen down the trench until they reached the downed soldiers. Van handed his weapon to Dan and began checking men for signs of life.

Meanwhile, Ryerson, Lebeau and Pierson wandered over to Fleming's squad. "Bad day," Ryerson said. "We lost ten people and five wounded."

"My whole fuckin squad is gone," Pierson cursed. "Fuckin Gooks killed them all."

Van found one man alive. He turned to ask for Dan's help and was horrified to see Dan stand and fire his weapon at the Americans outside the trench. Then Dan crouched and scurried down the trench for the jungle.

An American soldier took the bullet in his heart and fell over dead.

"That came from the trench," Flemings said.

Just then Dan ran the short distance from the trench into the jungle.

"A fuckin gook," Pierson shouted. "Did you see that?"

"Maybe there are more in there," someone offered.

"Let's check," Pierson said. "Hell, let's go after that motherfucker."

"We don't have the time," Ryerson said. "Our dust off will be here soon."

"The gook's got a big lead," Fleming said to Pierson. "We won't catch him."

Wounded man on his back, Van reached the trench's end. He dreaded the act of running into the jungle exposing himself to the enemy. He sprinted from the trench to the jungle.

"There's another one," Pierson yelled, gesturing wildly at the running V.C. "That son of a bitch's got a wounded man. We can catch him."

Fleming thought about it for a split second. Fuck it, he said to himself. "Let's go."

"No, you'll miss the dust off," Ryerson said.

"Sir, it can wait. They killed our friends and your men, sir." Fleming yelled, running off with Pierson.

"Get back here, Fleming!" Lebeau screamed. "Or we'll court martial your ass!"

As soon as they reached the jungle's edge, Fleming saw blood on the ground. He grabbed Pierson's arm and pointed to it. "We got a blood trail. This will be easy."

Pierson nodded his head in agreement and they started away.

Carrying the wounded man, Van soon tired. When he placed the man down for a brief rest, he saw blood pouring from the man's shoulder wound. It had to be stopped or he would soon die. Van applied pressure to the wound with a bandage.

Suddenly Van heard the Americans crashing through the jungle and realized they were chasing him. He hoisted the wounded man on his shoulder and started off.

Following the blood, Fleming and Pierson crashed through the jungle when they heard sound behind them. Both men quickly turned, ready to fire. They saw Rojas followed by Carlyle, Vines, and Washington.

"Damn, it's good to see you guys," Fleming said with a smile. A part of him knew all along that they would follow him.

Just then Ryerson and four other men reached the group.

"Sir, we can't go back,' Fleming said. "We can catch this gook."

"I'm not here to take you back. I'm here to help. Let's go"

They pushed forward with one collective thought: get the gook. After months of chasing an elusive, unseen enemy, they knew there was a good chance to catch this one man. They had all played the enemy's game and had observed his rules for too long. It was payback time.

Ten minutes later, Van dropped to the ground in an exhausted heap. He instantly saw that his comrade's wound was again bleeding profusely. Yanking away the battle dressing, he threw it to the ground and applied a fresh one.

Then he heard the Americans closing in on him. He hoisted the man on his shoulder and started away.

A minute later, Pierson picked up a bloody bandage. "A fuckin bandage," he yelled, holding it in the air. "It's got to be the gook's bandage, it says U.S. on it."

"There it is," every man called out.

Rushing madly through the jungle, Van's legs buckled and he fell, exhausted from moving at a breakneck pace while carrying a man. The Americans were following the blood trail and he couldn't stop the bleeding unless he had more time.

Then he once again heard the Americans approaching.

Fear consumed him. He had to go on as long as long as there was strength in his body. He picked the man up. He decided to cradle him in his arms as if holding a child. The wound would be pressed against Van's body and the blood would possibly stop falling so profusely on the ground. He started away.

He moved forward thirty meters when his legs buckled again and he fell. His legs were exhausted. Cover, he thought instantly. He had to hide, hoping that in their haste the Americans would rush past him. He placed the man under a thick growth of vegetation and draped palm tree branches over him. He made a quick check for telltale blood signs and saw nothing.

The Americans called to each other. They were so close. He turned to the sound and saw a large Black soldier leading them forward. Van dropped to his stomach, crawled, and hid behind a bush five meters away from where he had hidden his comrade.

Pierson saw Van just as he crawled behind the bush. "One of them is over there." Pierson pointed at the bush then ran toward it.

Suddenly, two V.C. rushed forward and fired at the Americans. They were followed by four others.

The most gratifying sight imaginable was when Van saw that some of his comrades had come to help him.

Pierson dropped to the ground, all the while firing his weapon at the newly arrived V.C. Then he started crawling forward.

Two more V.C. rushed from the jungle on Pierson's left.

Fleming fired and hit one of them. Carlyle fired an M-79 grenade into the other and he disintegrated.

Ryerson turned to the RTO. "Call in our coordinates and see if you can get artillery."

The firing intensified.

Fleming crawled to Pierson.

"Them fuckers are right around here," Pierson said to Fleming. "I can feel their slimy gook asses."

Van didn't dare move. The Americans were only meters away from where he had hidden his comrade.

Eight V.C. guerillas charged forward, firing their AK-47s.

Vines and Washington turned their M-60s on them, halting their progress.

Lying on his stomach, Rojas slithered to a bush. He aimed his M-16 and fired, killing two V.C.

Fleming felt satisfaction's warm glow. They were going to end this. They had chased the enemy for two months and finally had them out in the open in a firefight.

Suddenly a loud moan was heard; it came from somewhere nearby.

Pierson and Fleming were the only ones close enough to hear it. They exchanged surprised glances.

"A fuckin leg," Pierson said. He pointed to a bush where the calf of a leg was visible. He crawled forward a few meters and brushed away the camouflage. "The legs done got a body," he squealed gleefully. Then he fired a full clip into the V.C.'s face disintegrating it.

Horrified, Van moved reflexively and the bushes rustled.

Fleming heard it, looked in the sound's direction, and locked eyes with the enemy soldier.

Van scrambled backward just as the American fired his weapon. The rounds chewed up the earth just inches away from him.

Fleming started to remove his spent clip for a fresh one when Ryerson grabbed his arm.

"Fleming, we've been ordered to pull back."

"Sir, we're about to make these fuckers pay!"

Van saw the two Americans conversing. It was his one chance to escape. He stood and started running off into the jungle.

"We can't stay here," Ryerson continued, squeezing tighter on Fleming's arm. "We've crossed over into Cambodia."

He violently wrenched his arm free from Ryerson's grip and continued replacing his spent magazine. "It don't mean nothing. First we get these Gooks."

Ryerson pulled out a 45 and stuck it in Fleming's face. "I have no time to argue with you, soldier. We go now. It's over."

"But they're beaten. I ain't fuckin leavin, no sir." Fleming's eyes glazed over as if he was a different person.

Ryerson slapped Fleming's face. "Snap the fuck out of it. You're a good man. Don't fuck yourself up over this! We're leaving! Now!"

Fleming knew he was defeated. "FUCK!" he yelled out frustrated. Then he started scurrying backward, away from the fight.

Seeing the retreating Americans, the outnumbered, outgunned V.C. quit firing and let them back out, more than willing to let the battle end. In a few moments, the V.C. let out a cheer and start chattering and laughing.

It infuriated Fleming all the more. After crawling about twenty five meters, and crawling was the ultimate act of degradation, he and the others stood and started walking. Quaking with rage, he was incapable of speech; it didn't matter, no one else spoke either.

Fifteen silent minutes passed before they reached the jungle's end and the trench where the whole fiasco had started. When they reached the others everyone dropped to the ground, tired and depressed. It was a different kind of fatigue: their energy was drained, as if the spirit had been sapped from their souls.

While waiting for the dust-off not one man had taken a seat next to another. It was the first time Fleming had seen them sit so far apart from one another.

Pierson stared at the dead Gooks in the trench. "Bastards," he suddenly grumbled. He jumped into the trench, bent down to an enemy soldier and hacked off his ears and nose. Then he started on another.

"Pierson!" Ryerson shouted in righteous outrage.

Pierson turned back to him, a bloody ear clutched in each hand, a vacant look etched on his face.

Ryerson stared at him for a long moment. "Fuck it," he mumbled with a fatigued tone and looked away.

Then Pierson resumed hacking off body parts.

Fleming watched him with detached indifference. For months they had chased the enemy through insect infested jungles, over mountains and other impossible terrain, and they had finally cornered them. And just when they had their hands around the enemies' throats they were forced to leave the fight. Their own brass wouldn't let them win because of some insane rules. It was like playing an adult's version of tag. Today, the enemy was chased and he reached base, Cambodia, where he was free from being tagged. The death of their friends was a fresh open wound and they had to let the very soldiers who had killed them go free – it couldn't get any worse than that. Every day in Vietnam was more insane than the last and this last day was an insanity-laden twenty-four hours. Why are we here? He wondered for the umpteenth time. He had thought about it and thought about it and could never come up with one good answer as to what good they were doing in Vietnam. Fighting for their friends was the only motivation to fight and today that was taken away.

The noise of the approaching helicopter interrupted his thoughts.

The men climbed aboard the choppers. Fleming sat on the chopper's floor. Pierson sat across from him. He had already punched holes in the ears and nose and had hung them from his dog tag chain around his neck.

How ya gonna act? Fleming thought as he had thought so many times in the past.

It took Van a half an hour to reach the underground tunnel complex's entrance. Chi and Dan were outside speaking. They both turned to him.

"You made it back," Dan said with a tone of surprise and guilt.

Van hurried toward Dan and pushed him hard enough in the chest for him to stumble backward a few steps. "You stupid fool."

Dan attempted to rush Van, but Chi stepped between them. "Stop it, both of you. You are comrades, brothers. You don't fight each other."

"He almost got me killed. He is a stupid fool! He's a dumb ignorant– "

"Be careful of what you say, Van." Dan interrupted, grinning menacingly.

"Stop it," Chi said, pushing both men away. Chi waited a few moments for them to compose themselves then he said: "Tell me what happened."

Van told about the trench incident and everything that happened afterward.

Chi ordered Dan to leave so he could speak to Van alone. "He didn't mean to endanger you. He is enthusiastic to a fault. I will speak to him about it. But he's not the problem. Your friend Hoi is the problem. He is not fighting. I checked his weapon after the battle. It hadn't been fired. How does a soldier go through a battle and not even fire his weapon?"

"He was with me at the mortar. He had no opportunity to fire. I didn't even have a chance to fire my weapon."

"That may be true, but you've been protecting him ever since training ended. He shows no heart or desire to do what must be done in order to defeat the Americans."

Van couldn't think of anything to say in Hoi's defense.

"You are a leader. Your job is to speak to him. Get him to change. If you don't, I will take drastic measures." Then Chi turned to leave but turned back in an instant. "Why is Hoi your friend? Why do you protect him? He didn't come to help when the Americans were chasing you. Others did. He's using you. He knows that as long as you're his friend, it's to his advantage. It enables him to shirk his duty to his comrades and to the revolution. You are different. You would never use another person selfishly. You're responsible and a good soldier. Think about what I've said to you." Then Chi left.

Van sat on a large boulder. It upset him that Hoi had not come with the others. But the truth of the matter was he had never expected him to come. Hoi's internal make up would never allow him to seek out danger. It was just something that was beyond him. Maybe he was more spiritual than all of them. He had never killed a man in combat. Van had killed many. Hoi hadn't violated Buddha's law; Van had been living in flagrant violation of it. During the past six months he had changed into a completely different person. Who he had become had replaced who he had been. He liked the person he had been and now that person was gone forever.

CHAPTER 16

R&R In Nha Trang

The next morning Fleming returned from chow accompanied by his squad. Everyone entered the squad tent except for Fleming. He hoisted himself up on a sandbag bunker emplacement and raised his face to the sun. It was hot, damn hot. He had pitched countless baseball games on hot sunny days in Baltimore's unmerciful summer humidity. As a child he would play baseball all day long until his body was drenched with sweat. Baseball, he thought astounded. It was the first time he had thought of it in weeks. In the past, not an hour of the day went by without some thought of baseball

Then he saw two C-123 planes leveling off to the jungle about a mile outside L.Z. English's perimeter. He had frequently seen planes just like these, crop dusters, depositing the same load: silver trails of some unknown substance spewed out of these two planes and fell onto the jungle.

"Fleming," an approaching Ryerson suddenly called out.

Thoughts broken, Fleming jumped off the sandbags and saluted.

Ryerson saluted back.

Fleming hoisted himself back on the bunker. "Sir, you have any idea what the hell that is?" he asked motioning toward the jungle and the planes.

"Some new thing the Army is trying. It's called Agent Orange. It's supposed to kill the jungle so it will be easier to find the gooks so it will be easier for us to kill the gooks. Killing gooks being easy is never a phrase that should be used in a sentence, a paragraph, hell, the words themselves should be banned from any human, language, or dialect."

Fleming scoffed: "There it fuckin is. And good fuckin' luck with anything that claims it could waste that jungle. Good luck with that shit. Nothing could kill that jungle."

"I don't know. That stuff is supposed to be pretty potent."

"Yeah, well I still don't believe it will work.

A silent moment passed.

Ryerson lowered his head. "I'm here to tell you I'm sorry," he said sincerely. "I came here to say that."

Where the fuck did that come from? Fleming thought, astonished. "Sorry? Sorry for what, sir?" Fleming asked with utter confusion.

Ryerson's eyes widened with surprise. "For sticking a 45 in your face and slapping you, that's for what."

"Oh that," Fleming said with a laugh. "It don't mean nothin, sir."

"Well, I feel bad about it. I'm sorry."

A frustrated, smirking smile filled Fleming's face. "Sir, I just wish they'd let us fight this war so we could win. We could end this so easily. We could end all this suffering so easily."

Ryerson nodded his head in agreement. "The NVA is dedicated and Ho Chi Minh is for real. He cares. He is doing what he thinks is best for his country. There is power in all that. But the fact of the matter is we could march all the way to Hanoi, grab Hoi Chi Minh by the throat and demand he surrender. And he'd surrender. He'd have to. And meanwhile, we end all this carnage, all this death and suffering. The way we're doing it now, we're just prolonging the war. And I can't figure out why."

"Why would we prolong a war? Who benefits?" Fleming shook his head frustrated. "Thinking about it is enough to drive you crazy. I would know. I think about it all the time and I'm starting to get as crazy as all get out." Fleming thought about his first day when he thought Levine insane for wanting to stay on the battlefield. He chuckled and smiled. "Talk about crazy. Yesterday you forced me at gunpoint to leave a battle because I was all fired up about killing human beings. Sir, a year ago I was in high school sweatin' out getting a date for the prom. If you woulda' told me a year ago that yesterday was in my future I woulda' called you crazy."

"There it is. How did you get involved in all this madness anyway?"

"That's a story in itself. I was getting drafted when I though it might be a good idea to talk to a recruiter. You know to see my options."

"Mistake number one," Ryerson said with a chuckle.

"That ain't the half of it. The recruiter told me I was enlisting in a unit that wasn't in Vietnam."

"Jesus," Ryerson said, choking out a grunting chuckle.

Then Fleming told him the rest of the story, about the lost orders and being assigned to an Infantry Unit. "And I got a top-secret-crypto clearance," Fleming emphasized.

"Did you do anything about it?"

"I tried. I went to the 404th Radio Research Detachment. The C.O. said that he would look into it and that I should come back every month and find out if he learned anything."

"Did you go back?"

"Sir, they made me feel bad about myself. One of the fuckers over there, an MP, said I was a pussy coward trying to get out of the field. I'll admit, I was scared…of combat…when I went over there. But, I mean, what the fuck! Combat is something you're gonna' be scared of. I mean that's why it's called combat." A steel-eyed look of rigid determination filled Fleming's face. "I got used to it…Combat, that is. No. Let me correct myself. You never get used to that shit, you just learn to deal with it. I just said fuck it. I learned to deal with it, but I ain't lettin' some REMF fuckin' MP at the 404th call me a pussy-assed coward. I don't need that shit, especially from some MP that has never seen any shit whatsoever. I ain't putting up with that. I figure they know where I am. If they get it all straightened out they can come and get me."

Ryerson's brow furrowed, deep in thought. "You should go back. But I gotta tell you, the MP's harassment, the Unit commander's, remarkably bad attitude and behavior concerning this incident…I mean, none of that's right."

"Sure it's not right, but it's the way it is, sir."

"That's not what I meant." Ryerson shook his head, clearing it. "It's deeper than that. I'll talk to you about it later." He gave Fleming a huge smile. "Right now, I have something to tell you and this time it's good news. Where's the rest of your squad?"

Fleming hopped off the sandbags and motioned to the tent. "Sir, I'll take you to them."

Inside the tent everyone was lounging around, writing letters or reading.

Carlyle was the first to see Ryerson. "Hey everybody, it's the L.T. He's come to visit the slave quarters."

Ryerson smiled at him then took a seat on an empty ammo crate. The men gathered around him. Ryerson scanned the room. "Where's Rodgers?"

"Who knows," Washington said with a frown. "He never hangs with us, sir."

"He does seem to be the anti-social type," Ryerson said. "Anyway, I have good news. I got you on a detail. You're guarding a convoy."

A long moment passed. Fleming didn't think it was such great news. Convoys got hit, he thought.

"Sir, where's it goin, Hawaii?" Carlyle asked.

Vines and Washington cracked up in laughter.

"No, but it is going to Nha Trang."

"No shit, sir?" Fleming asked excited. When he first came to Vietnam he was in Nha Trang. It was where he learned about his lost orders. Nha Trang was heaven compared to where he had been ever since then.

"Where the fuck is Nha Trang?" Rojas asked.

Fleming turned to face Rojas. "Nha Trang is hot. It's got beaches, a town that's on limits, restaurants, and no real war. It's heavy."

Rojas smiled. "That sounds pretty damn good."

Vines smirked. "What's the catch, sir?"

"No catch. The first sergeant said I had to pick men to escort a convoy. I picked you guys. You guard it going down, that'll take a day. Then three days later it returns and you guard it coming back. You get three days out of the war. They got a real nice beach. You can swim. You can eat a good meal in a restaurant…boocco things."

"Yeah, like getting boccoo fuckin laid," Vines said and slapped palms with Carlyle and Washington. "And I'm getting boocoo fuckin laid, boocoo fuckin times."

"There's no problem with Rodgers going is there?" Ryerson asked. "They want six men."

"Oh, he'll go," Carlyle said with a threatening tone. "This is the Army we'll order him to go. He'll most definitely go."

Ryerson stood. "Outstanding, you leave tomorrow. Go to the C.O.'s office this afternoon and orders will be cut."

"Hey, my colored friend," Carlyle called to Fleming as he entered the transit barracks, Second Field Force, Nha Trang, Vietnam. "I got the straight shit from a brother over at Headquarters Company. The Paradise Bar's where it's all happenin in downtown Nha Trang."

"Tonight, we go. I'll tell the other guys."

"Where they at?"

"Howard Johnsons."

Digesting this information, Carlyle looked at him for a long moment before frowning. "Damn, I knew they got restaurants world wide, but I didn't think they had one over here."

"No, man, it's a snack bar over by the pool. They threw a sign on it that said Howard Johnsons. I was over there last night. They got good eats. Rojas, Washington and Vines said they are gonna' eat hamburgers and French fries till they die."

"No shit, they actually got real burgers and fries?"

"Damn right. Like I said they're pretty damn good. You oughta' go over there and pig out."

"I'm halfway there as we speak."

"It's over by the swimming pool, near–"

Carlyle holds up his hand silencing him. "Just point me in the direction, my nose will do the rest. Hamburgers and motherfuckin French fries! You gonna' go with me?"

"Nah, man. I'm gonna shower and take a nap."

"You already took two. You gonna' waste all this skate time taking showers and naps?"

"After we leave here, you know they're gonna' send us somewhere where we won't be able to shower for weeks. And did you see how thick these mattresses are. They ain't even like the skinny motherfuckers we got at English."

"Ain't that some shit when taking showers and sleeping is something ya' do for fun."

"It's called being in da' Nam."

"There it is," Carlyle said with a smile. "I better book outta' here. Fuckin' Rojas, Washington, Vines, them evil motherfuckers will eat all the fuckin' burgers and fries, I don't get over there. Catch ya' later, bro." Carlyle moved across the room and reached the door when Fleming called to him. Carlyle turned to him.

"What? I'm a bro' now?"

Carlyle eyed him a long moment before smiling at him. "You're getting darker every day." Carlyle ran his hands along his face. "I gotta' warn ya,' bro.' It ain't most people's favorite color."

He ran out the door leaving Fleming with a smile on his face.

"We goin' inside, or we gonna' wait out here all night?" Vines asked impatiently, standing in front of the Paradise Bar in downtown Nha Trang.

Fleming looked around nervously. "I guess we're goin' in. We're getting ready, that's all."

"Getting ready? To get laid?" Vines asked astonished. "It's real fuckin' easy. It don't take no getting' ready. We go in, talk some shit, and we get laid. Easy."

Fleming looked nervously up and down the street. "Man, I gotta' tell ya.' I feel fuckin' naked. All these gooks around and I ain't got a weapon. It's scary."

Washington frowned at him. "They're friendly gooks, Fleming."

"I feel weird, okay."

Carlyle gave Fleming a smirking smile. "There's boocoo M.P.'s around. Their job is to protect us. Now, relax, like the sign says." He pointed at the bar's sign. "We're in Paradise."

Fleming nodded his head yes. There was another reason, the real reason for his hesitatation but he wasn't about to let that secret out. He exhaled a long stream of air. "Okay, okay, I'm ready. Let's go."

They passed through the bar's courtyard and entered the Paradise Bar. A tape recorder was playing The Temptations song "My Girl." The bar girls were dressed in western clothing, predominantly mini-skirts, or the Vietnamese traditional dress the Ao-Dai. The women were busily working the room.

They were beautiful and alluring and Fleming couldn't take his eyes off them.

"Oh, man," Vines said, a huge smile on his face. "These foxes are super fine. Man, I'm gonna' lower my sperm count by millions."

'There it is," Washington said with awed reverence.

A huge African American, dressed in Air Force fatigues with sergeant stripes, approached their table. He engaged Carlyle, Washington, and Vines in a long stylized handshake known as the dap. When they completed the handshake the Air Force sergeant turned his gaze on Rojas and Fleming and frowned. "These two white motherfuckers, they come in with you good brothers?"

"I ain't white," Rojas said. "I'm Puerto Rican."

"You ain't black, that means you gotta' step back."

Caryle nodded his head to the man. "They with us."

The sergeant puffed his chest; it seemed as if he had just grown two feet taller and three feet wider. He's a big motherfucker, Fleming thought, looking around the room and seeing that everyone was Black.

The sergeant pointed at Rojas and Fleming. "These two ain't welcome in our place. They beasts, not part of the human race."

"Whatta ya mean?" Washington asked. "They with us."

"No way, they stay. We fightin the beast's war, don't mean we let the beast in our door. So, Beast, listen to what I'm sayin.' Leave now or start prayin."

The man could righteously rap, Fleming thought.

Washington looked at the man for a long moment. "You really think you're fightin' the war here? These dudes been fightin' the real war, in the field. They fightin' next to the black man in the bad bush. Saved our lives, too. Saved boocoo black asses boocoo times."

The Sergeant shook his head no. "Don't mean nothin.' They gotta' be movin.' They got bars for Whites and Spanish. Di-di outta here before ya' perish. You Brothers stay here, so we can rap in your ear. Gonna' re-educate you in the ways of the black man preparing for the revolution. It's the only motherfuckin' solution."

"You mean you really gonna' kick these guys outta' here?" Carlyle asked.

The sergeant grinned. "They cain't party here. Not even drink one beer. They try to stay inside. The brothers gonna' skin their hide."

Carlyle looked at the man for a long moment. His eyes narrowed.

Fleming knew they were seconds away from trouble. "No problem. Me and Rojas will go somewhere else. You guys can stay here."

Vines and Washington were frowning in protest.

Carlyle broke eye contact with the Air Force Sergeant and turned to Fleming. "You sure, man?"

"We'll be okay. No sweat."

Carlyle nodded his head. He began turning to the huge Air Force sergeant while saying: "Well, Brother, it looks like we're with you." On the grunted word you he finished turning to the man and punched him in the jaw.

The man's head didn't even move. Carlyle painfully rubbed his fist.

The huge Air Force sergeant eyed Carlyle for a long moment. "You shouldn'ta' done that, bro.' Now you gotta' go." A pleasant, yet sinister smile engulfed his face. Then he grabbed Carlyle, lifted him and threw him on a table.

The whole bar fell silent.

"You, motherfucker," Rojas growled with controlled fury.

The Air Force Sergeant smiled at Rojas. "Strong words, little man. But shut up while you can."

Rojas smiled at him. Then he fired a left jab, snapping the man's head back as if his neck were attached to a spring. He pounded two left hooks into the man's rib cage. The huge sergeant let out a loud gasp as he doubled over. A right uppercut to the chin sent the sergeant sprawling over a table. He landed unconscious in a heap on the floor. Rojas had moved so quickly that no one in the bar had time to prevent the onslaught.

A man tried to attack Rojas from the rear.

Vines slammed an elbow into the man's chest, sending him toppling over a chair.

Then everyone in the bar stood to face them.

"Let's di-di!" Fleming yelled.

While helping Carlyle to his feet, Washington kicked a man in the groin. The man fell to the floor, puking and retching.

Then the five men bolted for the door, followed closely by their pursuers. They were out of the bar and halfway down the street when they stopped. Vines and Washington doubled over out of breath. "Damnit, Carlyle," Vines gasped. "You almost got us killed. Why the fuck you hit that ape?"

"The prejudiced motherfucker pissed me off. Tells me I can't bring my colored friends into the bar. You see my man Rojas in action." Carlyle said, holding his palm to Rojas who slapped it. "He cut that fucking rappin' motherfucker like David cutting down Goliath's ass."

"You're fucking quick," Washington said impressed.

For a moment they all heaped praise on Rojas until Fleming asked: "What're we gonna' do now?"

"Go to another bar?" Carlyle suggested with a weak smile.

Fleming shook his head no. "It ain't too hard to figure how this night's gonna' go. We go to a White bar they won't let you guys in. We go to another Black bar, and they ain't letting us in. We find a Spanish bar the same bullshit."

Carlyle chuckled bitterly. "Great to know nothin's' changed – the closer you get to civilization the more fucked up people get."

A long moment passed. "You guys go and get laid," Fleming finally said. "Me and Rojas will find some place to go."

The ever-smiling Washington's eyes narrowed. His jaw tightened with determination. "Man, I wanted to party with you guys."

"Right on to that," Vines said with fierce conviction. "We party together."

"That's the thing, we won't party. We'll spend the night getting in fights. We will be doin boocoo fightin the next few months. I appreciate you guys sticking up for me and Rojas, but go get laid."

"We will fuck tonight til we can't fuck no more," Carlyle suggested. "Then tomorrow we'll all go to the N.C.O. Club and get piss assed drunk."

They spoke for a few moments longer then they broke up into two groups and walked in opposite directions. Carlyle turned back and yelled: "Hey, colored boy."

Fleming turned to him.

"Don't let your meat loaf," Carlyle said with a smile.

Both Rojas and Fleming groaned. Then they started walking in the opposite direction.

A few moments later Rojas asked: "What now?"

"Uh, man, I think I'm goin' back to the post. I'm gonna' let my meat loaf."

"I thought you wanted to get laid?"

"I can wait." Fleming looked cautiously up and down the street. He was about to reveal a well-guarded secret. "Man, I'm gonna' tell you something. You tell any of the other guys, I'm gonna' swear you're lying."

"If you ask me to keep something secret, I'll keep it secret."

Fleming took a last look up and down the street. "I ain't ever been laid," Fleming whispered. "I'm a...virgin."

"A virgin!" Rojas practically yelled.

Fleming shot quick glances up and down the street. "Keep it the fuck down! Someone could hear you!" He fixed his gaze on Rojas who is doubled over in laughter.

"Fuck you!" Fleming said angrily. "You ain't gotta' laugh at me."

Rojas took a moment to gain composure. "I never been laid either. I'm a virgin

too."

Fleming's eyes widened with astonishment. "Really? No shit?"

"No shit! I boxed, studied my schoolwork. My Mom always made me go to church with her and my sisters. I didn't have much time for chicks.

"No shit," Fleming said breaking up in laughter.

They continued down the street.

"What're we gonna' do now?" Fleming asked.

"Let's go back to the base, get piss assed drunk and lie to the other guys about the righteous ass we scored."

Fleming nodded his head and smiled. "Lying about chicks we scored on is almost as fun as getting laid." He pauses in thought. "At least I think it is." He'd never been laid, but he thought the theory was logical.

He and Rojas shared a smile then they hailed a taxi and started back to the base.

They drove in silence a few miles and Fleming asked: "Are you gonna' take up boxing again when you get outta' the army? You're really good."

"I ain't getting out. I'm re-upping."

"No way." But one look at Rojas' face was all it took for Fleming to know that he was serious. "You…a lifer?"

"I never had much back home. I didn't have friends. I wanted to stay out of trouble and out of gangs. It's the only reason I boxed, gangs left me alone. You guys are the first friends I ever had."

Fleming thought for a long moment. "Sometimes I think the guys you meet over here are the best friends you'll ever make."

"You being a big time baseball jock, you musta' had boocoo friends back in Baltimore."

"I had tons of friends, a few girl friends too. But I never had friends like the dudes I met over here. Like back in the World, man, your best friend is telling you how tight the two of you are. Then when you're not looking he's trying to score on your girl. Your girl friend tells you she loves you then you see her coming on to practically every guy she meets. It don't mean nothing, man. It's like back in the world there's so much bullshit talk. Over here talk is cheap. It's what people do that really counts. I mean over here people will actually die for you, man."

Rojas thought for a long moment. "You know somehow I feel we got it all here, right here and right now. We have friends and responsibility to our friends."

For the rest of the ride back to the base they said little. Fleming wondered why it took war and death to bring people together. But he knew that as soon as he got back home the same tired ass prejudices would start all over again. It was depressing.

Ten minutes later, they were back at the transit barracks where they found Rodgers lying on a bunk.

"Rodgers," Fleming shouted. "You're goin' with us and I don't even wanna' hear any of your bullshit. You're comin' with us to down some brew."

"Get your lazy ass in gear," Rojas said.

"No thank you," Rodgers answered, although he was surprised and pleased that they had asked him to go.

"You ain't got shit to do so let's go. You don't go, I'm gonna' make your life a bitch. So what's it gonna' be? You gonna' have a few beers with us or have me all up in your ass every fucking minute of the day?"

"I'll join you," he agreed with feigned reluctance. "What happened? I thought you all went downtown together?"

Fleming laughed. "We got in a fight, got run out of a bar. Rojas decked this dude. He was as big as King Kong."

"You got in a fight. Why am I not surprised? I have never been in a fight in my life."

Fleming and Rojas exchanged smiles. "You never been in a fight in your life," Fleming responded. "Why ain't I surprised? Is it my imagination or are you purposely trying to be weird?"

"I am different. I'm five years older than you. I grew up in a socially different environment than any of you. My economic environment is different. My schooling–"

Fleming grabbed his arm, interrupting him. "Okay, you're different in a lot of fucking ways. Now let's get some beers. We'll talk about how different you are at the N.C.O. Club."

They started for the N.C.O. Club.

Ten minutes later, they were all in the club. A Filipino band was singing the lyrics of a Three Dog Night song, Joy To The World.

Fleming leaned forward toward Rodgers. "This is your chance. Out in the field I ain't got time to listen to your bullshit. Tonight I can. What's on your mind?"

Rodgers looked at him for a long moment. "I can say whatever I want, no reprisals."

"No reprisals," Fleming answered. "Say what you want."

Just then a Vietnamese waitress came to their table and took their order: Fleming and Rojas ordered beers and Rodgers ordered a Scotch and Soda.

"Can you believe how easy these guys got it?" Fleming asked Rojas.

"God what I wouldn't give to be stationed here," Rojas replied.

Fleming smacked his hand on the table for emphasis. "There it fuckin is."

"You mentioned no reprisals," Rodgers said. "Is that condition still viable?"

"If that means can you still say whatever you want, yeah it's…" Fleming smiled: "fuckin viable."

Rodgers studied them a moment, trying to think of just the right words to say. "You just scoffed at how easy the soldiers stationed here have it compared to us. You expressed a desire as to how fortunate it would be if positions were reversed. But I don't believe you'd ever exchange your present Tarzan like existence for this one. It's a source of pride to you, some macho thing."

A look of unbridled wonder filled Fleming's face. "If you think for one moment that we'd rather be in the field than here, you're fucking wrong and there it is."

"I find that impossible to believe." Rodgers leaned closer to them, excited, supremely confident of winning this battle. "I heard that Lieutenant Ryerson drew a 45 on you and demanded you leave that last fire fight. A man who is forced, at gunpoint, to leave a firefight is a man who loves to fight. And that is only one example."

Fleming thought of all the friends he had lost because of this war. "It ain't what it looks like, Rodgers. There were reasons I wanted to continue that fire fight – personal ones. I ain't telling you or anyone why."

"Rodgers, you're a bit fucked up, you know that?" Rojas said.

"Did you ever consider that I am the only normal one here and maybe you're, as you so crudely put it, fucked up?"

Fleming took a long gulp of beer then leaned closer to Rodgers. "Okay, you're the only normal one. Why do you think we're fucked up?"

"You refuse to recognize what the system is doing to you. You refuse to acknowledge how wrong this war really is. It is blatantly obvious that you believe in it – you take such enjoyment when fighting it."

Fleming was flabbergasted. "Do you actually believe we enjoy war? You really believe we enjoy killing gooks? This war is about the most wrong thing I've seen in my life."

Rodgers looked at them a long moment clearly trying to determine if they were speaking the truth. He didn't know how to answer Fleming's statement. "Are you trying to tell me that you believe the war is wrong?" Internally Rodgers cringed. He could have thought of something better to say.

At that instant Fleming realized why the question had been asked. "I know why you believe what you do. You have to. It's the only way you can justify your actions."

"And just what are my actions that need justifying?" Rodgers asked stiffly.

"You're scared shitless," Rojas said matter of factly.

Fleming nodded his head in agreement. He signaled the waitress for another round of drinks. "You let fear control you because it benefits you. It lets you hide while we fight."
"Why would I put my life in danger for a war that is wrong?"

"Because the rest of us are doing it for a war that is wrong. Because, you, acting the way you do makes it easier for us to get wasted. You don't do your job and we have to take up your slack and that puts us all in greater danger. You're pissing all over the men who are keeping you alive. You're in this war and, wrong or not, you can't get out of it. You have to realize that. The reality of all this is this: your duty is not to the country or the flag. No one really believes we are fighting for freedom, country, or any of that horseshit they told us. But you still have to fight because your duty is to us, the men you serve with."

"But none of us should be here. Nobody back home cares about the war and whether we live or die. All our–"

"We agree with you," Fleming interrupted. "None of us should be here and nobody back home cares."

Rodgers has no idea how to respond. "But…uh, all our effort, our deaths, won't change a thing. We can die and when the war is finally over, it will still be wrong. And we died for nothing. When–"

"Are you hard of hearing?" Rojas interrupted. "Fleming said he agrees with you. I agree with you."

Rodgers' eyes darted nervously to and fro searching his mind for a response. "When, uh, when something is wrong you take a stand. You try to change it. It's a protest against indecency. The Vietnamese, not one of them, want us here. Yet we're here. Why is that?"

Fleming gulped another long swig of beer and signaled for another round. "Because we were told to come."

"Just because someone tells you to do something doesn't mean you have to do it."

"Fuckin-A," Rojas said. "They told me if I didn't go in the Army, I'd go to jail. I didn't want to go to jail so I'm here. Who told you, you had to come?'

"The draft board."

Rojas leaned closer to him. "Just because someone tells you to do something it don't mean you gotta' do it."

"Well, I uh–"

"Hell, for all your education, you're the same as me," Rojas said with a sneering smile. "You woulda gone to jail if you didn't go in the Army, same as me. And you think you're so special."

Just then the Vietnamese waitress returned. Fleming ordered another round for everyone. Rodgers was thankful for the interruption; it gave him time to think of what to say; however, nothing of substance came to him.

Then Fleming turned his gaze on Rodgers, demanding an answer.

Rodgers responded with the first thing that came to him. "When I was home I wasn't really convinced the war was wrong. It took my coming here to convince me."

"Yeah, when the first bullet whistled past your ear I bet you thought: motherfucker, this shit is wrong!"

"There it fuckin is," Rojas slurred, the alcohol starting to take effect.

The confidence Rodgers had at the outset of the evening had been seriously eroded. "No...it's just...when I got here all my knowledge of the war and the politics surrounding it, well...for lack of a better phrase – it kind of kicked in and I knew it was wrong."

Smirks of doubt filled Rojas and Fleming's faces.

Rodgers was filled with doubt; it was evident in his defensive tone when he said: "In College, I heard some of the brightest minds in the nation, the brightest minds of our generation, speak out against the war." Rodgers pleaded with a sense of urgency.

"Did you protest with them?" Fleming asked.

"Sure I protested. Everyone did."

"You said you weren't sure the war was wrong when you were home. What did you say? The wrongness kicked in once you got here. If you were protesting back home then it sounds like you were against it – unless the word protesting has taken on a whole new meaning."

Rodgers studied them for a long moment, desperately searching his mind for a rebuttal. "It's hard to explain but when a person comes here, sees it up close and personal, then the war is seen in its true light."

"How many of those experts, those brightest minds who speak in college – how many of them saw it up close and personal? How many had that true light turned on for them? How many of them were here?" Fleming wanted to know.

"Well...I doubt if many of them were actually here."

"None of them were "actually" here," Rojas countered with sarcastic emphasis on the word actually. "Yet they're experts, those bright fucking minds. You know what they are? They're whining assholes. They spend all their time protesting against the war, against society, and none of their time trying to change the things that are wrong. And believe me boocoo is wrong."

"Protesting is all we can do. We have no power, but that's only temporary. One day we will be the ones in the Senate. We will be running the corporations. Right now, we are doing what we can to make the world a better place, but soon we'll be in a position to make it a reality."

"Know what I think, Rodgers," Fleming said, pointing a finger at him. "I think when our generation is in charge nothing will change. Nothing. In fact, I think it will get worse. I think there will be more war. I think there will be more inequality, more greed and more paranoia in the government. I hear you people yelling about peace and changing the world and all that Age of Aquarius shit and I think you will be worse than the people in charge now."

"There it fuckin' is," Rojas slurred, the alcohol was taking a greater effect.

Rodgers scoffed at the evaluation. "That will never happen. We have seen this society's cruelty. We know the pitfalls to avoid and we will make sure it doesn't happen in the world that we rule."

"You'll make the world worse. You're all a bunch of rich spoiled kids living off your parents hard earned gains. The generation that started this war – they truly fucked up, getting us involved in Vietnam, but they had balls. They went through the depression, World War II. Character is built through adversity and struggle and most of our generation has experienced no adversity, no struggle."

"Except the motherfuckers here in da' Nam," Rojas said drunkenly.

"There it fuckin' is," Fleming concured. "And what are the peace-freaks doing to us. We are the villains in all this horror. When we come home they spit on us. They treat us like we're scum. If a man is a soldier you have turned him into an object of scorn. All those bright minds somehow came to the bright conclusion that eighteen year old soldiers should be shit on and blamed for this war – real fucking smart, those brightest mind motherfuckers."

Rodgers said nothing. He was speechless.

"Come on, Rodgers," Rojas slurred. "Ain't ya got nothing smart to say about that?"

"It is true soldiers have been scorned for their service. It is unfortunate. I have nothing to say about it."

"Are you telling me two dumb-ass soldiers have left you at a loss for words?" Fleming challenged. "You heard some of the brightest minds in the country speak."

They stared at Rodgers for a long moment.

"I am fuckin wasted," Rojas slurred while chuckling, breaking his and Fleming's eye contact with Rodgers. "Four beers and I am fucked."

Fleming downed his beer. "There it fuckin is. I'm fucked up too."

"Let's get outta here," Rojas stood. "I'm done. I don't want the hangover from hell,"

Fleming looks at Rodgers for a long, hard moment, waiting for a response. When none was forthcoming, Fleming decided to let Rodgers off easy. He smiled at him and stood. "Let's di-di."

Rodgers knew that Fleming's smile was an acknowledgement of his victory. Rodgers was more than eager to leave and end the debate. He couldn't think of one thing to say to counter them. He had been to Berkley – had the finest education money could buy. They had street smarts. They had had no formal education. But he had to admit it to himself that these two uneducated inner-city teenagers had beaten him in this debate.

CHAPTER 17

Medals

L.Z. ENGLISH

Two days later, Fleming and his men pulled into L.Z. English at 1600 hours. They exited their vehicles and hurried to their company area. When they entered their tent Fleming learned that White was looking for him. Fleming stashed his gear and exited the tent with Carlyle, who had decided to accompany him.

"Fleming, Carlyle!" Sergeant Lebeau yelled. "Get yer' asses over here. Lebeau was leaning against a sandbag bunker emplacement, smoking a cigarette and drinking a beer.

Fleming and Carlyle went to him; he reeked of beer and was obviously drunk. He eyed them for a long moment. "Our two fucking heroes, back from their skating trip in Nha Trang. I hope you assholes enjoyed yourselves, got laid, got shit faced drunk." His eyes narrowed. "All of you in this sorry assed platoon are some sorry assed soldiers! You don't listen! I tell you what to do, Fleming, and every fucking time you gotta argue with me."

Where did all this come from? Fleming wondered. Lebeau was aways on Fleming and the rest of the men for not representing his ideal of the model soldier, but this verbal attack came from nowhere. Fleming hoped it wouldn't turn any uglier. "Sergeant–"

"Shut the fuck up! You'll talk when I tell you to talk! From now on, you, and all the rest of the pussies in this platoon are gonna' shape up! You're gonna' take all the shit off your helmets and flak jackets! It's government fuckin property and you ain't allowed to write on it! You're getting rid of the love beads." He pointed at Fleming.

Fleming was fingering the beads around his neck. He had bought them in Nha Trang.

"I see you've taken to wearing them, Fleming!" Lebeau's face turned beet red; small beads of spittle flew from his mouth. "In the field you will listen to me! You'll put who I tell you on point and on listening posts. Where I tell you to put a listening post! Every motherfucking thing! Am I coming in loud and clear, Fleming?"

Fleming held eye contact with him for a long moment.

"Talk, asshole!" Lebeau demanded.

"I'm the squad leader. I'll do my job just like I've always done. But I ain't listenin to you when I think you're wrong."

"You ain't got respect for shit, you fuckin punk. Why you're squad leader God only knows."

"Captain Wiggins gave me the position. If he wants to replace me, there it is. But until then, I'm doing it my way. And, sergeant, my way has been working pretty damn good." Lebeau didn't have a leg to stand on. Captain Wiggins or Lieutenant Ryerson wouldn't remove Fleming from the position just because Lebeau wanted it so, and Fleming knew it.

Lebeau knew it too because frustration and defeat filled his face. Suddenly, he turned to Carlyle. "Get that fucking necklace off! You black motherfucker!" Lebeau's hand shot out to Carlyle throat. He grabbed a handful of love beads and yanked them off Carlyle's neck.

The beads spilled to the ground.

Then he grabbed Fleming's beads and yanked them off also.

It had just turned boocoo ugly, Fleming thought.

A smug smile of satisfaction filled his face. "There! You look military now! Don't even let me ever catch you wearing another fuckin necklace!"

Carlyle gazed angrily at Lebeau. "Sergeant," he whispered in a low ominous tone. "You shouldn'ta' called me that. You shouldn'ta' pulled my beads off. I get a chance, I'm gonna' come back on you, you can believe that."

Fleming couldn't believe his ears: Carlyle was actually threatening Lebeau.

Lebeau smiled as if welcoming the conflict. "What are you gonna' do, you black bastard. You gonna' frag me?"

Carlyle's eyes were hard, laser beaming at Lebeau. "I ain't sayin' nothin' else, sergeant. Not a fuckin' thing."

Lebeau grinned, a distorted drunken leer. "Just remember, two can play at this game." Then he turned and walked away.

"Damnit, Carlyle. What ·the fuck you mean by that?" Fleming asked.

"Not a fuckin' thing."

"Man, you don't wanna' do nothing stupid with Lebeau, you hear me?

"I done something stupid in Nha Trang when I belted that big ass nigger. I got rules, one stupid thing a year."

An expression of doubt filled Fleming's face.

"It was the first thing that came to my motherfuckin' mind and I said it," Carlyle said, trying to assure Fleming. "It don't mean nothin.' I ain't gonna' do nothing stupid. I promise."

Fleming was appeased, for the moment. Carlyle was the type who reacted spontaneously. Threatening Lebeau was a spontaneous explosion. Fleming hoped that there would be no more incidents between them. If more fuel were added to the fire then there would be no telling what kind of blaze would erupt.

A few minutes later, Fleming and Carlyle entered a nearly deserted orderly room and exchanged pleasantries with White.

"Where is everybody?" Carlyle asked looking around the room.

"Wiggins and the First Sergeant left for the day. I had to stay because I gotta type up some bullshit." He shook his head, frowning but then smiled. "I got good news for you, Fleming." White continued grinning, a long drawn out smile. "You won a Bronze Star."

Carlyle broke into a smile then clapped Fleming on the back.

Fleming gave Carlysle a somewhat embarassed smile. "For what?" he asked White.

"Whatta ya mean for what?" Carlyle snapped. "For all the shit you done over here, that's for what."

Fleming couldn't help but feel a warm glow of pride. "Seriously, White, what specificallly are they giving me this for?"

"For Operation Kansas City. A bunch of dudes got medals. Levine, Jenks, Garcia." White's smile quickly faded when he realized that all these men were dead. "Uh, boocoo guys that lived got medals too"

A long moment passed. "Boocoo guys?" Fleming asked confused. "Who, like Marsten and Garret?"

White looked at him a long moment. "Well, yeah they got medals" White's facial expression changed then his eyes narrowed. "I mean…who the fuck cares who got medals. It don't mean nothing. You got a fuckin' bronze star. Fuck it."

Fleming studied him for a long moment. White was hiding something; Fleming wondered what. "Who the fuck else, White?'

White studied him before finally frowning in defeat. "Everybody. Everybody got a fuckin medal – okay."

"Everybody? Fields and Doyle too?"

"They're part of everybody, ain't they?" White snapped, glaring at Fleming. "It's SOP. It ain't a big deal. It don't mean nothing. You earned that fucking medal."

Fleming shook his head in stunned disbelief. "So now they're giving out medals to everybody. How about Bradford? I suppose he got a shitload of medals!"

"What the fuck would he get a medal for?" Carlyle asked. "I know he didn't do jack-shit out there."

"There it fuckin' is," Fleming hissed. "But obviously ya' ain't gotta do jack-shit for medals. What the fuck he get, White?"

"An Air Medal and a Silver Star."

"He didn't do dick out there," Fleming said.

"He took enemy fire. The day you guys wasted all those Gooks in that ambush, Bradford's chopper took hostile fire." Throughout this conversation, it was obvious in White's manner and voice tone that he was genuinely concerned for Fleming's well being and his well being would best be served by taking the medal and keeping his mouth shut.

"The hostile fire was somebody in the platoon," Fleming explained. "He was trying to do Bradford."

"Well fuck it gave him enough combat flying hours for the Air medal. I guess they just threw in the Silver Star. Damnit don't be pissed at me. I didn't give him the medal."

Fleming tried to compose himself but he instantly had another bad thought. "What did Levine get?"

White exhaled a tired stream of air, as if he knew that the next few words would only add fuel to Fleming's anger. "He got a Bronze Star, just like everybody else."

"He saved boocoo lives out there, boocoo times. And I know for a fact that L T Bartstell put him in for a Silver Star. Jenks told me."

"They got allocations on medals like the Silver Star. They had one allocation left. The Silver Star went to Bradford."

Fleming was stunned. "Bradford downgraded Levine's Silver Star so he could take it?"

"Yeah that's exactly what happened, okay. Levine's dead, so it don't mean jack-shit to him. Bradford's a lifer puke. He's got a hard on for medals. So he took Levine's. It's how the game works. There ain't shit you can do."

Fleming glared at him for a long moment before he slowly broke into a bitter smile. "Ya wanna' know what I'm gonna' do. I ain't takin that medal. That's what I'm gonna' do."

"You can't do that. You'll get yourself into trouble for no good fucking reason. Lifers don't like you turning down medals."

"Watch me, White. I can guaran-fuckin-tee you I ain't takin that medal. Now is that it? Is that why you wanted to see me, to tell me about this bullshit medal?"

White stared at him with frustrated wonder. "Ryerson wants to see you. He said it's important."

"I gotta' sign any papers, anything like that, to turn down that medal, get them for me."

White nodded his head that he would.

Moments later, an angry Fleming stormed out of the orderly room and walked through the company area. He soon found himself standing in front of Lieuenant Ryerson's tent. He ordered himself to calm down, took a moment to gain composure and then entered.

He exchanged salutes with Ryerson.

Ryerson gave him a long, scrutinizing look. "You okay? You look pissed?"

"Sir, the minute we got back here shit started. Lebeau started beggin' all over me and Carlysle about the same old shit we've heard a thousand times. Then White tells me Bradford downgraded a medal on a friend of mine. It's given me a real bad case of the ass, sir."

"Lebeau got piss ass drunk the other night. His wife sent him a Dear John. She's divorcing him and marrying someone else. He was really broken up about it."

"Well, now I know why he jumped in my shit," Fleming said in an understanding tone. "That's a motherfucker."

Ryerson nodded his head in assent. "That other thing, the medal, I don't know anything about that."

"Sir, you wouldn't. It was before you got here."

"I am about to put a smile on your face. I have been thinking about the Army losing your orders. I know what to do about it. I know how to get you out of the field. I can put you in the rear with the gear."

It should have been good news, but Fleming was having a hard time making heads or tails out of anything. "Yes, sir. When do I get out?"

"Hold on," Ryerson said, holding up his hands in a defensive gesture while smiling and chuckling. 'It's not as easy as all that. There are a few things we have to do first. We need to talk with the JAG

(Judge Advocate General) and let them know of the error. It will take a couple of weeks but you'll get out. I hate losing you, Fleming."

A long moment passed with Fleming deep in thought. "You mean I gotta' ask them? I already done that."

"Ask them?" Ryerson said, at first confused. "Well, yes. I guess you ask. I mean you have to communicate with them. Anything wrong with that?"

Slowly and with deliberate purpose, Fleming shook his head no. "I ain't doin it, sir. I ain't goin to them."

For a long moment, Ryerson looked at him with astonishment. "Why...what do you mean you ain't going to them?"

"They lost the orders. They should come to me, sir."

Ryerson was not at all ready for Fleming's response. "We have to make them aware of the error. That's why we go to them, to let them know."

A sour expression settled on Fleming's face. "And that makes me look like I'm afraid to fight, like I'm begging to get out of the field. And, sir, I already told you – I tried that once. I went to the 404th, right here at English, and that son of a bitchin' MP called me a pussy coward. No fuckin' way, sir. I ain't goin' to them again. I ain't doin that, sir." Fleming stood. "Thanks for trying, I appreciate it, I do, but I ain't doing it, sir."

Ryerson was at a momentary loss for words. "This is not a question of pride. You know how rough it is out there. People are getting killed and that's a fact. You've done your share, way more than your share."

"Sir, I ain't askin' them for anything. If it's all right with you, sir, I'd like to go."

Ryerson's facial expression was one of confused bewilderment. "Okay, Fleming. Okay."

Fleming saluted Ryerson and left the tent. Each step through the company area his anger intensified. Suddenly he found himself in front of a bunker. He hurried inside, dropped to the ground, and leaned back against the sandbags.

From Lebeau, to the bullshit medal, then to this, he thought. He realized that L.T. Ryerson wanted to help him, but Fleming wasn't asking anyone for anything.

His whole life he had been told that he was different, and it was no secret why. It was because he cared. He cared for baseball – respected it – it was the reason for his success. Never, had he begged out of a clutch baseball situation – he was in all the way, win or lose.

Levine never asked for a job in the rear. He stayed till the end and although he met his death you could never take away who he had been, the type of man he was and how people felt about him.

No, Fleming thought. He wasn't asking for anything.

The next morning Fleming returned from morning chow and flopped on his cot. Rumor control had it that they were about to be sent back to the bush and rumor control was never wrong. If they were deployed there would be no time to do anything about his lost orders; not that Fleming had changed his mind about asking.

Just then, White walked in. "Hey, man, you okay?" White asked nervously.

"I'm fine."

"Uh, you still pissed off because of the medal?"

"It don't mean nothin," Fleming said unemotionally.

White smiled a wicked gleaming grin of genuine delight. He pulled a bag of marijuana from his pocket. "Let's party tonight! We're celebrating. You got a new man in your squad."

"A new man, who?"

White pointed to himself. "Me. I'm being sent back to the field."

Fleming was shocked. "Why they sending you back? Did you fuck up?"

"I asked to go back," White said with outrage. "I volunteered."

"You had it made in the shade in Vietnam. Back here you had an almost certain chance of lasting the three hundred and sixty five days. You get out there and your chance of dying or getting really fucked up are pretty damn high."

"I hate what I'm doing back here. I can't stand it."

"Remember, Operation Kansas City? How bad that was? What did you say; you smelled death, it was like the devil stepped out of hell and let out one bad ass fart. Guess what, White? The devil's still farting."

"I already told ya.' I can't stand it back here. Cut me some fuckin' slack. It's what I wanna' do."

Fleming studied him for a long moment. "Okay, you wanna' go back in the field.

Who am I to talk you out of it?"

"The first sergeant said I could choose whatever squad I wanted to be in. I picked yours. He okayed it, as long as you're fine with it."

"You're fuckin' dinky dau you know that?"

"We're all fuckin' dinky dau or we wouldn't be here. Am I in your squad or not?"

Fleming looked at him a long moment. He could tell by the look on White's face that he had made up his mind. "Yeah, you're in my squad. Tonight we party. I'll tell the rest of the guys."

That night the men of fourth squad met for their party. Fleming was more than surprised that Rodgers had decided to attend.

White lit a joint and passed it to Carlyle. "Why are we in Vietnam?" Carlyle choked out, coughing from inhaling too much pot.

"Our Country asked us to go and we obeyed," Vines answered. "Dumb fuckers we are."

Fleming frowned. "Our country asks a lot from a man. And one thing about our country – they don't ask everybody."

"Why do the gooks hate us?" Carlyle asked.

Rojas took the joint. "Cause we kill them." He hits on the joint.

"I mean the villagers," Carlyle said mildly irritated. "The V.C. steal their rice, make them join their army. They say no, the V.C. start choppin' off heads and shit."

"We do the same," Rodgers said with a smile on his face as if he is trying to bond with the men.

"Don't give me that shit," Carlyle fired back. "I mean I know there's been some incidents. But we give them food, everything. The V.C. just takes shit."

Fleming takes a hit off a joint. "We scare them, Carlyle."

"More than the fuckin V.C.!" Carlyle exclaimed with a bewildered falsetto tone.

"A typical gook is a farmer born in his village and eighty, ninety years later dies there. He's never been more than a mile away from home. Then one day a chopper lands. He ain't never seen a chopper. Out of that chopper comes Blacks, American Indians, Spanish, White dudes."

"Colored dudes," Carlyle replied.

Fleming smiled at him. "Colored dudes." He continued: "Everybody's wearing helmets and carrying rucksacks and rifles. A gook is five four and a hundred twenty pounds. An American is six foot, maybe taller. He's a hundred and fifty to two hundred fifty pounds. We got planes that drop bombs and spit fire. It's like we're from Mars or something. Now who do you think a gook's gonna identify with, us or the V.C.?"

General comments of agreement and understanding filled the room then Rodgers spoke: "We are in a foreign country trying to impose territorial rights by, for all intent and purpose, colonizing the indigenous people of that country. We cloud the issues with rhetoric, spewing out a constant stream of obscure idioms involving domino theories and Communist aggression. I said it before; in reality we are more concerned about our own potential political and economic gain than the welfare of the South Vietnamese People. And South Vietnam and its people intrinsically and spiritually sense this."

Carlyle groaned. "All they gotta do is talk to Rodgers for a few minutes and they'll think we're from somewhere farther out than Mars."

"And what's that supposed to mean?" Rodgers said in a tone loaded with defensiveness.

"You're all fucked-up. You got a college education and you don't know shit. You're selfish and spoiled." Carlyle paused a moment makes an obvious show of engaging each man in brief eye contact. "And we all can intrinsically and spiritually sense this."

Fleming exploded with laughter that he instantly tried to suppress but he ended up laughing with everyone else.

"You only think about your own self," Carlyle continued. "Like you're the onliest motherfucker over here. You let Carson die because you didn't have the balls to help him. He's white too. If it was my black ass I'd definitely be a dead motherfucker. You better pray you don't get fucked up cause I wouldn't piss on you if you were on fire."

"I am sorry about Carson, but apologizing to people like you is useless. You berate me because I'm different and I refuse to change. I can't justify turning myself into an animal just because I'm spending a year in Vietnam." Rodgers stood. "I knew I shouldn't have come here. I knew this was a mistake."

"Rodgers, sit down, man." Fleming said.

"Fuck you, Fleming. Get somebody else to join your brotherhood of killers!"

Rodgers stormed out of the tent.

"Damn," Washington said. "Rodgers' shit is getting flakier and flakier."

"I don't know," Vines said. "Maybe he's startin to grow some balls."

Rodgers walked aimlessly through the company area. He should have never come to this party. After the talk with Fleming and Rojas he thought he had come to some sort of understanding of them. Then today he learned that Fleming had refused a chance to be relieved of combat duties and that he was refusing a Bronze Star. What kind of man refuses to be relieved of a dangerous combat position? Then to complicate it all, the same man refuses to be honored for doing the job in an exemplary manner. He knew they didn't believe in the war: if truth were told, he had known it all along; he just never wanted to admit it to himself. Yet tomorrow they would charge through a wall of bullets if they were ordered. Their machismo, their bravery was not necessary in today's world of peace and love. Yet despite all this, he felt a primordial attraction to it all. Lately the same question kept running around in his head. He wanted to know what kept him from being like them and that longing meant that on some deep sub-conscious level he wanted to be like them.

CHAPTER 18

A Brush With The Past

The next day Fleming received word that tonight they would be deployed to the field, validating rumor controls flawless record of always being right. He told the squad and they became somber and pensive. They decided to go to chow but when asked to accompany them, Fleming felt a need to be alone and declined. He waited an hour then he went to the chow hall by himself.

Once inside he got his meal and took a seat. Just then he saw a tall, well built man walking through the mess hall searching for a table. Something was familiar about the man's confident gait and Fleming watched him until he got a good look at his face. I don't believe it, he said to himself. He stood and hurried to the man. Fleming approached and was a few feet behind the man. "Count's three and two, two outs and the bases are loaded."

The man turned to face Fleming.

"Whatta ya think I'll throw?" Fleming asked.

The man leaned closer to get a better look. Then his face broke into a smile. "Billy Fleming!" he nearly screamed. "Son of a bitch Billy Fleming," He grabbed Fleming, lifted him off the ground, and squeezed him with an affectionate bear hug.

"Ohh, let me down," Fleming choked and laughed at the same time.

With a mighty laugh, he lowered Fleming to the ground.

"Damn, Tony, you're still strong as an ox," Fleming said. The man was his baseball foe and sometimes teammate Tony Santoro.

"I heard you were in Nam, but I didn't know you were here at L.Z. English." Santoro studied Fleming. "Man, I almost didn't recognize your ugly ass. You look like shit."

"I lost weight. I came here at one seventy five and I'm down to one forty."

"Man, you got black circles under your eyes. You look older, too. What the fuck you been doing?"

"I ain't been sleepin much. I worry boocoo." Fleming shrugged his shoulders. "I'm a grunt."

"No shit," Santoro said, impressed. "You mean you've been fighting the gooks?"

Fleming chuckled mirthlessly. "When we find them we fight. But fuck that. You were at U.C.L.A. on a baseball scholarship – how the hell did you get here?"

Santoro frowned. "I got hooked up with the wrong crowd, some real assholes. I flunked out of school and lost my scholarship."

"You dipshit, you loved baseball. You were a shoo-in for the big leagues."

"Baseball and studying is about the last thing you do in College. Today, you gotta be one of the beautiful people." Santoro shook his head in frustration. "College was the first time I was away from home. I got lonely I guess. I got involved with protestors, war protestors. They recruited me. I was a big name in baseball so I was a feather in their cap."

"They actually recruited you?"

"About as enthusiastically as the Army. It was all bullshit. I went to a few protests. The leaders gave these rousing speeches. Man, they could talk. They'd get everyone in a protest-frenzy. Then we'd go on the warpath till the cops came and started kicking ass. That's when the leaders split, when the shit started. They wanted nothing to do with cops swinging clubs. But they were sure big on sending us out to kick ass."

"Sounds like the Army. Our leaders send us on these hairy fuckin missions and they sit in the rear safe and sound. And, for that, they get awarded medals for bravery."

Santoro shook his head and chuckled. "The peace movement has as least as much bullshit as the Army. The Army says we're over here fighting for peace. The protestors are smashing cops over the head with their peace signs. Fighting for peace? Clubbing cops with peace signs? I gotta tell ya,' Fleming, we live in a weird time."

"I hear that. So you enlisted?"

"Yeah, they were gonna draft me. So I said fuck it – I enlisted. After all the bullshit and bullshit people in college, I felt I needed something real."

"You got what you were looking for. There's enough reality around here to last a lifetime."

"I could've beaten the draft. The dudes back home are experts at it. They even got draft counselors. They show you how to flunk the physical. I knew this guy, graduated with a law degree. He wants to be a lawyer and go into politics. He got his draft notice. Before he took his physical, he drank two bottles of ink, gave him temporary spots on his lungs. Got classified 4-F. This fucker is gonna' be a lawyer and send people to jail. Yet he broke the law drinking that ink. He's a lawyer and they all go into politics. Imagine if he becomes a politician. What if he becomes president and he has to send people to war? When it was his turn to go to his war, he skipped out. I mean how could he do it – send people to fight? Send people to do something he was afraid to do himself?"

"From what I've learned about mankind and law, he will do it very easily. He won't lose one night's sleep over it."

Santoro chuckled mirthlessly. "You know you're probably right."

"So what the fuck they got you doin in da Nam?" Fleming asked.

Santoro frowned. "I'm a fuckin payroll clerk in finance. I'm stationed in Qui Nhon. I'm an airborne clerk." Santoro said apologetically as if embarrassed.

"You got it dicked," Fleming said to him. "You ain't missing much by being in the rear. It don't mean nothing. What are you doing here at English?"

"Damned if I know, but something big is goin down. A bunch of us clerks came here. I was hoping we were gonna have a last ditch fight with the gooks and I'd get to see some action." He gave Fleming a huge smile. "All those times we kicked ass in baseball. Over here, we'd be hell together as a team."

Fleming smiled back. "I tell you what, hurry up and volunteer cause I'm going on an operation in about four hours. Me and you, we'd end this war in about two months."

They both broke up in laughter.

"Hate to break this up," Flemings said standing. "I gotta di-di. Gotta' check on my men before we leave tonight."

"Check on your men! Are you in charge or something?"

"I'm a squad leader."

"No shit." Santoro said quite impressed. He stood and embraced Fleming. "It was good seeing you. Take care of yourself out there."

Fleming left. The fleeting brush with his past was satisfying. But his warm feeling was short lived. He wondered if he was walking away from his past forever.

Leaving his quarters to meet with Chi, Van knew the past few weeks of peace had come to an end. Chi was about to tell him that they were embarking on an operation. They had been in this underground bunker complex near Bong Son catching up on much needed rest and reinforcing the platoon with new men. It had been a relaxing, satisfying past six weeks. They had gone to the South China Sea and had fished and swam. Everyone joined in the activities even Dan and Hoi. Hoi had not spoken one word about defection. But each day the platoon added recruits; it was only a matter of time before they would be thrust back into the war.

Approaching Chi's quarters, Van passed by a new recruit who bowed deferentially to him. The recruit told Van that Hoi was in conference with Chi but he would tell Chi that Van had arrived.

The new recruits treated Van with respect. Stories were told of his and Dan's courageous deeds and bravery during battle. They were legends. Dan thrived on the attention but Van thought it curious that men told tales of his feats in battle while hardly a word was ever spoken of the lives he helped save assisting the doctors or his role as the platoon's medic

Then Hoi stepped from Chi's quarters. As soon as he saw Van he hurried to him. "I have to talk with you," he said, fear alive in his face.

The recruit rudely grabbed Hoi's arm. "Move! Sergeant Chi does not want us talking about the operation."

Recruits showed Hoi no respect and regarded him a coward. "Let him go, dog," Van said angrily.

The recruit's eyes went wide with alarm and fear. He mumbled an apology, bowed subserviently to Van, and slowly backed away.

"I'll meet with you after I speak with Chi," Van said to Hoi.

Van was sitting across from Chi when Chi suddenly stood and began pacing the room. "We've been ordered back into action. This operation is more than hit and run. Our mission is to aggressively engage the Americans and kill as many as possible." Then Chi returned to his seat. "You're valuable. If you do not perform to the best of your ability, our mission may not be successful."

Van knew that a comment was expected, but he chose to remain silent.

"I see you have little interest in what I am saying. Maybe this will interest you. Hoi is a disease – a disease that will spread unless I purify the platoon."

Chi paused waiting for a response. Not getting one, he continued: "Because he is your friend and because you're a good man I put up with him. But as I said this operation is more than hit and run. We all have to fight and I need you focused on killing Americans, not protecting your cowardly friend." Chi paused again. Malevolence in his ugly face glowed with unyielding intensity. "Hoi's behavior is your fault. He knows his cowardice is tolerated because you defend him. But that is ending. I am not spending another second worrying about him. I'll give you one chance, just one. Talk to him. Make him understand. If he does, I'll treat him like any other soldier. But if he makes one wrong move then I promise you I will sacrifice him for the revolution. I'm giving you a chance to help your friend. I can't do anything more than that."

"Am I dismissed?" Van asked in a tone loaded with contempt.

A moment passed while Chi studied Van. "Yes, you're dismissed."

Van got up from his seat and started to leave. He was halfway across the room when Chi said: "Van, wait."

Van turned to Chi.

Chi took papers from his desk and held them up to Van. "Propaganda leaflets. Read them."

Van returned to Chi, took the leaflets, and left the room. Reading leaflets was an exercise in monotoness futility. They all said the same thing. America was in turmoil. People were against the war and fighting in the streets. All the propaganda leaflets on earth and all of Chi's speeches could not change Van's mind. It was war. It didn't matter who was right or who was wrong. War was wrong and that made both sides wrong. He entered Hoi's quarters and found him waiting.

Hoi rushed to him. "I have to talk with you."

"No, I have to talk with you. You have to change right now. If you don't start fighting then Chi will go hard on you."

"Fight!" Hoi yelled out angrily. "I want to defect, like you promised. I don't want to fight."

"How many times do I have to tell you that I am not defecting until I am sure it is the right thing to do?"

Hoi's face seemed to drop; the desperate expression of a man who had lost his last shred of hope. "You lied. I know that now. You've been lying the whole time."

"I never lied. I was unsure and I still am."

"How long do you expect me to wait until you are sure? You deceived me. Why couldn't you just tell me the truth?"

There was honest sincerity in Hoi's facial expression and his voice tone; it affected Van deeply. "I am sorry if you were misled, but now we have to forget that. Chi told me to tell you that if you don't fight he will make it hard for you."

Hoi eyed him for a long moment then smiled mirthlessly. "So now you are Chi's messenger boy?" He turned and walked away.

"Hoi, wait," Van said. But he continued out of the room. Van sat on his mat. Defection would have never worked. Hoi would have become an infantryman in the American Army. It was his only skill. He had never once come to the hospital to help treat the wounded like he had promised and Van had asked him several times.

Van lay back on his mat. He had to clear his mind – the real enemy, the Americans, should be in the forefront of his thoughts. Frustrated, he grabbed the propaganda leaflets. Maybe he would read something that would distract him from his disturbing thoughts.

CHAPTER 19

The Battle

The sun beat down unmercifully as the platoon plunged through elephant grass. Every man felt a sense of impending doom. Every man felt the gut wrenching anxiety that combat could erupt at any second. The enemy was willing and ready to fight and had been ambushing relentlessly with great success. Yesterday afternoon, a combination of NVA and V. C. had uncharacteristically ambushed Charlie Company during daylight and killed every man. Alpha was also hit hard, losing thirty men and fifteen wounded, among them were three Lieutenants, platoon leaders.

Two hours passed before the platoon finally emerged from the elephant grass: Fleming figured they had maybe an hour of sunlight before they would have to stop and set up an NDP. Foxholes had to be dug before dark – the night belonged to the enemy. Up ahead, one hundred meters away, they saw their objective, a plateau bordered by a tree line. The plateau would offer excellent cover in case of attack during the night.

Third squad was walking point and had advanced within twenty five meters of the plateau when three RPD machine guns opened fire, killing the point man and the two flanks. Five other men were wounded. Their agonizing cries could be heard above the gunfire's roar.

"GGGRRR!" Doc Garret's familiar growl was heard amidst the screams and gunfire.

Rounds fell all around him. There was no way he would make it to the wounded men without being hit, so when Garret was about to run past him, Fleming stuck out his foot and tripped him.

Garret crashed down. A look of complete surprise filled his face until he realized what had happened. Then he reared back and punched Fleming in the face. "You motherfucker!" Garret said with unbridled hostility.

"Damn it, Doc! Calm the fuck down! There ain't no way you're gonna make it through three machine guns!" Fleming shot back angrily. He flicked his tongue at the warm blood trickling from his cut lip.

Garret's eyes darted left and right in uncertainty. "I got people up there!"

"L T called for artillery and air. When the gunships get here we'll get the men."

Garret nodded his head in agreement and thought a moment. "Okay, sounds good. Sorry I cold cocked you."

Fleming gave Garret a bitter smile. "You're a fuckin psycho, you know that?

"That ain't exactly front page news," Garret shot back.

Despite himself Fleming gave a weak, acidic smile then he rallied the men around him. "We gotta help Doc Garret get the wounded. When the artillery and gunships fire we're heading out who's going?"

Everyone volunteered except for Rodgers.

"I can't go out there," he said. "It's suicide."

Fleming gave him a long hard look. "We need to get our people out."

"I can't do it," he insisted, pronouncing each word slowly and distinctly.

Carlyle blew out a disgusted stream of air. "You gotta be getting tired of being the world's biggest pussy."

Rodgers looked away.

Just then Ramirez and another man made their way to Fleming's group. Ramirez pointed at the man with him. "We wanna help. This is a cherry. Name's Dunnigan, but we all call him Crazy."

No explanation of the man's nickname was needed. He had the huge arms and chest of a weight lifter. His eyes bulged wild with fury. He grinned cockily at each man as if sizing him up.

Fleming turned to Rodgers. "Find the L T tell him we're goin after the wounded."

"Okay, Fleming, okay," Rodgers said in a defeated tone.

Just then the gunships arrived and unleashed a murderous barrage of gunfire and rocket fire at the suspected NVA position.

Fleming looked at each man. "Let's go."

They sprinted twenty meters when small arms fire forced them to seek cover. They dropped to the ground, low crawled ten meters more, and reached the wounded. They hoisted them on their backs and started away.

Waving his arms like a traffic cop, Garret directed all the men behind a small hummock with a palm tree on top of it.

"Vines, Crazy, Washington lay cover fire," Fleming ordered.

They scrambled atop the hummock and started firing. An enthralled Crazy watched the artillery barrage hammer the tree line. Suddenly about twenty NVA soldiers fled the tree line heading for the plateau. "Awright," he whispered to himself. He took aim and opened fire.

Four enemy soldiers fell.

Excited, wanting a better look, Crazy peeked above the rock that was providing him cover. An enemy round struck him in the forehead. He tumbled backward, alerting Vines and Washington who immediately opened fire at the advancing NVA with M-60 fire.

A dozen enemy soldiers fell.

Fleming and Garret rushed to Crazy. Blood covered the entire left side of his face, "Oh shit!" Garret mumbled, fearing the worst.

From his supine position, Crazy smiled at them. "What? You think the gook's are gonna do Crazy Dunnigan with just one measly bullet? Ya think I growed a vagina or something? Fuck no." His smile grew larger. "I can't fuckin' believe this! Took one right in my fuckin' dome my first fuckin' ambush! Fucking far fucking out!"

Furiously examining the wound, Doc Garret learned that the round had only grazed the side of Crazy's head. "You believe this guy?" Garret said to Fleming. "He's getting off cause he got a head wound?"

Crazy touched his head, adoring the blood. "Oh wow! That's boocoo blood! Probably gonna leave a scar huh, Doc?"

"Yeah, Crazy, I think you're gonna have yourself a real nice scar."

A profound, almost reverent look etched on his face, Crazy grabbed Garret's arm. "You shoulda seen them gooks fall when I shot them. It was beautiful, man."

Garret rolled his eyes. "Yeah, I'm real sorry I missed that."

Crazy saw Ramirez approach and he bubbled with excitement. "Ramirez, got me four gooks and a ti-ti head wound my first fucking day out – can you believe that shit?"

Ramirez touched Crazy's arm. "Yeah, man, it's a great first day."

Crazy beamed a satisfied smile.

Ramirez turned to Fleming. "He's one highly motivated son of a bitch, ain't he?"

"He may win the war all by himself."

"Hate to break this up, but we gotta meda-vac these guys," Garret said to them. "Or some of them will buy it."

Fleming grimaced, not wanting to point out the obvious. "Doc, we're pinned down. We try to leave we're gonna have boocoo more casualties."

"We gotta do fuckin something and we gotta do it fuckin fast."

Suddenly there was a thundering, surprising outburst of M-16 fire.

Fleming turned to Ramirez and Garret. "That's Alpha firing on the other side of the plateau. "While they're hitting the gooks we can di-di."

"You think we should give it a try?" Ramirez asked.

"Damn straight," Garret said.

"It'll be dark soon. It would be suicide then. In the dark, we may even take fire from our own men," Fleming said. "Do it now while the gooks are fucking with Alpha."

Fleming and Ramirez instructed the men on what to do and then assigned men to carry the wounded. They sprinted off with the wounded and without incident made it back to the platoon and the company.

Lebeau rushed up to him. "Who the fuck told you to go out there like that?"

"Nobody told me. Those men needed help. I helped them."

"Damn it, Fleming, the Lieutenant and me were on the situation. We woulda' ordered men out there. Maybe we got another plan for you. Ya ever think of that?"

"We got the wounded, sergeant."

"That ain't the fuckin point. The point is you can't just do whatever you want in a firefight. Wait until you're given orders."

Lieutenant Ryerson was in earshot and had heard the entire conversation. He wandered over. "Okay that's enough. Sergeant, he got the job done. All's well that ends well."

"Sir, he does whatever he damn pleases. We gotta make sure we're all on the same page or it will hurt us in the future."

"He won't do it again." Ryerson turned and made direct eye contact with Fleming. "Fleming, in the future, you will wait for orders, right?"

Fleming smiled at Ryerson. "Yes, sir, in the future I'll do whatever the sergeant says."

Lebeau's face turned red with embarrassment.

"There, now everybody is happy," Ryerson said with a smile.

Lebeau was nowhere near happy. He knew Ryerson had just sided with Fleming and in Lebeau's mind that act successfully destroyed the tenuous hold he had on the platoon.

Fleming returned to his squad. They were in an upbeat mood after the successful rescue mission except for Rodgers. He sat with his head in his hands. He looked up at Fleming. "I really wanted to go that time." He looked away from them. "But I couldn't."

Carlyle looked at him contemptuously. "Rodgers, the day we gotta count on you is the day we're all fucked."

Rodgers heaved a heavy sigh as if life had been drained from him.

Just then Garret came to them. "Thanks for helping me, people."

"No sweat, Doc," Fleming said. "How's Crazy?"

"I told him he could be medavacced. He got pissed. Said no fuckin head wound was gonna stop him. I tried to talk him into leaving and he pulled his 16 on me – threatened to shoot me. Said he was stayin. He didn't want to miss any of the fun. He is one sick pup."

"Give him some time, his attitude will change. But I got a feeling he's right, the fun's about to start for real."

Chi halted his men inside a clump of palm trees situated near a fruit tree grove and a cemetery. He told them to rest. Tomorrow at noon they would join an NVA company and rest would be an expensive luxury.

Tired, but too anxious to sleep, Van wandered away from the others. American soldiers were swarming like so many ants in the surrounding area and the Viet Cong and the NVA were eager to engage them. The past few months' infiltrations had all been successful; Van had never seen so many NVA Soldiers congested in one place. It was as Chi had promised – the next few days they were destined to see much action.

Van lay down on a patch of lush grass. He stared aimlessly at the night sky. Stars twinkled like gold on a black background. Sitting by the village gate, he and Kim had spent many nights looking up at the stars, planning their future. For centuries the village had promised a life of harmony, love, and peace.

What happened? He wondered. Who was to blame? Or in any life situation was it senseless to search for someone or something to blame? What if he had done things differently these past six months? Would his situation be any different then it was today? Would it have been wise to have taken on Dan's persona; strike out at whomever was near simply because his life had been disrupted? Dan, the ferocious warrior, led like a small puppy dog by his master Chi. Dan acted but did not think. Right or wrong, good or evil were never concepts that stood between Dan and a violent action. There was a brutal honesty to Dan's behavior.

Should he have been like Hoi? Hoi, like Dan, did not think. Unlike Dan, Hoi did not act. Or was his inactivity really action in disguise? It was all so complex, so confusing. And to compound matters, his own behavior he found the most confusing and complex of all. He fought and he healed – a rare and unlikely combination. Then in the middle of a war he accepted Hoi's burdens, an action that was certain to fail. And fail he had.

But the time for wonder, for problems, for thought had ended. Questions still needed answering, but he now knew the correct path. He would concern himself only with this next operation. It was unlike anything they had ever undertaken; an all out offensive to kill as many Americans as possible. Now, he longed to kill them. The last propaganda leaflet had brought enlightenment. The leaflet began as every one he had read in the past: America was in upheaval; the people were fighting in the streets because of the immoral Vietnam War. He had heard it all a dozen times before. But this leaflet provided convincing proof. There was a picture of a famous American movie actress sitting behind an anti-aircraft gun. She smiled with unbridled joy; play-acting as if she were firing the weapon at imaginary American aircraft. She even wore a NVA helmet as if she were part of the Army. The leaflet had quoted her as condemning America's actions. She apologized to the Vietnamese. Her words and apology could have been lies put in the leaflet for propaganda purposes; however, no one could deny the picture of her happy smiling face. It seemed as if she were enjoying herself as she pretended to shoot down American pilots. Of course the woman would never kill, but he would kill. Kill for her, he thought, kill as many as possible. It was the right and honorable thing to do. It would be his last honorable action on earth. Until he died or the war ended he'd kill them all with a clear conscience.

The next day Fleming learned that Alpha's company commander and seventy-five other men had been killed during the previous day's battle. The company was decimated: all of their officers had been killed over the past week so Alpha was assigned to Ryerson, Bravo's senior field commander. Alpha was down to thirty-three men. Along with the thirty men in Ryerson's platoon their combined force was sixty-three men.

That morning they were sweeping toward the plateau when mortar rounds suddenly rained down on their position.

"Push for the plateau," Lebeau ordered.

Fleming was sure the mortars were being dropped in anticipation of the Americans doing just that, rushing to the plateau. He started to shout out a few words to counter the order when Lebeau butt stroked him in the stomach with his weapon. Fleming fell to his knees gagging and coughing.

"You cocksucker!" Lebeau said, standing above him. "I told you I'm in charge."

Ten men had almost reached the plateau when small arms fire cut them down; exactly what Fleming thought would happen. The NVA had set up an exact replica of their ambush the night before. Down on his knees, his breath slowly returning, Fleming saw the men fall. "There…it fuckin is…You just wasted those guys."

Lebeau glared at Fleming then turned and walked to the rear in search of Ryerson.

After catching his breath, Fleming hurried to his men. "We gotta take that plateau. Stay low and be fuckin' careful. Let's go."

Ramirez and Pierson's squad pushed forward toward the plateau.

Carlyle fired two grenade rounds then a crystal round into a NVA position.

Soon after, three Vietnamese vigorously rubbed their eyes, burned by the crystals, as they tried to crawl from the plateau's bottom.

Crazy fired on them, killing them all. "WHHHOOWEE!' he cheered. He turned to Carlyle. "Get some!" he screamed out enthusiastically.

The men inched forward. Men on both sides were dropping intermittently.

Rodgers lay near a small knoll, determined to charge forward – determined not to be the world's biggest pussy. But every time he tried to move small arms fire chewed the ground all around him. Small puffs of dust hit him in the face. Why move? He finally asked himself. It was all for nothing. Nobody cared about what happened on this stinking piece of earth. He had even seen Lebeau running toward the rear. It was senseless to die for nothing. Why???

Ramirez fired a burst at a half dozen enemy soldiers manning a RPD machine gun position. Two NVA soldiers fell, but the RPD continued spitting out round after round.

Ramirez crawled forward a few meters when machine gun fire ripped open his stomach.

Vines fired his 60 and killed the men manning the RPD.

Fifteen meters away, Pierson quickly crawled to Ramirez and turned him over. Ramirez's intestines hung outside of his stomach. Then Pierson was shot in the chest.

Doc Garret quickly crawled to them. Rounds fell all around him as he checked both men's wounds. He placed his arms around Pierson and crawled toward a knoll where he found Rodgers paralyzed and shaking with fear. Garret left Pierson and crawled back and grabbed Ramirez. Suddenly Garret felt the hot flash of an AK-47 round as it entered his leg. Gritting back pain and still dragging Ramirez, Garret reached the knoll and tore away his own fatigue trousers to reveal the torn flesh of his left calf. He quickly sanitized it then injected morphine into Ramirez. "Rodgers, get over here. I need help."

Reluctantly, Rodgers moved to Garret.

"Use your canteen, keep Ramirez's intestines wet," Garret ordered.

"How do you do that?" Rodgers said in a voice loaded with fear.

"Like this," Garret hissed. He cupped water in his right hand and slowly let it fall on Ramirez's intestines held in his left hand. Then Garret slammed the canteen against Rodgers' chest. "Don't go fuckin flaky on me, you hear? You keep his intestines wet or the sun will bake them! Now get the fuck to work!" Garret left Rodgers to the task then he went to work on Pierson.

It took a supreme act of will for Rodgers to force himself to touch Ramirez's intestines. Oh Jesus I'm in hell, he said to himself. I'm in hell.

Gunships strafed the plateau's eastern end. Fleming and his men made it behind a huge tree. He huddled the men together. "We're going around the plateau then we're climbing it. We'll hit the Gooks from the rear. Carlyle, cover us. Just pour on those grenade rounds." Fleming turned back to the others. "Let's go."

The men ran from behind the tree and made it safely to the plateau's other side.

Four NVA soldiers were at the bottom of the embankment.

The Americans opened fire, killing all four enemy soldiers.

"Be careful," Fleming cautioned. "They came from the plateau. They were trying to escape. There might be more Gooks trying the same shit." He paused and looked each man in the eye. "We're gonna waste these bastards."

Meanwhile Lieutenant Ryerson and a radioman took refuge behind the tree where Carlyle was firing rounds.

"Sir, Fleming took some men, they're trying to get on top the plateau. They left a minute ago, sir."

Ryerson nodded his head. The plateau was vital; capturing it would end the assault. "I'm going to try and catch them." Then Ryerson and the radioman sprinted away. They reached the other side and saw that the men were but a few feet up the thirty- foot rise. Ryerson and the radioman hurried to them. They climbed within five feet of the top. The position was perilous. Once on top they'd have to contend with the enemy and their own artillery that was bombarding the hill.

"Be accurate with your firing," Ryerson said to them. "We have to do this quickly."

They continued up and reached the plateau's top unseen. The enemy was fighting from foxholes and from inside four bunkers. Fleming's men opened fire and downed ten NVA firing from the foxholes. Then Fleming and some men charged the bunkers throwing hand grenades. They neutralized the first two bunkers, killing most of its occupants.

A gunship boldly flew within twenty meters of a bunker and released two rockets decimating it.

More gunships arrived and easily eliminated the last bunker in seconds, ending the battle for the plateau.

Fleming removed his helmet and sat atop it. He smiled watching Crazy rummaging like a housewife at a thrift shop through dead NVA soldiers, collecting war souvenirs.

Then Fleming's smile quickly vanished. Where's the L T? He said to himself. He jumped up, scanned the perimeter and saw Ryerson lying on the plateau's eastern end. The radioman was near him, writhing in pain. He sprinted toward them. A huge hunk of shrapnel protruded from the radioman's bloody right leg. When Fleming reached Ryerson he saw a human foot and eight inches of leg lying on the ground. Ryerson lay motionless on the ground minus half his leg. Fleming knelt down and turned Ryerson's body over.

Ryerson smiled weakly at him. "Glad it's you and not a gook. Guess we won."

Meanwhile Vines rushed over and attended to the radioman.

"Yes, sir, we won." With a bayonet and a piece of cord Fleming applied a tourniquet to Ryerson's leg. During the fire fight the enemy had only used small arms. There was a good chance that Ryerson had been hit by artillery fire from English. Probably the last fucking round, Fleming thought.

"They got my leg," Ryerson said. "Part of it is back there."

"Yes, sir. I'm really sorry, sir."

Ryerson smiled through gritted teeth. "It hurts like hell."

"White!" Fleming yelled over his shoulder. "Get Doc Garret. L T's been hit. We need another medic for his radioman." He turned to

Ryerson. "We'll get you outta here soon, sir."

Ryerson grabbed Fleming's arm. "I intend to be a politician one day, maybe even President. Want to be my V.P.?"

"Yes, sir," Fleming replied softly. "We'll teach those REMF's in the White House a thing or two."

Ryerson winced in pain. "I wonder what my Father will say. He didn't want me coming here. He was really P.O.ed that I went into the infantry."

Fleming touched Ryerson's arm. "Sir, it don't mean nothing. Everything is gonna be okay."

"Fucking-A. I don't mind this…not a whole lot." He coughed.

"Sir, I don't think I could ever have a better leader than you, sir."

"Thanks, Fleming. They're kind words."

Garret hobbled over to Fleming and Ryerson.

"You all right, Doc?"

"Yeah, got me a ti-ti wound." He looked closer at Ryerson. "Sir, how ya doin?"

"Fine, doc. Lost me a leg." He winced. "It hurts too."

"I got something for the pain, sir." He injected morphine into Ryerson's leg.

Vines motioned for Crazy to help him with the radioman. When Crazy reached him he hoisted the radio on his back.

Ryerson motioned to Garret's leg. "Doc, you sure you're all right? There's boocoo blood on your fatigues."

"Sir, I'm fine." Garret turned to Fleming. "You done a pretty good job with this tourniquet."

"Plenty of practice," Fleming said with a wry smirk on his face. "How many guys got hit, doc?"

"Five KIA. Got about ten medavacs. Seven are priority."

"How about you? You goin out?" The dried blood on Garret's fatigue trousers looked like red enamel.

"It's a through and through. Just boocoo blood, that's all. It's a ti-ti wound."

"Doc, a through and through means you got two holes in your leg. How you gonna hump the bush with a leg like that?"

"The way the Gooks are hitting us, we'll probably go a hundred meters and run into another ambush. I ain't gonna be doin boocoo humpin." Garret took off his helmet and sat on it. "You all right, sir."

"Man, I feel good." Ryerson slurred overcome by morphine.

"With the L T being medavacced, "Garret said. "That leaves Leabau in charge of the platoon."

A chill, as if a spider had just skittered across his spine, ran through Fleming. Lebeau was in charge until a replacement C.O. could be found and that could take a while. Lebeau would definitely not cut Fleming's squad any slack.

A medavac landed and Ryerson was put on board.

Crazy moved to Fleming.

"You know how to work that?" Fleming asked, motioning to the radio strapped on Crazy's back.

"I used it in A.I.T. and the radioman showed me a few things. But it sounds like it ain't working right. There's boocoo static."

"Well, it's better than nothing,"

Fleming and the others climbed down the plateau. Grim determination emanated from everyone. Months of chasing an elusive foe that had nit-picked at them made them eager to finally slug it out with an enemy who now seemed ready to stand and fight.

Hundreds of NVA Soldiers had been sighted five klicks from the plateau. Bravo's makeshift company of forty-eight men headed northeast to engage them. Two companies from third battalion were being flown in from English to engage the enemy from the opposite direction of Lebeau's men.

They humped two uneventful hours.

Fleming couldn't shake the nagging, haunting feeling that some really bad shit was about to go down.

Lebeau finally halted the column and the men dropped exhausted to the ground.

"Fleming, get your ass over here," Lebeau barked.

Fleming pushed his bone weary body off the ground and went to Lebeau.

For a few moments, Lebeau studied a map then looked up at Fleming. "There's a cemetery about a hundred meters past that mound. Take your squad and set up a perimeter defense in the cemetery."

The mound was two hundred meters away: it was fifty meters long, two meters high; high enough to make it impossible to see the cemetery from their current postion. A fruit tree grove was west of the mound and was approximately fifty meters in length. "That's way too fuckin far," Fleming blurted out. "You can't be fuckin serious."

"I know how fuckin far it is and I am fuckin serious."

Fleming took a moment to compose himself. He again looked at the proposed ambush site. "There're boocoo Gooks out here. We could be walking into something."

"And this is war, but I think you know that. I don't wanna hear any more shit – go out there and set up in that cemetery like I ordered you."

It certainly wasn't a well-guarded secret that Lebeau harbored ill will toward him and his squad, but this was such an insane order it had to be a joke. "Sergeant, that…it's crazy." He said exasperated.

"I am acting company commander and I want men in that cemetery."

Fleming couldn't help but think that Lebeau sounded like he was the little boy who owned the only football and no one was playing unless he was quarterback.

"Can we hump the company to that mound?" Fleming asked with a cautious, deliberate tone of respect. "Then I'll put some men in the cemetery.

"Take your men out there or so help me I'll bring you up on charges," Lebeau said slowly and distinctly. "I'll arrest your insolent ass right the fuck now and send you back to English. Now what's it gonna be?"

"If we're hit the company ain't gonna be able to support us!" Fleming nearly shouted. "And we'll never make it back to the company!"

"Get your men out there now!" Lebeau said softly but viciously.

A long moment passed. Fleming's eyed Lebeau angrily. Then defeat set in his face. "Would it be too much trouble to ask for a radioman?" he asked sarcastically.

"Sure, take Crazy," Lebeau said good-naturedly. "And there's one more thing. During that last firefight I saw Rodgers skatin' behind a hill. It's time he learned to fight. Put him on point."

Lebeau had seen Rodgers skating behind a hill because Lebeau was skating behind the same hill. "We can't put Rodgers on point," Fleming said, trying to suppress his anger.

"I am sick and tired of you trying to protect him. Put him on point. Now move out, or so help me God I'll put you under arrest for refusing to follow orders. I'll personally see to it that you end up in L.B.J."

Fleming eyed him for a long moment. "As soon as I get back to the rear, I'm talking to Captain Wiggins about this."

"Good, asshole. Now move out."

Fleming stormed away. He grabbed Crazy then called the squad together. "Lebeau wants an OP in that cemetery. Guess what squad he's picked?"

Everyone turned to look at the cemetery.

"That's too fuckin far," Carlyle said. We get hit we're cut off from the platoon!"

"I told him that and boocoo more. It don't mean nothin. He wants it there. Crazy, you're my radioman. You're in my squad."

Crazy took a second to look at the ambush site. "Fleming, that's a little fuckin far for an OP."

Fleming was getting tired of hearing the obvious. "There it fuckin is! I can fuckin see! I know it's too far! I told Lebeau it's too far! It don't mean nothin, we still gotta do it."

A moment of silence passed.

"And, there's one more thing. Lebeau wants Rodgers to walk point.

"Me?" Rodgers bellowed. "I have never walked point, not once. Why now?"

"Lebeau thinks it's time you learned. Let's go."

Rodgers' facial expression was a mixture of protest, confusion, and fear.

The squad began its walk to the cemetery. Two hundred meters later they came to a huge bomb crater just a few meters from the mound. They stepped up and over the mound.

Fleming scanned the area for possible cover sites. A huge tree lay broken on its side right next to the mound. Thirty-five meters ahead another broken tree lay on its side; it was fifty meters from a clump of palm trees and the cemetery.

Hiding behind the second broken tree, Hoi, the lone guard, shook himself awake from a momentary catnap. He was astonished to see Americans walking straight toward him. Fear coursed through him like a current. He looked back to where his platoon was laagered, approximately fifty meters behind him in the clump of palm trees.

Americans hadn't been sighted in this area so, at dawn, Chi had posted one man guard shifts; allowing the men extra rest for the upcoming battle that he had promised would come today. Hoi had started his shift an hour ago. Now, silently, he cursed his luck. He didn't want to kill them. Why did he have to be the one to sight them? He shouldered his weapon and fired, purposely intending to miss the point man.

"Back to the mound!" Fleming screamed. It only took Fleming a few seconds to run to the mound and scramble over. He turned to watch as one by one his men climbed up and over the mound. Everyone had made it except for Rodgers, who was only twenty meters away.

"RUN! RUN!" Everyone screamed at him.

Hoi fired his weapon, aiming his rounds at the ground behind the American. Run, run, he mentally cheered for the American to make it behind the mound before Chi and the rest of the men arrived.

I'll never make it, Rodgers said to himself, running for all that he was worth. A second ago, Vines, the last man, had jumped over the mound. It was the loneliest second of his life. Run! Run! He ordered himself. He had a vivid mental picture of his father running in the open field with a football. Suddenly it felt like a huge mallet hammered down on his back. He was slammed to the ground.

Tackled!

Aiming his rounds in the dirt, Hoi was surprised when the American fell. One of his rounds must have ricocheted off the ground and struck the American. Then he heard footfalls behind him. Quickly he turned and saw Van, followed by the others, running toward him.

Rodgers attempted to stand but there was no life in his legs. Tackled, he thought again. And that instant he realized that today just might be his last day on earth. To his surprise he felt no fear, even though he might die and die alone, in a field, bleeding to death. He suddenly realized how tired he felt and tired felt strangely liberating. Death meant he was through fighting. He was through arguing with his Father and with his platoon members. He was through with facing firefights and the mind numbing fear that left him frightened beyond reason. Dying, it don't mean nothing, he said to himself, the first time he had used the phrase. At that moment he realized that it was fair and just that he die and die alone. So many others had died and nobody gave a shit. He never gave a shit. Carlyle said it: he was selfish and spoiled. And realizing all this left him feeling new and refreshed.

Van was the first to reach Hoi.

Hoi's face was a landscape of anguish and despair. He looked into Van's eyes. "I shot that man. I…" He bent over and vomitted.

It was just like when they were children when Dan had crushed the bird's skull and Hoi had gotten violently ill. And at that moment, Van realized that no power on earth would make Hoi change. He hated hurting anything and no amount of American invaders, glorious revolutions, or self-proclaimed honorable causes would ever change that.

Just then Chi, Dan, and the others reached his position.

A blur of a figure ran past Fleming just as he screamed: "Open fire!" The order wasn't necessary. Everyone had already opened fire.

"Fire! Fire your weapons!" Chi screamed maniacally. "Kill the Americans! Kill them!"

But the Americans unrelenting cover fire made it impossible for anyone to take time to aim at the second American who had gone to aid the downed American.

Rodgers felt someone grab his fatigue shirt, drag him behind the large broken tree in front of the mound, and turn him over.

"You dumb, motherfuckin,' honky dipshit," Carlyle screamed at him. "How in the fuck did you get to be such a fuck up?"

Rodgers smiled warmly. "Thanks, man, but you have to be stupider. You have to know that I wouldn't have done the same for you."

"Think you're telling me somethin new, asshole?" Then Carlyle gave him a bitter smile. "You don't like niggers do you?"

Rodgers winced in pain. "The...crux of my problem is I'm anti-social. I don't like people."

"What the fuck does crux mean?" Carlyle blurted out. "Christ, Rodgers, why do you always talk so funny?"

"I think funny," he replied. But not anymore, he said to himself. Now, he understood. He knew why he had a negative attitude toward his Father and toward his squad members. It actually went further than that – he held ill will toward the human race. He was always obsessed with ideas and the way things should have been but seldom were. Here, men lived for each other. There were no theories concerning how things ought to be. These men never judged whether it was good or bad, right or wrong, yet they always exhibited a high degree of morality. They weren't animals. They weren't stupid. They weren't even brave. If they were anything they were young men who cared for each other and were secure in the knowledge that their actions would be reciprocated. They did for each other, he thought, using their vernacular, and now they were doing for him.

Carlyle was the last person anyone had expected to go after Rodgers. But, in reality, Carlyle acting spontaneously was a surprise to no one. "Carlyle," Fleming yelled. "You okay?"

"I'm fine. But Rodgers can't move his legs."

Fleming turned to Crazy. "Get Lebeau on the radio. Tell him we've been hit. Tell him Rodgers is hit and Carlyle is with him. Tell him, we're cut off and we can't leave till we get them. Tell him we're pinned down and we'll be overrun if we don't get help. Tell Lebeau to hurry."

At the observation post, Chi quickly assessed the situation. The fruit tree grove was sixty yards away on the right flank. The Americans were occupied with their wounded man on the left flank and the fire that Chi and his men were putting on them from their position. There was a good chance that if men left from the palm tree clump they could slip into the fruit tree grove and flank the Americans. They could fire on them unseen and from behind perfect cover. His decision made, Chi ordered some men back to the palm tree area where they would then enter the fruit tree grove.

"Where's Lebeau," Fleming yelled. "Crazy, you get through to him yet?"

"I'm talking to him now. He wasn't near the radio. They had to go get him."

Fleming couldn't believe it. Lebeau was acting platoon commander: his job was to be near the radio.

All of a sudden Doc Garret was seen running toward the mound on his gimpy leg; it was more a fast limp than anything that resembled running. When he reached the men a breathless Garret wheezed out: "Lebeau's taking his sweet old time...said it's too dangerous to send help unless he knows support is coming."

Fleming turned to Crazy. "Tell him we can't get back till we get our wounded man."

"I did," Crazy fired back angrily. "He said he's trying to get here."

"He ain't comin for awhile!" Garret emphasized. "I mean if I could make it on one leg don't ya think he'd be here by now if he was comin? And Raines, Pierson, Ramirez, the old squad leaders, they've been medavacced out. They were your brothers. The guys from Alpha don't know you from shit. They ain't even gonna come out here, especially when Lebeau ordered them not to."

Static and crackling sounds suddenly burst from the radio. Crazy took it off his back and began examining it.

"Damnit! He knows I'll go to Wiggins about this. If we're all dead he'll be in the clear." A sudden thought flashed in Fleming's mind: he could bypass Lebeau and call in directly for air and artillery support.

Crazy ran his finger across a small hole on the radio's back. "Fleming, the radio's fucked."

Without a radio, they couldn't call in for artillery or air support. "Son of a bitch! It was working a second ago! What the fuck's wrong with it?"

"It ain't my fuckin fault! I told ya I thought it was fucked a while back," Crazy yelled back. "It was hit by a round or a piece of shrapnel or something. We were lucky to even make contact with Lebeau."

Suddenly approximately twenty V.C. run across the terrain, heading straight for the fruit tree grove.

Vines opened fire and downed a few but at least a dozen made it inside the trees. "Fleming, some gooks ran into the fruit tree grove. They're gonna have us dead in their sights in ti-ti time. We'll be fucked for sure."

Fleming looked at the grove and realized the situation's severity. He instinctively turned to the bomb crater behind them – it would offer excellent cover. "Carlyle, you gotta try to get over the mound and you gotta do it now or we're all fucked. Can you carry Rodgers?"

Carlyle unslung his M-79 and threw it over the downed tree. It landed on the other side of the mound. Then he threw his ammunition bag. Without the added burden and weight the task would be much easier. "I can carry him, no sweat. Just lay down cover fire."

Fleming turned to the others. "You heard him. Rock and roll or we're fucked."

Each man shouldered his weapon.

"You ready, Carlyle?"

"Lay down that cover fire."

They opened fire on the V.C. in the cemetery. Carlyle hoisted Rodgers on his shoulders and ran from behind the tree.

A sudden outburst of American gunfire chewed the ground all around Van and the others. Everyone dropped down for cover except for Van. Rounds fell all around him scattering debris in his face. Then he saw the American run from behind the tree carrying the wounded man. He took quick aim and hastily pulled the trigger.

In a split second Carlyle reached the foot of the mound. He took two steps up when a round hit him in the foot. He crashed to the ground and slid down the embankment. In the next few seconds everything seemed to move fast and slow at the same time. The other men were furiously providing cover fire while Vines and Fleming reached for Rodgers. They grabbed him just as he was about to slide down the mound and pulled him up and over.

Carlyle scrambled to his hands and knees, crawled quickly up the mound, and stretched his arm out.

Fleming reached for Carlyle's hand.

Van took quick aim and fired.

Fleming grabbed Carlyle's hand. Then he felt a tremendous blast in his right shoulder, as if a car had hit him, but it was only a round, breaking his grip on Carlyle's hand. Fleming had the curious sensation of being transported as he was flipped in the air and came to rest on his stomach, straddling the mound. All the wind had been knocked out of him. His shoulder bled profusely and felt dead. He was disoriented and watched helplessly like a spectator at an event.

Carlyle had slipped a few feet down the mound. He scrambled back up. Vines reached for him.

Van took aim again and fired.

THUD! THUD! THUD!

The sound reminded Fleming of when he was a child and he and a friend were pitching rocks at a watermelon. When the rocks penetrated the melons there was a dull thudding sound. This time the sounds were rounds striking Vines tearing off most of his face and head killing him.

Fleming reached again for Carlyle.

Carlyle scrambled to his hands and knees and reached for Fleming's outstretched hand.

Van fired multiple rounds.

Fleming grabbed Carlyle's hand.

AK-47 rounds slashed holes all across Carlyle's mid section, disemboweling him, spilling his insides. He fell to the ground his face inches from Fleming's. His lifeless eyes were the epitome of nothingness.

The death of both Fleming's friends was overwhelming; it felt as if a hot knife had just pierced his heart. He suppressed a powerful desire to surrender to fate and just sit here and cry. Instead he rolled down the mound and yelled: "Into the bomb crater!" At the same time he wiped away the tears that were streaming down his face.

Rojas and Garret lifted Rodgers and started toward the crater, twenty feet away. White and Washington stayed behind and laid down cover fire. Fleming grabbed Vines' 60 and ammo, Carlyle's M-79 and ammo, and jumped into the crater, followed by Crazy. Then Fleming scurried back to the crater's top. "White, Washington, get the fuck in here!" he screamed.

Washington turned to White. "Get in the fuckin crater, White."

"Fuck you, you go!"

"Get the fuck out of here, White."

"Get your asses in here! Now!" Fleming hollered.

White looked back at Fleming then turned to Washington.

"Go, White, now!" Washington said. "You're wasting time."

Confusion flitted across White's face. "You come right after me, you hear?"

"Yeah, go!"

White took off, running toward the bomb crater.

The V.C. just finished setting up an RPD in the fruit tree grove. The machine gunner pulled the trigger, sending out dozens of rounds at the running American.

RPD rounds hit the backside of White's body, sending him on a face first, belly flopping slide. He came to rest inches from Fleming's face. His vacant dead eyes stared at eternity.

Fleming turned away from the sight. "Washington, get the fuck in here!" Fleming knew it would take a miracle for Washington to reach the crater, but it was his only chance. Out in the open he would surely be killed.

Washington stood and slowly backed away firing his M-16 from the hip.

The RPD machine gunner took aim and opened fire.

Rounds ripped through Washington's chest and shoulders. He jiggled and shook and flew backward fifteen feet before falling to the earth. Small holes all over his body fountain sprayed miniature geysers of blood. He looked like a human hot water heater that had sprung several leaks.

Fleming dropped his head into the dirt at the crater's lip. They're gone, he thought. All of them just about every friend he had. Gritting his teeth, he lifted his head from the dirt and wiped away the tears that were streaming down his face. Don't mean nothing, he said to himself. Not a motherfucking thing! He needed to say those words; it took the edge off just how much it all really meant.

Fleming slid down into the crater and saw that Crazy and Rojas were bunched together near Rodgers and Garret. "Spread the fuck out!" he ordered.

They did so instantly, realizing they had violated the old adage of one grenade getting them all.

"Fleming, Rodgers is bad, man. We gotta get him outta here?" Then Garret surveyed the bomb crater. "Where the fuck is White and Washington?"

"Wasted, man. They're gone."

"Lebeau wants all you guys gone, I know it."

"Somebody oughta make him pay," Crazy said softly.

Aware that the Americans had retreated into the bomb crater, Chi, Van, Hoi, Dan and four others raced to the mound and took cover behind it. "We will charge into that bomb crater and kill the Americans!" It was a bold, risky move. The Americans failed to leave a sentry at the crater's lip. Possibly because they were too busy caring for their wounded they hadn't the time to post one. Whatever the reason they were open to surprise attack. Chi turned to Hoi. "You will lead the charge."

"He can't do it!" Van said angrily.

Hoi smiled warmly at Van. "This time I want to do it." He had spoken softly, a peaceful expression rested comfortably on his face.

Chi grabbed Van's arm and pulled him a short distance away from the others. "He's in no danger," Chi whispered so no one else could hear. "You will follow immediately after him, then I follow and then Dan. All of us will be at the mound's top within a second firing on the Americans. Hoi will be safe. He just goes first."

Van turned his head to look at Hoi.

Hoi smiled at Van then he charged up the mound.

"NOT YET!" Chi screamed. "WAIT!" It was too late. Hoi's suicidal charge had ruined the element of surprise.

Van immediately ran after him.

Fleming was surprised to see the lone V.C. standing at the top of the mound rifle held harmlessly at his side. Fleming fired a half a dozen rounds into him.

Hoi was propelled backward off the mound. He crashed into Van knocking him backward. They both tumbled down the mound. Van hit his head on a rock and the world went black. He lay on the ground unconscious with Hoi lying atop him.

Dan ran up the mound and fired a burst.

Crazy screamed as several rounds tore through his leg.

Both Fleming and Rojas opened fire on the V.C.

Multiple rounds shredded the magnificent body that had always been Dan's chief source of pride. Dead the second he was hit, he was propelled backward off the mound.

If Fleming hadn't moved the men minutes earlier, the V.C. could have killed half or possibly all of them. But Fleming also realized that he had committed a major mistake by not leaving a guard at the crater's lip right after Washington had died.

"HE LEFT TOO EARLY!" an outraged Chi screamed at the four other V.C. "HE RUINED THE AMBUSH!" Chi was livid and didn't know what to do. Charging up the mound now would certainly be a death sentence. He had to come up with a plan, quickly.

Hearing the Vietnamese voices, Fleming wasn't about to make another mistake. He grabbed the M-79 and shot a round high into the air. Then he and Rojas both threw grenades. The M-79 grenade round fell to the earth just as the grenades detonated.

A huge chunk of shrapnel penetrated the side of Chi's head killing him instantly. The other four men were also killed. Lying on the ground with Hoi's dead body covering him, Van was shielded.

Doc Garret hurried to Crazy and began examining his leg. Rojas reached for a new magazine while Fleming moved toward Crazy.

Van regained consciousness and pushed Hoi's body from atop him. He saw Dan's lifeless body and the four dead V.C. Chi lay dead a few meters away. What matters in this world of death and destruction? Van knew he was also about to die, but he didn't care. He grabbed his weapon and charged up the mound. He opened fire, sending rounds into the back of an American's head.

Van swung his weapon toward another American.

Fleming saw the V.C. with his weapon trained on Rojas. Fleming fired round after round into him.

Rounds struck Van's hip, shoulder, and leg. He spun crazily and slid a few feet down the crater's lip into the bomb crater. He lay there unconscious.

"Rojas, watch for Gooks," Fleming ordered.

Rojas hurried to the crater's top.

For a moment, a stunned Fleming looked down on Doc Garret's dead body. Fleming turned him over. Rounds had exited the front of Garret's face. His chin hung grotesquely on his neck and chest. Broken teeth and bone lay like small kernels of corn inside his mouth and on the ground next to him. His mother would be taken care of, Fleming thought.

Fleming moved to Crazy. His pants leg had been removed revealing a mass of torn muscle tissue and nerves.

"Christ, Fleming, it hurts."

"Your leg's all fucked up. We gotta get you outta here or you'll bleed to death."

"What's taking Lebeau so long?" Crazy asked softly.

"He wants us dead," Fleming answered unemotionally then moved to Rodgers. "How ya doing, man?"

Through dreamy morphine induced eyes, Rodgers gazed up at Fleming. "I never hated you guys. I wish I would have gotten to know everyone a little better. I know how that sounds saying it now but it needed to be said."

"It's okay, man," Fleming said. "It's okay."

"My legs…I can't feel a thing…. I know I'm hurt bad."

Two V.C. charged up the mound. At the crater's top, Rojas opened fire and killed them. He quickly reloaded.

Van regained consciousness and knew that he was dying. Lying there, wounded, he saw an American a little more than arm's reach away reloading his weapon at the crater's top. He pulled out a knife and raised it over his head.

Fleming turned to see the V.C. attacking Rojas. He aimed his 16 while simultaneously screaming: "Rojas, behind you!" He squeezed the trigger and heard the horrible sound of metal clanking against metal. There was no time to reload the empty weapon. He thought of using his weapon like a club but with his wounded shoulder he couldn't effectively swing it. So he dropped it and started running toward Rojas.

Crazy grabbed the M-60 and a belt of ammo and began reloading the weapon.

Rojas turned.

Van plunged the knife downward.

Rojas shifted to the right.

The knife pierced his side.

Van raised his knife ready to strike again.

Fleming ran three feet up the crater's side and crashed his left shoulder into the enemy knocking him off Rojas. Then Fleming fell to the ground next to the V.C. He scrambled to his hands and knees and found himself face to face with the Vietnamese. They locked eyes for a long moment.

Van had only one thought: kill the American. Van raised his knife and sprang at him.

A one armed Fleming braced for the assault.

Rojas pressed the trigger and released the switchblade's steel. He stretched out his right hand and sank six inches of blade into the V.C.'s mid section. The movement left Rojas off balance and he rolled down the crater's side.

The V.C. fell on top of Fleming.

Fleming frantically rolled the V.C. off him. He took out his bayonet, grabbed the V.C., and rolled him over and saw the switchblade sticking from his stomach.

Holding his blood soaked side, Rojas grabbed Fleming's M-16.

Just then, three enemy soldiers appeared at the crater's top.

I am dead, Fleming said to himself seeing them.

Crazy fired the M-60, decimating the three enemy soldiers and sending their bodies flying from the crater's lip.

Rojas crawled to Fleming and handed him his 16. They begin reloading their weapons.

'They keep coming," Fleming said. "And this animal!" They both looked down at the V.C. and saw that life was still in his eyes and he was staring up at them.

In his mind's eye Van saw Kim smiling at him. She was so close that he could smell her skin; it was so clean, so refreshing a scent. She had never looked more beautiful then she did right now. And he knew that he was about to join her in a place far more beautiful and far more peaceful than the village or anywhere else on earth. She reached out and touched his cheek. Her hand was soft and her light silky touch healed his troubled mind. He knew that he had finally found peace. He looked at the Americans staring down at him. He saw through their young, dirty, blood stained faces and grim eyes to the innocence and humanity that burned alive in their souls. The war had stolen all that was good from these two men. We are the same, he thought, except that their pain would go on and his was about to end forever. He had the incredible, irresistible urge to ease their misery and suffering. He smiled at them, wishing he could do more. And while smiling, Van died.

Rojas and Fleming look at each other for a long moment. "Did you see the gook's face?" Fleming asked Rojas.

Rojas nodded his head yes. "He was happy like he was at peace."

"Watch for more gooks," Fleming said softly.

Rojas started back up the crater's lip then turned back. "Wash the blood off the gook's face," he said.

The request needn't have been asked. Fleming had already grabbed his canteen. He poured water on the face and gently rubbed away the blood with his dirty hand. He looked at the face of his hated enemy; this enemy, this man that Fleming had been sent twelve thousand miles from home to kill couldn't be more than fifteen years old. Only a boy, Fleming said to himself. He folded the boy's arms and hands across his chest. Then he reloaded his 16 and climbed to the crater's top to Rojas.

Suddenly about thirty V.C. charged from the fruit tree grove.

"Here they come," Fleming said. Both he and Rojas took aim.

From behind them they heard M-16 fire.

They both turned to the sound. "It's Lebeau," Fleming said savagely. "Another two minutes and we'd be dead."

The V.C. were caught in the open by the approaching Americans. Choppers suddenly appeared and opened fire. A Spooky plane dropped Napalm in the grove – it erupted, sending flames high into the air. The sharp stinking odor of gunpowder and cordite was everywhere. Within minutes the enemy was eliminated. Fleming and Rojas returned to the crater's bottom.

A medic from Alpha Company was the first soldier to jump into the bomb crater. He administered morphine to Rojas, Fleming, Rodgers, and Crazy.

Five soldiers and Sergeant Lebeau entered the crater. Lebeau and Fleming immediately locked eyes. "I'm telling Wiggins about this and why it took so long for you to get here."

"I didn't know the enemy's strength," Lebeau explained with a smile. "I couldn't take the chance on losing the few men I had."

Fleming was covered with blood from his shoulder wound. It was his pitching arm. Baseball was the only thing in life he ever wanted to do and maybe that was gone and it was all Lebeau's fault. The death of his friends that was also all Lebeau's fault and Fleming knew that somehow Lebeau would get away with it all.

Then he turned to look at the dead V.C., lying undisturbed. He was the luckiest man of all, because he was out of the madness that was war.

The morphine started to kick in. He turned to Crazy and stared at his leg – a meaty, bloody mess, as if a huge creature had bitten a large chunk out of his thigh. Fleming thought he saw the strangest hint of a smile resting on Crazy's face but he couldn't be sure. He had no idea what tricks the morphine was playing on his mind.

"Hey, sarge, I got me four KIA's," Crazy's speech pattern had slowed about two speeds and he slurred badly.

Lebeau's face erupted into a huge smile. "Crazy, you are a true soldier. I mean you're lying here all fucked up and not a word of complaint." He looked at Fleming. "Not like others." Then he turned back to Crazy. "You did fine, son. I'm gonna get you a real nice medal."

Crazy shivered and stuck his hands inside his shirt as if he were cold. "Sarge, Fleming fucked up. That's why everybody's dead."

With his morphine-addled brain, Fleming wasn't sure if he had heard correctly.

The huge smile on Lebeau's face widened. "This is one outstanding fucking day." He turned to Fleming. "You're gonna report me and Crazy says you fucked up. Ain't this what them hippie college professors call poetic justice – all them fucking months I put up with your hippie bull shit and now it looks like I'm gonna get the last laugh. God, this is an outstanding fuckin day! Tell me how he fucked up, Crazy?"

"You got a cigarette, sarge?"

"Sure, son, sure," Lebeau said, making his way to Crazy.

The morphine kept kicking in and Fleming didn't know what to think; then he flashed back to when he had failed to post a guard at the crater's lip. Was Crazy referring to that?

Lebeau bent down to him and held out a cigarette.

Crazy shot his muscular arms from underneath his shirt and wrapped Lebeau in a bear hug. He easily pulled him into an embrace.

"What the fuck!" Lebeau blurted out.

When Crazy's right hand interlocked with the fingers of his left, Fleming saw Crazy's index finger and the ring with the pin dangling from the end.

"You're a gutless prick!" Crazy said with a rattling voice tone.

A muffled explosion was heard, and Fleming realized that the ring on Crazy's finger had been a grenade firing pin.

Lebeau's body lifted in the air and was freed from Crazy's embrace.

The medic rushed to both men fully knowing that nothing could be done. Their upper bodies had been torn open; pieces of intestine and stomach had exploded from their stomachs.

The bomb crater was an ocean of blood and resembled something from a slasher horror movie: there was Garret's dead body with his head and face blown away – his jaw hanging on his chest like a puppet with a broken face. Rodgers and Rojas lay in an enormous pool of blood. The medic was covered with pieces of human stomach and intestines. Hundreds of flies covered and feasted on the dead men. A small army was on Fleming's shoulder wound. The idea of brushing them away seemed too great for his morphine induced body and mind to handle.

Suddenly a whistle shrieked. A bugle sounded a charge followed by a tremendous thunder-clapping roar of gunfire erupting everywhere.

A helicopter landed nearby. Men jumped into the bomb crater. Frightened faces and excited voices screamed that the L.Z. was hot, and they had to get out and get out fast.

Fleming was lifted and placed inside a chopper. Rojas was loaded next to him.

Rounds buzzed like so many locusts all around the chopper, some ricocheting off the chopper's metal frame, an eerie, tingling, whining noise. Freshly wounded men screamed in agony. Despite the morbid symphony, despite being weakened by loss of blood, the numbing effects of morphine had given Fleming a strange sense of comfortable peace.

An unconscious Rodgers was placed aboard. With what seemed like a supreme effort, Fleming drunkenly turned his head to see the dead bodies of Garret, White, Vines, Carlysle, Washington, and what was left of Lebeau and Crazy.

The helicopter shook and took flight.

No, Fleming immediately said to himself. He didn't see the dead V.C.'s body and thought it highly inappropriate that he hadn't been taken out with them. The gook had earned it, he thought. His body shouldn't be left to rot in a crater. He tried to scream out in protest, but no words came from his mouth. Then he passed out.

CHAPTER 20

Recovery

The following morning at 0900, Fleming awakened and was surprised to see Lieutenant Ryerson in a hospital bed next to him.

They spoke a few moments then Fleming said: "Sir, I'm fuzzy as hell…and I sound like a drunk. This morphine is kicking my ass."

"It's not morphine. It's Thorzaine. The doctors give it to everyone who comes in. They figure it'll help us catch up on some much needed rest."

A moment of silence passed.

"You got shot in the shoulder," Ryerson said. "I'm sorry."

"My pitching arm, the dream of playing big league ball is now a nightmare."

"Wait till you know for sure before you count yourself out."

"Yes, sir." Fleming looked around and saw that the room was filled with wounded men. Rojas and Rodgers were asleep in their beds right next to him.

"What happened, Fleming?"

Fleming told him of the suicidal mission and the men's deaths. He said nothing of the V.C. and his smiling, peaceful face. No one would believe it. Fleming was still having a hard time believing it himself.

"I wish I had been there to stop Lebeau," Ryerson said.

"Sir, Lebeau had it in for me and my squad paid for it. I shouldn't have shot my mouth off to him all those times. It's my fault."

"Don't blame yourself. You always did all you could for your men."

"Yes, sir, but in the end I got them all killed."

"Your men loved and respected you. You did nothing wrong. It's war and people die."

"Yes, sir," he said unconvincingly. "Sir, what's gonna happen with you?"

"They're sending me to Japan for my new leg." Ryerson reached under his pillow where he had placed a magazine. "Do me a favor. Read this article and tell me what you think." Ryerson handed him a Time Magazine.

Fleming started reading. The reporter went to great lengths describing today's deranged young adults. America was going to hell from pot, rock and roll, and long hair. American youth were irresponsible and mistrustful. They wouldn't listen to an adult and cared about nothing. Racial unrest was rampant, creating a rift between black and white that would never be repaired. Fleming had absolutely no interest in the article and wondered why the L T had asked him to read it. "Done, sir."

"What did you think?"

"Don't mean nothing, sir."

Ryerson's eyes widened. His jaw dropped open. "Don't mean nothin?" he said astounded. "I don't see it that way. No, I don't see it that way at all. That reporter doesn't know the whole story. He has never seen nineteen year olds, like my men, march for hours in the hot sun then crawl through automatic weapons fire to secure some stupid no name piece of land for God knows what. He's never seen them go on ambushes and LP's and never complain when they know that at any second they might get maimed or wasted. He's never seen a black man crawl through enemy fire to help a white man simply because that man was his friend."

Fleming had seen all of this and more. In the end, all those men had died. "So? What's the big deal, sir?"

"I feel sorry for him," Ryerson said softly.

"Sorry. He's had it good. The REMF ain't seen his friends die."

"No, that's not it at all," Ryerson said. "Don't you understand?"

Fleming shook his head no. "Sir, I don't know what you want me to say."

Disappointment filled Ryerson's face. "The REMF hasn't seen how men really live. That's what he missed. It's not about dying. My men, your squad, they were like saints. The Reporter is older than me and he knows nothing about men like them. I feel sorry for him. He's missed out on a lot of life."

Fleming handed the magazine back. "Sir, I'm played out, must be this Thorzaine stuff. I think I'll go to sleep."

Ryerson studied him for a long moment then his features softened into a facial expression that Fleming thought was filled with pity.

"Sure, you need rest," Ryerson said.

Fleming lay back on his pillow. The L T was right. Deep down, where it all counted, Fleming was proud to have known these men, but they were dead. And the truth of it was that he was sick and tired of seeing dead men, sick and tired of going deep down. In the past seven months he had dug deep down to that place where it all counted, too many fucking times. Deep down was all used up – an exhausted fucking wasteland. He had scraped and scrounged and had managed to endure but no more. Memories of his friends were much too depressing. How could they all be dead? What would happen now? He would go back to the field, unless his shoulder was too fucked up. It would probably be adequate enough for killing human beings but not good enough to pitch a baseball, he thought bitterly. And returning to the field was a death sentence. He would never make it out alive or with all his body parts intact. The only thing certain in this country was death or severe maiming; the type of maiming that left one praying for death. Maybe his next lieutenant or platoon sergeant would be like Lebeau. Damn Lebeau, he thought. Why did he do it? But every why question boiled down to one – why were they here? He wasn't the smartest person in the world; all he ever wanted to do was pitch a baseball. But one didn't have to be a Magna Cum Laude' or even intelligent to realize there was nothing to win in Vietnam. The best and the brightest, people with College Degrees and Doctorates were responsible yet not a one of them felt responsible enough to serve here. They were all enjoying life back home. And back home, back in America, they were not exactly welcoming home men that L T Ryerson had called saints.

Suddenly his eyelids felt heavy. Thank God for Thorzaine, he thought. He didn't want to think anymore. He embraced Thorzaine's comforting heaviness and soon fell asleep.

"GGOOODDD MMORNNING VIETNAM?"

Fleming was startled awake by the sound of a blaring radio.

"This is Army Specialist Joe Flowers and it's time for an early morning attitude check." Then the sound of The Animals song "We Gotta Get Outta This Place" filled the room.

Fleming wanted to strangle Army Specialist Joe Flowers, his "Good Morning Vietnams" and his attitude checks. He was a REMF and all REMFS had good mornings. Let him try just one operation in the field, and Flowers wouldn't be wishing anyone an exuberant good morning.

Fleming turned to L T Ryerson, who motioned with a head nod to look behind him. He turned to see Rojas and Rodgers sitting up in their beds awake.

"How ya doing?" Fleming called out to them.

"Hey, man," Rojas said excitedly. "You been asleep like for fucking ever."

"They drugged the shit out of me. You guys okay? Your wounds?"

"I'm fine," Rojas answered. "My side hurts like hell, but I am fine."

"I'm paralyzed from the waist down," Rodgers said. "The Doctor said I'll never walk again."

Just like Marsten, Fleming thought. A dude I met like a thousand years ago. "I'm sorry," Fleming said.

"At least I'm alive. I'll make out. I know it. I guess I have to make peace with my father and work in his advertising agency. He's been after me for years to do that. I have never been fair to him. He's a good man."

Ryerson studied him a long moment. "You're different. You've changed."

Rodgers gave him a weak smile. "Sir, I've learned much since coming here. From now on I will be a better man. I owe that to the men who died trying to save me, especially Carlyle. Then maybe they all wouldn't have died for nothing."

"That's good way to look at things," Ryerson said.

"Yeah, he ain't so fucked up any more," Rojas piped in.

Rodgers and Rojas exchanged smiles.

Rodgers seemed at peace with himself. He had changed. He wasn't the only one who had changed, Fleming said to himself. It don't mean nothing. He turned away from the men and lay on his side, hoping they didn't include him in their conversation.

That afternoon a Sergeant entered the ward and told the wounded they were about to be visited by their battalion C.O. Colonel Bradford.

What the fuck does he want? Fleming said to himself.

Bradford and two aides entered the hospital room. Bradford made his way around the room speaking words of encouragement before handing each man a Purple Heart.

When Fleming received his medal, he suppressed an intense desire to throw it across the room.

After distributing the medals, Bradford assumed a modified parade rest position and spoke. He commended the men on a job well done defending the South Vietnamese. "Now it is over for you and the rest of the gallant soldiers of the 173rd Airborne Brigade."

Over? Did we win? Fleming wondered sarcastically. It was highly unlikely that the North had surrendered.

"President Nixon, our commander in chief has said that we have accomplished our mission. We have pacified the area. Now it is up to the South Vietnamese to maintain the peace that we have won for them. As part of the President's plan to end our commitment in

South Vietnam the 173rd is being deactivated as a combat unit. Men, we are going home victorious. You soldiers will be part of the 101st Airborne Division at Fort Campbell, Kentucky. The war is over for you. Years from now you will be able to tell your Grandchildren that you helped make South Vietnam a member of the Democratic Nations of the free World. Gentlemen, you have every right to be proud." Bradford went silent for a moment expecting the men to cheer his announcement, but it didn't come. He cleared his throat. "I will leave you alone with your thoughts. This last statement comes from the President himself. Great job and feel pride at what you have accomplished here."

Fleming clenched his fists. Bradford and the President were truly fuckin head cases if they believed that bullshit. It was a classic case of simply declaring victory without actually having won anything. Fleming couldn't remember an operation when the South Vietnamese did anything other than offer support. Not one operation, he thought. They had no chance against the North without Americans leading the charge. Yesterday, his friends had died because the mission of liberating Vietnam was vitally important. Twenty-four hours later it was so vitally unimportant that the entire Brigade was leaving the country. Make sense of that, he thought. He and his friends had fought in that stinking hole and only two of them had come out in one piece. All along, the people who had sent him here, the same people who had never fought, the best and the brightest, were planning to leave the country.

Just then, Fleming's thoughts drifted back to the day he had eaten with Santoro in the mess hall. He had said something big was going down. Now he knew what he had meant. How long had they been planning this? He wondered.

Where's the medic? He asked himself. I need another fuckin pill! I need to sleep! Cause being awake was one bad, never ending, fucking nightmare.

He called for a medic and got his pill. Thorzaine, he thought.

They were probably giving it away so freely because they hoped the men would forget the past year. They wouldn't want soldiers returning home and telling the truth. He took the pill and fell into a drug-induced sleep.

Hours later, Fleming awakened. He was groggy but felt surprisingly rested and refreshed. He lay in bed for a few minutes contemplating his thoughts. Maybe sleep had put things in a newer light. The thought of returning home and visiting old friends, seeing his parents, his sister, and the rest of his family left him eager with anticipation. Life was long and Vietnam was only a small bitter part of it. The goal now was to make the rest of his life happy and worthwhile. Maybe he could still pitch. He was looking forward to finding out. Baseball had gotten him over some of life's nasty humps. It could do so again.

"Fleming, Sergeant William Fleming."

Fleming scanned the room and saw a man in crisp, starched fatigues, a REMF's uniform. He immediately felt anger, seeing someone who had never served in the field; someone who had never suffered. He ordered himself calm. He was going home soon. He needed to stay calm. "I'm Fleming," he called to the man.

The man came to him. He was a Lieutenant. He wore aviator sunglasses and carried a briefcase.

Fleming had to do his best to stifle laughter. The Lieutenant didn't walk he waddled.

"You're Fleming?" He asked.

"Yes, sir."

"You're a hard man to find. I'm Lieutenant Darrow, from personnel." The Lieutenant had a high-pitched squeaky voice and sounded like someone's nagging Mother. They exchanged greetings and handshakes then the Lieutenant craned his neck, scanning the room as if he were looking for something. Then he motioned for them to walk to a desk in the room's corner.

Once there the Lieutenant said: "I'll get right to the point. You shouldn't have been out in the field with infantry types."

No shit, Sherlock, Fleming said to himself. "Sir, I went where the Army sent me."

"Yes, your orders were lost so there was some confusion as to your status. I am happy to tell you we now know where you really belong. With the Herd (nickname for the 173rd Airborne) pulling out we found a lot of men who were in the wrong M.O.S."

Fleming couldn't help but wonder what stories this man would tell back home about his service with The Herd. "Yes, sir, but what's this got to do with me?"

"I am pleased to inform you that you will be going back to your original M.O.S. The job the Army trained you to do. I have your new orders here." The Lieutenant patted his briefcase. "Of course you'll have to recuperate first, but the Doctors assured me you'll be fit for duty and your new assignment in about a month."

"New…. Colonel Bradford said we're going to Fort Campbell to be part of the 101st."

"True, but you're no longer a member of the 173rd."

"Sir, what are you saying?"

"I'm saying since your orders have been found, you're no longer be part of the 173rd. You're being re-assigned."

"Re-assigned? Where? Where am I being re-assigned?"

"You're being re-assigned to the 330th Radio Research Field Station."

Radio Research – A.S.A., Fleming said to himself. "Where is the 330th Radio Research?" he asked, but he already knew where it was.

"It's in Nha Trang."

"Vietnam!" The word burst forth like a crackling thunderbolt. "Viet-fuckin-Nam! Why the fuck's everyone else goin home and I'm staying in Vietnam?

The Lieutenant's eyes darted nervously inside his head. "Well, uh, the Army trained you for a specific job. The Government spent a lot of money training you. They need a sufficient return on the taxpayer's money."

His voice had an irritating tone of self-righteous indignation that did nothing but fuel Fleming's anger. "Sufficient return on the taxpayer's money! Did you really just say that? How about all I've done so far? Ain't that a sufficient return on the taxpayer's money? Christ, why did they lose my orders in the first place? Why?"

The Lieutenant's eyes searched the room, as if he were looking for help. "That I don't know. An organization as large as the Army is bound to have administrative blunders. Unfortunately that's what happened to you."

"Administrative blunder! Is that what I am? An administrative fuckin blunder? Why don't you just say the truth – the Army fucked up and fucked me over!"

"That's enough. In the Army you're not permitted to question orders. You took an oath. You promised to follow orders." The Lieutenant quickly opened a briefcase and took out a manila envelope. "Here are your orders."

Fleming snatched the envelope out of his hands.

The Lieutenant stood and said in a nervous tone: "You have an attitude problem. You have no respect for authority." Then he turned and briskly walked away.

Fleming opened the envelope and saw the orders. He was indeed being sent to another duty station in Vietnam. The orders were for a Specialist Fourth Class William Fleming – the final indignity. He was no longer an acting Sergeant. He had just gotten busted back to Spec. 4.

He walked back to his bed, threw his orders on his cot, and flopped on it.

"What happened, Fleming?" Ryerson asked softly.

"They found my original set of orders, sir. I'm goin back to the unit I was supposed to be with in the first place, the 330th Radio Research Field Station in Nha Trang, Vietnam."

"You're staying here?" Ryerson asked in disbelief.

"Yes, sir. I won't be goin home with you guys."

A moment passed as Rojas, Rodgers and Ryerson all exchanged glances.

"It won't be so bad," Rodgers volunteered. "At least you won't be fighting."

Fleming shook his head with frustration. "Most of my friends are dead or fucked up. Somebody has to tell me why. It was supposed to mean something. Now we're just leaving. I need to know why and I need to know why the Army lost my orders? And now they find them. It all seems a little too fucking...I don't know."

Rodgers' face is a mask of sympathy. "I wish there was something I could think of to say to you."

Rojas looked at his friend. The Army or the system had heaped injustice after injustice upon Fleming. "Hey, Man?"

Fleming turned to him.

"There it fuckin is." Rojas said.

THE END

About the Author

Tim Davis served seven months with the 404th Radio Research Detachment (ABN.), 173rd Airborne Brigade at L.Z. English, Bong Son, Binh Dinh Province, Republic of South Vietnam. After seven months the 173rd Airborne was deployed back to the United States. He finished his one-year tour serving with the 330th Radio Research Unit, Nha Trang, Vietnam. He also spent a one-year tour with the 7th Radio Research Field Station at Udorn Thailand.

Since his army days, Tim Davis has been active in the Health Club Industry. He has managed health clubs and has worked as a certified personal trainer.

While in the Army in Nha Trang, Vietnam he began learning the Korean Art of Tae Kwon Do from Korean martial artists in the Republic Of Korea's White Horse Division, a Korean Army Unit also stationed at Nha Trang.

He continued Tae Kwon Do training while stationed in Udorn, Thailand with the 7th Radio Research Field Station. Upon returning home from his army overseas tours of duty, he continued Martial Arts training reaching the status of third degree black belt. He also took up American Boxing which served him well during his career as a Professional Karate Association (P.K.A.) kickboxer. He fought most of his bouts in Atlantic City Casinos. He was also an accomplished karate tournament competitor competing in both forms and fighting.

He worked for a time in Houston, Texas as a Martial Arts Instructor and Personal trainer. In Houston Texas he began writing and won an award for the novel The Eagle And The Tiger. He also took up acting in Houston and acted in many plays at the Actors Theater Of Houston.

He moved to Los Angeles, California and continued acting and writing. He has appeared in stage plays in Los Angeles and has been in commercials and has acted in some television shows and movies – most notably the Television show *Criminal Minds*. He credits acting for much of his success at writing.

He also studied the art of Massage and currently works as a Professional Massage Therapist.

34524991R00233

Made in the USA
San Bernardino, CA
31 May 2016